# TERROR TALES OF
# THE COTSWOLDS

# TERROR TALES OF THE COTSWOLDS

## Edited by Paul Finch

# TERROR TALES OF THE COTSWOLDS

First published in 2012 by Gray Friar Press.
9 Abbey Terrace, Whitby,
North Yorkshire, YO21 3HQ, England.
Email: gary.fry@virgin.net
www.grayfriarpress.com

Typesetting and design by Paul Finch and Gary Fry

ISBN: 978-1-906331-26-9

# TABLE OF CONTENTS

# IN THE QUIET AND IN THE DARK
## Alison Littlewood

T he street was dead. Steph looked up and down it and saw honey-coloured houses, a quiet church and, behind everything, sleeping fields. She wrinkled her nose. 'Street' didn't seem the right word for it, not really; she didn't know what was. 'Lane' was too small – this was the centre of Long Compton – and 'road' implied it was going somewhere. Anywhere.

She thought again of the way her mother had said goodbye, walking down the platform after the train as if she hadn't wanted Steph to go. Then she'd turned before she was out of sight, and taken her new husband's arm and walked away, a spring to her step, off to live in some cheap bar on an unfashionable stretch of Italian coastline. Steph scowled. She had asked if she could go too – just once – and she didn't really remember the words her mother had used, but she remembered the look in her eyes. Steph knew, when she saw that look, that it wasn't any use. The flat in London was already sold – the one that lay on a street, a proper street – and now she was here with her dad, nowhere to go and nothing to do, in the far reaches of the back of beyond.

*But it's beautiful,* a voice said in the back of her mind, and Steph shook the thought away. She didn't want it to be beautiful, didn't want the sun to be pressing down insistently on the top of her head, shining on the mellow stone of the church. It was late summer, nearly time for school, and that meant everything starting, her life here; everything beginning again.

A bell rang behind her, tinny and shrill, and Steph jumped. A bicycle flew past, its tyres whizzing against hot tarmac. "Watch it," a voice said, and there was a flash of yellow hair. The girl braked, set down her feet, wheeled the bike around. "You moved into Willow Cottage," she said to Steph. She made it sound like an accusation.

Steph nodded.

"We're off to the Rollrights," the girl said. Her hair was pale, her skin tanned to honey, a tone darker than the buildings behind her. "You want to see the Rollrights?"

Steph shrugged. She didn't know what the Rollrights were, whether they were things or people, and didn't much care either way.

"You got a bike?"

Steph shook her head. She hadn't needed a bike, had always used the bus or the tube.

"You should have borrowed one, like me." The girl grinned. "Well, get on then."

Steph got onto the back, found herself reluctant to hold on but didn't have much choice; she put her hands around the girl's waist as they headed away, strangely intimate, the shadow of their wheels churning on the pavement, and realised that she didn't even know her name.

\*

The girl was called Holly, and the other part of the 'we' was Anne. They were Steph's age – fourteen – and would be in her class in school. The three of them walked up a path from the warden's hut, where an information sign informed Steph that the Rollright Stones were a thing, not a family; but the place was green and empty and she wondered why they had come here, where there was nothing. They passed a few walkers on their way, and all of them were Steph's father's age, and they didn't seem particularly excited about anything much.

"Race you," said Holly, and they charged up the rest of the slope under the late summer sun, until they doubled over, laughing, and Steph looked up to see a stone circle at the top of the hillside.

She pulled a face. It was smaller than she'd imagined when she'd seen the sign at the bottom. The circle was wide, but the stones were nothing but a jumble of worn-down teeth. She had imagined something like Stonehenge, towering, formed into rough arches.

"The King's Men," said Anne, and she ran to the nearest stone and slapped it before weaving in and out of the next few.

"They're supposed to be soldiers, turned to stone by a witch," Holly said. "Stupid, really. But it's pretty cool up here. You can see for miles."

Steph looked out over the landscape. It was green and rolling and went on and on. A few small villages nestled into it, calm and cosy and safe. She couldn't see her old home at all. She wondered if her mother was out there somewhere, looking back towards her, and felt a pang of homesickness.

"Witches come here," said Holly.

"They're not witches, idiot," said Anne. "They're druids, or pagans or something. They have rites."

2

Steph thought she'd said *rights*, frowned as Anne mimed pulling a knife from her jeans and cut her own throat. Then she got it.

"They *don't* do that," laughed Holly. "They just – I don't know, greet the dawn or something."

"Freaks."

"Weirdos."

Steph grinned at the pair as they joined hands and spun each other around, moving towards the centre of the circle. Then they stopped.

"You can't count the stones," said Anne. "If you count them three times and get the same number, you get a wish."

Holly snorted. "I thought it was 'the man will never live' who can do that," she said. "I always thought that meant, if someone managed it, it means they'll die."

Steph laughed, but she wasn't really looking at the girls any more. She was looking around at the circle, the whole empty place, nothing to do, nothing to see, but it didn't feel like that, not really; she had a sudden sense of people coming here, century upon century, because there was something here after all; something important. She wondered for a moment if maybe they *had* killed people here, put them to death while they sang and the stars wheeled overhead, but then she shook the thought away. It was a pile of rocks and empty fields and nothing more. If she was in Italy, there'd be the sea. She could swim. There would be shops and things to do and people, lots of people. She looked back at Holly and Anne and found they were staring at her.

Holly shrugged, as if Steph had asked her a question she couldn't answer. "Come on," she said. "Let's go and see the Knights."

\*

The Whispering Knights were a collection of tall stones, four or five of them together, a distance away from the main circle, and they didn't look like knights to Steph. There was a fence around them, each black strut ending in a blunted arrow.

Holly and Anne walked together, talking about what their friends had been doing, Janey and Finch and Tom, names Steph didn't know. She cut away and went towards the stones. They were taller than she had thought, broad and powerful but rough, their skin pocked and pitted.

*Their skin,* she thought, and smiled at herself. They weren't knights; the name was more exciting than the place.

3

"They can tell your fortune," Holly said close to her ear, and Steph jumped. "They see the future. If you sit and listen, they'll tell you who you're going to marry."

Anne, behind her, laughed. "Jason Dereham," she said. "That's who Holly's going to marry."

Holly hit out at her friend, and judging by the face she pulled, Steph gathered that Jason Dereham would have been her last choice on the planet.

"I wonder who you'll get?" Holly said. "Hmm, Cal Parker might do."

"Get real," said Anne. "Maybe Ben Hodson."

"Or *Marcus*."

The two joined hands, laughing, and Steph pulled an uncertain smile, unsure if they were mocking her or if the boys they named might actually be someone she could like. Then she shook her head. She wasn't going to fall for some local kid, *marry* some local kid; she wasn't going to stay here at all.

"You should try it," said Holly.

Steph shook her head. "I'm not getting married."

Holly shrugged. "Maybe you will, maybe you won't. It's fate. It's up to the stones to decide."

Steph snorted.

"Let the stones decide!" chanted Anne. "Let – the – stones—"

"Fate," said Holly. "Come on, we'll all do it, won't we, Anne."

"I don't believe in fate," said Steph, "or any of that. I don't believe there's one person we're supposed to be with. It's all bullshit."

Holly pulled a face, half shocked, half amused. "Don't insult the stones," she said, "or *you'll* have to marry Jason Dereham. And you don't know how bad that is, but take my word for it, it's pretty bad."

"I don't believe my mum was *supposed* to marry my dad. Look how that turned out."

"But then you'd never have been born. Everything was *supposed* to happen," said Anne. "Come on. It's only a laugh, anyway."

Steph tried to smile. Anne was right, it was only a bit of fun, and she wanted to be friends, didn't want to be labelled the boring one or the miserable one before school even began. The three of them sat with their backs to the railing, sinking into the long grass that grew around its base.

"Close your eyes," Holly said. "Close your eyes and be quiet and wait until you hear a name."

Steph's nose itched, and she scratched it. She heard a soft titter at her side: Anne. She wondered if the others still had their eyes closed or if it was all some stupid trick, whether they were making fun of her. Then she heard a voice: Holly's voice but deeper, full of barely suppressed laughter. *"Jason Dereham . . ."*

Anne giggled. "Stop it."

And they fell quiet again. Steph felt the sun warm on her face, the soft breeze a cooler note. She could smell green things, sap rising through the grass, a sourer tang from the fields. It was different, here. There was no sense of presence, of layers of things past just beneath the surface. There was nothing at all, and it wasn't home, and she didn't know any boys and didn't have to and it was alright because she didn't have to stay.

The sunlight stopped shining on her skin. She opened her eyes and there was a figure standing over her, someone tall, silhouetted by the sun. She felt Holly's hand on her arm.

"So," said the voice. It was a boy's voice, full of amusement. "Who's it going to be?"

*

The boy gave his name as Kix, short-for-something-boring, and he sat next to Anne and pulled a packet of cigarettes from his pocket. He was good looking in a thin, bony kind of way, and had pale hair that hung over his eyes. From the way Holly and Anne hung on his every word, Steph gathered that he was the popular kid in school, the cool kid. Then he flicked his hair and held out a cigarette. She didn't take it, didn't like the smell, never had. He shrugged and passed it to Holly and she took it, breathed in deep, and from the way the girl tensed, Steph could tell she was trying not to cough.

"So, you were asking the stones a question? Don't let me stop you." Kix smiled a sardonic smile.

"She's going to marry Jason Dereham," Holly said and laughed, the forcefulness in her voice almost trying to make it true.

The boy breathed a plume of faint smoke that vanished into the air. "No," he said after a while, drawing the word out slow; "no, I don't think so. I don't think Jason Dereham would do, at all."

Steph found her cheeks colouring. "I'm not getting married," she said. "Marriage is a joke. It's all a joke. I'm going to travel; I'm going to see the world."

5

"The world, eh?" he leaned forward, peering at her from under his hair, so that she wondered why he didn't brush it aside; that way, she could have seen his eyes. "Maybe. Maybe not. It depends what fate has in store for you, doesn't it."

Steph pushed herself up from the grass. "This is crap," she said, knowing as she said it that she was burning her bridges, marking herself out as no fun and no use before she'd even started her new school, but she couldn't help herself. "It's all crap. If you think it's fate – why did my mum leave my dad? Why did he even let her go?" And she was walking away, fast as she could, knowing she'd have to walk all the way back on her own, and she didn't care about that either; she had nowhere else to go, nowhere else to be. Only the quiet, sleeping village, where nothing seemed to happen and she knew no one.

She looked at the King's Men as she left the site, still in the places they had been for centuries, but looking more like people now that the sun was lower; motionless people looking back at her, their expressions nothing she could read.

*

Holly caught her as she walked along the lane, *chinging* her bicycle bell as she stopped. Anne was nowhere to be seen.

"Wait up," she said. "What'd you go chasing off for?"

"Sorry," said Steph. "It's just—"

"I got what it was. I gather things aren't all contentment in Willow Cottage."

"Not exactly." Steph thought of the quiet house her father had bought after the divorce, its small rooms, the quaint thatched roof. It was the image of contentment; her father, indeed, seemed more than resigned to it. It was Steph who was angry, who had brought a note of discord into the house. *But it's their fault.*

"Kix really likes you." Holly's voice took on a more teasing note, and something else – jealousy? Steph wasn't sure.

She shook her head. She remembered the way he'd looked at her through his hair, his eyes nothing but two bright points. She didn't think he'd looked as though he liked her, wasn't really sure if she liked him.

"He said so," added Holly. She moved aside on the bike, making room for Steph. "He's gorgeous, isn't he? Maybe it's *him* you're

6

going to marry." She looked mock-startled at Steph's expression. "Just kidding."

Steph slipped onto the bike. "What's his name anyway?" she asked as she took hold of Holly's waist. "Kix isn't a name."

"No idea," Holly said, giving a quick *chirr-chirr* of her bicycle bell. "I never met him before in my life."

*

The tallest of the King's Men was bony against Steph's back as she closed her eyes and listened to the tour guide. She wasn't with the tour guide, wasn't really with anyone – she'd walked to the Rollrights this time, just for somewhere to go. She didn't have any money but the warden hadn't been there so she'd come in anyway, and was now sitting out of sight of the guided tour while they went on about megalithic structures and burial chambers and thousands and thousands of years.

Then she heard familiar words, and opened her eyes, startled. "The man will never live who can count the stones three times and arrive at the same number," the voice said. "Either that, or they'll get their heart's desire. Do you want to try it?"

Steph heard murmurs of assent and footsteps edging around the stones, and caught her breath. Would they know she hadn't paid? And then someone was close, really close, and so she stood and pointed to the nearest stone and the next, counting them herself, just another one of the group.

She glanced around and started. It was Kix standing there, watching her with an amused expression. "Three, four, five," he prompted, and grinned.

"What are you doing here? I thought you were—"

"Not me."

"How'd you know what I was going to say?"

He tilted his head, and she got the distinct impression that he'd winked at her, though she couldn't really see his eyes.

"So let's do it," he said. "Let's count them. You go that way, I'll go the other."

Steph let out a splutter of a laugh, and nodded. She turned her back on Kix, continued around the circle, counting each pillar and boulder and stub, stepping out of the way as she crossed paths with various tourists. When she was halfway round she glanced up and looked for Kix; saw only the tour guide looking at her with narrowed

7

eyes. She put her head down, kept going. Thirty-three, thirty-four. On around the circle, focusing on the ground so that she began to feel dizzy. When she looked up she was almost back at the tallest stone and she found that Kix was waiting for her, grinning that broad grin.

"Seventy-four," she said, triumphantly.

"If you say so," he said. "Now, the other way. Come on!"

Steph doubled back, already growing tired of this. It was getting boring, counting the stones. But still – twenty-six, twenty-seven. It wasn't difficult, wouldn't take long. She finished the circle and once more Kix was there ahead of her.

Steph smiled at him, ready to count the last few stones before the tallest – she'd counted that already, hadn't she? And she drew alongside, and looked puzzled.

"Problem?"

"Seventy-six," she said. "No, that can't be right. I must have missed – when—"

"Never mind. Once more, back the other way."

And so she did, she made her way around the circle, making sure to count each stone. And she'd counted the tallest already: definitely. This time there could be no mistake. When she reached the starting point, she wasn't surprised to see that Kix had beaten her to it; she had taken her time. She counted the last couple of stones and her smile faded.

"Seventy, but …"

He grinned again, that knowing grin she wasn't sure she liked.

"So it's true," he said. "And no heart's desire for you, young lady."

"Or you."

"What makes you say that?"

"You got the same number? Three times?"

He tapped his finger on the side of his nose. "That'd be telling."

"So what did you wish for?"

"I have no need for wishes, Stephanie. I have everything I need. And the things I want, I can take."

She looked at him uncertainly. "What do you mean?"

He tilted his head on one side, as though he was listening. "I have to go. See you later, Stephanie who wants to see the world."

"It's *Steph*. What did you mean?"

But he just did that quick gesture again over his shoulder, the slight bob of his head that could have been a wink, could have been

8

anything at all. And his words floated back, so faint she could hardly tell what he said: "Which world did you want to see?"

Steph stared after him. She'd meant to ask who he was, whether he lived here or was just holidaying, whether he would be in school come the autumn. Instead she'd let him walk away, having discovered nothing at all.

*

"He was weird," Steph said, her voice rising. "He said if he wanted something he'd just take it. What do you think he meant? I don't know what he meant." She had found Holly and Anne sitting by the church, drinking cans of coke and tapping their feet against the wall.

Holly frowned. "Probably just confident," she said. "I like that in a man, don't you, Anne?"

"He was *weird*."

"Why? What else did he say?"

"He said – he asked – I dunno." Steph subsided. Maybe Holly was right, maybe she *had* overreacted. She wasn't really sure Kix had said anything all that odd. And it was nice having someone like that, cool, confident – yes, *confident* – choosing to spend time with her. Not that he'd spent much of it. She remembered how he'd walked away, and wondered if, after all, she'd been a little disappointed.

"You like him," Holly said, and Steph met her eye, startled.

"No, I don't. I – I don't think I do."

Holly giggled. "Steph and Kix, sitting in a tree . . ."

"Don't." Steph laughed; caught Holly's eye and laughed harder. "Really, I *don't*. Let's talk about something else. Tell me about the stones."

"What, the Rollrights?"

"There are legends about them, aren't there? What are they?"

Holly pouted. "Not much to tell. It's boring, really. They're king's men, invading England, only a witch stopped them and turned them to stone. There's some story about them all going off to a stream to drink when the church clock strikes midnight, but it's all rubbish."

"And there's the one about how they can't be moved," said Anne, "or misfortune will strike."

"And the one about fairy-folk living under them, waiting to drag you beneath the stones and turn you into some sort of slave."

"Plus the one about the knights telling your fortune," said Anne. "That's about it." She shrugged. "We told you. Boring."

Steph thought of the circle and wondered what it would look like now the daylight was fading. She imagined they would look more like people than ever, huddled in the half-light. But the others were right, it *was* boring. The fact that she had ever felt interested – it was a sign of her horizons shrinking, of having nothing else to do. She should remember she was leaving this place as soon as she could. She could go to university or get a job, or do as she'd boasted to Kix and travel the world. And then she remembered the thing she'd almost thought she'd heard, as he walked away: *Which world do you want to see?*

"Course," said Anne, "It wouldn't be so boring if we went up there at night."

Steph stirred. Holly was staring at her friend. "Yes! We could sneak out, take candles, and dance round the stones in the dark, like the nutty witches."

"Pagans."

"Whatever." Holly turned to Steph. "And we can ask the knights to tell our fortunes." She laughed. "We'll know for sure if you're going to get married then."

\*

Steph sat on the wall and waited, watching for Holly, but she jumped anyway when the shadow of a bike appeared in the road. The moon was fat, almost full, and Holly's face was a pallid oval in the dark. They didn't say anything, just headed away. As they went, Steph stretched out her legs to either side of the bike, feeling an unaccustomed sense of freedom; as though she was leaving Long Compton and her father and everything behind, nothing to think about, nothing holding her back.

The warden's hut was locked up but they crept past anyway, and waited for Anne at the top of the path. She arrived at last, out of breath. "I nearly got spotted," she said. Her voice sounded loud on the hillside. Above them, the sky sparkled with stars. The breeze was cold but felt good on Steph's face.

"Come on," whispered Holly. "The King's Men, first."

They stood in the centre of the circle. Stones stood out eerily in the dark, their paleness catching the moonlight. Holly pulled a candle from her bag, but it was cold, and she found she hadn't brought any

10

matches – she started to shiver. "Sod this," she said. "Let's go to the Knights."

They headed down the hillside. Steph felt the circle of stones like a presence at her back, and she turned and saw them, still there as they had been for centuries. She remembered the story of them going down to a stream to drink, and her lip twitched. When she turned back she could see the Knights and found she had been right: they *did* look like human figures leaning towards each other, whispering their secrets. Seeing them now, in the quiet and in the dark, she didn't find it surprising that the story had been told.

"Sit down," said Holly, "like before. We can close our eyes and chant or something."

"No," said Anne. "Be quiet: if we're quiet, we might hear them."

They sat as they had before, Steph sinking into the long grass. She immediately felt chilled through, the ground cold beneath her. *So* cold. It had been a warm day, the sun shining, and it surprised her it should be so cold.

"Right," said Holly. From the sound of her voice, she wasn't finding this so much fun as she'd expected either. "Shut it."

They did, and Steph leaned back against the railings. It wasn't comfortable and it didn't help with the cold, but she didn't want to change position and annoy Holly. Somewhere, out over the hillside, an owl hooted. Someone – Anne – let out a spurt of air.

*"Shh,"* Holly said.

Steph let her mind drift. She told herself she could be anywhere: France or Spain or Italy. Anywhere.

There was a sound at her back. Steph started: tried to turn. The others still had their eyes closed. After a moment, she settled back down. It hadn't sounded like Anne, messing about. It had sounded like someone whispering behind her back. She didn't like sitting here like this, not any more. She would have preferred it if the stones had been in front of her.

She felt a sharp elbow in her ribs and forced her eyes closed.

It was a short while before it came again, a soft sound gradually getting louder. There was a strange feeling too, a numbing feeling that rose from the ground. It must have been the cold, but it didn't quite feel like that.

"Sssss . . ."

Steph started up again, spun around. There was only rock and nothing more.

*"Steph!"*

But Steph no longer cared if Holly was annoyed. She jumped to her feet and walked around the stones, checking if someone was hiding behind them. There was nothing. No one.

"What is it?" Holly was standing now too. "Did you hear something?"

"No," said Steph. "Just a bird, maybe." She went back to her place and sank down. This time, when she closed her eyes, the voice was there. She knew it wasn't Holly. It didn't sound like anyone she knew, wasn't the *kind* of voice she knew. This was something else. It sounded at once deep and sibilant and close and distant, and older than any voice had a right to be. "Kixxsss . . ."

"Jesus," said Steph, jumping to her feet.

Holly's eyes snapped open. "What's up?"

"I heard it. Didn't you hear it?"

"Seriously ... you heard something? What did it say?"

Steph didn't answer.

"Tell us," said Anne.

"She's fooling about."

"She's not. Look at her face."

Steph put a hand to her cheek. She didn't know what Anne meant, but she felt pale; very pale. "It said 'Kix,'" she stammered, "but it wasn't real. I must have fallen asleep or something."

"No, you didn't." Holly stood. "You really heard something, didn't you? And – Kix!" Something about her voice changed. "Score."

"No – I mean, it isn't real. Or it isn't *right.* Something isn't right." Steph wanted to explain, but didn't know how: none of this made any sense. "I don't even like him," she finished.

But then they fell silent, because they heard a new sound; footsteps swishing through grass. Someone was coming towards them. "Shit," hissed Holly, but it was too late, they had nowhere to go. A dark figure stalked down the hillside. After a moment it started to whistle, and then pale hair caught the moonlight. It was Kix.

"Speak of the devil," said Holly admiringly.

"But – but how ... "

"Kix!" Anne cut in. "You'll never believe what ..."

"*Anne!*"

But Kix didn't seem interested in what Anne was going to say. He stopped in front of them and looked at Steph. "Hey," he said. "I saw a bike at the bottom. Thought you rebels must be up here somewhere."

12

"Well, you found us," said Holly, her voice full of smiles.

Kix kept his eyes fixed on Steph. "I was wondering if I could talk to you." He reached out a hand; let it fall again before touching her. "I wanted to apologise for something I said earlier."

Steph shook her head. "Sorry, but it's late, and it's dark. I need to be getting back. Holly, we should go."

Holly spluttered. "Already? You've got to be kidding." She took Anne's arm. "Come on. We'll wait for you at the circle, Steph."

"No, but …"

It was too late. They were already heading away, and Steph was left alone with Kix.

"Walk with me," he said, and his voice was soft; he made it sound like a question, and Steph nodded.

They headed down the hillside, away from the Knights and further from the circle, and soon Steph could hear a stream. She remembered the story about how the King's Men would come and drink, and it made her smile.

"The things I want, I can take," said Kix, and sighed. "I said that, and I wanted to say I'm sorry."

"It … it's okay."

"It's true, of course. But I prefer them to come willingly."

"What?"

He smiled. "Willingly," he said. "Please do come willingly, Stephanie." He put a hand to his brow, pushed back his hair. She stared at him.

"I asked you a question, once," he said.

*Which world did you want to see?* Steph heard the words, though his lips didn't move. She didn't move either. She felt she could never move again, as if she was rooted to the spot. Her legs were heavy, lifeless. She couldn't look away from his eyes.

"We were both right," he said softly. "You and I – we'll always be together. But you're never getting married, Stephanie."

His eyes were gold. *Gold.*

"You're mad," she said, but her voice faltered. "Let me go."

He held up his hands, the palms turned outward.

"Please." Steph could feel coldness rising from the ground, creeping up her legs, penetrating deep into her knees, wrapping itself around her thighs. It rose higher and she gasped, felt its tendrils easing under her clothes, finding her spine. Soon she wouldn't be able to move at all. She looked down and saw a peculiar thing; her clothes were glowing in the moonlight, the same pale sheen as the

13

stones. She blinked. *Like* the stones. "No," she whispered. "Kix, don't." She looked at his face and his eyes shone and there was no mercy in them, only amusement, and understanding, and age-old knowledge.

He mouthed something: *Be with me.*

It was rising higher, freezing her; it was killing her. Soon the cold would reach her heart and it would stop, just *stop,* while all around her the years would pass and she would still be there, just as now, except she wouldn't be able to move or breathe or speak. *Speak.*

"Please," she said, her thoughts running wildly. Let me go. I'll give you anything."

He smiled, as if at the antics of a child.

"I'll count the stones," she said. "Just give me a chance. Let me count the stones, and if I get it right – three times – you'll let me go."

He laughed, loud and sharp, and suddenly she could move again. "Done," he said. "I knew there was a reason I chose you, Stephanie. I knew, if nothing else, you'd make this interesting."

\*

When they reached the King's Men, Steph looked around for Holly and Anne. They weren't there. She scanned the site, back and forth, but she couldn't see them. They must have decided to wait by the entrance, or left her alone, thinking it a fine joke to leave her with Kix.

"Holly!" she shouted, starting to run, and suddenly Kix was in front of her, and he was laughing. When she heard that laughter, she knew it wasn't any use. Tears sprang to her eyes. Kix put both hands to her shoulders, not holding tightly but steadying her.

"There, there," he said. His voice was kind, but those eyes were hard. He indicated the stones. "Count," he said. "That's all you have to do. Count them."

Steph took a deep breath. He was taller than her, and she knew he would be faster; there was no use in running. She looked around, found the tallest stone, and began to count.

She had thought it would be harder in the dark, but somehow it was easier. Each stone shone in the moonlight, standing out clearly against the dark grass. Kix stayed in the middle of the circle, turning slowly like the hand of a clock. She glanced towards him, almost lost her place; but no, she'd counted the small one, was on to the next.

She went slowly, carefully. Then she was back at the starting point and she opened her mouth, but Kix spoke first.

"I'll give you a clue, little Stephanie," he said. "There are seventy-seven. Have you counted them all? I'll know if you're lying."

She met his glance. "You're the liar," she said. "There are seventy-six."

He made a slight bow. "Again," he said.

Steph's heart beat faster as she made her way around the circle for the second time. When she reached the end, she let out a long breath. "Seventy-six," she said.

"Again."

And she began. This time, as she went, she started to remember the things Holly and Anne had told her: that the stones could tell fortunes. That they were soldiers turned to stone. That fairy-folk lived beneath them, waiting to drag prisoners down under the ground. *Which world do you want to see?*

She shook her head, terrified she would lose count. No: she was up to that one, the reddish stone that stood a little apart from the others. She forced herself to concentrate, knew she was reaching the end when she started to count into the seventies. *Seventy-three. Seventy-four. Seventy-five . . .* no, that wasn't right. The seventy-fifth stone was the tallest, the starting point; she had counted it already. *Seventy-four.*

"Well?" Kix was there.

She stared at him. *I'll know if you're lying.*

"Seventy-six," she said.

He reached out, quicker than she could see, and grabbed her arm. His fingers were long and narrow and hard as steel. "Liar."

She tried to pull away.

"How many?"

Steph was crying now, crying and struggling. "Seventy-four. Seventy-four."

His grip on her arm relaxed, and he started to laugh. Steph pulled back, hard, almost fell; and suddenly she was free, she could *move*, and she was running, careering down the hillside as fast as she could.

Two figures rose in front of her. They didn't look like the figures she knew. They were taller somehow, and their shapes were wrong, too thin; and they were blocking her path, and their eyes were cold.

Steph stopped in front of them, gasping for breath. It *was* Holly and Anne, but they were different: different in a way that reminded her of Kix.

"Bring her back," came a commanding voice from the stones: and they did.

Holly and Anne held onto Steph and she couldn't shake them off. Kix stood in front of her, peered into her eyes as if he could see through her. He smiled. "Do you see?" he asked. "Do you see now?"

Those eyes bored into her and she couldn't look into them. She looked away, saw instead the stones; motionless, silent stones.

"How many are there, Stephanie?"

"Seventy-seven," she whispered. "I get it now. But one of them was you, and you weren't in the circle: and then two more were gone. But there were always seventy-seven."

He smiled that knowing smile. "Wrong again," he said, and he stepped forward and breathed on her, and he put the cold inside her, and it grew; and Steph only heard him faintly as everything began to dim.

"Seventy-eight," he said.

*

The days passed, and then the seasons. Autumn came, and it felt like everything was dying: and then winter with its hollow slowness, and the struggle began to sap from Stephanie's being. Not that she had struggled, not really; not only because she couldn't move, *didn't* move, but because struggle was no longer part of her make-up. And then winter melted away and spring came, and summer, and after a time the seasons flickered by like days; one after the next as the world turned, and she turned with it, her roots sinking deeper into the earth and becoming one with it, as a tree might.

There was no hunger, no thirst. Only the endless cold.

She saw people, too. They came and went, momentary darting things like dragonflies settling for a moment before moving on. Sometimes they stayed by the stones; they came and lit candles, or sat in a ring with their eyes closed, or sang, or dressed the stones with flowers. She wondered if her mother missed her, if her father did. And then she noticed, somewhere in the back of her consciousness, that the visitors began to appear different as their styles and modes of dress began to change.

*Which world did you want to see?*

Always, she felt Kix's presence. She dimly remembered a time when she had railed against it, but as the days passed she found she couldn't remember why; and after a time, it became a comfort.

On some occasions, when visitors came and walked the circle, she would feel Kix leave her side and he would walk among them. Sometimes they saw him and sometimes they didn't; sometimes he was older and sometimes younger, but Steph always knew it was him.

Sometimes Holly and Anne left the circle and spoke with some wanderer they found there. At those times Steph would remember how it had felt to ride on the back of a bicycle, her legs outstretched to feel the rush of freedom: to talk about the future, to plan, to laugh.

Sometimes, in the quiet and in the dark, the stones moved. Sometimes, they danced.

She wondered if, one day, she would learn the trick of it.

# FURY FROM BEYOND

The Cotswolds of England are well-known as a cradle of ghost stories. The verdant landscape is dotted with old market towns, medieval castles, Tudor manor houses, the ruins of Roman villas and the mounds of Dark Age hill-forts. Though lush, green and sedately agricultural, it is a veritable smorgasbord of historical fact and fantasy, not all of which is entirely edifying. The violent haunting of Little Lawford in Warwickshire is a particular illustration of this. At first glance it follows a familiar pattern, but it is better attested to than most legends of this sort, and it has many twists and turns.

The story begins with the Boughtons of Little Lawford Hall, a building which no longer exists in the modern age (the current village contains only a handful of dwellings). The Boughtons were a respected baronial family, but there is a mystery about them – for at some stage in their past a bloody hand was incorporated into their heraldic livery.

In general terms, the symbol of the red hand, more famous now as the defiant 'Red Hand of Ulster', was in earlier days taken as a sign that an aristocratic line had defaulted in its service to the realm and had to bear forever this mark of shame. One tale explains the Boughton bloody hand by naming one particular member of the line – known to us only as 'Boughton' – who, during the reign of Elizabeth I (1558-1603) suffered the loss of his hand as a punishment for illegally enclosing his neighbour's land. But this story is deemed to be unlikely, as mutilations of this nature were rarely imposed on the nobility. A more plausible explanation is that Boughton had his hand severed in battle, so the Boughton Red Hand might actually be a badge of honour.

Whichever is true, it seems that Boughton died shortly afterwards and his one-handed spectre commenced a fearful haunting at Little Lawford Hall, which all but drove the family out of their ancestral home. Why his ghost was said to be so angry was never explained, but by the $18^{th}$ century the hall was deemed to be uninhabitable. The then owner, Edward Boughton, attempted an exorcism by assembling twelve clerics, all chosen for their great piety. The ceremony was almost a disaster. It lasted for many hours, during the course of which the interior of the hall was virtually destroyed by poltergeist activity. One by one, the clerics either collapsed with fright or fled.

Soon only one remained whose name has come down to us as Parson Hall. Obviously a man of stout character, Hall persisted with the exorcism alone and at last brought the grisly phantom to heel. It is said that Hall even communicated with One-Handed Boughton face to face.

Boughton gave no explanation for his presence, but agreed to reside in a bottle, from which he would not emerge except for two hours every night, when he would ride around his former estates in a carriage. Before he left the blighted premises, he warned Parson Hall that if he ever encountered a closed gate while making his rounds, the treaty would be broken and he'd return to the building with full ferocity. Boughton then complied with Hall's wishes, and the bottle was sealed and thrown into a deep pit.

From this point on, it is said, Boughton's ghost only reappeared in a dark carriage, drawn by semi-invisible beasts, prowling the highways and byways around Little Lawford. Phantoms in spectral carriages are a staple of English superstition. Often the carriages were said to be ablaze and under pursuit by a hellish pack – all 'proof' to the gullible populace that the soul in question was evil and therefore damned. It's no coincidence that many who were executed for treason – Ann Boleyn, Walter Raleigh and Guy Fawkes, for example – were said to appear in this fashion. But the case of One-Handed Boughton is a little different. Folk took the story so seriously that local farm gates remained open at night until well in to the 19th century.

As an addendum to the tale, around 1800, after the hall had been demolished, a sealed bottle was found in a nearby pond. There was widespread speculation that this was the bottle in which Boughton's soul had been confined. Not surprisingly, nobody opened it to find out. The bottle was eventually passed to Boughton's descendents, the Boughton-Leighs, whose own home, Brownsover Hall, near Rugby, also became the haunt of a spectral carriage – a disturbance which only ended when the family moved away in 1945.

# STRAW BABIES
## Gary McMahon

"I think Fred West lived near here."

Derek glanced over at Samantha as he spoke, watching her struggle to pull the final bag from the back of the Range Rover. She asked for help with her eyes and he ignored her. She sighed and continued to unload the car.

"In Much Marcle. We passed the road sign a little while ago."

"Huh? Who? Where?" She stared at him. Her hair was mussed, framing her small, oval face; she could see the fringe drooping before her eyes. Her brow was damp, sweaty.

"You know, Gloucester's most famous son. The serial killers. Fred and Rose? He was born around here, might even have played in this forest when he was a child."

He was clearly excited by this piece of local history.

Samantha shook her head. "I have no idea what you're talking about." She looked down at the bag, dismissing him, and shut the boot of the car. "No idea ..."

At times like these, more than any others, she was painfully aware of the twenty year difference in their ages, the often unbridgeable gap it created: cultural touchstones – songs on the radio, films released before she was out of nappies. And famous serial killers. Their pop culture references were not the same; when he was celebrating his eighteenth birthday she wasn't even born.

Was that why he was always drawn to such sombre topics? Did being with her make him more aware of his own mortality, drawing attention to the fact that in all probability he would die before she did?

Just then a souped-up Ford Escort pulled up on the other side of the one-lane road, and parked in the passing point opposite the lane where they'd stopped to unload their gear. Three young men sat inside the vehicle, staring at the couple. Dance music blared from the car stereo, turned up so loud that it was distorted by the cheap speakers.

Derek walked to her side and slid his arm around her waist. "It's okay," he said, but she could tell that he was on edge. He'd never liked confrontation; fighting was something that was not part of his psychological makeup. "Just some nosey kids."

Samantha walked around to the other side of the car and stared across the short stretch of potholed tarmac, directly at the boys. The driver – wearing a dark blue baseball cap pulled down low over his eyes – spat out of the open window and revved the engine. Then he wheel-spun the car and drove away, the rear wheels churning up the loose gravel and dirt.

Samantha stood and watched them go.

"Come on," said Derek, leading the way along the barely visible public footpath that branched off from the road. "They won't come back. The car will be fine here. It's just a short walk to the cottage."

"That sounds like a line from a horror film," said Samantha, grinning as she slung her rucksack over her shoulder and followed him.

Derek shook his head.

"Be dark soon, too." She trotted, just to catch up with him, and punched him lightly on the arm. "Promise you'll protect me from the naughty boys, big man?"

He turned around. His face looked pained. Perhaps it was the low sun or the shadows caused by the close-knit trees. "Yeah. Promise."

She saw so much in his eyes that she almost felt sorry for him. She felt his pain; the regret, the heartache. Then she remembered that it was her pain, her heartache that should be more important. She was the one who'd carried the baby for three months – not long enough to show, but enough time to be aware every second that she was carrying another life. All he'd done was watch from the sidelines, promising that he'd leave his wife when the time was right.

She followed him along the overgrown pathway, pretending that she could just about manage to keep up when in reality all she wanted to do was run ahead. He was older then her, yes, but sometimes he seemed ancient. He used to be fit; even when they'd first met he was captain of the local rowing team. These days his only concession to exercise was lifting pints of real ale.

The cottage appeared up ahead, stepping forward from the screen of trees directly behind. Its lopsided walls were dirty white, the rendering peeling away in patches. It was a single-storey timber frame building with a low roof. The windows looked black, but it was simply layers of dirt. The old wooden door was scarred and pitted.

"Quaint," she said, stopping before the small structure.

"Yeah, it's a bit run down. But it's very private. No neighbours for miles. This part of the Forest of Dean is about as quiet as it gets."

For some reason his words made her feel oppressed, as if there was a secondary meaning hidden beneath what he was saying.

"Come on," he said. "Let's go inside and get the lights on before it gets too dark to see."

*

The cottage was not equipped with electrical power. The lights were old fashioned oil lamps; the stove was a wood burner; extra warmth would be provided by a combination of blankets and body heat.

"There we go." Derek stepped back from the final lamp. Its glow pooled on the floor at his feet and cast his face in an eerie light. "Cozy, eh?"

Samantha was sitting in the old rocking chair by the window. She hadn't taken off her coat. Her unlaced boots sat at her feet like a couple of well-behaved cats. "If you say so."

Derek turned to her. "Oh, come on. Give it a chance, would you? I went to a lot of trouble to get this place. The guy was going to close it up for the season but I managed to convince him to let me have it for the week. Let's go easy on each other. We have a lot to talk about." His smile was genuine, she was sure of that, but it looked faked.

She stood and walked across the creaking bare boards, stopping a few inches away from him. "Okay, let's have a truce. No more winding each other up. Let's get the wine out and see what happens." She grinned. Her hand strayed to his belt, her fingers flicking the buckle. This felt faked, too.

They were on the second bottle of wine before he told her the story.

"There's a lot of history here," he said. "Witches and demons – all kinds of spooky stuff." His face, in the unsteady light from the lamps, looked old and lined.

"Oh, yeah? You trying to scare me into bed?"

He ignored her and continued. "There was a deformed old woman once in this part of the forest. Some say she even lived in this cottage. Her name was Mother Stagfoot and she was a healer. She was also into all kinds of occult nonsense. The guy who told me about it said that the locals hanged her as a witch."

"Nice." She sipped her wine, settling back against his chest. His voice was soft, mellow, as he warmed to his subject.

"She would arrange abortions for the women of a nearby village."

Samantha stiffened against him but she doubted that he even noticed. He was too caught up in his tale.

"People said she was also a wet nurse to demons. That she took in infant devils and raised them as her own, letting them suckle at her breast."

She pulled away. "Jesus, Derek, how could you tell me this?"

He looked confused, as if someone had just turned on a bright light in a dark room.

"Abortions? Devil babies? How insensitive can you get?" She stood and went to the kitchen, ran the tap and washed her face with cold water. She didn't want to cry; she didn't want him to see how much he'd upset her.

"Ah," he said, rising from the chair. "Sorry ... I'm an idiot. I didn't think."

Samantha stepped away from the sink and cupped her hands across her belly. Her flat, flat belly. There was a gap there, an absence. How could he not be aware of it every second of every day, in the same way that she was?

She felt his arms as they went around her from behind. She wanted to walk away but she was unable to leave. It was always the same: he was like glue; she stuck to him.

Later that night, as she lay in the darkness listening to him sleep, she pressed her fists into her stomach. At one time she'd thought the baby might act as a catalyst to make him leave his wife, but then it had all gone wrong. Three months: a tiny thing, really; barely a human life at all. But it didn't feel that way to Samantha. It felt like a part of her own life had been scraped out of her when she had been in the clinic getting rid of it for him.

She stared up at the exposed beams of the ceiling, watching the shadows. The wind gusted in the eaves. The ancient timbers creaked. The darkness above her seemed to take on form and substance, like a thick gel. She watched as it dropped and coiled around the beams. Then, gradually, she became aware of the sound: a gentle thudding noise, like someone beating against the roof. Or was it more like footsteps? Yes, that was it. Weird clip-clopping footsteps scampering across the roof outside, like some crazed circus performer on stilts.

Just the wind, she thought, drifting away.

Then the stilts began to hammer madly against the roof tiles, as if trying to break through.

*

23

The next morning was fresh and crisp. The air was cold but the sun was trying its best to get through. She jogged along the path back to the car, warming up her muscles, and then followed a narrow bridle path that headed west. Samantha never went anywhere without her running gear. Running had saved her sanity after the termination and she'd been addicted ever since. And nothing cleared her mind better than an early morning run.

She thought about those sounds last night, and the way she'd expected the roof to fall in. Even in daylight, and out in the fresh air, she was convinced that there had been someone messing about on the roof. Perhaps it had been local youths, tormenting the outsiders … maybe it was a common game in these parts?

She ran for fifteen minutes and then turned around and ran back the way she'd come. It wasn't like the photographs she'd seen online. The forest here was much denser, and darker than she'd expected when they'd been planning their trip.

The trees seemed to have moved closer to the edge of the crude path and the leaves and branches were thicker than during the outward run. She started to sprint, and by the time she reached the cottage she was breathing hard.

"Morning. Good run?"

Samantha was bent over, hands on knees, and panting like a dog. She looked up and saw Derek approaching from the direction of the cottage. "Not bad," she said, straightening. "Hey, did you hear all that banging last night?"

He shook his head. "No. When was that?"

"Late. You were asleep, I suppose. I'm pretty sure that someone was farting about, climbing up on the roof and rattling the tiles. Maybe you should take a look?"

"Okay." He turned back towards the cottage. "Come on."

Inside, she pointed at a spot directly above the bed. "There. I heard them. It was … unnerving." She smiled, putting on a brave face like always.

"That's strange." Derek stood on the bed. The mattress groaned.

"What is it?" She walked around, to the foot of the bed, and stared at the place he was inspecting.

"Can't you see it?"

"No." She climbed up beside him. The bed groaned again.

"Look … see it now? A tiny trapdoor."

24

"Wow … yes. That *is* weird." Her eyes found the outline of a small door or panel in the fabric of the roof, between two exposed joists. "Do you think it's, like, a little loft space, or something?"

Derek stretched his body, reaching up towards the hatch. "I don't know, but we can easily find out."

It took them only minutes to move the bed and Derek positioned a kitchen chair beneath the hatch. He stepped up and reached for the hatch, pushing it with his fingertips. At first the wooden square didn't budge, but then, slowly, it began to lift inside its frame. One more push and it came loose; dust fell into his hair. He blinked, coughed, and wobbled on the chair. "There's something carved on the hatch. Just a faint outline … I think it's a five-pointed star. Isn't that meant as protection from evil, or is it a curse? I can never remember which."

Samantha couldn't help but notice the mild note of glee in his voice.

The hatch fell, clattering on the floorboards, and something else came down after it – a small dirty bundle; a dusty sackcloth package. The bundle hit the floor and rolled over towards the bed, then came to rest.

"What the hell is it?" Samantha walked over, dropped into a crouch, but didn't touch the bundle. It was old; the material was filthy and torn.

Derek bent down and picked it up. Tiny fragments of rotten material came away from the whole, shredding and flaking like dry skin. "Let's see." He took the bundle over to the dining table and set it down. There were strange markings on the wrappings, stained or dyed onto the material.

"I don't like this. Whatever it is, somebody hid it up there. It wasn't meant to be found."

Derek was smiling. "Oh, come on. Where's your natural curiosity? There could be old church gold wrapped up in here, or ancient bones."

"Why do you always have to be so damned dark?" Her voice was louder than she'd intended. The words sounded more like an attack than a simple question.

"Because it's interesting," he said, unrolling the sacking. It came away in layers, each one breaking off in sections rather than peeling away as a single sheet. It didn't take long; the thing wasn't bound too tightly. Under the final layer there was a handcrafted figure – a doll – made from carved wood, old netting, and with a body made of dull

25

rag stuffed with dry straw. The head was smooth and round and oversized like that of a baby.

The old stitches along one side of the body were coming loose, the thread failing, and beneath the torso each sticklike leg ended in what looked like a wide double toe, or split hoof.

"Wow," said Derek. "This is cool. It's like an old fetish, or something. The kind of things witches used to lay curses." He turned the doll in his big hands, inspecting it. "It even has a little face, drawn on in charcoal. It's amazing the details have lasted this long … like it's been preserved up there for centuries."

Samantha was backing away, clutching at her stomach. "I don't like it, Derek. I really don't like it."

"Oh, come on. It's actually kind of cute." He turned around, holding the doll against his chest. It looked wrong; blasphemous. "According to the story, Mother Stagfoot used to make these little straw babies for the women she helped; grim mementoes to take away with them. I wonder if it's one of hers?"

"Throw it away. It's horrible."

"No," he said, gently stroking the doll's smooth wooden scalp. "I'm keeping it."

*

She rarely ran twice a day, but today was different. She needed to stretch out, to feel as if she were in control. Exercise made her aware of her body in a way that she treasured. It was a form of empowerment, but it was also a sham: nobody was ever truly in control, even of their own body.

Just before it started to get dark she ran the same route she'd found earlier that day, but faster, following the path for longer. After twenty minutes she became aware of somebody trailing her in the trees, moving alongside her and mirroring her pace.

*I'm losing my mind*, she thought, stretching her legs, trying to outrun the paranoia. *It's the doll … that stupid doll, it's spooked me.* She pushed on, damp leaves slapping her arms, the side of her face, and the path became narrower, less easy to define.

She knew that there were still wild boars roaming in the forest, but there was definitely somebody following her. She could hear their footsteps, feel their eyes upon her. Was it the same person who'd been climbing around on the roof last night? Was this some

26

kind of joke, a little friendly persecution by those boys who'd watched them from the Ford Escort yesterday afternoon?

Not for the first time in the last twenty-four hours, she wished they hadn't come to somewhere so isolated that they couldn't get a phone signal.

She stopped running and stood with her hands on her hips, breathing heavily. "I know you're there." She turned in a slow circle, watching the trees. The sky was dark; the air felt heavy. "I know you're following me. You were on the roof last night. I'm not scared of you."

Was that laughter? A soft sniggering sound somewhere off to her left?

"*Here, pretty-pretty*," whispered a soft, high-pitched voice. It could have been either male or female; she wasn't sure which.

Samantha spun around, her hands clenched into fists. "Leave me alone. We have a gun back at the cottage." Laughter again: short, sharp and abrupt. Then there was the sound of someone rushing away from her through the undergrowth, stepping on twigs and branches in their haste, unconcerned about being heard.

Samantha ran full-tilt back in the direction of the cottage, and stopped off at the car on the way. She could see that the bonnet was open before she even reached the vehicle. When she got there, she walked around to the front of the car, staring at the mess inside. Whoever had done this, they'd done a good job. She didn't know engines but she knew that this one was wrecked. It looked like they'd used a large rock, bashing away at the mechanics, and tearing out plugs and wires with their bare hands.

She walked into the middle of the road. There were no cars in either direction. She couldn't even hear the sound of distant engines – the main road was nowhere in sight.

She walked back to the cottage, watching the trees intently.

It was growing dark.

*

"We can't leave yet. It's about five miles to the nearest village." Derek was pacing the floor, walking from one wall to the other like a prisoner in a cell. "Are you sure about the car? I mean, could you have been mistaken?"

She closed her eyes, rubbed her forehead. "Go and take a look if you don't believe me." She waited.

Derek nodded. "I'm sorry. Of course I believe you."

"What are we going to do? There's somebody out there and they're messing with us, trying to scare us. That must've been them on the roof last night. Now they've trashed the car. This is serious. They're not playing games."

Derek stopped pacing. He looked at the door, at the windows. "This place is secure. Nobody's getting through that old wooden door without a bazooka and there are shutters on all the windows. I say we barricade ourselves in here tonight, just in case, and then set off walking early tomorrow morning. We should reach civilisation in three hours. There'll be a police station. A shop. Something."

Samantha started closing and locking the heavy wooden shutters across the windows. "Have you checked your phone again? I still can't get a signal."

Derek's footsteps banged across the boards as he dealt with the windows on the opposite side of the room. "Yeah, I've checked it. Same for me, I'm afraid. That was part of the charm of this place, remember? No phone, no internet, no disturbances."

"Who knew?" she said, trying for humour but falling short.

They stood facing each other across the room. The distance seemed huge and unnavigable; safety was not within easy reach.

Samantha turned away and walked into the kitchen area. The doll was on the table, propped up against an empty wine bottle. It's horrible, pinched little face stared at her from the bulging round head, and the straw was hanging out of its badly stuffed torso, making it look as if it had been partially disembowelled by a particularly clumsy child. She tried not to look at the legs, those horrible cloven feet ...

Her stomach ached and when she glanced down, for a moment it looked swollen, distended ... but it was simply the shadows playing tricks on her, plucking at the chords of memory until they chimed.

Outside the cottage walls, the forest seemed to respond to her feelings. The forest was out there, waiting, but it was also inside, nestled within her barren womb.

Once she returned her attention to the doll, she became convinced that it had moved. Not much; just an inch or two, a tilt of the bulbous baby-head or a subtle change in the positioning of the limbs.

"Come here."

She went over to where Derek was standing, beside the front door.

"Did you hear that?"

She waited. "Hear what?" There was a loud bang, which was followed by another.

"That. Someone's knocking."

The banging sound moved around the walls. Somebody was walking around the cottage, slamming their fists against the door, the outside of the window shutters, the walls themselves. The banging became frantic, and then after a few seconds it stopped.

"Why are they doing this?" She reached out and grabbed his hand. "Why don't they leave us alone?"

Derek squeezed her hand, let go, and shuffled forward to stand right next to the door. "I'm armed," he said. "I'm a hunter. I have guns. Leave us alone or I'll use them."

Gentle, mocking laughter from the other side of the door.

"I'm warning you. I'll shoot you."

The soft laughter continued for a while and then the sound moved slowly away, as if whoever was out there had started walking backwards, retreating from the door. Samantha could still hear the sound, even as its owner backed farther away. It stayed in her ears, a mocking echo.

"I'll check the bedroom windows," she said, suddenly realising that they'd forgotten the small room. She moved quickly in the flickering light, across the floor and into the bedroom. The shutters were open. There was a face at the window. She couldn't make out any features because of the darkness and the fact that the figure was wearing a hat – a dark blue baseball cap. She ran over and slammed the shutter, blocking out more laughter.

"*Heeeeeeeere*, pretty, pretty, pretty!" The voice on the other side of the shutter was high-pitched, a nightmarish imitation of a child's singsong tone.

Samantha stood with her back against the wall. She was breathing hard.

Derek appeared in the doorway. His face was pale. There was sweat on his forehead and his upper lip. She'd always known that he lacked courage, and here was yet more evidence. He should have stood by her – he should have been with her when she got rid of their baby instead of sitting at home and eating dinner with his wife.

"It's kids," she said.

"What? How do you know?" His voice was soft. Like his hands. Like his resolve. Soft and useless. She could see that now. Why had she never seen it before?

"I saw one of them, at the window." She pointed. "A young lad in a baseball cap. They're trying to scare us. Spooking the outsiders."

The banging sound started up again. And then, inevitably, she heard those same clip-clop footsteps making their way across the roof, the ones she'd heard the night before. They were slow, dainty, and deliberate. Not the clumsy, excited steps of a young kid out to give someone a scare, but the careful steps of somebody who knows exactly what they are doing, where they are heading.

"Mother Stagfoot," she said, not quite understanding why or even how she knew. She looked over Derek's shoulder and saw an elongated shadow cast against the wall. She told herself that the doll wasn't moving in an uneven gait, stomping off in search of its mother. But she could hear its little cleft-hoofed feet as they tip-tip-tapped across the hard wooden floor.

She pushed past Derek and went into the other room; glanced at the dining table, where the doll had been sitting only moments before. The doll was no longer there.

"What's happening?" Derek's voice was even quieter. It sounded almost as if he were awed by what was going on around him.

Something slammed with great force against the side of the cottage, hard enough to make the timber frame creak and buckle. Dust puffed and drifted across the room. The oil lamps flickered violently, threatening to go out.

"I think Mother's coming," said Samantha. She felt like giggling.

There was a loud, plaintive cry; somewhere out there in the forest darkness, another one of their attackers was being dealt with. She heard a prolonged growl, like that of a lion, and then the sound of what she could only think of as rending. Something was being torn apart.

Then there was silence, blissful silence.

They both waited, expecting something else. But there was nothing: just that awkward quiet, the sense that something had finished its business but was still out there, waiting.

"What should we do?" Derek walked to her side and grabbed her hand. She pulled away, unwilling to even touch him.

Samantha licked her lips. "I think you should open the door. It's safe now. They're gone."

"What?"

She didn't even look at him, just kept her eyes on the front door. "It's fine. Trust me ... those kids are long gone. They won't cause us any more trouble." The forest reached out to her; she felt a gentle tugging at the pit of her stomach.

Derek walked slowly to the door. He looked back, seeking reassurance. Their roles had reversed; he took his orders from her now. It was much too late to take back what she'd done in the clinic, but still, belatedly, she could make a stand.

She nodded. "That's right." She smiled. "Just open the door."

When he did so, the little straw doll was standing outside on the stone step, leaning against the door frame. It was turned towards them, its charcoal features looking inside. She had no idea how it had got out there, past their fortifications. It wasn't possible.

Derek paused for a moment, and then bent down to pick it up. When he stood upright, she was there, standing right before him.

She was broad yet thin, and easily a couple of feet taller than Derek – and she was motionless. She seemed composed of the darkness, but with ragged edges, as if she'd been cut out of the night; the dark template of all Mothers.

The forest had shuffled forward behind the figure, crowding out the flat spaces, eating up the terrain. Her long, strong legs were wide at the top and narrowed towards the ankle.

She looked fast, agile, comfortable at speed.

"Oh, God …" That was all Derek had time to say.

She took him in one swift movement. Her arms went up and out, as if she were taking him into an embrace. She opened her hands wide, displaying a lethal fan of razor-like claws. Then she curled around him, folding him over at the waist and, mounting him like a rider climbing onto a mare, rode him madly across the black ground and into the trees.

Derek did nothing but run, with the dark billowing shape attached to his back, steering him deeper into the waiting forest. He was a man possessed. His mind was no longer his own. He was in her thrall; he belonged to her completely.

He scampered between the dark trees and vanished from sight.

The doll remained on the doorstep.

Samantha didn't know how to feel, but she certainly did not feel afraid. Something had been released; an appetite had been set free, unleashed upon the world.

Outside, something screamed, and it sounded pitched somewhere between agony and ecstasy.

Derek had found his voice at last.

31

Samantha stood there for what felt like a long time, watching the darkness. But nothing stirred outside. Finally she turned around to face the room and saw the formless shape of Mother Stagfoot standing there, squeezed tightly into the kitchen doorway. She was so large that she filled the frame, creating a crooked rectangle of black.

The patch of darkness that was her face writhed and she clomped noisily forward on her cloven feet, swaying from side to side and breathing heavily, like a horse at the end of a race. A light mist rose from her body; cooling sweat, from the exertions of her ride.

As the large, spindly-legged creature shifted into the flickering lamplight, Samantha saw the dolls hanging from her bloated multiple breasts. Dozens of those straw dolls, each one a replica of the one Derek had found in the roof space. The Mother was suckling them, giving them sustenance.

These were her babies, the remnants of all the children she had ever brought dead into the world.

Samantha felt her stomach swell. She looked down and saw that she was clutching the doll – her own straw baby – and that it was climbing slowly up her body, making its way towards her chest. Its small head tilted upwards; its tiny mouth was open.

She looked up again, tears on her cheeks.

"Sister," she said, opening her mind to all the possibilities of darkness.

Outside, the forest waited.

# A BIZARRE AND TERRIBLE EVENT

A macabre tale, which has never been explained to the satisfaction of historians or folklorists, comes to us from the village of Besford in the Wychavon district of central Worcestershire. It concerns a certain Church Farm, located in a region of wooded countryside now known as Dog Kennel Place.

In times past, the occupants of Church Farm were charged with kenneling the various packs of foxhounds belonging to the local lord of the manor. On an unspecified date sometime in the 1750s, the kennelman and his wife were woken in the middle of the night by a frantic baying from the kennels. It was an uproar such as they had never heard – something had disturbed the dogs badly, and was continuing to do so because there was no let-up in the furore.

Eventually the kennelman decided to go out and investigate, but his wife was frightened and begged him to stay indoors. The kennelman insisted that he had his duty. Though still in his nightshirt, he put on his boots, loaded a blunderbuss and ventured outside, locking the cottage door behind him. His wife remained indoors, listening intently. The dogs continued to bark and howl madly, and then there was a detonation – the blunderbuss had been discharged. However, the kennelman did not return and his wife was so frozen with fear that it was only at first light, long after the hounds had finally fallen quiet, that she was able to pluck up the courage to go out and look for him.

She made a terrifying discovery: her husband's two legs, both apparently torn from his body, though still wearing his boots. There was no sign of any other part of him.

Not surprisingly, this event caused a local sensation. Numerous theories abounded. Perhaps the kennelman had been murdered by a band of wandering rogues – but if so, why would they take away his head, torso and arms, and why not assault the cottage now that it was undefended? Perhaps he had been attacked by some fierce animal which might have escaped from a local circus, maybe a bear or tiger? But no such escaped animals had been reported at the time, nor were they reported afterwards. Perhaps he had been killed by his own hounds? Had they failed to recognise him in his nightshirt, and thought him an intruder? This explanation was also dismissed – the dogs were still in their kennels and the kennelman's remains were outside. In any case, even in the extremely unlikely event that his *own dogs had mauled and partly eaten him, there would have been recognisable leftovers.*

*The grim mystery was never solved, though there was brief excitement in 1930, when the skeleton of a man without legs was found buried in close vicinity to Church Farm. This might have provided an explanation, but then other similarly mutilated skeletons were also found and identified as Civil War casualties.*

*To this date, the strange and brutal death at Church Farm is unexplained. As an epilogue to the story, the kennelman's ghost is said to wander around the old farm buildings at night, his spurs jingling in the darkness.*

# CHARM
## Reggie Oliver

S tonehill Manor stands on gentle slopes of the Cotswold ridge a few miles East of Broadway, looking down into the fertile mists of the Vale of Evesham. On a clear day from its front lawn you can just see the notched summit of Bredon Hill far away across the valley. A faint echo of Housman's poem used to stir in my mind whenever I caught sight of it:

> *In Summertime on Bredon ...*
> *My love and I would lie,*
> *And see the coloured counties*
> *And hear the larks so high*
> *About us in the sky.*

This was quintessential England, just as Stonehill was the quintessential small Georgian Manor House: perfectly proportioned, spacious without being rambling, set in two or three acres of manageable grounds. Its charm was self-evident, so why was it so inexpensive to rent? I'm afraid there is no simple and obvious answer to this question, but there is an explanation, of a kind. You must allow me to give it in my own way.

My name is Arthur Bertram, I am a Professor of Constitutional History at Oxford, and I am in my late fifties. I have a wife, Pauline, and two grown-up children. (When I say grown-up, I mean they have left home, not that they are 'grown up'. My son, Edmund calls himself Zack, wears a stud on his lower lip, and claims to be a 'rock musician'. My daughter Fanny dyes her hair green and edits a tabloid gossip column. I rest my case). At any rate, about three years ago, Pauline proposed that I should take a sabbatical to finish a book I had long been writing on 'The Souls'. The ignorant had better be informed at this point that The Souls were an influential group of aristocratic writers, artists and political thinkers who flourished at the turn of the century. One of their main meeting places was at Stanway, not far from Stonehill. That is all I need to say: they play no further part in my story.

We decided to let our house in the Woodstock Road, and move to the country for which Pauline has always had a hankering. We chose the Cotswolds partly because it was comparatively near Oxford, but also so that I could have easy access to the archive of Souls' papers at Stanway.

Nothing sullied our first sight of the Manor. We came to it in early January on a day when the cold sky was a pure pale sapphire blue, and a light covering of snow gilded the ground. The local Guiting Yellow Limestone with which the Manor had been built glowed golden in the far off winter sun.

Our guide was a young assistant from the estate agent's in Winchcombe, fresh, to judge by his manner and accent, from a minor public school. He may not have been clever enough for university, but his newness to the job made him keen. I noticed how closely he observed all our reactions.

We liked the elegant classical portico with its Tuscan pillars. We liked the English Palladian Hall and the modest grandeur of its sweeping staircase. We loved the library which opened off the hall, still tenanted by ranks of unread books, with its slackly comfortable armchairs and its bow-windowed alcove at the end. We approved of the numerous airy bedrooms where Edmund and Fanny could come at weekends, bringing with them their customary retinue of unsuitable friends and lovers. There was nothing to which we could object.

The place was to be rented 'furnished' and the furniture was undistinguished but suitable: mostly early twentieth century reproductions of eighteenth century, in addition to the usual baggy armchairs and sofas in faded chintz covers. There were portraits on the walls – of the family who owned the Manor, I assumed – but I noticed that the only two that might have been valuable, a Gainsborough and a Raeburn, were actually photographic reproductions printed onto canvas to look like the real thing. After the briefest of tours Pauline and I had decided.

The young estate agent looked very relieved when we told him, but he showed some signs of nervousness when I asked about our landlord. The landlord, he told us briskly, lived in the little lodge or gatehouse at the entrance to the drive leading up to the Manor: his name was Sir Rodney Foxe-Walter, a Baronet. The name stirred a faint memory somewhere in my mind but I could not grasp it.

Pauline, to her credit, did raise some doubts about having a landlord practically on our doorstep, but the young man quickly dismissed them by saying that "he keeps himself to himself," and "he's hardly ever there anyway." These two statements struck me as being slightly self-contradictory, but I did not pursue the matter. I don't like to use the term – it sounds so sentimental – but the fact was we had 'fallen in love' with Stonehill. We elected to take it on a six month short-hold tenancy from April 1st.

Our first few weeks there were spent getting to know the place. It was a mild, kindly spring. Pauline and I dozed over books in our new library. We went for long walks through the elegant grey villages on the slopes of the Cotswolds. We dined at the overpriced restaurants of Broadway and poked about in the overpriced antique shops of Stow-on-the-Wold. I was reminded that there was more to life than Oxford and the academic world. It was a spring in many ways.

Occasionally we would speculate about our landlord. Pauline in particular was intrigued and kept an eye on the Lodge at the end of the drive. She would report on signs of his presence. A battered Landrover sat on the side of the drive whenever he was in residence.

"He's definitely around," said Pauline one evening. "His lights are on and I thought I saw a shadow moving about in there just now. You don't think it would be polite to ask him up for a drink or something?" My wife subscribes to the belief that everyone needs looking after and 'taking out of themselves' in some way or other. It is one of her many endearing qualities; I take a less activist approach to life.

"The man is obviously a recluse," I said. "I think we should let him be until he chooses to reveal himself." I couldn't help feeling curious, though.

The following afternoon my sister-in-law, Trish, rang me up. Strictly speaking, I should say she is my ex-sister-in-law. After about five years married to my brother, Jim, a London dentist, she decided he wasn't good enough for her and went off with a man who lives in Temple Guiting and is something to do with horses. In spite of this, she has kept in touch with me; I suspect because Oxford professorships in her eyes possess a certain social cachet. My feelings for Trish are mixed; but Pauline actively disliked her, insofar as she was capable of disliking anyone. Trish is a very lively, horsey woman, and speaks in one of those loud, assertive upper class voices, as if she were permanently addressing a roomful of deaf underlings.

"Hello, Arthur! Trish here! Why didn't you tell me you'd moved to my part of the world?"

"How did you find out we had?"

"Nothing escapes me, darling. Now you must come over for drinks or lunch or something and I'll introduce you to everyone who matters in the Cotswolds."

"But we don't want to be introduced to everyone who matters in the Cotswolds."

"Nonsense! Don't be such a fearful academic bore, Arthur. By the way how are you getting on with your landlord?"

"We haven't seen him yet. Do you know him?"

"Roddy Foxe-Walter? Of course I know him! Now then, why on earth didn't you consult me before renting somewhere here?"

"Why should we? Anyway, we're very happy with Stonehill."

"H'mm...! Now then, when can you come over?"

Eventually, I was bullied into accepting an invitation to drinks the following evening. Pauline was not too happy when I told her, but she said: "At least we may find out something about the mysterious Sir Rodney."

The next morning I woke up early. Pauline still slumbered beside me but I felt I had been aroused by something. Pale sunlight filtered through the curtains: it would be another fine day. I put on dressing gown and slippers and quietly left the bedroom.

Our bedroom opens onto a balustraded landing which leads to the main staircase down to the hall. As soon as I was on the landing I could distinctly hear a faint murmuring sound coming from below. I went to the top of the stairs.

I looked down into the hall and saw that the door to the library was half open. I was sure I had closed it the night before. The noise I had heard was now identifiable as that of conversation: casual talk interspersed with laughter as at a party. I was not in the least alarmed but I was puzzled that some people should be having a get-together at half past six in the morning in my library. I trod softly down the stairs, crossed the hall and entered the library.

A large man in a green Barbour and mud-coloured trousers was wandering aimlessly round the room with a glass of whisky in his hand. The glass was mine and the whisky also: my bottle of Famous Grouse was open to the elements on the console table.

I had entered the room silently, so that for about fifteen seconds I was able to watch him unobserved. He looked like someone making a circuit of his acquaintances at a drinks party and what I could hear of his talk corresponded with this appearance.

"How are you, you old bugger, eh ...? Still rogering for England? Ha ha ...! My dear, you look positively radiant ... Well, I've been away ... Out of things ... Suffering from the dreaded lurgy ... Better now ... All the better for seeing you ... And the more of you I can see, the better, I shall feel, eh? Eh? Ha, ha!"

At that moment he turned and saw me. I think he was mildly embarrassed, but he was soon over it.

"Ah! Hello, there. You must be Bertram. I'm Roddy Foxe-Walter. Your landlord. How d'you do? Call me Roddy." I shook a damp, flabby hand. "Just dropped in to check up on the old place. See how you're getting on."

"We're doing fine, thank you."

"Splendid! Splendid! Excuse the unseasonable hour. As my friends will tell you, I have a pretty individual sense of time."

He turned away from me, drained his whisky quickly and returned the glass to the tray on which stood the bottle. He muttered something as he struggled to replace the screw top of my Famous Grouse.

Rodney Foxe-Walter was in his fifties: not all-round obese, but with a sagging belly that flopped over his trouser belt and pendulous jowls. He had a longish, square-jawed face and a shiny red complexion. Tiny scarlet thickets of broken veins were beginning to blossom on his nose and cheeks. He might, when younger, have looked like a handsome rugby player, but those days were now over. He turned back towards me with a grin, having finished with his rather feeble attempts to conceal the theft of my drink.

"So ... Look, I can't keep calling you Bertram, like a bloody beak. What's your other name?"

"Arthur."

"Arthur ... And you must call me Roddy. None of that Sir Rodney here. I've always been an informal sort of bloke, as my friends will tell you. You here with your better half, then?"

"She's upstairs asleep."

"Fine, Fine. We won't disturb her. Look, you two must come down to the Lodge for a drink. Welcome you officially to Stonehill. How about this evening?"

I explained how that evening was out because we were already spoken for where drinks were concerned. He seemed mildly offended by this and asked who I was having drinks with. I told him. He laughed.

"Good God! Trish Parker-Wimbourne! Trish Sutherland as was before she briefly married some ghastly fellow whose name I forget! Dentist, I believe! Bloody Hell! Oh, I knew old Trish very well. Biblically too, once or thrice. Eh? Ha! She was a bit of a hot-knickers in her day, you know. Oh! Beg pardon. Shouldn't have said that."

I made a dismissive gesture to show that I wasn't offended. (I wasn't: not even by the allusion to my brother). We arranged to meet for drinks the following evening.

"Well," said Roddy when these arrangements were concluded. "Must be off. Things to do ... People to see ... Arthur ... Bertram, is it?" I nodded. "Do I know you from somewhere?"

"I don't think so."

"Feel sure ... The old brain must be going ... Well, pip pip. See you tomorrow evening. Don't do anything I wouldn't do, eh? That'll leave you some scope, as my friends may tell you. Ha!" And he left.

I went upstairs and told Pauline about my encounter. She murmured: "Poor old thing, he must be lonely," and then turned over in bed to sleep a little longer.

*

Trish lived on a stud farm run by her husband Dickie. Apart from horses, there were also a great many dogs. In her late middle age Trish had become strangely androgynous, as some country women do. Though I would never have described her as a "hot knickers" in her young days I do remember an unusually slender and attractive young woman. Now she had become chunky and amorphous, a quality emphasised by her puffer jacket and sensible tweed skirt. Her skin was weather-beaten and scribbled over with fine lines: she no longer affected make-up.

Our welcome was hearty. "Come in! The place looks like a bloody tip, as usual, I know. One has to make these choices in life: either one has dogs and horses, or one has house beautiful. One can't have both. I prefer dogs and horses." We were shown into a sitting room that smelled – not too unpleasantly – of wet dog. A pair of liver and white spaniels eased themselves off a sofa to sniff at us. "You'll have to excuse my husband. He's out somewhere with the horses. The fact is, Dickie's a darling, but he generally can't stand people. Only really likes horses. Used to be a pretty good amateur jump jockey. Just about tolerates dogs. On the whole I don't blame him. Now then, darlings, what's your poison?"

I chose whisky and soda; Pauline and Trish had gin and tonic. Conversation was relaxed. I had the feeling that Pauline's ancient aversion to Trish was evaporating. Though she was not at all "our sort of person", Trish seemed to be at ease with herself in a way that she never was when she had been a brittle and beautiful debutante in the Seventies.

It was inevitable, I suppose, that the subject of our landlord should come up. I gave Trish a carefully edited account of my encounter with Roddy that morning.

Trish nodded as if the incident I had recalled was typical. "One barely sees him around these days," she said. "I think he's rather horribly gone downhill. There are some people who simply won't speak to him. I know what they say about him, but he could be the most tremendous fun in the old days, you know. Buckets of charm. All the charm in the world. He'd let you down in some appalling way and the next time you'd just forgive him. You couldn't help yourself."

I asked Trish if he had ever been married.

"Stayed bachelor as long as possible, then got hitched to the Kleinman girl. Catriona Kleinman. We all called her Cats. She was pretty dippy, but quite sweet and she had stacks of the wonga: father in oil, I believe. Can't remember. Anyway he was rolling in the stuff. By all accounts, Roddy didn't treat her very brilliantly after they were married. When Cats got pregnant he just buzzed off, leaving her at Stonehill with an old nanny. By the time she was about to give birth he was in the Bahamas living it up with Princess Margaret and the Dorsets. Well she lost the baby which was ghastly and there were frantic calls to Nassau summoning him home. Eventually the Dorsets literally had to shovel him onto a plane back to England. When he got home poor old Cats was suffering the most terrible depression and I don't think Roddy helped. He stayed with her for a couple of days then buggered off to London for a bit of shagging and boozing. While he was there Cats did herself in."

"At Stonehill?" Trish nodded. I am not superstitious; this ought not have troubled me, but it did. "How?"

"Chucked herself out of a window, I believe. I can't remember the details. I think Roddy was hoping he would come into some of Cats's money, but it was all tied up in a trust and he got practically nothing. Old man Kleinman had always loathed him anyway. Well, by this time he was rapidly running out of money, but he still had some faithful contacts. He got a job as a sort of host at the Egremont – you remember, the high class gambling joint in Duke Street – pulling in the rich punters with his title and his charm and all. He was quite successful at it for a while, but most of his earnings went back into gambling at the Egremont. He attracted all sorts to the club, including the Freeman brothers – you remember, those South

London gangsters who kept getting themselves into photos with minor royalty? Well, that was a big deal for a while, but it all went sour and Roddy was sacked from the Egremont. I don't know the details. Then Roddy began to drink a lot more than was good for him and was always on the cadge. Suddenly he just wasn't fun anymore. And he used to be a scream, you know, in his day. Such a hoot: really! Some of the things he came out with, I can't remember them now, but they could be absolutely killing. Basically, he just ran out of friends, I suppose. Money and drink – lack of and too much, respectively – were the main reasons. But there was something else. Something that happened at Stonehill. I don't mean the suicide: this thing came later. A few people know what happened but they won't say anything about it, it's so utterly ghastly, apparently. I've tried to worm it out of them but they just won't spill the beans."

A silence followed. Suddenly, I became aware that a man was standing in the room by the door: small, wiry, self-possessed, now past his prime but still fit, with a shock of curly iron grey hair. He looked like an elderly jockey: this must be Trish's husband, Dickie. I had the impression he had been listening quietly to our conversation for some time without drawing attention to himself. In a low, tired voice, he punctured the silence with a single sentence:

"Roddy Foxe-Walter is a complete and utter chateau-bottled shit."

Having said this he went to the drinks table and helped himself to four inches of neat Glenfiddich in a glass.

"Dickie darling – this is my husband Dickie, by the way." Dickie turned and waved at us genially. "Dickie, do you know what this ghastly thing was that is supposed to have happened at Stonehill that nobody talks about?"

Dickie swallowed most of his whisky and shook his head. I could not be sure whether this meant he did not know, or was unwilling to say. He came and sat down on a sofa. One of the spaniels immediately occupied his lap. For the rest of our visit he said nothing, but he did not abstract himself from our conversation. He listened to us intently, a slight smile on his face. I had the impression that it was not other people he disliked, as Trish had said; it was the sheer tedium of having to talk to them that irked him.

Pauline was unusually silent as we drove back. I asked her what was the matter.

"Poor old Sir Rodney. He really seems to have blotted his copybook." She sighed. I refrained from saying anything. Long years of marriage have taught me when and how to be silent.

It would be useless to deny that knowing about the suicide did not affect our attitude to the house. It took the shine off it, certainly. I'm not saying that we were immediately aware of something sinister about the place: none of that nonsense; but now we knew, and there was no way to unknow it. Reason unfortunately has a very limited capacity to regulate one's emotions.

Pauline and I said nothing about it at the time, but much later we compared notes. Our reactions were similar. Whereas before small noises in the house were ignored, now we listened out for any deviation from normality. All houses, particularly old ones, have their repertoire of clicks and creaks, and you think nothing of them: from that time onwards every single one was mentally checked. We did not hear anything untoward, I don't think, but the very act of having to pay attention to these sounds set us on edge.

There was another thing which we both felt, but did not communicate to each other at the time. Whenever one of us entered a room in the house alone, we became conscious of its emptiness. It is a little hard to explain. Yes, if we had been aware of an 'unseen presence' in a room, that might have been more obviously unnerving, but it was the opposite. It was the unseen *absence* that we disliked. It was no more than a fleeting impression and very nebulous, but sometimes it was as if when we entered a room – in particular the library and the drawing room on the ground floor, someone or something had just left it.

I do not want to exaggerate these feelings. They were slight and transitory for the most part, but they were present.

The evening after our drink with Trish we went down to the Lodge for the same entertainment with Roddy. I was not looking forward to it but Pauline was full of curiosity.

Arriving fairly punctually at six we rang and knocked on the front door but received no response. Lights were on and he was definitely there. The sound of music – I think, the *Rolling Stones* – thumped in the background, heating the warm summer evening. Eventually the *Rolling Stones* were switched off, a curtain was drawn, and a window opened from which Roddy's head emerged.

"Sorry chaps, I should have told you. I never use that door. Come round the back," he said pointing to the kitchen door.

We squeezed past Roddy's Landrover and found the back door

open. The kitchen with its Aga showed little sign of practical use. The pedal bin overflowed with tin foil receptacles that had once held prepared meals from the local supermarket or takeaway. There were tins of baked beans lining the shelves and hosts of empty bottles. In the middle of the floor on a sheet of newspaper squatted a female mallard duck. The duck had defecated several times on the newspaper, and seemed mildly agitated by our presence. She opened her beak to let out a hiss and released another little viscous pool of coffee coloured liquid.

"Come on in," said Roddy. "Don't mind Bloody Mary. A duck I rescued. She's got stuck in a barbed wire fence during a shoot. Just negotiate your way round her and come into the sitting room."

As we were doing so Pauline said: "Isn't it a bit unhygienic, having her in the kitchen like that?"

"No, no, my dear. Life's too short. We're all going to die anyway," said Roddy. "Now then, what's your poison? I've got a bottle of The Widow in the fridge. Went to a cousin's wedding on Saturday and liberated a case. It was just sitting there outside the marquee, asking to come home with me. Waste not want not. That's my motto. Come in and sit down."

It was a warm night but there was a fire burning in the sitting room. Roddy threw open a window to alleviate the atmosphere a little, then left us to fetch the drinks. It was a low-ceilinged, poky room whose pokiness was enhanced by the fact that it had rather too much in it. I noticed some valuable pieces of Georgian furniture and a bookcase crammed with gilded leather-bound volumes. The yellowing walls were teeming with small family portraits, human and equine from the eighteenth and nineteenth centuries. A couple of Georgian silver candlesticks stood on the mantelpiece on either side of a row of miniatures. The place was stuffed with last remnants of ancient family wealth.

"This is where I keep my dwindling hoard of treasures," said Roddy, noticing our interest. He carried a bottle of Clicquot, with its distinctive orange-yellow label, perspiring from its stay in the fridge, a bottle of Brandy and three Champagne flutes. He poured us each a glass, lacing his own with a generous shot of brandy without making mention of it. Talk was anodyne. He was solicitous about our comfort at the manor, particularly towards Pauline. His manner was practised and gracious, with the slightest hint of aristocratic condescension. I could tell that my wife was rather more enchanted than I was and he must have become aware of this because soon he was turning his full attention on me.

"You know, I could swear we've met before. Were you on the deb scene at all in the Seventies?"

"Not really. I went to a few drinks parties with my brother, Jim that's all."

"Of course! Jim Bertram who married Trish. Briefly." His eyes were off me now and had a faraway, almost wistful expression in them. "Those were the days, eh? People knew how to throw a decent Cockers P."

"Cockers P!" Good grief! I had not heard that rather nauseating slang expression for a cocktail party in almost forty years. It conjured up all the glittering vapidity of that world, its greedy evanescence, its falsity and pretension.

"It's not the same now. Nobody has any style any more. The scene is full of the most ghastly *nouveaus*. Back in the Seventies there was still a bit of old money knocking around which made all the difference. They set the standard. Now it's all X Factor and instant celebrity. I mean, who are all these ghastly people? Chavs and spivs. Most of them seem to come from Essex. That's why I gave up the whole party scene. Frankly I've become a bit of a recluse because of it. I have a few good friends like the Dorsets and that's it. I'm always being asked to go back on the scene, of course, give a bit of class to their gruesome gatherings, but I won't do it. Still, I had a good innings. Work hard, play hard. That was my motto. Maybe, I played a bit too hard, but that was my style. I was known for it. Still, no use crying over spilt vino. Ha ha! I must remember that. No use crying over spilt vino. That's a cracker."

He drained his glass, then replenished it and ours. Conversation meandered on. Roddy showed flashes of amused interest in us and our doings, but he lapsed more and more into maudlin reminiscence. During a suitable pause we took our leave and threaded our way past the duck which was still sitting on its newspaper (*The Sporting Times*) in the middle of the kitchen floor.

As we walked back from the lodge Pauline said: "I think he's lonely. I think he's really lonely."

Later that night Pauline and I were in bed. I had been thinking about Roddy when suddenly, as these things do, an image from the past came back to me.

My elder brother Jim, the dentist, had been something of a socialite in his young days. (Have you noticed how many dentists are snobs? I'm not saying all of them are, but it is a tendency among the orthodontic profession. Hairdressers are rather similar. Perhaps it's this concentration on the external physicality of people that compels a certain shallowness of attitude. I don't know.) I was never quite sure how Jim managed to get in with the kind of people whose parties get photographed in *Tatler*, but he did. Perhaps he fixed their teeth at special rates; I don't know.

Occasionally, for his own amusement, Jim used to take me along with him to the drinks parties of the Seventies. The age of the Deb and the Deb's Delight, which is what Jim considered himself to be, was coming to an end, but there were still drinks and canapés to be had most evenings in the week in London, provided you were young and pretty and well-connected. I went with him, partly out of interest, partly because I was a student, too poor to pass up the opportunity of a free drink and a pretty girl.

The occasion that I suddenly remembered took place on a warm summer's night in the June of – I think – 1976, that scorching summer. There was a drinks party going on in the garden of some rich person's house in Chelsea and Jim took me along, though I was uninvited. "Everyone ought to have a pet 'crasher'," he used to say "and you're mine." The trees of the garden were festooned with fairy lights which came on as the sun graciously left the sky to the stars. The party was just beginning to wind down and a certain amount of rowdiness had entered the proceedings, but nothing seriously out of order. Among a crowd of young people in their silk frocks and velvet jackets, a young man was standing on one of the garden tables conducting an impromptu rendition of Paul McCartney's song *Hey Jude* with an empty Champagne bottle. He was good-looking in a beefy sort of way and his face glowed with high spirits. Everyone – even the older guests – seemed to be carried away by the moment and were singing along, or at least swaying in time. The conductor, in a dark blue velvet suit and an Old Harrovian bow tie slightly askew, seemed at that moment like the master of all the revels.

I remember turning to my brother Jim who was standing beside me and asking who it was.

"That's Roddy," he said, as if I should have known. I was too cowed to say "Roddy who?" So I never knew who it was until that night thirty five or so years later when I remembered the incident and realised that it could only have been Roddy Foxe-Walter in the days of his glory. For some reason the memory of it gave me an acute pang of sadness.

In the weeks following I began work in earnest on my book and was away a good deal doing research. I did not feel I had to worry about Pauline who is quite capable of making her own amusements. She gardens; she reads; she bottles fruit. Besides, Trish had decided to take her up and Pauline did not reject her advances. They went shopping together in Winchcombe and Evesham, and occasionally journeyed as far as Cheltenham to see a matinee or go to a concert. I gathered that Dickie had no interests other than equine, and Trish sometimes felt the lack of a little culture.

One thing troubled me, though very slightly at first. Whenever I returned to Stonehill from my researches, I would often find Roddy there. He and Pauline might be having a drink or a cup of tea together, perhaps even a scratch lunch. When I interrupted them Roddy would always be talking and Pauline listening, sometimes, I thought, with undue attentiveness. I came to – 'dread' is too strong a word – but intensely dislike the sound of my wife's laughter, as I came into the house, because I knew that the cause of it was Roddy. He seemed to be good at making her laugh, better than I ever was, as a matter of fact.

Whenever I came upon them like this, the laughter would immediately subside. Roddy would become subdued, almost sullen. Soon after, he would leave. Once, when he had just left, I asked Pauline what they had been talking about.

"Oh, you know," she said with a sigh. "Just chit chat. Gossip and that sort of thing. He can be quite amusing. Tells the most outrageous stories. I expect they're pretty well all lies, but I feel sorry for him. He gets lonely." She looked at me, smiling, as if she were amused. "You're not jealous, are you, Arthur?"

Of course, I had absolutely no reason to be jealous. I have never been a jealous man, and, naturally, Pauline has never given me cause to be. It was ridiculous, but it was annoying all the same. I had the feeling I was being treated like a child by Pauline, rather as she seemed to treat Roddy.

One evening I came home to be told by Pauline that she had invited Roddy over to supper. I tried hard to conceal my irritation, but of course Pauline was not deceived. It was a fine warm evening. Rather briskly she told me to get out the garden table and chairs and lay for supper on the stone terrace which runs along the back of the house outside the library.

The terrace was accessible by a pair of French windows which opened onto the spacious kitchen. As I laid the table these were open and I could hear and see Pauline and much that went on in the house.

I heard Roddy enter noisily by the front door and greet Pauline as "dear lady," a rather pretentious form of address that I noticed he had recently adopted for my wife.

I hurried in from the terrace to find Roddy hugging Pauline in the hall, with a bottle of Burgundy in one hand and a white plastic bag in the other.

"I come bearing gifts, dear lady," said Roddy. A slight blur in his voice told me he had already begun drinking.

"What's in there?" Asked Pauline pointing at the bag.

"Aha!" Said Roddy. With a flourish he took out the plucked carcass of a bird. "It's a wild duck. Mallard. Got the old butcher in Evesham to pluck it for me. In fact, it is *the* Mallard. You remember Bloody Mary who used to hang around my kitchen? Well I got fed up with her crapping on the floor and generally making a nuisance of herself. She never laughed at my jokes as you do, dear lady. So yesterday, I rung her little neck. Et voila!"

Pauline was rather stunned by this revelation. She took the bird gingerly. "I can't cook her tonight, you know," she said. "We're just having shepherd's pie."

"Good grief no, dear lady! Some other time perhaps. With a spot of the old orange sauce maybe. *Duck á l'Orange*: why has that gone out of fashion? Sign of the times. Meanwhile, shall we discuss this rather fine old burgundy? One of the last bottles left of the cellar my dear old father, the late Sir Walter Foxe-Walter, laid down. With it you shall drink to the last of the Foxe-Walters. That's me. There'll never be another."

"Well, come through and we'll have it on the terrace."

"The terrace?" I had never seen so rapid a change in a man's face. Roddy turned pale; the scarlet traceries of broken veins stood out lividly on his cheeks and nose. He began to sweat.

"It's such a lovely evening, I thought we'd eat outside," said Pauline, looking enquiringly at Roddy.

"Um ... Yes. Delightful. But if you don't mind awfully ... The thing is, I get this bad back if I sit outside too long. Old rugger wound, you know. We could sit in the kitchen, my back to the old Aga. Sorry to be such a pain in the BTM. Would you mind awfully?"

So I moved all the cutlery indoors and we ate and drank at the kitchen table. Roddy recovered his spirits a little after his first glass of the Burgundy, which was superb, but I could tell he was not on top form. All the same, he did enough to make me understand his appeal. He told stories about the people he had known in his world.

Often he featured himself as the hero of some amusing prank or other. The world he depicted was careless, raffish, sometimes scandalous; the only villains were solemn and middle class. Working class people were relegated to the status of comic extras, as in a film from the 1930s, who actually said things like "Cor Blimey, Guv'nor." The inhabitants of his world were not quite real people: they were types, players of some obscure and infinitely trivial game; and he, Sir Roddy, had been their puppet master. There was something compelling about Roddy's fluent narratives, so that you were drawn in to his view of things. Judgement was temporarily suspended.

It was only towards the end of the evening, when he became maudlin, that I regained my perspective. By this time two further bottles of our own rather inferior wine had been broached. Roddy began his familiar complaint that society was not what it was. It was now a world of wags and chavs and C list celebrities from worthless television programs. He had actually been to a party recently at which "some ghastly little oik" had refused to believe he was a baronet.

"That's why I give up. I'm practically a recluse. I have a few good friends, like the Dorsets of course and your good selves; otherwise I keep my own company. Talking to yourself is just about the only way to have a civilised conversation these days, eh? Ha, ha! I'm thinking of writing a book, you know, about the decline of standards, the decay of the aristocracy, that sort of thing. You wouldn't know a good publisher, would you, Arthur?"

I gave him a dusty answer. Soon after, Roddy rose unsteadily to thank us for "a most delightful evening." Pauline and I watched him stumble down the drive and decided to leave the washing up till the following morning and go to bed.

While she was undressing in the bedroom Pauline said: "What was all that nonsense about the terrace, for God's sake? Why didn't he want to go near it? I've noticed it before."

I was standing at the window and looking down. I could see the terrace below me in the moonlight. I said: "I'm guessing that we are in the master bedroom. The one that Catriona – Lady Foxe-Walter used to occupy. It could be that this is the window she threw herself out of. If she had thrown herself out of any other window she'd have landed on a flower bed. She must have broken her neck on the stone terrace."

"Shut the curtains," said Pauline, "and don't ever, *ever*, say anything about it ever again! Understand?"

I nodded, but she was not looking at me.

*

That little incident marked a further stage in our disenchantment with Stonehill Manor. The following morning I overheard Pauline ringing up our children, Edmund and Fanny, inviting them down for the weekend. Both declined. When we first took over Stonehill they had come eagerly, but no longer. Their visits had become briefer and less frequent. They offered no reason, other than the vague one of being "incredibly busy just now."

Through Trish we began to be invited to one or two drinks parties in the area. I went because Pauline wanted to go. I think this was because she felt her isolation at Stonehill more than I did, not because she particularly revelled in the Cotswold drinks party circuit. There was a remarkable uniformity about the people, their houses, even the canapés – usually from the same firm of caterers – that they served on these occasions. Their reactions to what one said were fairly predictable as well. When we mentioned that we had rented Stonehill for the summer, they tended to say "Oh, really," and then slid neatly onto a safer topic of conversation, like the iniquities of the Fox Hunting Bill.

We were attending one Saturday morning occasion, not far from Stonehill, designed, if I remember rightly, to raise money for the East Cotswold Hunt, when something unpleasant happened. Roddy turned up. I am pretty sure he had not been invited, but he had somehow got wind of the event, though not through us. It had been a bright sunny morning and we were almost enjoying ourselves. We had even bought some raffle tickets for the hunt, and had found a couple to talk to who had some interest in the world outside that of hunting and shooting.

Our first intimation of his presence was a sort of braying sound from across the room. It was Roddy's laugh. We looked to see Roddy at the other end of the long drawing room waving an empty champagne flute in his hand. He had obviously arrived at the party with a few drinks already inside him and was proceeding to get himself badly drunk, or "thoroughly rat-arsed," as he would probably have said. At the moment, he was just being a bit loud, but that was embarrassing enough.

"Do you know that man?" Asked one of the couple we were

50

talking to.

"I'm afraid so," said Pauline. The couple looked at each other, perhaps wondering whether they should continue to talk to us.

I saw our host approach Roddy and gently try to steer him towards the door. Roddy took violent exception to this and a sort of scuffle began. Roddy's protestations became louder. Our host was doing his best to be quiet and dignified with him, but it was useless: Roddy began to shout. I heard the words: "Get your filthy hands off me, you dirty bloody Jew!"

This was followed by a silence. A ripple of shock, as palpable as any I have ever felt, passed through the room. The loose boundaries of what was regarded as acceptable behaviour in Cotswold society had not simply been broken, they had been smashed. Most people there, I suspect, including myself, had been completely ignorant of our host's ethnic origin and would have been indifferent to it had they known. I am not saying that Cotswold people are free of prejudice; simply that anti-Semitism was a disease which had long since fallen out of fashion among them. I saw two burly men in regimental ties bundling Roddy out of the room and the house. Conversation was resumed but at a greatly subdued level. A man in a pin striped suit with the self-important look of a senior civil servant came up to us. He looked at me disapprovingly.

"Are you responsible for that man being here?" he said.

"Good God, no! What on earth makes you think that?"

"Well, you are living at Stonehill, aren't you? You are his tenant."

"But not his keeper," I replied firmly.

The man stared suspiciously at my Oxford don's leather-patched tweed jacket and my shirt without a tie, but eventually decided he had no more to say. Pauline was staring out of the window.

"Look," she said, "those men are trying to get him into his Landrover. Roddy can't possibly drive in his condition. He'll kill himself. We have to give him a lift."

At that moment I suspect every person in that room except Pauline would have been glad to see him dead, but I recognised, however reluctantly, my wife's moral imperative. We made our excuses and ran out of the house. In the drive Roddy had just backed his vehicle off the drive onto the lawn and knocked over a small stone statue of a cherub in the process. He was about to drive forward and do damage to the rear of a silver Jaguar when I climbed aboard his Landrover and removed his keys from the ignition.

Much protest followed but Pauline and I managed to get him into the back of our car and home. I supposed this must have confirmed the civil servant's suspicion that we were somehow looking after Roddy, but I didn't care. I was done with Cotswold drinks parties anyway.

When we had dumped him semiconscious onto his sofa at the Lodge, Pauline said: "There! He'll have to look after himself from now on." I was glad of that at least, though we did, at Pauline's insistence, go back to fetch his Landrover. The following morning the Landrover was gone and the Lodge was empty.

We were relieved. Though I had told the civil servant at the party that we were not Roddy's keeper and this was true, there was no doubt that we, and particularly Pauline, felt a kind of responsibility towards him. Roddy's absence seemed to exonerate us.

A tranquil week passed, then, one evening after dinner, we were in the library when there was a knock at the front door. "Oh, God! It's Roddy again!" said Pauline echoing my own fears.

I went to peer out of a window which looked into the portico over the front door. Standing there in the gloom was a thin, twitchy man in a leather jacket: certainly not Roddy. I went to open the door.

The man was not just thin, he was emaciated. He was pale and looked to be in his late forties, possibly fifties with a few thin straggles of curly black hair clinging to a skull-like bald head. In a dull, flat voice, he said: "Are you Foxe-Walter?"

"No. I am Professor Bertram."

"Where is he?"

"I don't know."

"What do you mean, you don't know?"

I explained that Roddy lived at the Lodge but had gone away three days ago, and we had not seen him since. I was prepared to be polite but the man had not put me at my ease and I was about to shut the door on him when Pauline behind me said: "Won't you come in and have a cup of tea or something? You look absolutely frozen."

We sat him in the kitchen next to the Aga and Pauline put a cup of tea and a sandwich in front of him. He looked at these wistfully for a moment, but did not touch them, then he began to talk. His name was Nick – he would not give his surname – and he had just come out of prison where he had been for the last twenty four years.

I asked him why he wanted to see Roddy.

"Because he murdered my brother and ruined my life."

I have no way of knowing if what he told us next was true. He

52

said that he was the elder by three years of two brothers who grew up in South London. Their mother was a single parent, the father absent for unknown reasons. Nick had embarked on a career of petty crime at a young age, followed, somewhat reluctantly, by his younger brother Leo. Whereas Nick was dark, Leo had been fair haired and angelic looking. Nick wondered if they had had different fathers.

When Nick was eighteen he had come to the notice of the Freeman brothers, a much feared pair South London of gang leaders. They had caught Nick thieving on their manor and had beaten him up severely, then taken him under their wing. He had become part of their organisation. Though Nick claimed that he had tried to keep his brother out of their orbit it was inevitable that Leo should have been drawn in. Leo's good looks attracted the attention of one of the brothers, Charlie Freeman, who was homosexual, and he became, for a brief while, a favourite. Nick objected to this and unwisely allowed his displeasure to be widely known.

This was in the period when the Freeman Brothers were at the height of their power. They began to show themselves abroad and mingle with 'posh people'. They were photographed by Snowdon for *Vogue* and could be seen in the crowded pages of *The Tatler* sharing a joke with the rich, titled and famous. They began to spend their money in fashionable places, in particular the Egremont gambling club which is where they met Roddy Foxe-Walter. Roddy became very thick with the Freemans and used to invite them down to Stonehill for riotous weekends.

"The way I heard it," said Nick, "Foxe-Walter, or Foxy as the Freemans called him, invited the brothers down for one weekend and they brought along a few tarts and a couple of their heavy men and Leo. I didn't want Leo to go, but I didn't have any say no more, because I was in the doghouse for shooting my mouth off about queer Charlie. So I got to hear about this later. Anyway, there was the most almighty piss-up here. Drink, drugs, women, the lot and one night Foxy suddenly takes a fancy to young Leo. Foxy wasn't queer like Charlie, I heard, but he was a mad bugger and he would help out if they were short-handed, if you know what I mean. Now normally Charlie went bloody mental with jealousy if anyone took a fancy to his boys, but this time he just thought it was the funniest thing he ever heard. So he says to Foxy: 'Right, you have him.' But Leo didn't want it. He just about put up with queer Charlie, but he wasn't having nothing to do with Foxy. He threw a big fuss and tried to get out. The way I heard it, Foxy chased him all over the house and Leo was screaming to get away, but the rest of them thought it was some kind of a bloody game. Then Charlie Freeman got two of his heavy lads to help Foxy get him. They caught Leo in one of the bedrooms and Foxy said, no not here, so Charlie's goons dragged the boy out onto the terrace and held him down, while that bastard took his pants down and …"

"You don't need to say any more."

"Fucking raped him."

"Terrible."

"Terrible! That wasn't the half! That shithead buggered him so bad, Leo started to bleed inside. It wouldn't stop. He was carted off to London by Freeman's men and they dumped him in my gaff and called the police. Leo was dead when they came round. Freeman's heavies made it look like I'd come back and beaten him up. My own little brother! I was fitted up. Just 'cause I'd called Charlie Freeman a poof. Well, he was. Maybe I shouldn't have said so, though. Anyway they banged me up for it. I've been away a long time."

"So you've come here for your revenge. Is that it?"

"No ... Yes ... No, it's not like that. I don't want to go back there for that toe-rag. I just want to see the bastard. I want to tell him to his face what he's done. I want to see him when I tell him. That's all."

"Well, I'm afraid, we honestly don't know when Sir Rodney will be back," said Pauline. Her use of his title puzzled me. "Of course, you're welcome to spend the night here. I'll make you up a bed, but there's no guarantee you'll see him in the morning and you can't stay here indefinitely, you know." She put her hand reassuringly on his. "Goodness, Nick! Your hand's freezing! Aren't you warm enough yet? You must have very poor circulation."

"I'll be alright," said Nick.

Just then we heard a bumping sound, though whether it came from inside or outside the house was impossible to tell.

"Heavens! Was that the door again?" said Pauline. We both looked at Nick. His eyes were shining and he was smiling triumphantly.

"Look," I said to him. "It may be Roddy; it may not be. Either way, you stay here, you understand? I want no trouble in this house."

Nick did not respond, but he stayed sitting at the kitchen table, his back to the Aga. Pauline and I went to the front door and opened it. We looked out and saw nothing but the full moon silvering the trees on the front lawn. The world was silent. We went round the house looking to see if there was anyone there. When we returned to the kitchen, Nick had gone. We opened the back door and called for him but there was no response.

"Perhaps he's gone upstairs to bed," said Pauline.

I shook my head. "We would have heard him. And he seemed too alert to want to sleep."

There was another bump, faint, but in that silent house clear enough to be heard. I thought it came from the library. It was nearly dark outside. We went to the library and turned the lights on.

At the far end of the room is a bay window which reaches almost to the floor. From where we stood we could see, pressed against the glass of one of the lowest panes something pale, almost white. It was Roddy's face and it appeared to be alive. At any rate it was moving.

We stood staring at it, fearful, undecided. Suddenly it disappeared. Pauline was gripping my arm.

"What do we do?" She said. Now I was angry as well as frightened.

"We lock all the doors and windows and go to bed. I'm fed up with this."

We did so, together because we did not want to be left alone. Besides, the noises in or outside the house, were increasing, little bumps and knocks, little reverberations of what sounded like laughter, or subdued chatter. The place seemed to be rousing itself to persecute us. We turned off all the lights on the ground floor and began to climb the stairs, not looking behind us.

When we reached the landing at the top of the stairs I turned round and gripped Pauline's hand hard, then let go when she gave a little cry of pain. We had both seen it, or him. Roddy was at the bottom of the stairs. He was naked, a vast pale slug of a body, and he was beginning to climb the stairs on all fours, looking up at us as he did so, with a dumb, pathetic appeal in his eyes, like a sick spaniel.

As he crawled upwards, the whole of the ground floor slid into shadow and then darkness. I heard noise coming from the darkness, like the noise that comes from a crowded room when the party has begun to wear down your nerves and your mind retreats even from the words of the person you are speaking to. I saw movement in the darkness, black on black, the restless movement of an endless futile revel. The voices no longer made sense even to themselves, and the fumes of alcohol that drifted upwards no longer consoled. The darkness from below had become tendrils of smoke that reached up like long thin arms trying to grab Roddy's ankle and drag him down into the abysmal vortex. I saw him look round once with wild terror on his sweaty face. With a huge effort he pulled himself out of reach up the stairs, now fixing his eyes on Pauline behind me. I told her to go into the bedroom and shut the door, frightening myself by the hysterical anger in my voice. Pauline looked shocked but stood still.

Roddy had reached the top of the stairs still on all fours and was crawling towards us, one arm outstretched in supplication. The darkness had climbed with him and was threatening to engulf the whole house.

"Pauline, dear lady!" His face glistened with sweat, dead white apart from the scarlet grog blossoms on his nose and cheeks, jowls quivering. I turned and pushed Pauline violently down the passage and through our bedroom door which I then locked and bolted behind us both. Pauline looked at me in terror then went and hid her face among the bedclothes.

From beyond the door things were coming nearer. I could hear Roddy crying out my wife's name: "Pauline! Pauline!" My mind recalled the pleading cries of our children when they were young and had just woken from a nightmare and were calling out to their mother. Roddy's appeal came again and again, and each time the articulation of "Pauline" decayed a little more until it was no more than an incoherent whimper. I stopped my ears, telling myself that the man was beyond pity. I could hear him come closer and closer to our door, sobbing, snuffling, whining, retching.

There was a small silence, then it felt as if the lower part of the door were being smoothed, almost caressed by a hand. I saw a mouth trying to insinuate itself through the draughty crack below the door. Lips were pushing their way in. The noises coming from them were not words, merely the sounds that words make when they are wheedling, coaxing, attempting to charm, the noise of sickly persuasion.

Pauline had left the bed and was at my side clinging to me, frozen. There was nothing we could do except not to let it in. The lips began to make strange sucking and pouting noises as if they were trying to blow kisses. It was then that Pauline finally lost her temper. She stamped. I believe she muttered "Go to Hell!" – even though that is not like her at all.

Another moment of stillness followed, then a melancholy withdrawing sigh and an all-pervading odour of whisky-soaked vomit. The silence continued and seemed to stop our ears. After an infinite hour I unbolted the door and looked out. The house was quiet and as normal as it would ever be again. Roddy was nowhere to be seen.

Pauline and I went down stairs and looked into every room, turning on all the lights in the house as we went. In the end we found Roddy outside, lying on the terrace, naked still, knees drawn up convulsively almost to his chin, his face cast upwards, eyes staring, sweat-slicked skin glistening in the moonlight. He was dead, but we summoned an ambulance for formality's sake. When we entered the kitchen again later that night we found a cold cup of tea undrunk and an uneaten sandwich on a plate on the kitchen table as before. Nick was nowhere to be found.

We left Stonehill as soon as the authorities allowed us, never to return. We did not even look back at its perfect Georgian contours as we went down the drive, past the little Lodge and out of the gate. Strange how beauty fades, how subjective it is. Nowadays I can't even read Housman's *Bredon Hill* without a slight shiver.

There is nothing so repulsive as the charm to which one is no longer susceptible.

# THE GRIMMEST CASTLE IN ALL ENGLAND

The murder of King Edward II in 1327 is one of the grisliest tales in English history. And in the shape of Berkeley Castle, in southern Gloucestershire, it boasts one of the most ominous backdrops imaginable – a lowering structure which so emanates menace that even today it is associated with monsters, witchcraft and evil spirits.

Berkeley Castle was built in 1067 by a powerful Norman family, the FitzOsberns. Such strongholds had appeared all over England in the wake of the Norman Conquest, and were rightly viewed by the population as symbols of oppression, but Berkeley Castle was more feared than most as it was constructed on the site where an infamous Saxon witch had once made her home, and stories were soon circulating that the evil lurking within its mighty walls was more to do with the black arts than with the cruelty of foreign despots.

The story of the Berkeley Witch was already a famous folktale when the Normans arrived in England. It concerned a wealthy Saxon matron who, after living for many years in a fine timbered hall – on the exact spot where the castle would later be built – confessed to her family that her good fortune was the result of a pact with the Devil. After her funeral, it was reported that the chapel where her coffin was kept was inundated with nightmarish demonic forms – one of which finally broke open the casket and bore the woman's corpse away on a horse covered with spikes. The corpse was said to have been impaled on these spikes, and witnesses claimed that it screamed in agony. In an associated legend, a supposed monster, a gigantic toad which fed on human flesh – possibly the witch's familiar – was also believed to inhabit the site and in later decades, after the castle was built, it would reputedly wander through secret passages and spring out on the unwary. And indeed, an immense, unnaturally bloated toad was recovered from a recess in the castle cellars and killed during the reign of Henry VII, (1485-1509).

Of course, none of these stories are provable, but the one tale of Berkeley horror for which there is much documented evidence concerns the fate of Edward II.

Son of the famous warrior king, Edward I, who conquered Wales and was also known as the 'Hammer of the Scots', Edward II made enemies on all sides simply because, by comparison, he was very weak. He was supposedly fonder of poetry and sailing than of *fighting, which in the early 14<sup>th</sup> century were ·not kingly activities. And when he was defeated by Robert the Bruce at the battle of Bannockburn in 1314, few of his nobles were surprised – though many were furious, as they'd lost friends, relatives and retainers en masse, and more importantly, they'd lost their holdings in Scotland.*

*Edward also incurred hostility by showering favours on ambitious but unpopular young courtiers like Piers Gaveston and Hugh Despenser. There was no proof that Edward was homosexual. He had at least two female partners, and fathered five children. But accusations of 'sexual perversion' were a useful scandal to spread when one was stirring discontent. His barons' real gripe was that, despite his many failures, he refused to subject himself to the will of Parliament. When in 1326, Roger Mortimer, a powerful marcher-baron, with the full connivance of his lover, Queen Isabella – Edward's aggressively opportunistic wife (so aggressive that she was known as the 'She-Wolf of France') – rose in rebellion and deposed Edward, there was general satisfaction.*

*But this was not to last.*

*Edward's eldest son, also called Edward, was a minor. And his mother, Isabella, and her lover, Mortimer, intended to rule England from behind his throne – which was not widely popular. This made it problematic for them that the older Edward was still alive, even though he had officially abdicated. As long as he lived, even in custody, the former king could be the rallying point for a counter-revolt.*

*It was unthinkable that one of royal blood should be murdered, so Isabella and Mortimer opted to bring about Edward's demise by 'natural means'. He was imprisoned in Berkeley Castle, and put in the custody of two extremely brutal gaolers, Gurney and Maltravers, who were charged with literally mistreating him to death.*

*Edward was enclosed in an odious cell, which only a metal grille separated from the castle's main cesspit. The stench was said to be suffocating, but to make matters worse, Gurney and Maltravers also piled rotting animal carcasses in the pit. Edward lingered for months amid these foul humours, weeping and begging for release. In addition to this torture of the senses, he was given only decayed food to eat and stagnant ditchwater to drink. But somehow he survived. Mortimer, becoming increasingly uneasy as opposition to his haughty rule grew, finally ordered the two gaolers to do their worst. Edward had to die – by any means, so long as there were no telltale marks left on his body. The wicked duo thus stripped their captive naked, and one held him down on his bed while the other inserted a metal funnel into his anus. A red hot poker was then thrust through the funnel, burning out his innards.*

*The grotesque act was said to have lasted for minutes on end, and Edward's shrieks could be heard in the countryside beyond the castle walls.*

*Initially the plan was successful. Edward's unblemished body received a royal burial at Gloucester Cathedral, but still there was resentment towards the new government. When in 1330, the young Edward turned eighteen and was crowned Edward III, he immediately had the conspirators arrested for the murder of his father. Roger Mortimer was hanged, drawn and quartered at Tyburn, a process which in the Middle Ages was no less gruesome than it sounds, while Isabella was imprisoned for life at Castle Rising in Suffolk, where she finally died shrieking with insane laughter.*

*This laugher is still reportedly heard on dark winter nights at Rising, just as the unfortunate Edward II's appalling screams can be heard ringing though the gloomy passages of Berkeley Castle.*

# HOXLIP AND AFTER
## Christopher Harman

A soft jolt and Kevin was in the coach again. The engine died. Un-clicking of seatbelts and murmurs in the otherwise heavy silence. The same white-haired gent was once again the first to rise and fiddle around in the overhead rack. Kevin prepared for another long wait while people cleared the central aisle.

"Okey dokey," Ron the driver's miked voice said, for the hundredth time. "We're in Slodshill ... but not for long. Just waiting for someone who knows a lot more about the area than I do." He'd parked on an indeterminate area of shaved grass that blended towards table tombs and stone crosses. Here was another of those enormous village churches funded by some wealthy medieval wool merchant. Past the church and some cypresses filled with rooks, a great space of air dropped to a mile or so of woods covering the near end of the Vale of Butterlode and lapping up the sides of neighbouring low hills.

Kevin felt refreshed. The passing landscape had kept him awake for a time; riotous hedgerows, the shock of yellow rapeseed, like a field in Oz, a spattering of red poppies on a verge, a bloody battlefield of them in a meadow. Then came successive waves of smooth green uplands with topknots of trees and strung with stone walls. The back wheels had gently vibrated beneath him. Villages blurred by, tawny as lions. The warm air conditioning and blend of voices had his chin bouncing off his collar-bone.

But for their arrival he might have continued to dream of places like the ones they'd passed. Two minutes of nothing before Ron's enhanced tones sounded again, "Ah, here's the rescue party." Whispering like a snake the doors opened and everyone, as well as the coach, was taking her in.

Her smile was like the sunlight that had spun off the River Windrush during that stop in Bourton-on-the-Water – and was as meaningful, though Kevin approved: insincerity made the world go round. Like him, she must be a good fifteen years or so younger than anyone else on the coach including Ron, who was standing up, pear-shaped next to her slenderness.

What was that he said? Kate *something*. Kevin was too intent on the straight, coppery hair, the light brown eyes which saw right to the back. Some anodyne miked patter from her as Ron started up the

61

engine. Nice to see them all and were they enjoying their holiday? Some fulsome 'yes's in reply. "Not too hot?" "No …" "Well wait 'til you get outside." That seemed addressed directly at Kevin. Good practice to include back rows; he did the same with his classes to keep the difficult ones in check. But he never button-holed just one. He felt privileged. Hoop earrings glinted and, yes, a nose ring. The sheepskin coat was stylishly worn-out and a puzzle on such a warm day.

She bobbed out of sight and the interior was several shades darker as the coach groaned by the church and out of the village before rising gently to the right. After a quarter of a mile the road levelled off. "Slodshill Common coming up," Kate's amplified voice told Kevin, her attentive pupil. Cows grazed and a gang huddled under the inadequate shade of a lone arthritic tree. The coach stopped and there was another interminable wait as passengers filed off to view parallel ditches and swells of grassed earth of what, Kate informed them, were the remains of an Iron Age fort. With one or two intelligent questions lined up, Kevin glared at Kate and Ron staying in the cool of the coach while everyone else roasted. Twenty minutes later the coach was full again and swinging around to head down into the vale.

At the front, some repartee with the driver as trees closed in on each side. "Make sure you get a photo before you run like hell," Ron said, chuckling over the microphone. "That's the 'Beast of Hoxlip', folks, as read about in the newspapers every umpteen years or so. Talk of flattened ground – a big beast by all accounts, probably drunk ones." "Not you is it?" a female wag called out. Ron didn't hear or had no witty reply to hand. "Glimpsed, always glimpsed, never seen full-on. Roast pig's back high as the guttering on a cottage."

"I'd show you around Hoxlip but nobody's seen it in four hundred years," Kate said over intrigued murmurs.

Dense woodland; odd vistas into dells where sunlight was contained like honey. "Can't just vanish," someone said to nobody in particular.

Kate said Hoxlip had been a hamlet. A man called Edmund Hobbs started up a school there. One day a girl returned to her home in Slodshill covered in burns and gashes. She couldn't or wouldn't speak. Men of the village went down into the vale and saw a burning deep in the woods and assumed it was Hoxlip. They followed the track but soon realised they had gone far past where it should have fed them into the hamlet. There was no longer any sight or smell of a fire and, more strange still, no sign of Hoxlip or any indication that it had ever existed. Pupils, Hobbs and other residents of Hoxlip were never seen again.

Kevin guessed holiday coaches were the biggest beasts to ever roam the Vale of Butterlode. The coach slowed and creaked massively into a roadside clearing. There were some parked cars, benches and tables in the shade of scattered trees.

Warm outside; the blinding sun winked between leafage. Pine cones and soft chippings underfoot. Fellow travellers divided, one line to a toilet block the other to a tiny shop with an outside counter. Ron stayed ensconced in his bucket seat on the coach like an egg in an eggcup. Kate wasn't with him and nowhere else was she visible. A path bent off into the woods; Kevin set off purposefully as if the trees farther off might be more interesting than the ones near to hand.

Ron had allotted them three quarters of an hour; after a few hundred yards Kevin thought that would be half an hour too long. He took a narrow side path and pursued it for several minutes. The trees thickened, pushing the blue sky higher; on the edge of visibility, birds trembled like midges. No birds down here; silence, no fluttering, though something ran above eye level, suddenly and stumpily, and twigs crackled. Like a squirrel, in respect of its size and colouring. Leggy, compact body the size of a human head. Kevin was vaguely glad it was legging it away and not approaching.

The underbrush trapped the heat. Sweat ran into his eyes. Trees flickered like fire between his quivering eyelashes. He blinked hard, thought he was losing a contact lens. That was a minor worry when something swung like a censer high in a tree.

A nest come loose—no, the edges were too defined. Too high for a hive, he'd have thought. Dark against the bright sky it swung at the ends of two branches for a moment more before dropping lower. No longer visible, it thudded to ground level. A stumping gait commenced from about the same spot. Gratifying that this animal too thought it best to flee.

Three quarters of an hour were barely adequate. Looking at his watch as he turned, he jerked, shocked.

Kate was directly behind him. "Seen the time?" he said, tension collapsing like a house of cards. That smile again; teeth more buttery than white here.

"Thought I was the Beast did you?" she said. Healthily pink about the face, despite the sheepskin coat. Rings at nose and ears shone like solid gold.

"You're far from that," Kevin said. Her steady gaze had him babbling. "I've been exploring. Must have been foundations where Hoxlip was. Or some open ground."

Kate shrugged at the trees. "Church records mention the place. People have photographed the woods from aeroplanes—nothing." She looked like she wouldn't have it any other way. Kevin supposed it was good for the tourist trade.

"You look so lost," she said unexpectedly. Stern sympathy in her face.

"No, just outnumbered," he said, casting a glance at the trees.

"I meant on the coach. Not happy. I can always tell the ones who aren't." No pity there; he'd have hated that.

"I'm the youngest by twenty years." Adding five or so would do no harm. "I'm by myself. I prefer beaches, sun hotter even than this … the sea." Annually, when he'd been married. "But this year …" He explained. Mother had booked with Hotline Tours, but then her oldest pal had inconsiderately died just a week before. The funeral was in the middle of the holiday. Well, she couldn't miss Elsie's send-off, now could she? A minimal refund offered by the company at this late stage. Come on Kevin – *you* go. It'll be a change. And you've talked about retiring somewhere rural. And yes, he had.

"We'd better hurry," Kate said, not hurrying herself. Kevin suspected she'd linger were it not for her obligations to Ron and the party.

They were four minutes late and the coach grumbled. Ron stood outside, mopping his pink dome, a capital D with his straight back and large paunch. Expressionless stares in the windows, which were laughably large – like on a hearse. Someone checked their watch or was winding it. Kevin and Kate climbed onboard. He felt a thrill of transgression mixed with defiance, and could hardly stop himself smiling. He was like the back-row kids in some of his classes. As the coach moved off he joined in fervently with the 'yes's in answer to Kate's "hot enough for you?" Five minutes later the coach squealed to a standstill on the same spot by the church in Slodshill.

After thanks from Ron on behalf of the passengers Kate walked swiftly away from the coach. Kevin watched while he could. She'd be gone as irrevocably as all the places in the Cotswolds he'd never see again. She entered a street end, stopped there. Handles, a hood opening; yes, a pram, the big old-style kind. But for the hood, the baby would have fried. She stooped to check on its well-being. No, too cursory; she must have merely released the brake. At any rate she now gripped the handle and pushed away and out of sight.

When Ron said they had half an hour in the village, Kevin was out of his seat. Prams meant babies though not always. Kate was no bag lady but might she be using it to transport stuff? That was far more likely than her leaving a child unattended during the three hours she spent being a guide. More likely still was that someone else, concealed around the corner, had been waiting with the pram. Kevin didn't like that theory. Either way, he had to know. Outside he headed for the intersection.

No sign of Kate in the street that curved away. Slate and thatched roofs, broken only by square dormer windows, sloped lengthily to ground floor windows and window boxes overflowing with colour. Past the curve there was nobody as far as the end of the street where hedgerows began.

In a post-office embedded under dark thatch he bought postcards without taking in the scenes and trudged back to the church.

Fellow travellers moved desultorily within sight of the coach; a couple sat on a tomb and ate sandwiches, a man fanned himself with a baseball cap, another aimed a camera at the church and the hills beyond. The cypresses were baked black as the watching rooks. Attended by neat puffs of vapour, the sun was a fierce unrelenting white. Light showered the tower. Kevin's eyes prickled and gargoyles swam in water under the tower's roof rim; their indistinct features seemed randomly set-out around their heads. Other than to escape the pupil-less white eye of the sun, Kevin had no other reason for entering the church.

Cavernous inside, cool. Discreetly deferential sounds; the scrape of someone's footwear; a devoted little throat clearing from a far-off pew. He walked along a side gallery, stepping in and out of pools of colour cast down from stained glass; he recognised the Garden of Eden, a crucifixion, a resurrection; elsewhere various groups of robed and haloed figures looking anguished or earnest. He glanced in a side chapel. Ochre limestone was almost black in the light compromised by the luridly coloured glass.

Two windows; in one, rows of pupils behind square school desks, sinuous red flames rising from their shoulders to fill the frame. In the other window a single figure had black and red rents in her white smock. Grey billows rose from her. Her hands covered her eyes – but not her smile.

If there were details in the story too X-rated for the coach party, he didn't doubt Kate knew them – but *he* never would. She had been a welcome diversion, a piquant memory to take home to Yorkshire.

Kevin leaned his head against the window glass. The hills were an interminably extended body of haunches, shoulders and several long slopes of thigh on the way back to the hotel. Sheep bundled in wool chewed philosophically. Stone walls ran down hills to whip at the coach before falling back, defeated for now. Some white clouds were frozen against powdery dark blue. A crow eased itself over blackened woods. As the coach rose to Stow-in the-Wold a pulp of yellows and oranges rested on the darkening land.

Ron double-parked on Market Square until everyone had gone into the hotel. Kevin felt a thousand miles from Slodshill and further still as he watched television in his room. In the dining room later there was no space at any of the Hotline Tours tables. Some professional etiquette concomitant on his calling meant Ron ate alone at a separate table. Tonight he didn't and Kevin felt all the more cut-off from his fellow vacationers. Under the table the hotel cat sympathetically rubbed its silken flank against his shin. Ron was taciturn and distant now that he wasn't playing to the audience in the coach. "I was intrigued by that missing village," Kevin said.

"Yeah, looked like you were," Ron said, eyebrows slightly raised in his heavy, expressionless features. "Thought the Beast had got you – turns out Kate had." Assuming a lot from Kevin's short spell with Kate, but now that they were on the subject – "Lives in Slodshill does she?"

"As long as I've known her," Ron's gaze was uncomfortably direct; Kevin tried not to flinch from it.

"Puzzled by the pram though," Kevin said. From Ron's extended chewing of duck pate and toast this was unexpected. Kevin described his last sighting. "Looks like it had been left waiting there for her while she was with us."

Ron scratched his stomach overhanging his tight black trousers. "Kid in it?"

"Not that I could see. Unlikely, unless someone was waiting there with it."

Ron concluded his thoughts. "A lot can happen in a year – and it only takes nine months." He dabbed his lips with a napkin. "She's not mentioned a kid. Still, it's obvious she's still got the plumbing for one. And the clock's ticking. She was first on our books twenty odd years ago." He pondered. "Hasn't changed much. Neither have the clothes and metalwork come to think of it."

Conversation was sporadic after that. Kate had been the only subject of mutual interest. Tea-dance tonight, Ron said when Kevin got up to leave. He swallowed his indignation at Ron thinking he might be interested.

Watching television in his room was like being at home. He switched off and was back in the Cotswolds mentally as well as physically, but something seemed held back from him.

He opened the window and sounds stepped in from the square; a lumbering coach, a car over-revving into a parking space. A squeaking had him leaning out. To his left, in the narrow street branching out from the square, someone headed away, hunched, pushing. Clearer now, entering the light beneath a bracketed lamp high on a shop front. A bronze sheen of hair. Thin wheels and fluffy white at the coat's hem were gloomed over and the narrow way was empty again.

Here, nine, ten miles from Slodshill and at this hour? Leaving the hotel, running to resolve the question was a holiday madness he wouldn't succumb to. He reminded himself that woman and pram was not a promising combination. Best to forget.

An easy decision the next morning to forgo the optional trip to Cheltenham and Bredon. He was already paying the cost of the whole holiday to his mother without handing out more to Ron. Besides, he was weary of the travelogue Cotswolds in the great TV screens of the coach windows. He decided on a leisurely day in which he might take the trouble to find out more about Hoxlip.

The information office had nothing. He could forget about Hoxlip as well as her. Aimlessly he wandered along a narrow alleyway walled with rough stone and tall wooden entrances to rear properties. Something moved with greater urgency – a lopsided gallop.

Nothing behind him. Forty feet ahead the alleyway opened out into a street. That's where whatever was responsible for the galloping steps was about to appear, maybe to swerve into the alley. Apprehension growing, he was on the point of heading back the way he'd come. Then the steps stopped, and he became conscious of the squealing that had accompanied them. What was briefly visible crossing the alley-end didn't surprise him unduly.

Kate had been pushing the pram. It had a raised black hood. Set on great spoked wheels, the metal bowl had been the delicate colour of oyster flesh. By the time Kevin was out of the alley and looking left, she was some way ahead.

He battled impatience. Running would be creepy, desperate. Coolness was more likely to get results. He stopped at paintings in a window; the reflection outdid them, a moving picture of Kate tipping up the front wheels of the pram and feeding it into a shop doorway. Kevin strolled, shooting the cuffs of his jacket in the sunshine; he took in clean, sunlit air, he felt great volumes of it were all rooted here.

The window was filled with shelves of toys and ornaments – tourist fare. He'd remark on the coincidence of seeing her here. Reminisce over their Hoxlip sojourn yesterday?

A bell alerted staff. Kate was one of them – the only one? The proprietor even? She'd been sitting and stood now with no particular surprise evident at his entry.

"Another string to your bow?" he said

An intent look. "I just help out here in the season."

A follow-up dodged out of sight. He considered the merchandise unwillingly. There were snow globes, various scenic mugs and tea-towel maps, sticks of rock lettered through with 'Stow-on-the-Wold', a tee-shirt emblazoned with 'I'm a Cotswold Lion'. A deep, glass-fronted shelf was full of, full of …

Kevin had half glanced away as Kate said with something like pride: "Hoxlip devils. Sewed them myself."

"Do they sell?" A want of tact he realised too late.

"Some children like them," she said.

What kind of children? Kevin couldn't help wondering.

"They're cute," she said, watching him steadily. Sensing she'd detected his reservations he reserved judgement and looked again.

Pink, red and puce blobs sprouting tubular limbs of varying numbers. Noses, ears and eyes were strikingly human, but arrayed seemingly randomly, as onto a plastic potato head by someone who'd never seen a face before. A movement and Kevin narrowly avoided stepping back a pace; nothing animate had stirred amongst the devils, a resettling more like. He was reminded of huge crabs he'd seen in a tank in a French hypermarket – not dead and not quite alive.

"Offspring of the big Beast?" he said, not entirely seriously.

"They've been seen in the woods," she said through a sigh, as if those that had seen them were to be envied.

"If you'd mentioned them on the coach I might have stayed on board."

"The Hoxlip Beast didn't keep you there."

"You could leg it away from that before it got a chance to flatten you but these ... Bet they can run like the clappers." He smiled at them for as long as he could bear. They were as cute as spiders. He was thinking what to say next while she didn't appear to be trying.

"Well, better not keep you from your work." Yeah, really busy he could tell, but he was more adept these days at the art of knowing when to conclude things. Now, carefully does it. "When do you finish?"

She said any time he liked, a better reply than he'd hoped for. He blessed Mother's deceased friend. He was thinking of tonight; an afternoon meeting would mean drinking and yawning alone through the evening while the others tea-danced. He was aware of her saying "Maybe tonight's best", and he pictured strange shapes in a complex game fitting perfectly into allotted slots. "Your hotel bar, about nine?" He'd a better idea, The Sheepfold Inn. No point encouraging the gossip of fellow travellers, not that he'd set eyes on them again after Saturday.

He left. The pavement felt springy as a mattress underfoot. He expected the afternoon to drag and it did. He walked down a steep path outside the town, sweated and wheezed back again. The pram rolled into his mind several times. No sign of it in the shop, no cry from the baby. Baby didn't cramp her work or social life. Father went one better and was completely absent, as far as Kevin could tell. A matter for regret he wasn't travelling independently; he could have driven her back to Slodshill afterwards.

The coach returned around five. There were red pates and noses from too much sun. Faces were haggard and elderly limbs stringy from too much exercise. There were bags trumpeting obscure retail outlets. Cheltenham must be richer by a few hundred quid.

At dinner he laughed at hoary anecdotes, embellished one or two of his own; he felt the satisfactions of the evening ahead seeping back into the present.

At nine o'clock Kate was waiting in an alcove in The Sheepfold Inn. Kevin pointed at her mostly empty glass and she said, "Anything. So long as it's fiery."

She didn't back away from his not entirely serious offer of whisky and took a long sip when he brought it back to her. "I get so cold," she said, hugging her glass. Still buttoned up in the sheepskin coat. Wearing it during the heat of the day she was hardly going to feel the benefit, but telling her he'd only sound like his mother.

She seemed content not to talk. Kevin wasn't. Okay, Hoxlip then – at a tangent. "Ever get bored trotting out that Hoxlip stuff?"

"It happened," she said, whether it bored her or not.

"But what happened? That girl was mute wasn't she? Never described her ordeal?"

"Maybe indescribable," Kate said, her expression warm, secretive.

"She's smiling in that stained glass in the church. Is that because whatever it was she escaped from, it was worth smiling about?"

Kate was smiling at the question, or happy with the company or the pleasant surroundings – the ship's oak beams, framed old maps of Gloucestershire, ruby lights in sconces: the one above them made her fine features ripple. He felt vaguely defeated by her lack of conversation until stepping outside later she slipped an arm in his, said, "Cold", and he felt her shudder. A brisk walk would cure that and delay their parting. They turned into Fleece Alley. Kevin commented on the name. Educating him, shuddering the while, Kate said alleys snaking out from the town centre were called 'tures'.

Something ran: Kevin couldn't place where. "Hear that," he said. "Skipping, or learning to. Bit late for a young girl to be out." His heart skipped.

"How do you know it's a girl?"

"Boys don't skip."

She smiled as if he'd said something endearingly naïve. "Let's go back to your hotel." Because she was evidently feeling the non-existent cold, not to get out of hearing of the skipping, which Kevin was keen to do. And he forgot about it as she stepped into the hotel ahead of him. Ignoring the bar, she proceeded to the stairs. With incomparable timing, Ron was descending them. A proprietorial glance, as if whatever might follow was of Ron's own devising and part of the holiday package.

In his room Kevin gestured at the tray with its dried teabag, the stained cup and saucer. One measly chair in the room, so he sat on the bed – it was only polite. "Sorry, can't offer you much."

"Oh you can," she said. She interrupted her undressing to turn out the light and draw the curtains. Kevin began to unbutton. Under the bedcovers next, and strangely not alone. A sense of hurtling. The coach plunging down a smooth golden hill, not stopping at the valley floor, burrowing further. He worked hard, sweated. Kate was hot as a loaf fresh out of the oven, and as dry. A butting low against the other side of the door, a soft tapping. Claws sheathed, the hotel cat must want to get reacquainted. A roughness to Kate's skin alternated with a curious smoothness like scar tissue. *What the eye can't see*, Kevin thought. He was more than satisfied and more than once. Later a break turned to sleep. Sleep turned to light under the curtain, the mutter of a car. Alone in the bed, he'd every excuse to seek her out again.

After breakfast, Kevin told Ron he was hiring a bike for the day. They were in the foyer; fellow travellers were gathered by the coach thrumming at the kerb. "What about all those hills? Think you're up to it?" Ron said.

*More than you would be.* "No problem."

Ron spoke confidentially. "If you were thinking of heading back to Slodshill, we're going to the fete there tomorrow." Kevin shrugged. With deliberation Ron began polishing the silver buttons of his black jacket. "Kate works here in Stow on and off. Don't suppose you'd want a wasted journey."

"Fresh air. A nice trip out – what more could I want?"

With a look, it was clear Ron had thought of something. Kevin watched him soft-whistle towards the coach and park his bulk in the driving seat.

Kevin wasn't surprised to find the souvenir shop closed. Opening times weren't even indicated. It didn't matter. He headed for the cycle hire shop then was free-wheeling down the first slope. He was off the bike within yards up the facing one, thinking Ron's doubts had been sound. When the road levelled off he found a rhythm and could stop thinking of the mechanics of cycling. Not passively watching the landscape through windows, he felt inside it. He enjoyed the rush of opposing air and the slow shift of green slopes with their fingertip-sized sheep. He began to make better headway up some killer gradients and there were fewer than he'd feared. The road skirted valley sides, had him skating over long low rises. Sheep that had ignored the coach, noted his passing. He stopped once to drink in an ancient inn and watched shaving-cream clouds steal across the sky.

The climb to the Slodshill took a good ten minutes of alternate walking and cycling. Sunshine made the ancient stonework of the church look edible as fudge mortared with honey. A breeze fiddled in the cypresses. Rooks pecked a stone cross. The bike's wheels ticked and he turned right into the street. He went the entire length. No voice called. The rooks drew him back to the church.

A bed of white wool absorbed and tamed the bright sunlight. He could see the tower clearly. He scratched his moist scalp.

Harsh sunlight had tricked the other day. There were plain stone corbels at intervals under the base of the tower roof. If he'd seen any actual gargoyles, today they were taking advantage of the shade inside, maybe having lunch. He'd overlooked that consideration himself. No eating places here as far as he could tell.

He remounted the bike. He ignored the fork right, down into the vale. Leftwards, the road began to feel steeper than all the previous ones. The woods below dragged at his eye-corner. He was rising out of the seat and pressing hard on the pedals when the van passed close, blasting him with warm air. His foot slipped off the pedal and he was toppling. Recovering himself, standing either side of the crossbar, he gasped at the van which had stopped a little way ahead. He'd little breath to give directions even if he knew any. A further reason to gasp as Kate appeared around the back. "Where are you going?" she asked, looking faintly amused. She was in the sheepskin coat again under the beating sun.

"Thought I'd look at the woods from a safe height." 'Safe' sounded sincere, not sardonic as intended.

She opened the van's back doors. He noticed the pram inside, presumably empty. "Come on," she said. She helped him manhandle the bike to join the pram then slammed the doors.

He was in the front passenger seat as the van speeded to higher ground.

"Just happened to be passing?"

"I come up here a lot." Another of those answers tangential to the question.

"As well as down there?"

A glance let him know she liked that; it spared her the bother of answering. She edged the van onto an area of worn grass, got out and opened the back doors. He went to join her, a twist in his gut at the prospect of being sent on his way again.

She didn't get out the bike, she extracted a wicker basket. The slams of the doors made two resounding and triumphant handclaps over the woods. Kevin followed her to bitten grass downhill from the van. Further on, sheep-patched meadows banked drastically down. Kate dispersed a bottle, plastic glasses and paper plates onto a rug.

72

Ginger beer burned his throat. By the time she'd torn off pieces from the loaf it looked less like a Hoxlip devil. He didn't feel like asking if the resemblance had been intentional.

He asked if the girl had just kept quiet the rest of her life and Kate said she'd disappeared "barely out of her teens". She unbuttoned her coat, lay back and stared at the sun. "Hot, hot, hot," she said, chest rising like a baking loaf.

Remote as the sun. He'd have to start again – if he started at all. He realised he did want to. No point pretending he hadn't seen the pram just now, and on previous occasions. "Baby being looked after?"

"Baby is fine," she said, no defensiveness, no bluster. Was there anything he said that could surprise her? "Separation does no harm. You ask my other children. They're thriving."

Kevin was startled and impressed. Kate wasn't raddled, though now he recalled that oddly disparate texturing of her skin last night. He told her they were all going to the Slodshill fete tomorrow. "I know you are," she said, contentedly rubbing her shoulders into the short fine hairs of grass. Kevin did the same until the blue vault made him vertiginous, about to fall away from the world and roast in the sun. "Will you be there?"

"I'll be around," she said.

Kevin tipped on his side and looked down to the woods. Branches were like wires in the lumpy green stillness. Movement then, within a fifty yard radius: a kaleidoscopic folding and rolling of foliage. There was a blush of colour. When flecks and puffs of grey appeared, Kevin stood, said, "You should see this … Kate?"

A gear-change break in an engine note. Below, the van disappeared around a shoulder of hillside. She'd assumed rightly he had no mobile phone with him; neither had she or why else would she go careering down to Slodshill? He looked back desperately to the woods.

Still as coral now. A breeze must have turned up a reddish underside of leafage. No smoke, no fire. And Kate had simply gone – after dumping his bike outside the van.

At the fete, he'd gingerly chide her on these unexplained vanishings; exasperating, so why was there a smile under his frown? At the thought of the ride back to Stow the smile disappeared.

He ached the next morning. A night at Slodshill would have spared him that had Kate offered it. He might have had the same dreams though, of suffocating greens and blistering reds. "Warned you," Ron said later as Kevin boarded the coach like one of his less sprightly fellow travellers.

Sights recalled his heroic cycling. A fine afternoon for a fete, with the hills clear-edged and supple under the cloudless sky. Meadows were freckled with colour. There were gooseberry pickers, rucksacked hikers. Distant stone walls lay on the hills like abandoned ropes. Clusters of buildings were gone as suddenly as they'd appear, leaving memories of mullioned windows in ancient stonework, roofs sloping to worn and deserted greens.

Fingerposts reminded everyone of where they were heading. Cars gathered ahead and behind as the coach rose to Slodshill. Ron followed the road as it swung in a horseshoe around the village and continued towards the glints of many windscreens. On the common, people milling around stalls, tents and mini arenas. The coach nudged its bulk into a space; then there was the rigmarole of Ron's instructions and the queuing to get off.

Outside, Kevin buried himself in the crowds. He took lungfuls of air. He felt a benign, superior interest in everything, anticipating a greater fulfilment later. He strolled by judges presiding over tables jewelled with jam and honey jars. In a white marquee he sipped Pimms and kept watch on the entrance for as long as his patience allowed. He went to the edge of the fete where birds of prey rose from stiff-gloved hands and floated over ditches and mounds of the iron-age fort. He entered the melee again, stopped for a chorus line of puppets raising their legs on a small stage. Sweet-scented candyfloss covered an odour of roast meat coming from nowhere he could identify. A wheel of fortune spun. A boy with gold stripes and whiskers on his face snarled up at him and ran off. A whole bunch of kids were having their faces painted. Children everywhere, running in lines between adults and stalls.

He realised Kate's absence didn't surprise him. Too detached a personality to immerse herself in all this. As a long-time resident a fleeting visit might suffice – or even none at all.

He spotted Ron by the entrance to the beer tent. A faceted glass in one hand was balanced by a cigarette in the other. Kevin approached him, said, "Don't wait for me. I'll make my own way back." Ron nodded minimally, shrewd-eyed. Kevin guessed he wasn't the first in Ron's experience to have had a programme running parallel to that of the rest of the party.

Once he was past the parked vehicles, he headed quickly down a high-hedged lane to the village. At the end of the curve of low, sweeping roofs he stopped. A pram was on the worn slabs outside a closed door.

Kevin approached. Yes, Kate's pram; rust scabs on the bodywork, rusty gold spokes. The raised hood was frayed at the edges, black as bat-wing. The baby must be indoors – and mother would be too. The van was parked elsewhere, the picture book street unspoiled.

His knocks resounded up the street. He listened hard; voices from the common, a crackly loudspeaker. Nothing from inside the house. Not on the common, not in the house – where then? A sourness at the base of his throat. The pram offered itself as a handy object on which to vent his frustration. He stood behind the handle and looked inside. The bright air made a black cave under the hood. The blackness churned and he swayed until he saw that the head was a lump of pink pillow.

He walked away aimlessly. The dark under the hood clung to his shoulder until he was in sight of the church.

A bulge of stone under the lip of the tower roof might well have been a gargoyle, had its features come anywhere near to forming a face. He sat on a bench. Rooks' continuous cawing was like laughter and becoming unendurable. He'd go back to the fete.

Rounding the curve of the street, he was startled to see the pram had gone. The door opened directly on his hard knock. "Been up at the fete," he blurted, teeth together in his near-smile. Her smile was open as if she'd expected him. She said she had the rooms above and turned for the stairs immediately opposite. Dark, creaking and airless, like a slanted chimney flue, it can't have been easy getting the pram up them. Off a tiny landing was a large room.

Kevin was struck by the heat. All the bars of an electric heater glowed red. The off-white linen top Kate wore was a layer too many. A single dormer window was embedded in the long slope of ceiling. She invited him to sit on a worn-out sofa. "You look hungry," she said, noticing his hunger before he had. She went into a tiny kitchen. He heard cutlery clash and smelled raw meat.

"Didn't see you over there," he said, not letting his curiosity go.

"No," she said. Meat began to fry and his mouth watered. She came in with two tall glasses. Kevin tasted a peppery, spicy liquid.

"Baby sleeping?" There was one other unopened door.

"It'll wake up later." She went away and came back with steaming plates and laid them on a low table. Thin steaks were cooked close to burning. They were covered in soft lengths of red pepper. They ate in silence, Kevin sweating from the heat off the bar heater. Sounds drifted down from the common. "Hear that?" he said.

"It'll be passing down here," she said. "The parade I mean, on the way to the vale."

Topics he raised she acknowledged with a sweet indulgence, but there was no attempt to engage with any of them. He sensed talk held no particular appeal for her. Interested in him in a generalised sort of way, perhaps, but incurious as to his background, his likes and dislikes. He made his mind up to interpret the silences as companionable. Refreshing in a way; he could just 'be'.

"I'll just check on baby," she said, going to the other door and closing it behind her.

Kevin drowsed, woke suddenly. The room was darker. He went to the window. The sun was lower, a deep orange button nearly lost in wedding veils of cloud. The hills were stained in sandy hues; vivid greens were speckled with sheep. To his right, over the roofs opposite, he could see the common. Surrounded by particles of motion, one thing dominated. Kate re-entered the room and closed the door behind her.

"That a bouncy castle? Didn't see one earlier."

"Hmm?" She sat on the sofa; a shapeless piece of gammon-coloured material covered her hand. In the other a needle and thread.

"Beloved of fetes, club days," he said. A dull reddish colour – a block of a thing with a domed top. Things clinging to it were like ticks – children?

He turned back into the room and loosened his collar. "I'm sweltering."

She poised her needle and thread over what he now saw was one of those Hoxlip things probably destined to remain unsold in the shop in Stow. "Open the window then," she said, pleasantly chiding. He pushed out one leaf of the window and voices were clear; a scratch wind band *harrumphed*, an amplified voice made some comment. Cool air made his face feel hotter.

He sat down beside her. "I was thinking about the other night." He hadn't been – he just wanted to remind her.

"Tonight will be better," she said, mild and sympathetic as she laid down the fabric thing on her lap. Kevin chose to believe she meant 'even better'. He'd be as insouciant about that previous encounter as he would be about this one. Kate cocked her ear to the window. "It's coming."

76

"Oh, the parade," he said, not much interested. Once it had passed out of sight and mind there would be silence and the low beams overhead to play under. "'S funny. Where I come from, parades usually begin the festivities."

"This isn't where you come from," Kate said, concentrating, head bowed.

"Made anything for baby?"

"No." A slight wrinkling of her nose, as if that would be a worthless enterprise. He leaned a little against her, ostensibly to get a better view of the thing in her lap. It was some way from being finished; he hoped she didn't intend to tonight.

He listened to the silence from the other room. "Not a crier. That's something. I'm told I was. Could raise the rafters."

A fleeting consideration of him for that inept solecism chilled his damp brow. His past, maybe her own, meant nothing to her. Better this than that subtle interrogation he'd sometimes endured during rare new encounters. He should be grateful.

She laid the sewn thing down and went to the window. Her nose-ring glinted, red-gold. "It's at the top of the street." A slow rhythmic thud: Kevin couldn't be certain if he were hearing it or feeling it through the floor.

"Let's go down and watch it," she said, pulling at one of her earrings. A rosy light played on her features. Not street lights or the faint sunset. Torches? Enthusiastic paraders giving it their all?

"Can see just as well from the window, can't we?" he said.

He couldn't be certain she'd heard. Her teeth gleamed in her intense smile. From her fiercely proud eyes, looking towards the baby's room, he thought she was on the point of fetching it out. Kevin might demur at going out to watch the parade, but the baby couldn't. So he was surprised when she went to the main door of the flat and was gone. He listened to her thumping lightly down the stairs. The ajar door whined and was still. He noticed the sheepskin coat on the hook. *Don't get cold*, he thought, a little chill of abandonment in his chest.

The noise outside grew. He didn't want to face all those people. The scratch wind band tried to keep in time. Excitable youngsters laughed and shouted. A tambourine was bashed. He felt the wide-spaced beat through the floor; the white-plastered walls blurred with each elephantine step. He touched his forehead and considered his glistening fingertips. It was getting hotter in spite of the half-open window. In a moment the head of the procession would pass directly and loudly below. He closed the window, keeping his gaze on the sunset draped over the darkening hills. Kate should appreciate his ensuring of the baby's continuing repose. That was assuming the window was shut in the baby's room.

Maybe it wasn't. A high harsh wail; it pierced like knives through the cracks around the doorframe. Kevin put his hands to his ears as the cry went on as if breath weren't involved in the sustaining of it. He stood outside the door to the room, half expected to hear mother's steps running up the stairs. The horrible sound conjured in his brain the lumpy pinkness in the hollow of the pram hood. Had that been a pillow? There was no accounting for a mother's love, and he was bewildered by Kate's continuing failure to take heed. He was thinking the cry was like a call to something many times more troubling than the crier, when it abruptly ceased. So too did the enormous slow-stomping tread.

A sharp *crack*, and glass tinkled. A murmur of voices stole in and a stream of hot air.

At the window, his vision was filmed by the heat. He looked over the great bulk that had drawn up a matter of yards from the house. Wielding flaming torches like in an old horror movie, revellers filled the street way past the border of the village and as far as the common.

An impact, a single massive stamp, shook the building. It demanded he acknowledge the thing directly outside, which had dominated the distant common. This close it bore only a superficial resemblance to a bouncy castle. Red, raw, glistening: its highest point, at his eye-level, sizzle and smoked. Partway down, a studious, bloodshot eye, in a sink-sized socket, considered him. Yards away, on the monster's back, a singed hirsute ear unfolded like a car-seat. Children played hide and seek around a number of legs the shape and size of wheelie-bins. Smaller bulbous shapes played too, skipping on long brachiated limbs.

Kevin forced himself to recognize that it was in fact Kate leaning back naked against the thing's great blunt prow. Her body was scored with crimson welts like insignia.

A fold beside her opened suddenly. It was like a melting cathedral archway and there was a furnace within.

"Come on down," she shouted up at Kevin over the windy bonfire bellow the great mouth made. Her face was burnished red as an apple.

The meat he'd consumed wanted to come back and choke him. He looked to the partially open door of the flat. Yes, he'd come down. Find a back way. Run between the browning hills, through black-flowered meadows and crops of shadows in the fields, run far away.

Another door creaked open as he got up. With a squeal of un-oiled and rusted wheels, the pram emerged and trundled in the direction he had wanted to go. It butted the quarter-open front door of the flat, knocking it shut.

He was feverish, trembling. He wiped sweat from his eyes. He'd taken two steps towards the pram when the thin, pink and pliant limb reached out. Its fingerless extremity held a key and was sufficiently dexterous to fit and turn it in the lock. The lock engaged. The limb withdrew with the key into the hood.

His face was teary with sweat. His vision swam, but he had to get to the door. He took one step – no more as the pram began to rock violently back and forth, turning gradually, with regular squeaks, until the black opening within the hood faced him. He backed away to the window.

The stupendous tread again – not going anywhere. It denoted an eager and immense prancing. He didn't dare to look away from the blackness under the hood – but then he had to. "Come on Kevin. You mustn't keep us waiting," Kate called up. "We're all ready to go." He looked down.

Sunset filled the street. Everyone was looking up at him. Kate was poised at the furnace yawn, looking with amber eyes over her greasy golden shoulder at him, teeth like Cotswold stone in her smile.

Then she was gone.

Loss whistled through him. It was inescapably apparent where he had to go to find her again. The pink-hued darkness under the pram hood nodded sagely in agreement. Kevin pushed open both leaves of the broken window and the heat masked him. And still he hesitated. But then the pram squealed briefly. Irregular impacts approached, and he knew a decision of any kind was no longer his to make.

# THE UNDEAD WHO WANDER THE WYE

Old legends of Herefordshire tell of Herla, one of the ancient British kings, whose court was located on the banks of the River Wye. No factual record exists in the modern day of any king called Herla, though this does not mean that no such person existed.

Herla was regarded as a wise monarch, whose realm was fair and prosperous. He was also known for the lavishness of his feasts and celebrations. However, his reign was to end abruptly in the midst of a bizarre and frightening event which would have weird repercussions for centuries to come.

In early middle-age, Herla married the daughter of a neighbouring potentate and held a magnificent wedding banquet. Half way through, an unexpected guest arrived: a diminutive man riding a goat. Baffled but always beneficent, Herla invited the new-arrival in and offered him a seat at the table. The new-arrival gratefully accepted. He did not give his name, but said that he was a king also. At the end of the feast, before departing, the small guest told Herla that he too was soon to be married and that he would send an invitation, which Herla said he would be glad to receive.

Herla soon forgot the curious incident, but a year later a wedding invitation arrived – not just for him but for all his leading courtiers. The diminutive fellow then returned to Herla's court, offering to escort the guests personally. The merry band departed, following their guide along the River Wye until at last he brought them to a cave in a cliff-face. Some of Herla's men became uneasy, but Herla felt that any withdrawal would be deemed an insult, and insisted they continue.

Beyond the cave, they followed a narrow passage which led deep into the Earth, eventually to a wondrous subterranean kingdom filled with palaces and pavilions. All manner of handsome but diminutive folk were there to receive them. By now Herla's followers felt certain they were in the faerie realm, and were on their guard for trickery. But everything happened as their host had promised. They were treated to a royal feast and sumptuous entertainments, which lasted for three whole days. When they finally departed, they were plied with every kind of gift: fine raiment, jeweled vessels, hunting hawks, gold and silver plate. They were also given a bloodhound, and were told that on returning to their homeland, none of them must dismount from their horses unless this dog had been placed on the ground first.

Herla and his men travelled back along the passage in good spirits, and re-emerged into the upper world, where the king stopped a shepherd, introduced himself and enquired how things were in the kingdom. But the shepherd was not able to understand the king. Herla and his courtiers were Britons and spoke the old Gaelic tongue. The shepherd appeared to be of a different race altogether. At last they managed to make some sense of what he was saying. It seemed the Saxons now ruled England, and the only king called Herla whom the shepherd knew about had ridden out of his kingdom 200 years earlier with his leading retainers, and had never been seen again.

Horrified, several of Herla's men leapt from their horses, paying no heed to the warning that their new bloodhound must touch the ground first.

All of them crumbled to dust.

From this moment on, Herla and his followers were known as 'the Herlethingus': a solemn, pale-faced band of undead warriors who would endlessly roam the benighted countryside, never laughing, never speaking and never ageing. Their mere presence, it was said, caused such a sense of despair that many who saw them did away with themselves. Others simply died of fright. Some stories suggest that these casualties would then join the eternal wanderers – whose number grew steadily as a result.

Much English folklore describes a faerie realm which appears to occupy a different time-zone to our own. There have been many myths and legends about those who have spent time in this otherworld, re-emerging to discover that centuries have passed, though the story of Herla was taken more seriously than most. Until the late Middle Ages it was widely believed to be true, and the rural folk of west Herefordshire were careful not to travel the roads at night in case they met the doomed band.

The last reported sighting dates from the year 1191, when the chronicler Walter Map described the party riding through a village after dusk, their wedding finery reduced to rotted rags, their skin white as snow, their ageless eyes gazing without seeing into the autumn murk.

# THE SHAKESPEARE CURSE
## Simon Clark

### DESPAIR AND DIE

C live read the words on the secret door. "Despair and die." He grinned back across the bedroom at his wife. "Not very welcoming, is it?"

"This is a listed building." Verity sounded uneasy. "Are you supposed to be ripping walls down without permission?"

"Despair and die," he murmured, as he ran a finger below ornate letters painted in black on white door timbers. "This looks like old-style writing. Way, way old. What do you think?"

"Shakespeare."

"You think he painted this?"

Clive rolled his eyes in surprise, and she wasn't sure if he was teasing her, or genuinely believed that the Bard had got busy with a paint brush to daub this graffiti four centuries ago.

"Despair and die," she said. "It's from a Shakespeare play."

"*Richard the Third*, I know. We were tortured with the bloody thing at school."

"So you knew where the quote came from all along?"

"I'm not as stupid as I look, Mrs Cheadle."

"I never said you were stupid."

Clive closed his eyes as he recited, "*Richard the Third* by William Shakespeare, first performed circa 1600. Tells the story of evil King Richard, who murdered the princes in the tower, possibly poisoned his wife, assassinated his brother, and bumped off a few more beside. Royalty, huh?"

"Tudor propaganda; they portrayed Richard the Third as an evil monster."

"Ah ... and bloody King Dick was indeed a monstrous humpback." Clive hunched one shoulder, screwed up one eye, and lisped theatrically, "His soul was as ugly as his crookbacked frame. Rudely stamp'd... deform'd, unfinish'd ... Everyone turned against him in the end, even his own mother. He was the last English king to be killed in battle ... and before he died King Dick was visited by the ghosts of people he'd gruesomely murdered. They pointed their spectral fingers at him and uttered: '*Despair and die ... Despair and die!*'"

Clive lurched across the bedroom toward her, gurning with relish, while keeping one shoulder hunched up as high as he could manage. Despite the face-pulling, he looked much younger than his forty-six years; although now his high forehead was smeared with black dust from his enthusiastic, if potentially illegal DIY, here in the bedroom of the seventeenth century house picturesquely known as 'Glover's Yarn'. Then Stratford-upon-Avon was an amazingly picturesque town.

"Fair maiden." He acted with gusto. "Fair maiden, unbutton thy bodice and repose thy comely flesh upon yonder bed, so that I might ..."

"Clive ... not while you've got cobwebs in your hair, and ... ugh! Something horrible's stuck to your eyebrow."

"That's the ghost of King Richard's moldy old eye wart."

"No, it's a bloody spider," Verity shrieked – the shriek turned to laughter as he tickled her ribs. "Don't you dare come near me with a spider stuck to your face."

"It's dead." He picked the miniscule, shrivel-legged corpse from his eyebrow. "Dead, just like poor crookbacked King Richard at Bosworth Field." He play-acted being heart-broken and rolled his mournful eyes up toward the ceiling. "The last king of the House of York is no more."

She smiled. "If you don't get your cobwebby fingers away from my new sweater, you'll be joining him."

"Ha! What's important now is to solve this mystery: *why is there a secret door behind these plywood panels in our bedroom?*"

"No, Clive." She returned to the real purpose of why she'd interrupted his demolition work. "What's important now is that you look at this email." She held out the tablet pc with those stark and frankly bitter words on the screen. "You can't ignore it in the hope it'll go away."

"Later, my sweet. I want to see what lies behind our secret door."

"Clive ..."

"Do you think this message, *Despair and die,* is supposed to be a general reminder of our mortality, or is it a specific warning? The olde worlde equivalent of *High Voltage: Do Not Touch.*"

"Forget the bloody door. Your brothers and your mother are extremely annoyed with you. In fact, they're furious at what you've done."

"Well, it is done now. Can't be undone."

"But you've got to deal with the consequences, Clive."

"Nope."

"I love you … but I feel like strangling you."

"Love you, too, my English rose."

His lively brown eyes twinkled as he smiled his charming smile – the very smile that had ignited a warm glow inside of her the first time they'd met when they were office newbies in the same department twenty years ago. Although she had since learned to resist his charmer's smile when the occasion arose – and, damn it, the occasion had risen now.

Clive hummed as he ran the tip of a screwdriver around the edge of the sealed door in order to score away accumulated dust and paint.

Verity knew that her husband intended to evade his responsibilities. Clive's policy of avoiding troublesome issues always annoyed her. However, she wouldn't let him charm his way out of this one.

She spoke firmly, and in such a way to impress upon his boyish soul that she was determined to deal with this problem that her husband had created – and that he must deal with it, too. No evasions. No excuses. "I'll leave the tablet here on the bedside table. Read Jonathan's email. I'm going to make some coffee then we'll decide how we put everything right."

"Will you pop to Urswicks for a malt loaf?" Cheerfully, he poked the screwdriver tip through a knothole in the door. "They do the finest malt loaf in all of ye olde Stratford."

"No malt loaf – at least not until we find a way to stop your family hating you."

"Scones, then?"

"Read the email, Clive."

Verity Cheadle could still hear him reading the words on the door as she went downstairs.

"Despair and die." Clive was enthralled with his discovery. "Brilliant. Absolutely bloody brilliant."

She shivered as if something cold and wet had just slithered down her back.

*Despair and die,* she thought. *It sounds like the words a hangman would use when he puts the rope around your neck.*

## THE SCREAM

"I love him. I like him." That was the rhythm of Verity Cheadle's feelings as she filled the kettle and set out the mugs. She knew plenty of married couples who although they clearly did love each other didn't exactly like each other – that may be an odd situation; it was one, however, that she'd seen with her own eyes. Some couples didn't relish spending time alone with their other halves. On the other hand, Verity and Clive did enjoy being alone together. They had long conversations, they laughed at the same things, and enjoyed the same films and music.

After clicking the kettle switch, she stared dreamily out of the window. Shoppers could be glimpsed passing by the end of the alleyway as they scurried along busy Wood Street. Clive and Verity enjoyed one another's company so much that she wasn't at all surprised when he suggested they take a sabbatical – one whole year away from their respective office jobs. That way they'd have more time together to enjoy visiting museums, exploring the countryside, searching out the perfect pub lunch; in fact, indulge any whim that came their way. Their twin sons were at university, so why not?

They'd sold their house in Harrogate and bought the two-bedroomed cottage in Stratford-upon-Avon – a place they'd fallen in love with when they'd honeymooned here two decades ago. The black and white timber-framed house with that charming name, Glover's Yarn, lay in an alleyway just off Wood Street in glorious proximity to ancient inns, tea-rooms, restaurants and enchanting architecture galore. Painted on one of the black timbers on the front of the house was the year of its construction: 1623. It was a beautiful home. They loved it.

But that silver cloud had a dark lining, as it were. Cash from the sale of the house in Yorkshire had dwindled alarmingly. So Clive, being Clive, found a quick-fix solution.

He'd sold his twenty percent share in a warehouse that his family owned in Bradford. However, he'd not consulted his mother and three brothers, who owned the remaining shares. Not telling them was bad enough, but Clive had sold his share to the tenant of the warehouse, and now the man had decided he wouldn't pay his rent. Result: fury. Utter fury. Clive's brothers had tried phoning him – no doubt to remonstrate … well, more accurately, play merry bloody hell with their inconsiderate brother for dropping the family in the karzi.

For the last two weeks his mother had assumed a regal if icy silence. Clive screened the calls on his mobile and didn't answer if his brothers' names popped up on screen. Steadfastly, he refused to check his emails. So now Verity had to check them for him.

"You're not a child, Clive," she murmured to herself, as she poured boiling water into the mugs. "Take responsibility for what you've done."

Clive – playful, boyish Clive – always on the look-out for a jolly adventure that wouldn't be out of place in an Enid Blyton story, had been overjoyed to find the secret door in their bedroom. It all started that morning when he'd begun scraping off wallpaper that just fair-yodeled 1975, with its yucky brown roundels on a black background. Beneath the wallpaper were hardboard panels. Clive had soon pried these modern-ish boards off to reveal some very old white plasterwork, gorgeous black timbers, and *that* door. The secret door with the disturbing message: *Despair and die.*

So, while Clive's family grew angrier with him by the day for what they clearly saw as a betrayal, Clive himself would use the excitement of finding the hitherto concealed entrance as a distraction. That, in turn, would mean he could avoid the uncomfortable reality of apologising to his brothers and his mother for selling his share of the family business to a swindler.

After stirring the coffee, she placed the mugs on the tray *(No malt loaf! No scones! No way!)*, she then headed for the stairs. Coming from the upper-floor was a staccato squeaking – possibly nails being pried from timber with a claw hammer.

Then came the sound of her husband's scream. Long and loud and terrifying.

### FROM SUCH DARKNESS

Verity clattered the tray of mugs down onto the blanket box at the top of the stairs and ran into the bedroom. *Dear God, what's happened to him? Why had Clive shouted like that?* Her heart pounded and she felt physically sick, because she expected to see him lying there hurt in such a shockingly awful way.

"Clive … Clive?"

The first thing she noticed was the door – the secret door – it yawned open. Nails poked from the wooden frame where it had once been sealed shut. So Clive *had* been prying free the nails. She ran round to the other side of the bed, expecting to see Clive lying there on the floor, perhaps clutching his chest as a blood clot or a ruptured artery overwhelmed him with agony. God, yes, her imagination fired all kinds of scenarios of hurt and tragedy.

She stared at the floor.

Clive didn't lie there. What did show itself on the bare boards were round drops of blood the size of pennies.

"Clive, where are you?" Panic made her yell crackle with energy. "Clive, what happened?"

There was no answer. So she walked toward the yawning doorway that had once been closed-off for goodness knows how long. Cobwebs smeared the inside of the panels. While on the woodwork at the edge of the door were a cluster of bloody fingerprints – they were moist and crimson, and clearly fresh.

"Clive, what's happened?" She felt a sickening mixture of anger, frustration and downright fear. *Why doesn't he answer me? Is he willfully ignoring me? Or can't he answer? What if he's ...* With an effort she stopped her imagination layering horrific imagery upon her already fraught nerves.

Verity stepped through the doorway into a narrow passageway, which appeared to run between the other side of the bedroom wall and the outer wall of the house. Far too gloomy to see much, although she could tell the timber floor was gritty underfoot – no doubt years of accumulated dust and dirt – the soles of her sandals made a light scrunching sound when she moved her feet. There was a tarry smell, too. Probably the aroma of the black stuff they painted on the house beams all those centuries ago.

"Clive, talk to me. Just let me know where you are."

*Dark ... too dark to see much ... walls, a low ceiling ...* she made out those. Then there was only the darkness of the corridor, leading to some mysterious, hidden part of the house.

*No! Wait ... something's happening ...* Because there, directly in front of her, the darkness was no longer still. She couldn't explain what she saw, but there seemed to be a shadow moving in front of a mass of darker shadows.

"Clive, is that you?"

The shadow lunged forward – and she suddenly realized that shadow had become a bulky figure that raced along the passageway toward her: a massive shape that moved with fury and evil intent.

Closing her eyes, and putting her hands in front of her, she held her breath and waited for the creature to strike.

Verity Cheadle stood there, muscles clenched, holding her breath, eyes scrunched shut. She expected to feel a massive blow as the intruder barreled into her.

Only the impact never came. All she felt was the cool, stale air on her face. Her thudding heartbeat was the loudest sound right now.

Verity opened her eyes. She stood alone in the narrow void that ran between the bedroom wall and the party wall of the neighbouring property. So where was the figure? The burly trespasser? She was certain that someone had sped toward her from the darkness at the far end of the passageway, yet it had been too gloomy to see their face. Though surely it wasn't Clive playing some ridiculous joke, was it? A cruel joke at that. She thought she was going to have a heart attack when that terrifying figure had appeared.

*But think this through ... it can't have been Clive*, she told herself. *He's slightly built.* A 'wind and wafer chap' was how her mother sometimes disparagingly referred to him. So who'd darted toward her before vanishing into thin air? She wasn't going mad, was she? After all, a symptom of insanity must be seeing things that simply aren't there. The mystery of it all sent electric shivers tingling across her skin.

"Clive!" she called in a loud voice, despite the fact the intruder might hear (and might be encouraged to come back). "Clive, are you in here?"

Clenching her fists in determination, she moved along the corridor. Her eyes were adjusting to the gloom now. The walls were rough, unplastered stonework. There were no windows, no electric lights of course; there were, however, cobwebs galore. They formed something that resembled dusty curtains, hanging limply from the ceiling, threatening to adorn her hair if she got too close.

Quickly, she discovered that the corridor came to a dead end. However, halfway along the corridor she noticed an opening. Beyond the opening was a narrow staircase: one so narrow that she had to turn sideways to use it. Maybe the shock of hearing her husband scream, and of almost being attacked just now, generated a big enough shot of adrenalin to make her feel brave, because she didn't hesitate.

Verity descended the stairs with a clear sense of purpose. *Find Clive. Then get out of here, and telephone the police.* Those all-important thoughts dominated. Nothing else mattered.

She went down the final section of staircase in a rush; seconds later, she burst through a doorway into a room. A light suddenly blazed into her face, dazzling her.

"You should take a look at what I've found … it's amazing."

"Clive? Are you alright?" Her heart pounded.

"Come and see what's on the wall …"

"Clive! There's someone in the house. We need to call the police."

Clive shone a flashlight onto the stonework. "Remember, we were talking about Richard the Third a few minutes ago – the evil hunchbacked king?"

"What on earth …"

"Well, here he is."

"Didn't you hear me? There's an intruder."

"Oh that …' His voice was dismissive. "I thought I saw someone, too. That's why I shouted."

"Shouted? You screamed!" Her face felt burning hot. She was all knotted up inside with outrage and shock. What she'd experienced a moment ago had rattled her nerves more than she could say; now Clive was prattling about something he'd found. Verity Cheadle wanted to scream with sheer, bloody exasperation. "We can phone the police from outside in the street; we'll be safe there."

"Verity, there aren't any intruders. It's just an optical illusion when you walk through the secret door. The light from behind throws your shadow down the corridor."

"That was no shadow."

"Must have been shadow. The stairs only lead down here into this room. There's no other exit. So, unless your scary burglar became invisible, he must have never existed in the first place."

The knots of tension began, at last, to unknot themselves. Verity sighed as she started to relax. Even so … "What about the blood?" she asked

"Punctured myself on a ruddy nail." Clive held up his left arm. He'd made a fist of the hand so that a wad of tissues stayed pressed against the palm. "Don't worry … just a nick."

"Come upstairs, I'll take care of it."

"See what I've found first. You're not going to believe your beautiful eyes."

"I've had enough excitement for one day, thank you very much."

He grinned. "Isn't it brilliant? I discover a secret door in our bedroom, now I've found secret stairs to a secret room in *our* house."

"Where are we?" Despite the recent shocks, she began to take an interest in the strange chamber.

"We must be on the ground floor. See the stone slabs? On the other side of that wall is our kitchen ... on the far side of *that* one is the wine bar next door. The round grate in the floor must be the opening to a well. Probably the household's water supply, until the mains were installed a hundred years or so ago."

As her husband swept the flashlight round, she realised that she stood in a void that was perhaps twenty feet long by six or seven feet wide. There were stone shelves on the end wall. No windows, no furniture and no other doorways.

"It's amazing, isn't it?" His grin broadened. "But you haven't seen the best bit yet."

"You said you'd found Richard the Third?"

"Or someone who resembles him." He directed the light at the stonework. "Take a look, there's dozens of them."

*'Them'* referred to drawings that had been scratched on the wall. Indeed, there were dozens. Each image had been laboriously engraved with the point of a knife, she surmised – and each image sent shivers down her spine. They were a catalogue of horror.

"These are awful," she gasped.

"And, look ... in each picture there's a hunchback. I've named him 'Hunchie'. Sort of suits, doesn't it?"

"Clive. Something terrible happened down here." Her blood ran cold in her veins. "These aren't just pictures, they're someone's autobiography."

"Uh, how?"

"Look closer – you can follow the images like they're frames in a comic. Here, give me the torch. See? They start up there at the top of the wall. The first picture shows a boy with a swollen back. He's standing in a garden with trees; the man and woman at either side of him must be his mother and father. The next frame shows him ..."

"Hunchie."

"If you like. The next one shows him sitting alone in a room that looks uncannily like this one. See those dots on his face?"

"Acne."

"No, they're not spots – they're tears."

"Blimey."

"He's been locked up in here ... he's crying."

"Poor Hunchie."

"If you're going to act the clown, I'm going."

"Sorry."

"This is serious. Someone was kept prisoner here." She glared at him, ready to storm out if he made another silly joke.

He drew a cross over his heart. "And hope to die ... Go on, you're good at this."

She shone the light on each etched image in turn. "The poor man, whoever he was, spent a long time producing these ... notice how detailed they are." She worked her way along that chilling narrative in stone. "So, the first one: he's a boy – happy in the garden with his mother and father. Next one: crying ... alone. The next: reading a book ... now he's mending his clothes."

"*Making* his clothes," Clive corrected. "Look he's wearing a new coat."

"But he's still alone in this room."

"So, Hunchie ... sorry ... the *victim* ... was locked up here; he spent his time scratching these self-portraits, which showed how he lived his life. What a wretched existence."

"I wonder when he was imprisoned here."

"The style of clothes suggests three or four hundred years ago, do you think?"

She nodded. The hunchback's billowing coat had distinctive sleeve cuffs, bearing a chevron pattern. The man seemed to hold this pattern in high regard, because he'd carefully scratched the >>> design onto the cuffs in every picture after the tailoring scene.

"He must have been here for years," she murmured. "You can see him ageing in each portrait. As you get toward the end of this line, his hair vanishes as he starts to go bald."

"And, if anything, his hump grows bigger. It's like he's walking round with a hill between his shoulder blades."

"But keeping a poor, deformed man in this miserable little cell without windows? What a terrible thing to do."

"Blame Shakespeare. He equated physical deformity with evil. You know, like that old wives' tale? About how people who have their eyes set too close together must be criminals."

She shuddered. "The Shakespeare curse."

"Absolutely. Because this guy had a hump people would assume that he was evil, just like Richard the Third."

"So, lock him up before he does anything bad." When she illuminated the next line of images she found herself uttering a shocked, *"Oh."*

Clive let out a whistle. "Maybe Hunchie wasn't a goody two-shoes, after all?"

The remaining images revealed the hunchback waging a one man war on the townspeople. Picture after picture depicted that striking man, with the mound of bone and flesh on his back, rushing through Stratford-upon-Avon. There he was in his coat with the distinctive >>>> motif. In one picture, he plunged a knife into the eye of a man, wearing a lavish cloak and a hat. In the next, he placed a hangman's noose round the neck of a well-dressed gent in knee-breeches. Then he was in a ballroom, eagerly beheading elegant ladies in their long dresses with embroidered bodices. Heads were bouncing across the floor. Sprays of blood splashed the walls. Other grisly images showed the hunchback drowning priests in the river, or burning thatched inns full of weeping townsfolk, or crushing what appeared to be soldiers between two huge circular millstones.

"Our Mr Hunchie broke out," Clive declared. "He got his revenge on Stratford."

"Then he lost his mind." Verity shuddered as she directed the light at the final graven portrait. "Just look at what he's doing to that naked woman."

Clive's eyes narrowed as he examined the stark image. The hunchback had drawn himself as a strangely distorted giant, where the hump had grown bigger than the rest of his body. There he posed in his billowing coat with the chevron pattern cuffs. He'd torn the naked woman to pieces, much as you could pull a roast chicken apart. This last self-portrait was cleverly rendered. Hunchie gazed out of the picture into the eyes of anyone who viewed it. Happily, he munched on his victim's leg – just as if it were a chicken drumstick.

The sight of the cannibalism, together with the aura of insanity that surrounded the final image, made Verity feel panicky and claustrophobic.

*Oh God... oh my dear God.* Something strange was happening in that hidden chamber – and something very strange was happening to her. The walls appeared to be closing in. What's more, she felt incredible pressure being directed into the centre of her forehead. This was followed by the sickening impression of a barrier giving way. A frightening moment of surrender – of yielding to some force of immense power. Her stomach churned in disgust as she experienced a sensation that she could only describe as the feel of cold fingers stirring the living matter of her brain: weaving her thoughts into new patterns, and threading bizarre ideas through her mind.

Suddenly, she had a dazzling vision of the hunchback. He was staring at her with a gloating expression as he ran his tongue under a torn flap of skin on the butchered woman's leg. The pictograph had come blazingly to life right there in front of her.

"Thank you, my lady," oozed the hunchback in a whispery voice. "Thank you for breaking my shackles."

His eyes burned with such evil madness. To Verity they were the brightest objects in the universe: twin infernos that poured the fire of his insanity down upon her once sane world.

Then the nightmare vision was gone.

Quickly, she splashed the torchlight around the walls to make sure they weren't really inching closer to crush her. She heaved a huge sigh of relief. Those strange events just now must have only lasted a few seconds; Clive hadn't even noticed that anything unusual had happened to her. So what had happened to her? Hallucination? A momentary lapse of consciousness?

Verity Cheadle managed to shrug off the sense of terror, and yet she was gripped by this powerful revelation: *nothing's ever going to be the same again. Everything will change…*

"Wait." Clive caught her arm. "There's something stuck in the grate. Keep the light on it."

He bent down where the iron grill capped the well shaft. A piece of rag had been jammed between two of its crisscross bars. Between finger and thumb, Clive fished the cloth out before holding it out so she could see more closely.

On the grimy fabric was a distinctive chevron pattern. A series of embroidered marks like so: <<<<

Clive swallowed. "Something tells me that Hunchie ended up down the well."

*CRUDELY STAMP'D … UNFINISH'D …*

The raging argument that culminated in them sleeping apart that night could be traced back to when the skeleton was found at the bottom of the well. Press and TV people invaded the house. Verity wouldn't have anything to do with the media circus. She detested the way that the hunchback's bones were awarded the freak-show treatment.

The police were satisfied that the death had occurred at least three centuries ago and announced there'd be no homicide case to investigate. So the bones were laid out in the *DEVIL HUNCHBACK'S DEATH CELL* (as one tabloid screamed from its front page). Verity Cheadle loathed the invasion of privacy. She resented the way reporters and camera crews tramped through her home, getting her new carpets dirty, and using the toilet without asking. Filming the malformed skeleton in such pornographic detail revolted her. The way the camera lingered over the strangely splayed ribs; the manner in which the lens zoomed in on a spine that was almost as bent as a fish hook – how disrespectful, how callous.

If anything, Clive gloried in the attention of the TV crews. What's more, he saw this as the perfect excuse to forget that he'd alienated his own family by selling his share of the business. Problem solved (at least that's what his self-satisfied expression seemed to say). Verity grew increasingly annoyed with her husband. The point where annoyance erupted into anger was when he gushingly tried to impress a pretty, dark-eyed TV reporter by clowning round with the skull, live on-air, then claiming, "When I first opened that hidden door, I thought I saw the ghost of Hunchie. Huge he was – with a hump that came up higher than his head." He'd comically hunched his own shoulder as high as it would go. Right on cue, the reporter laughed prettily, and Verity's husband almost preened himself because he was so flattered by the woman's attention.

Verity suddenly saw another side to Clive – a side she did not care for at all.

Later, after the newshounds had gone, and the skeleton had been collected by museum officials, the long-running argument culminated in: *"Clive! You're on the sofa tonight!"*

"What have I done wrong?"

"It's a wonder you didn't sit up and beg like a lapdog for that woman."

"It was just a bit of fun, Verity."

"Well, you can have a bit of fun sleeping on the sofa."

After stamping upstairs, Clive returned to the lounge with pillows, a blanket, and an extremely sulky expression. "My mother and my brothers have turned against me, Verity … and now you've turned against me, too."

"You've only yourself to blame. Don't you realise how stupid you made yourself look on television? You pretended you'd seen the hunchback's ghost. You were laughing and joking about the death of

94

a poor deformed man: someone who'd been locked up for years in that cell downstairs. Can't you begin to imagine how much he suffered?"

"He ran amok and killed people. You saw the pictures."

"They were probably just his fantasies of revenge."

"Well, you can't turn the clock back and save Hunchie now."

"My God, I wish I could, Clive. The poor devil suffered in *our* house. So, yes, I wish I could turn back the clock … I wish it with all my heart. Then I could prove to him that not everyone in this world is cruel and heartless."

"Careful what you wish for, Verity." He lay down on the sofa and pulled the blanket up to his chin. "Careful what you wish for."

Verity Cheadle woke as the downstairs clock struck midnight. She'd gone to bed alone. Now, however, a figure lay beside her. *Clive waited until I fell asleep,* she told herself, *then he sneaked into bed with me.*

The figure lay very still. She reached out to put her arm around Clive's shoulders. What she found there with her fingertips was a swollen mound of flesh – nothing less than a giant tumulus of a ribcage. The hump was smoothly rounded and very firm. Verity had never believed in ghosts before. Oh … but she did now. And she believed that with the right encouragement the dead could return … and return as solidly, and as viscerally, as any living human being.

If it ever occurred to her that she was descending into madness, then she suppressed the notion. After all, do the insane know that they are insane?

What's more, Verity Cheadle remembered what she'd wished for. That she longed with all her heart to prove to the poor wretch, who'd been entombed in the well, that not all men and women were bereft of compassion.

So she felt no fear when she whispered, "It's okay. I promise to make you happy. But first we need to take care of Clive. What do you think about the secret room downstairs? He'll be out of sight there. We can keep him out of trouble."

Then she kissed the bare shoulder of her crookbacked man.

# OXFORD'S BLACK ASSIZE

The city of Oxford is regarded universally as a seat of culture and learning. It doesn't just boast the second oldest university in the world, an institution famed for its excellence, but the entire city centre is rich with ancient buildings, ivied cloisters and an air of scholarly academe. It is difficult when wandering around Oxford's dreaming spires to imagine that anything dreadful, bizarre or horrifying could ever have occurred there, but like so many apparently tranquil places in England's beautiful Cotswolds, this façade can be deceptive.

For a brief time, Oxford became famous for reasons few of its citizens would like to be reminded about today. In 1555, during the reign of Mary I, known as 'Bloody Mary' for her eagerness to persecute Protestant heretics, three prominent bishops – Hugh Latimer, Nicholas Ridley and Thomas Cranmer – were tied to stakes at Balliol College in central Oxford, and burned alive. A fanatical Catholic, Mary's roll-call of anti-Protestant vengeance was quite chilling, though most who perished in her fires did so at Smithfield in London. Only Ridley, Latimer and Cranmer died at Oxford. However, this shows that the city already had a tradition of dispatching heretics when, by 1577, one Rowland Jenkes was brought to trial for a similar crime.

By this time, Elizabeth I, an arch-Protestant, was on the English throne, though she had a known distaste for the use of burning as a punishment. Nevertheless, heresy was still a capital offence, and to be accused of this could have a serious outcome. No-one could have foreseen that the trial of Rowland Jenkes would have an outcome so serious – not for him, but for many others – that it would become known as 'the Black Assize'.

There is some confusion about who Jenkes was and what form his heresy supposedly took. Possibly he was a follower of Arianism, an off-shoot doctrine which led several other free-thinking religious folk to die at the hands of their fellow Anglicans during the reigns of Edward VI and his sister Elizabeth I, though this may actually be giving him credit he didn't deserve. Other pamphlets of the time suggest that Jenkes was little more than a foul-mouthed seditionist, and maybe even a seller of 'saucy books'.

There is also the possibility that he had some mastery of the dark arts.

He was tried at the Assize Court at Oxford Castle in July 1577, convicted and sentenced to have his ears cut off. This was a relatively mild penalty given the standards of the time, but it was too much for Jenkes, who was furious and, as he was led from the dock, passed a curse on the entire courtroom. Within minutes, a choking stench filled the building which led to scenes of pandemonium. The jury, magistrates and many of those present as witnesses, began screaming and raving – apparently behaving as if they had gone mad. One by one, either there on the spot or over the next few hours, they died. Among their number were several illustrious names, including Sir Robert Bell, who was Lord Chief Baron of the Exchequer, and Robert D'Oyly of Merton, who was Lord High Sheriff. Almost everyone involved in the trial had expired before the end of the day, with the exception of Rowland Jenkes, who walked free. But it didn't stop there. Whatever the epidemic he had started was, it raged on through the city of Oxford and claimed a total of almost 500 lives before suddenly, inexplicably, disappearing.

Initially it was thought that Jenkes had summoned a demon to destroy his enemies – devilish manifestations were believed to be accompanied by odious smells, though this kind of lurid rationalisation was not accepted by everyone, not even in the credulous age of the Elizabethans. A later witness gave evidence that, shortly before his trial, Jenkes had visited an apothecary who had made a candle for him composed of poisonous materials, and that he had somehow managed to smuggle this into the court and lit it – though why he himself wasn't struck down by the toxic fumes has never been stated.

A more prosaic explanation may be that Jenkes was only one of several prisoners brought up from the castle dungeons, and that some kind of contagion – possibly typhus or cholera – arrived in the courtroom with them. Though why it was so fast-acting and again, why Jenkes himself was not affected, are questions that remain unanswered.

Jenkes went on to live until well into old age. Despite his seditious tongue and saucy books, no-one could be found who was willing to put him on trial again.

# THE SCOURING
## Thana Niveau

"Is it a dinosaur?"

Natalie smiled. The strangely disjointed white figure etched into the hillside could easily be mistaken for a dinosaur. It certainly bore little enough resemblance to the horse it was supposed to be.

"No, sweetie, it's a horse."

Charlie squinted and cocked his head to the side as he tried to rotate the animal in his mind. "But it looks like a fossil and its head's turned around like the one at the museum."

Now it was Natalie's turn to screw up her eyes and try to see what her son was seeing. If she imagined that the horse's spike of an ear was instead its lower jaw, then the hollow square of a head below it could be inverted, with its weird beaked mouth representing some kind of reptilian crest. Some people insisted that the horse was actually the dragon slain by St George, so a dinosaur wasn't that far off.

"Well," she said, "I don't think anyone is a hundred percent sure what it is, so if you want to call it a dinosaur, you go right ahead."

But Charlie shook his head. "No," he said earnestly. "White Horse."

She nodded, responding to him in kind. Sometimes he could be so serious, so formal. He'd been that way even before the funeral. He had a set of internal rules that he followed with an almost religious devotion.

"Very well. White Horse it is."

Sitting down in the grass at her feet, he pulled a battered notebook from his rucksack and set to work on a sketch.

Natalie moved away discreetly, not wanting Charlie to feel watched. He was always so protective of his drawings. Although they were quite good for his age, he was reluctant to share them. Perhaps that was what they called the 'artist's temperament'. His father had certainly had it and Natalie's heart twisted as she recalled the immaculate flowers she used to find sketched in the steam of the bathroom mirror or on the dewy windows of her car. Michael never committed them to paper, despite her pleading, but seemed content to let them fade. *Just like real flowers*, he'd told her once.

She blinked back tears. Just like you.

A breeze ruffled the grass, transforming it into a blurry green lake through the liquid sheen in her eyes. The flowing white lines of the horse swam above, as though trying to escape the pull of the grassy current. Natalie wiped her eyes and glanced down at Charlie. He was working industriously on his sketch, peering hard at the figure for several seconds before dipping his head again to the paper. His pencil scratched with vigour.

Natalie closed her eyes against the thought of Michael working just as hard on the ephemeral blossoms he had painted in glass for her over the years. She remembered the first one most of all. It was their third date and the first night they spent together. The hotel had been beyond both their means but everywhere cheaper was full and they were too tired to make it back to Bristol that night. So they had made the most of the elegant room, spending the entire night getting to know each other better, talking, laughing, making love and sharing secrets. By the time they finally slept, the sun was up and they were madly in love.

An hour before check-out Natalie jumped into the shower to wash her hair. And as the steam drifted up around her she saw an image begin to form on the shower door. A rose. Its delicate petals unfolded for her like a secret message and she was surprised to find herself crying. Michael must have done it while she was asleep. A year later they were married.

And six years after that, Natalie placed a single red rose on top of Michael's closed coffin. She leaned down to the polished wood and exhaled against it, then sketched a clumsy heart in the stain of her breath.

Charlie had stood by her side, clutching her hand bravely as he peered around at all the sombre grownups. He didn't fully understand what the strange ceremony was about; he just knew that Daddy had gone away and wasn't coming back. He made her think of a Christmas puppy dumped by the roadside, watching with wide, trustful eyes for his new best friends to come back. For several months after the funeral Charlie had talked to his father, openly and un-self-consciously at first and then later in reserved, private whispers as the finality began to sink in.

A small monetary settlement from the accident had been enough for a trip to Disneyland in Paris. It had been Michael's mother's idea, something to help take Charlie's mind off the loss. But Natalie should have known better. Being there without Michael only magnified their grief. There was a hole in their family, a wound that

99

worsened at the sight of all the happy and intact families hooting with laughter on the rides and posing for photos with Mickey Mouse. They had cut the visit short and returned home to their cold and empty house.

Natalie was haunted by what she could see of Michael in their son. His artistic leaning, his introspective nature and most of all his eyes. Michael's eyes had been somewhere between green and brown, changing colour with the light. Natalie had been mesmerised by those eyes throughout their too-short marriage and every time she looked into Charlie's eyes she saw her husband gazing back. She had been a widow now for a little over a year and the pain in her heart had shrunk from a dagger to a splinter, but she didn't dare to hope it would ever get any smaller than that.

It was an unusually quiet day and, despite the sunshine and mild weather, only a handful of people were at the site. Uffington was an easy journey from Bristol but she'd never been before. She'd taken the week off for a mini road trip with Charlie. The poor kid deserved a break after the past year of being smothered by her.

The Cotswolds were lovely this time of year and the original plan had been to show him Oxford, with detours to Stonehenge and Avebury on the way back. But Charlie had spotted the numerous 'White Horse' references in the road atlas and insisted that they investigate.

It was a strange figure, that horse, and the only one of several white horse hill carvings that was authentically old. According to the guidebook the Uffington horse was the oldest hill figure in Britain. No one knew for sure who had put it there or what it was meant to represent, although their guidebook favoured the idea that it was a representation of the Celtic horse goddess Epona.

There was something otherworldly and vaguely unnerving about it. Natalie couldn't shake the feeling that its single eye was fixed on them. But that was silly. A single white dot, what else could it possibly fix on but the person looking at it? It was like the eyes in old portraits that seemed to follow you. As she stared at the sprawling chalk figure she found it harder and harder to see it as a horse. Now she could only see it as a dinosaur, a dragon or some other monstrous beast, its head upside-down and its ugly mouth gaping hungrily.

She hugged herself against another chilly breeze and went back to where Charlie was still hard at work on his drawing. It was such a simple figure she was surprised he hadn't finished it already.

"Are you drawing the whole county?" she asked with a laugh.

"No, just the horse."

When no further explanation was forthcoming she suggested they climb the hill to see it up close. Charlie was quiet as they made their way towards the figure. He'd always been a peculiar little boy, more introverted than most, but Natalie was used to his silent, contemplative ways. Michael had been shy too, but he had been positively extroverted compared to his son.

They reached the top and Charlie approached the horse. He frowned down at it, looking puzzled. "It's different," he said.

"How do you mean?" Natalie asked. "Different from what?"

He knelt alongside the horse's back and hesitantly touched the chalk. "I thought it would be ..." He shook his head, unable to find the words. He held his cupped hand above the lines of the carving and mimed stroking a raised figure.

"Oh, I see. You thought it would stick out. No, it's carved into the hillside. The guidebook says it's filled with chalk."

"How old is it?"

Natalie flicked through the book. "Hmm, well, this just says it's been here since the Bronze Age."

"When's that?"

She blushed, feeling horribly ignorant. "I don't really know, sweetie. But it's pretty old."

"About three thousand years old."

They both turned towards the voice. An elderly man stood there, leaning on a walking stick and smiling down at Charlie. He wore the sort of tweed suit and flat cap that Natalie imagined English country gentlemen wore to shoot grouse on the moors. He had a kind, weathered face with sharp features of almost birdlike fragility.

"Is that older than the dinosaurs?" Charlie asked, fascinated.

"Well, not quite," the man said. "They were long gone by the time this horse was put here. But 1000 BC is still a very long time ago. And it wasn't always here either."

"Really?" Charlie asked. "Where was it?"

"Not far. Just a little further down, on the side of the hill below us. It's climbed up here over the years, you see."

Charlie's eyes widened as he peered down the hillside in amazement.

"Is that true?" Natalie asked.

"Absolutely. The horse was cut into the side of the hill so it could be seen for miles. But time takes its toll on things like this. Weeds, weather, invading armies … Sometimes the picture would disappear almost entirely and need re-carving. So each time it was re-cut it inadvertently moved a little higher up the hill. There used to be a festival based around it that lasted for days. The 'Scouring of the White Horse', it was called."

"That doesn't happen anymore?" Natalie asked.

The man shook his head. "No, that was well before my time. English Heritage looks after it now. The festival grew out of pagan ritual, some ancient rite said to bring it back to life. The horse would get hungry, you see, and its guardians had to release it from the hillside so it could feed. They would make offerings, chant songs, that sort of thing. All sadly lost to time now."

Charlie was still staring intently down at the side of the hill as though trying to see the original lines of the horse. The man crouched beside him.

"You see that valley down there?"

He pointed down the hill towards a jagged depression below the horse. Charlie nodded.

"That's called the Manger. They say that's where the horse goes to eat."

Natalie smiled at Charlie's reaction to that. Everything the man was telling him was pure magic and it was wonderful to see her son so spellbound. She hung back while their companion pointed out the other interesting features of the site and Charlie peppered him with questions about castles and hill forts and particularly the horse. Of course, she couldn't help but feel a pang of remorse that it wasn't Michael, but at least Charlie seemed to be enjoying himself. That was the whole point of the trip, after all.

She rejoined the pair and Charlie excitedly pointed out the Giant's Steps to her. Already she could see his creative mind at work. Giants and spectral horses. He was happier than she had seen him in a long time. She wanted to kiss the old man.

"Well," he said at last, "I must be off. It's been a pleasure, young man."

Charlie beamed up at him and gave a salute which the man returned. Then he immediately sat down and dug out his notepad to work on a new drawing.

Natalie trotted after the old man. "Thank you so much," she said. "He probably won't be half as impressed with Stonehenge now, but hey – so what?"

The man chuckled. "It was my pleasure."

"Before you go, you wouldn't happen to know of a nice B&B around here, would you?"

"As a matter of fact, I do. And I'm sure your boy will approve." With his walking stick, he pointed across the green patchwork of the landscape towards the nearest village. "Down in Woolstone," he said. "The White Horse Inn. You can't miss it."

Natalie smiled. "Sounds perfect."

"You can walk there if you're up for it. Just follow the valley and skirt the edge of those trees. Take you about forty-five minutes."

But Natalie was shaking her head. "No way," she laughed. "I'm starving and we've only got another half hour before the pubs shut."

He shrugged. "Another time perhaps. Well, you take care, now." He waved goodbye over his shoulder as he headed off down the hill.

Natalie returned to her son, who was sitting cross-legged by the horse's head, just at the crude V of its open mouth. He was working excitedly on a new sketch and Natalie was loath to rush him, but she didn't want to miss the chance to eat.

"Hey there," she ventured. "How's it going?"

"Fine," he said distractedly. He was gripping the pencil in a strange way, clutching it in his fist and pressing down hard on the paper.

"What are you doing?"

"I want to make it right," he said, "now that I've tasted it."

"Now that you've what?"

He froze and looked up at her, blinking. "Huh?"

Natalie shook her head. "Nothing." She must have misheard him. "Aren't you hungry?"

Charlie thought for a moment, as though eating were a foreign concept. Then he nodded.

"Well, if you're almost finished, how about we get something to eat? Your friend suggested a place we could stay and I'm sure they'll feed us too."

"OK," Charlie said agreeably and folded the notebook closed.

Natalie caught a glimpse of the sketch as he did. It looked as though he'd improved the creature, adding some details to make it look more like a horse. That was unusual for him. Normally he was very literal with his pictures, trying to recreate them as faithfully as possible.

"Can I have fish and chips?"

"Of course you can."

"And ice cream?"

"If they have it."

"Hooray!"

She smiled at his enthusiasm and then glanced back at the horse. For a moment she could have sworn she'd heard a soft chuff of breath, a kind of horsey snort. But it was only her imagination, no doubt stimulated by the old man's stories.

\*

The White Horse Inn was almost as deserted as the hill had been and Natalie was glad of the peace and quiet. Oxford would be bustling and touristy, so it was nice to be somewhere tranquil for a while. They found a table near the window and she left Charlie to hold the fort while she went to the bar to place their order.

"Good looking boy," said the woman behind the bar, nodding towards Charlie as she filled one glass with Diet Coke and another with lemonade. Her enormous hoop earrings jangled with every movement.

Natalie beamed proudly. "Thanks."

"I've got two of my own. Teenagers – ugh! Right little tearaways, they are. Didn't have a single grey hair 'til they came along. Now look at me." She laughed, but it was a harsh, brittle sound. Although she couldn't be much older than Natalie, the years – or perhaps her children – had been unkind. She had the hard-bitten look of someone who'd never had a day off in her life. Her hair was dyed a garish red in an effort to hide the copious streaks of grey.

Natalie shuddered companionably. "Well, Charlie certainly has his energetic days but he's pretty quiet most of the time."

"Sensitive type, is he?"

"Artistic. He loves to draw."

"You're lucky. All mine want to do is blow things up on their PlayStation."

Unsure what to say to that, Natalie merely said "Mmm" and took out her credit card to pay for the food. The waitress handed her the drinks and a wooden spoon with TABLE 4 scrawled on it in black marker. "I'll bring your food out to you," she said. "Shouldn't be too long."

She had filled both glasses right to the top and Natalie had to walk at a snail's pace to avoid sloshing the drinks over her hands. She always wondered why pubs didn't simply use glasses that were a

104

bit larger and not fill them quite so much. She'd gladly have one less sip of Diet Coke if it meant less risk of spilling it.

As she neared the table she noticed that Charlie had taken out his notebook and was staring intently at one of his drawings. There was something wrong about the way he was sitting, the way his arms lay folded over the page. His lips moved rapidly, as though he were talking to it. A chill slithered up her back. No, she thought. As though he were *praying*.

She broke the spell by setting the drinks down and Charlie turned the notebook over and pushed it aside.

"Whatcha doing?" she asked, trying to sound casual.

"Nothing."

"Oh? I thought maybe you were working some more on your picture."

"Not really."

That appeared to be all she was going to get out of him so she reluctantly let it drop. She got out the guidebook and showed him the pages devoted to Stonehenge, but he seemed unimpressed when she told him they wouldn't be allowed to climb on the stones.

"They're much too high and anyway, they're roped off to keep people from damaging them."

"But they're stones," he said. "You can't break them."

"No, but people can chip bits off them or carve their name to say they were there. That ruins it for everyone so it's best to just keep people at a distance."

He frowned in disappointment.

"You can touch the stones at Avebury, though," she added hopefully.

"I like the White Horse. She let me touch her."

"Oh, it's a she, is it?"

"Uh-huh."

She smiled indulgently and picked up her glass. "How do you know it's a she?"

"Daddy told me."

Natalie nearly choked on the sip of Diet Coke she'd just taken. Charlie's offhanded tone was almost more disturbing than the idea that he'd been talking to his father again. She'd been assured that it was something he'd grow out of once he came to terms with the loss.

"Daddy told you?" she repeated, her voice wavering.

"Sure. He goes for rides with her. He said she likes me."

She was silent for a few seconds. *Relax*, she told herself. *He's an imaginative kid. He comes out with stuff like that all the time.*

But another voice in the back of her mind qualified that. No, not quite like that.

"Charlie? Do you think I could see your drawings?"

His brow creased thoughtfully and for a moment she felt unaccountably frightened. Then he shrugged and with a cheerful "I guess so," he flipped the pad over and turned it around for her to see.

The first drawing was a fairly faithful representation of the horse as seen from the base of the hill, and she turned the page to look at the second one. This one bore only a passing resemblance to the actual figure. Charlie's version was more obviously a horse, if still rather stylised. He had connected its two floating legs to its body and lengthened them. Now the horse appeared to be rearing up. He had turned the beaked square into a long thin head with a proper mouth. He had also given the horse a mane. Natalie was puzzled by the animal's torso, however. Instead of widening the thin line of its body to make it more realistic, Charlie had drawn a row of jagged ribs.

She wasn't sure what to say about it. Clearly it was good, if a bit weird and not at all his usual style. Had the old man told him something to inspire it? Perhaps he was just experimenting with technique. Surely that was a good thing.

"Fish and chips," the waitress sang.

Charlie held aloft the wooden spoon. "That's for us," he said.

The older woman pretended to be confused as she looked from the large plate to the smaller one. "I wonder whose is whose?"

Charlie giggled. "The big one's for me!"

She grinned and made as if to oblige, then set the plates down in front of their rightful owners. "What a little angel," she said, sounding wistful.

"Well," Natalie said playfully, "maybe not an angel all the time." She ruffled Charlie's hair.

This earned her a grimace as Charlie swiped his hand back through his hair to mess it up again.

"Hey," the waitress said, suddenly catching sight of the notepad. "Your mum said you were an artist. Is that some of your work?"

Natalie wasn't sure how he would react to a complete stranger seeing it but to her surprise he seemed fine. He nodded as the woman turned the notepad around to see the drawing.

"It's the White Horse," he said helpfully.

She bent down to look at it and the smile immediately melted from her face. She stared at the picture in horror until she got hold of herself and wiped her hands on her apron with a nervous laugh. "Do you know, I think I forgot to close the till!"

She hurried away leaving Natalie staring after her in bewilderment. Charlie didn't seem to have noticed anything amiss. He was already besieging his chips with a lava flow of ketchup.

"Charlie, stay here," Natalie said, getting to her feet. "I'll be right back."

She hurried back to the bar where she found the waitress fiddling with the closed drawer of the till.

"Hey, what happened over there?" Natalie asked.

"Huh? What do you mean?" The woman's friendly tone had turned gruff.

"Charlie's picture? Your reaction?"

"Oh, that," she said distractedly, then forced a laugh. "I'm not much of a one for art. I'm sure it's a good picture though. Don't take offence."

Natalie eyed her firmly. "That's not what I meant and you know it."

The woman pursed her lips and glanced over at Charlie. For a few seconds she looked as though she were about to say something. Then she shook her head fiercely. The earrings clanged like bells. "It's nothing. Just reminded me of something else, that's all. You go on and enjoy your lunch. We shut at two."

She wouldn't meet Natalie's eyes and eventually she turned and walked into the back room. Natalie felt disturbed and excluded. The waitress was being as circumspect as Charlie now.

They ate their lunch, chatting about inconsequential things. From time to time Natalie glanced over at the bar, but the waitress was nowhere to be seen. A younger man had replaced her.

"Still want that ice cream?" Natalie asked as she pushed her half-finished plate aside. Charlie had eaten his like a starving animal.

"Yes!"

His exuberance made her smile. She returned to the bar and told the man they wanted dessert. "There was a lady here before," she told him. "Older. With bright red hair."

He nodded. "Susan. Yeah, she had to leave early."

Natalie chewed her lip, not sure what she was going to say but still too haunted by the weird encounter to let it go. "Well, she was friendly at first, but then she reacted very oddly to my son's drawing and when I asked her about it she turned to stone and wouldn't speak to me."

The man shuffled his feet and looked confused. "So ... you want to complain to the manager?"

"Oh no, nothing like that," Natalie said hurriedly. "It's just that I had hoped to speak to her again. It sounds silly, I know. Only she looked absolutely terrified and I just ... well ..." She made a helpless gesture with her hands.

A look of sympathy crossed the man's features and he glanced over his shoulder as if to check that no one was listening. "I probably shouldn't be telling you this but Susan's had a hard time these past few years. She lost her little boy, you see."

"Oh my God. What happened?"

He shrugged. "No one knows. He wandered off one night and was never found. She hasn't really been right since."

Natalie felt ill at the thought of the woman's pain. No wonder she had called her son an angel.

"Maybe seeing your little boy," the man suggested, "just stirred up the past or something?"

"Of course," Natalie said. "I'm so sorry. I feel terrible."

He sighed. "Well, what can you do?" He punched a button on the till. "What can I get you?"

She glanced back at Charlie, who was staring out the window. "Ice cream," she said. "Just for one." The thought of eating made her feel queasy.

Afterwards they carried their bags up to their room and Charlie bounced happily on the bed nearest the window. "This one's mine!" he crowed.

"Fine with me. I'd rather be near the loo."

Natalie unpacked a few things and surreptitiously took some Paracetamol. Her head was pounding, but she didn't want to dampen Charlie's mood. He would worry about her if he sensed anything was wrong. She wanted to lie down and rest but she knew she'd only fall asleep and then be out for the rest of the day.

"What would you like to do now?" she forced herself to ask.

"Can we go back to the White Horse?"

Her head throbbed. "No, sweetie. We just spent the whole morning there."

The look of disappointment on his face made her heart twist. She may as well have told him there was no Santa Claus. "How about

108

this? We'll have a wander through the village and then before we leave tomorrow I'll take you back up there. Will that do?"

He considered this and then his smile returned. He held out his hand and she shook it once, firmly, sealing the deal.

\*

The moon was visible before the sun went down. Not quite full, it was still big enough to light the way for any midnight ramblers.

Natalie's headache had disappeared at some point during the afternoon and they'd found a nice little café for dinner. It had been a strange and difficult day for her so she treated herself to a glass of wine. Charlie had demanded a taste and made an extravagantly horrible face in response.

"Yuck!" he exclaimed loudly, wiping his mouth as though he'd sipped sulphuric acid instead of alcohol.

Natalie laughed. "You're a real connoisseur," she teased and then had to explain what that was.

Charlie had insisted on a few postcards of the White Horse, which Natalie gladly bought for him. She wondered at his fixation, but then, it was an unusual bit of history and mythology. The old man had really got his imagination going.

He was still wide awake when they returned to their room and Natalie parted the curtains enough to let in some moonlight so they could find the loo without crashing into things in the middle of the night. Charlie was sitting on his bed with his notebook open to the first drawing as he compared it to the image on the postcards.

Natalie snuggled under the duvet and picked up her book but she only managed a couple of pages before the words began to blur and a yawn overtook her. "That's it for me," she said, switching off her bedside light. "I'm out, kiddo. Don't stay up all night, OK?"

"I won't. Good night."

"Good night," Natalie echoed. "Love you."

"Love you too." Charlie smiled at her and then returned to his drawing.

\*

Natalie was dreaming of the seaside, hearing the gentle slosh of waves as they washed up onto the shore and then slipped away again. It was soothing and hypnotic, the most peaceful sound in the world. But there was something harsh in the splash of these waves, something rough and sandpapery.

*Scratch, scratch …*

Her eyes fluttered open and she found herself in pitch darkness. She had absolutely no idea where she was.

*Scratch, scratch …*

She shuddered. There was a rat somewhere, scrabbling in the walls. She reached across to her left. "Michael, wake up, there's a …"

Her hand struck a wall, shocking her fully awake. Where the hell was she? She stared helplessly into the darkness, frightened and confused. Then she remembered. She stretched her arm out to the right and found the bedside light. She switched it on and the shadows retreated to the corners of the room.

Charlie was sitting up in bed, drawing in his notebook. No, 'drawing' wasn't the word. He was *gouging* the paper, tracing over the same line again and again.

"Charlie? What are you doing?"

He didn't respond and she sat up, wincing with pain. Her headache had returned. With a vengeance.

"Scouring," Charlie said absently, not taking his eyes off the page.

*Scratch, scratch …*

She moaned and covered her eyes with her hand, in too much pain to register what he'd said. "Come on, it's late. Turn out the light and go to sleep." She flailed around until she found the lamp and switched it off, plunging the room into soothing darkness again. Then she laid her head gingerly on the pillow and tried to return to the tropical beach in her dream.

The waves returned, sloshing up onto the shore and foaming against her bare feet. She waded further out and the warm water covered her ankles, then her knees, then her hips. As she sank blissfully into the azure depths she felt a thought tugging at the edge of her mind. Hadn't she left the curtains open a bit so she wouldn't wake up in the dark? And Charlie, digging his pencil into the paper like that, as though he were trying to cut the image free. How could he possibly see what he was doing?

*Scratch, scratch …*

The waves were up to her chest now. Natalie closed her eyes as the heavenly warmth enveloped her.

*

It was the silence that woke her later. The silence and the cold.

Natalie sat up and the room was flooded with the blue-grey moonlight that streamed in through the open window. The curtains billowed languidly, letting in the chilly night air.

"Jesus, Charlie," she muttered, hurrying across the room. She pulled the sash down and glanced over at her son's bed.

He wasn't there.

"Charlie? Are you in the loo?"

But even as she asked, she knew he wasn't there. And with a sick, sinking feeling, she realised where he was.

*Daddy told me. He goes for rides with her. He said she likes me.*

Her stomach plummeted and she raced back to the window and yanked it open. A rose trellis ran up the side of the inn next to the window. He must have climbed down that. Panic flared brightly in her mind and she quickly dragged her jeans and fleece on over her nightshirt. Her fingers shook violently as she knotted the laces of her trainers. Charlie's shoes lay where he had kicked them the night before and she felt her eyes glaze with tears.

She grabbed her handbag, slammed the door and raced down the stairs and out the front door, calling Charlie's name. But she knew he wouldn't answer. Some clear-headed part of her brain reminded her of something the old man had said: they could walk to the inn from the site. She had no way of knowing how long Charlie had been gone. He could already be on the hill or he could be lost in the woods trying to get there. In a heartbeat she'd made a decision; she ran for the car and drove. If Charlie wasn't there yet she would make her way back towards the inn on foot and hope to intercept him. It was all she could do.

She reached the site in no time and clambered over the gate. The moon was high and bright in the sky and she had no trouble finding the path they had taken earlier up the hill. Down on her left was the Manger, the valley where the old man had said the horse went to graze at night. Her heart fluttered as she saw movement there, but it was only a fox.

"Charlie! Charlie, where are you?"

The ragged desperation in her voice alarmed her. It was how she had sounded that night when the police knocked on the door, removed their caps and looked at her with unbearable pity before telling her that her husband was dead.

111

She stopped calling Charlie's name and simply focused on getting to the top of the hill.

She was near the summit when she heard the awful sound. A terrible ripping, like the noise it made when you wrenched something out of the frost in a too-cold freezer. An unearthly light bloomed at the top of the hill, a shimmery bluish white, as though moonlight had bled into the grass. Then she saw it.

The horse snorted as it tossed its long skeletal head, its tangled mane flying. Just as Charlie had drawn it. She watched in horror as it peeled itself up from the grass like a fossil come to life. It pawed at the ground with spindly legs, gaining purchase. Then it heaved its torso up and she gasped to see her son's depiction before her.

A row of spiky ribs stuck out where its belly should be and she remembered something else the old man had told Charlie. He'd said that the pagan ritual was meant to free the horse when it got hungry. So it could eat.

The white beast towered over her, twisting its too-thin body around and lashing its long tail. Its single terrible eye swivelled in its head, then stopped. It had seen something.

Too late she saw Charlie approaching the summit from the opposite side. She ran for him but the horse's tail slashed her aside, knocking her to the ground. She lay dazed and winded for a moment. Charlie seemed unafraid. He walked right up to the monster, a smile playing at the corners of his mouth.

The horse reared, waving its long spidery legs above his defenceless form. She saw its razor-sharp hooves flash in the moonlight in the second before the creature brought them down. Natalie screamed.

She clambered to her feet and ran for her son but the horse's vicious tail swatted her again – just like a fly, and this time she tumbled down the hill. Fistfuls of nettles came away in her hands as she scrabbled for purchase but the force of the blow had been astonishing. She fell hard on her right hip and heard the sickening crunch of bones as she sprawled headlong in the grass near the base of the hill. She moaned and began dragging herself back up towards the summit, only vaguely aware of the pain as her right leg hung limp and useless behind her.

She could see the horse at the top of the hill. It stood still, its head down, grazing placidly and occasionally pawing at the ground with one slender leg. After a while it lifted its head and snorted. Its muzzle was stained with blood.

*

A group of hikers found Natalie in the morning, lying alongside the belly of the carving, curled into a foetal position. She was delirious and murmuring to herself. At first they thought she was praying, but she kept repeating certain words: ritual, scouring, ribs, Charlie. Her fingernails were broken and bloody and it looked as though she'd spent hours clawing at the horse's chalk belly, trying to dig into it.

Someone called an ambulance and the paramedics bundled her off to the nearest hospital, where her broken leg was put in a cast.

The police searched the area but could find no sign of her little boy. She didn't seem surprised by the news. The doctor said she was in shock.

A nurse came to check on her that night and found her sitting up in bed. She had a photograph of her husband and son and she was painstakingly tracing the outline of their faces with a pencil. No, not tracing. She was digging the pencil in, pressing down hard.

"Oh, be careful," the nurse said gently. "You'll cut right through the paper."

Natalie didn't look up. She continued to trace the lines, her eyes shining with fierce determination. "I know."

# THE CANNIBAL FEAST

Back in the pre-industrial age, there was nothing like the dishonouring of pretty young village maids for creating catastrophe in England's rural heartlands.

In 1703, a certain Mary Williams – beloved by all as the beauty of Alvington, a market town close to Gloucester – embarked on a love affair with the handsome son of a local well-to-do farmer whose name has been lost in the mists of time.

In the way of so many country tales, this lover was something of a rake. Mary was far from being his only sexual conquest, and, as she came from simple peasant stock, she would not be his last. According to a pamphlet published shortly after these tragic events, Mary was bedded on a number of occasions by her lustful beau, and only a very ghoulish incident helped bring a halt to it. Apparently one night, while the young couple were engrossed in each other, Mary's deceased mother appeared at the bedside – in her shroud, covered in grave-dirt, gasping as though struggling to escape from a coffin – and screamed a warning at her daughter that she was being used and abused.

Mary was understandably horrified. She fled her lover's bed and stumbled all the way home in tears, refusing to see him again for several days. However, this relatively short period was all he needed to acquire himself another mistress – this time from a wealthier family, and he quickly realised that it would be in his best interests to treat this one more like a lady.

Mary, meanwhile, was wallowing in misery. Not only had she now learned that her lover had turned to another woman, but she'd discovered that she was with child, which revelation was enough to ostracise her from friends and family. After a poverty-stricken pregnancy and a very difficult and lonely labour, she delivered twins – two little boys. Thinking this might be sufficient to restore her former lover's favour, she sent a message to him. But his reply was uncompromising: he no longer knew her; he was now betrothed to his new lady-friend and was shortly to be married.

Driven mad with despair, Mary killed her two babies. One she drowned in a pond, and the other she dismembered and baked in a pie, which she took to the country house where the wedding feast was to be held and concealed among the other consumables. According to the story, it was the cheating lover himself who made *the grim discovery, finding portions of his own infant son in the slice of pie he was eating.*

*A hue and cry was immediately raised. The distraught Mary, who had made no attempt to conceal her involvement, was soon arrested, charged with infanticide and convicted. As she stood on the gallows, a wronged, wretched and broken woman in every sense of the phrase, there was nobody at all to offer her support or even a kind word.*

*Before our readers allow themselves to be too distressed by these events, it should be mentioned that there is very little historical basis for this story. Mary Williams, a poor woman from Alvington, may indeed have hanged for infanticide in 1703, but no legal document records it. The pamphlet in which the case is described in such lurid detail is one of several which were circulating at the time, all written in the gaudy and sensational style of fictional frolics 'Fanny Hill' and 'Moll Flanders'.*

# WASSAILING
## Steve Lockley

"You on holiday then?" George Harry asked as he held his glass out for the landlord to refill, and Charlie Grissom took it from him without saying a word. The man at the other end of the bar was as out of place as a dancing girl at a wake. It was easy to spot the ramblers and holiday-makers from those who had just made a trip out from Hereford or Gloucester in search of a quiet country pub. This man belonged to one of the first groups but it was clear that the clothes he was wearing were new; his boots never having walked through so much as a puddle, marking him as a real fish out of water.

"Not exactly," the man said, his voice exactly as George had expected; another refugee from London. George had heard the story so many times with only slight variations that he hardly needed to listen to the man's history. "I've just bought a house here. Orchard Cottage. Do you know it?"

"Ah. I heard it had been sold. When are you moving in then?"

"I'll just be using it at weekends and holidays to start with," the man said.

Of course he would. That was the way of the world at the moment. Outsiders came in and snapped up houses that would then lie empty for most of the year while local kids were forced to move away because there was nothing for them to buy. It pushed prices up and of course meant that it was one less family who would be buying their groceries from the local shop. One less barstool that could be occupied in the The Black Bull on a weekday night

"Family?" George found it hard not to ask questions of strangers; it was something he had done all his life and helped pass the time when he had needed to get away from the house for a couple of hours

"No, I'm happily divorced and have no plans to plough that particular furrow again. This is all part of the new start if you like."

"You got any plans for that orchard then?" The one thing that George was sure about was that the incomer had no chance of getting planning permission to build on it, at least not as long as *he* was on the planning committee and had breath in his body. The orchard had been the heart of the village for generations, giving so much each year as long as its needs were tended to.

116

"I was hoping to get some advice on that," the man said, moving around the bar to site beside George. "Alex Carmichael." He extended a hand and George accepted it, the man's flesh soft and limp against his own hard-worn skin.

"George," he replied simply. "So what do you want to know?"

"The orchard seems to have been neglected for a while and I wondered what was needed to get it back to the way it used to be?"

"The trees are still pretty sound," George said, trying hard not to let the relief show in his voice. "Wouldn't take much more than a little love and care to tidy them up a bit. The grass needs a bit more attention but there are a couple of people in the village who would get that sorted out for you if you like. Might be just as easy to stick a few sheep in there for a couple of weeks to take care of the worst of it."

"Sheep? I would never have thought of that."

Of course he hadn't, that was because he was a townie and his first thought had probably been to turn it all over with a rotovator and re-turf it. It wasn't his fault but someone had to put him right. And if was going to be done right then George suspected that it might have to be *him*.

"Will you be around here for Christmas?" George asked.

"That's the plan. I've got to go back to London for a while, but then I'll be back to spend Christmas and New Year here. Lock myself away and forget about work for a while."

"There's worse things you can do, and worse places to be doing it in," George said. "You'll be here for the Wassailin' then?"

"What's that? Carol singing isn't it?"

"Some places it is. Here it's a kind of blessing for the fruit trees. If you want a good harvest next year, you'll want to make sure that your orchard is on the list of them that will be visited."

"Local custom eh? Well I suppose I should join in the spirit of things shouldn't I?"

*

George hadn't seen the man for a few weeks. The *Sold* banner had gone up over the *For Sale* sign, but there had been no sign of any possessions being moved in for some time. Winter had taken hold and most of the weeds that had choked the meadow grass in the orchard had turned brown and died back. He had been tempted to get a few of the sheep from one of the local farms installed even without the new owner's agreement but the fence required too much work to make it secure. It would have to wait. He was as neighbourly as the next man but wasn't going to go to a lot of time and effort in case the man had completely changed his mind about what he was going to do with the orchard. Besides if people like Charlie Grissom had his way then Carmichael would not be here long.

It would be good to see the orchard cared for again though; it was part of their heritage and it was a shame to see it fall into ruin. The orchard stood to one side of the cottage with the trees closest to the road having branches that hung over the fence, inviting passing children to help themselves. There were fewer children in the village now though, and the narrow path was often littered with windfalls in the autumn. For sometime the path had only been used by anyone walking between the cottage and the pub. For most of that year it had not been used at all.

There was snow in the air and the tips of the Malvern Hills had a dusting that gave them a Christmas card look. It would not be long before a heavier fall descended on them, perhaps even enough to cut the village off from the outside world for a day or two; it happened most winters and there seemed no reason that this one should be any different. Christmas was still a week away but the chances of it being a white one were rising by the day. George was gazing into the orchard, remembering the ghosts of Christmas past, when the removal van pulled up outside the cottage. There was no sign of Carmichael but that didn't surprise George. He had not expected the townie to do the shifting of furniture himself when he could pay someone else to do it. That seemed to be the nature of the man. The surprise came when Carmichael pulled up behind the van, there to supervise if not to do his own fetching and carrying.

"Good afternoon George, how is everything?" Carmichael said, a broad smile on his face as he breathed in deeply, making a show of enjoying the cool, fresh air. It was something outsiders did far too often.

"Everything's fine. You having Christmas delivered then?" George nodded at the men who were already lifting furniture from the back of the van.

"Just a few things. I picked out some bits and pieces from my flat. Enough to make it feel like a home."

"If you'd left a key with someone we could have made sure that the house was aired for you. It's going to take a day or two to get the feel of damp out of those old stone walls."

"I'm sure I'll be fine. Besides, there's always the pub." A smile spread across his face again and, in other circumstances, George felt that he and Carmichael could become friends.

There were others who would turn against him purely because he has was taking the place that could have been a home to one of their sons or daughters, but the truth was that none of them would be able to afford it, at least not for a while to come, by which time the cottage could easily be on the market again.

George had seen people come and go over the years and no matter how much the locals complained about people buying houses as holiday homes, sooner or later they would be up for sale again. It was all a matter of time.

*

George saw the young man in the pub a few times over the course of the next week; he had even thought of inviting him to have Christmas dinner with him and his wife but Carmichael pre-empted the invitation by telling him his plans over a pint.

"For the first time I finally have the chance to spend Christmas Day doing what I want, when I want, without being tied to the clock and the whims of family."

"And your Christmas dinner?"

"I'll eat it when I want, not when someone else tells me I have to eat."

"That sounds like quite a rebellion."

"More like growing up," Carmichael said. "A chance to be myself, not what everyone else wants me to be."

"I know what you mean. Everyone wants a piece of you at this time of year don't they? Well if you change your mind and want a little company, you'll be more than welcome in my home. Anne's not a lot of company at the moment, she's not been well, but I'm sure she'd be more than happy to see you."

"Sorry to hear that, and it's kind of you, but just this once I'm going to be sure to enjoy my own company."

"You'll be around for the Wassailin' though, won't you?"

"Of course, I've been looking forward to it. I've been reading up about it on the internet. When do you do it around here? I know that different places have a tradition of doing it on different nights."

"Christmas Night."

"Then I'll try to stay fairly sober," Carmichael laughed.

119

"We'll be meeting outside the pub at eleven, so wrap up warm. There'll be plenty of cider, so even if you haven't drunk enough by then you will have by the time we're done."

*

Snow had been falling lightly for most of Christmas Day and now lay crisp and fairly deep on the fields and hillsides around the town. A few cars had driven through the High Street during the day, compacting it to a layer of white ice but that was not going to bother anyone that night. There would be a few who might have plans for trips out on Boxing Day and they may be disappointed that they'd have to cancel their arrangements, but it was not the end of the world.

Open fires had been roaring in cottages and farmhouses, and central heating systems had been working overtime but, even so, people still wrapped themselves in heavy coats, hats, scarves and gloves before opening their doors a little before eleven. Even the sturdiest of boots slipped and slid on a shiny, ice-coated road, turned orange by the streetlights. Couples held onto each other for support even though each was in danger of bringing the other down. And there was laughter. It was Christmas and now it was time for the Wassail.

George held an old oil lantern on a pole that had been used in the village for generations and, although a few carried torches, releasing the light of a million candles, they would be switched off inside the orchards themselves. The village orchards were special places where tradition was everything. Things had to be done the way they had always been done. The way they should be done.

Carmichael came striding down the road, his hands thrust deep into a Barbour that was feeling its first kiss of snow. George remembered the first time he had seen him in the pub, all decked out in new clothes ready for his life in the country. This was obviously another recent addition to his wardrobe.

"George!" Carmichael waved as he grew closer, attracting the attentions of most of the assembled villagers who politely tried to hide their amusement at the sight of him struggling to keep his footing while slightly the worse for wear with drink. "This your wife then?"

George felt embarrassed to even know him at that moment. Anne was a quiet woman, reluctant to come out on a night like this even

120

though she had done it since she was a child. Tonight reminded him how old she was growing, how frail her illness had made her, and if she was getting old then so was he. He looked around at all his friends and knew only too well that they all were. So many of the people around him he had known for most of his life. People who had been born in the village, grown up here and would die here. That was the way of this place. Even those who had left for a while had returned as if drawn back, never really able to escape. There was something about this place that was ingrained in them; you were either part of the village or you weren't and that made it harder for outsiders to settle. Even those who married those who had been born here didn't always find life easy. So many failed marriages littered these streets but George had no idea if they were more or less than the national average. George and Anne, though, had both been born within a mile of the place they were standing on at this moment, and that in itself had kept them bound together for so long, as if they were two parts of a whole.

"That's right," he said after a pause. He made the introductions even though he would have preferred not to have done it when Carmichael was so obviously drunk.

George was relieved when the newcomer gave little more than a smile in return. He did not object to men who enjoyed their drink a little more than was good for him, but that did not mean that his wife did, and he would always do everything he could to protect her sensibilities.

"So what happens now?"

"I think we are heading to your orchard first. It needs wassailing more than the others in the village. It's been neglected for far too long."

"Then what are we waiting for," Carmichael said, turning a little uncertainly though it was hard to tell if it was the drink or the slippery surface that caused it.

Villagers were already starting to make their way past him and in the direction of the orchard, clutching onto each other to maintain their footing on the ice. George was happy to watch Carmichael's back as he joined the others, reaching an arm across the shoulders of strangers as they made their way along the road. Anne said nothing, even when the man was out of earshot, and George was glad of it. He was already afraid that he had started to like Carmichael even though everyone else in the village was either indifferent to him or detested

121

what he stood for. They were happy to accept his company tonight, though.

The lantern seemed to grow heavier each year, but George was not ready to hand it on to anyone else. If he had a son of his own it might be different, but it had not been meant and so he would carry it every year he remained strong enough to do it. By the time he and Anne reached the orchard gate, the rest had already formed a circle around the tree. Not any tree, but *the* tree, the special tree, the father of the orchard.

There had been a time as a boy when he had been afraid of it, its twisted and entangled branches casting eerie shadows when the moon rose behind it. None of the other trees had that effect on him and other boys had teased him about it, but he had known that it was best to fear something you did not understand. Who knew how far its roots spread through the orchard, or beyond. If they stretched as far as its influence, then they reached into the foundations of every home. This was the only tree that was never cut back, never restrained in its growth, and the bigger it grew the more it reminded him of how he had felt as a boy. It was a special tree and even if it was not feared, it needed to be respected.

Only the men had entered the orchard itself; the women were no more than bystanders in this particular ritual. This was a special Wassail; there would be no Wassail Queen this year and no King either, only Carmichael.

George took a glance around him, unsurprised to find that apart from the new owner of the orchard there were no other outsiders amongst the gathering. Those who were married to outsiders had kept their partners away. It was better that they stayed at home. George had wanted Anne to stay inside in the, warm but she had insisted that she came; it was her duty to bear witness just like the other wives. It was not the same here as in other villages, it never would be.

"So what happens then?" asked Carmichael, shuffling in the soft snow.

"You have to climb into the tree and place this piece of toast in the branches," someone said.

"A piece of toast?" He laughed but seemed more than willing to go on with it. George wanted it all to stop. It was one thing to humiliate a newcomer but another to do what was planned. He wanted to walk away from it, but he could not leave now; he was part of all this.

A couple of the younger men stepped from the gathering and lifted Carmichael up into the lower boughs of the tree, as he giggled uncontrollably. While he was held suspended in the tree, the men began to wind rope and ribbon around him, binding him to the tree, pulling the ropes tighter and tighter with each turn, until the two who had been supporting him could step away leaving his legs thrashing for something to hold him up. George held the lantern closer so that everyone could see how hard Carmichael was trying to free himself.

"What the hell is going on now? Is this another part of the game?" He was laughing at first but it did not last for long.

No-one responded and he began to grow more agitated.

George was not sure who started the chanting but the chances were that it was Charlie Grissom, the pub landlord; his voice was certainly the loudest by the end of the first line.

> *Apple tree, apple tree, we all come to wassail thee,*
> *Bear this year and next year to bloom and to blow,*
> *Hat fulls, cap fulls, three cornered sack fulls,*
> *Hip, Hip, Hip, hurrah,*
> *Holler boys, holler hurrah*

"Come on, join in," Grissom called, not to the gathering, but to Carmichael. It was better if the man joined in as a willing participant not as a victim drawn into this against his will.

Someone pulled back Carmichael's sleeves, exposing bare skin to the cold of the night. Metal was pressed against flesh and a thin, dark line appeared, then another and another. Carmichael called out but no-one took any notice of his cries, which were drowned by the chanting.

> *Apple tree, apple tree, we all come to worship thee*
> *Take this blood, fill the bud, to grow and to show*
> *Arm fulls, leg fulls, all around the neck fulls*
> *Hip, Hip, Hip, hurrah*
> *Holler boys, holler hurrah*

George struggled to hold the lantern still and he started to shake as the first of the blood started to run down the trunk of the tree. He had seen this too many times before and it could not continue.

"Please," Carmichael screamed. "Let me down.

His appeals did nothing to stop the men, though, as they began to turn around the tree in a circle, all except George who still held the lantern to reveal the snow melting to a red slush. He couldn't look for a moment longer and glanced towards Anne for support. But she had turned away, no longer able to watch either, while other mothers were cheering on husbands and sons, baying for more of Carmichael's blood even though he had done nothing wrong.

He had not murdered anyone. He had not stolen. He had not even slept with another villager's wife. All he had done was buy a house that maybe one day one of these young men would have wanted it. It would have been enough to make it known that he was not welcome, that they would rather than the house had been sold to someone from the village – not this.

They knew that the man would not be missed for a while, and somebody probably already had plans to drive his car off one of the country roads and make sure that it caught fire. It wouldn't be the first time that a car had come off those treacherous roads in winter, and wouldn't be the last. There would be no signs that anything untoward had happened; nothing that would point a finger back towards the village; nothing that would raise suspicion. There never was and George doubted that there ever would be.

The fact that Carmichael might not be missed did not make it right. This was not about whether they could get away with it. This wasn't about tradition this was about sacrifice and the benefits it brought. But still it had to stop.

"Enough!" he cried eventually, not sure if he had even intended for the words to be spoken out loud.

The men fell silent, their chant forgotten in an instant as if a spell had been broken.

"If you don't want to watch then get yourself back to your cottage, old man," one of the younger ones finally said.

George waved the lantern and saw the unmistakable freckled face of Danny Trower, who had only turned eighteen that summer. This was his first time, and he had the look about him of a man who was caught up in the moment and could not stop his own actions. George had known his grandfather; a bully of a man who had believed that the old ways were the only ways and, in the absence of a father figure, the boy had hung onto his grandfather's every word. His father had not been able to settle in the village, forcing his mother back into the arms of her family; his mother now stood at the fence. She was not caught up in the bloodlust, though; instead she held onto

Anne, no doubt wishing she did not have to witness this. But it was expected of her; she was part of the village and the village was part of her.

Danny Trower took the old knife, the blade stained red from the use of ages and waved it in the air. "This has to be done. These trees are the village, these trees are our life."

"That doesn't give us the right to take life away from others."

"Hypocrite! How can you stand there holding the lantern to show us the light? You are part of this. You have always been part of this."

"And that's why I have to be the one that says that it's time we have to stop."

"And why should we listen to you, old man?"

"Because if you don't, I will make sure the whole world knows about it."

"You wouldn't do that," Trower laughed but there was an element of fear in the laughter. "You'll spend the rest of your life in prison."

"I don't have many years left, so I have little to lose."

"And your wife? You'd do that to her?"

George looked at Anne, wanting to share her secret, but knowing that it was not his to give.

"I have even less time than him," she said. "But he's right. You have to stop!"

Anne stepped through the gate and walked towards the men but it was clear that it was an effort for her. George reached out and she took his hand and let him guide her to his side. "George has always done this for me, not for the village. Every time some poor innocent is treated like this, the apples grow bigger, the cider tastes better and I grow a little stronger, know that I will live a little longer. But no more. It has to stop."

"What the hell are you talking about, you old bat."

"Don't talk to her like that," said George taking a step closer to Trower but finding himself restrained by his wife.

"It doesn't matter anymore," she said to him. "You've spent your whole life looking after me."

The young man still held the knife in his hand and looked in no mood to stop on the say-so of a couple of pensioners.

"Do you think we do this just to get a good harvest of apples? Just so that people like you have cider to drink?" George said.

"It's the way things have always been done," Trower replied, as if that was the answer to everything, as if the most important thing in the world was resistance to change. Things were the way they were because that was the way they had always been. It wasn't an argument that held water, even George could see that, but the young man had blind belief in what he was saying.

"It's what we've always done because of what it gives us," George said. "Haven't you noticed how long people live in this village if they stay here, how they rarely fall ill? The trees give us life, but is it worth the price?"

"Price? What price?"

"Well, if you can't see that, then this poor man's life is worth nothing. Cut him down."

"Are you going to make me?" Trower asked.

"If I have to," Anne said, slipping free of George's arm and taking one unsteady after another towards the knife-yielding young man,

"Anne!" George tried to stop her but she shrugged him off. He knew that there was nothing he could say that would stop her, not now that she had made her mind up. He could only watch helpless as she took another step and another.

"It has to stop now," she said, losing her footing and stumbling towards Trower, falling against him and then going limp.

*"Anne!"* Gorge thrust the lantern into someone else's hand though he had no idea of who had accepted it. He took hold of his wife and tried to support her weight, lifting her away from young Trower, only to reveal the knife buried deep in her chest.

"I couldn't stop her. I didn't mean to …" the young man said, holding out his bloodstained hands, showing them to everyone who was gathered around – though few were paying him any attention. They were more concerned about Anne. But it was too late for her. It had been too late for her for a long time.

"Cut him down," said George quietly, and then more insistently until his voice reached a near-scream. They released Carmichael, lowering his body to the ground. He was still breathing but it was shallow, his heart-beat weak.

Charlie Grissom crouched beside Anne, a small glass of cider in his hand at the ready. "It's too late," said George. "Give it to *him*. He needs it more than she does."

"It can save her George, you know it can."

"It's time to let her go. She couldn't stand the thought of anyone else dying to keep her alive for another ear or two; to keep any of us alive. She's been wanting to die for such a long time but it even though she hasn't taken a drop of it for so long her body would not give up the fight, no matter how bad the pain."

"What should we do about him?" Grissom nodded at Carmichael.

"Give him the drink, and look after him. Take care of him tonight, and I'll speak to him in the morning. I need Doctor Ellison. Are you there Doc?" he called into the darkness.

"I'm here, George. Still as much part of this as you are."

"She's gone, Doc. Will you sign the death certificate; say that it was her cancer that took her? I'm sure that a friend will bury her quietly without asking any questions. She wouldn't want there to be any fuss."

"Of course, George. I'll take care of it."

Of course he would. George had lost count of how many times the doctor had helped arrange funerals for people who were older than they had any right to be, without any questions being raised. He hoped that there would not be many more.

\*

George didn't get to speak to Carmichael until after the funeral. It had been a quiet service in the village, attended only by a handful of people, each of them probably knowing that their own days were numbered. There were embarrassed looks from some of the younger residents of the village, especially Danny Trower who could not look George in the eyes. George had tried to talk to him, tell him that it was not his fault, but he knew that it would haunt the young man's dreams for many years to come.

The doctor had kept Carmichael sedated for most of the last couple of days, but he had been conscious long enough to take regular drafts of the cider, and each day he had grown stronger. He was still weak but there was no lasting damage.

"What happened?" Carmichael asked when George sat by his bedside with a mug of tea in his hand.

"Things got a bit out of hand and you'd had a little too much to drink..."

"Ah," said Carmichael. "That sounds about right. I hope no-one else got hurt."

"Nothing for you to worry about, but one of your old apple trees will have to come down I'm afraid."

Carmichael raised a weak smile. "That's a shame," he said. "Never mind. We'll have to find something else to put in its place."

Danny Trower was already cutting the tree down when George left the pub; it had only taken a quiet word with his mother and, despite offers of help, Trower had insisted on dealing with it himself. The snow had already melted and washed away the last of the evidence, and soon there would be nothing left to stand as a reminder of what had happened. George did not need a tree to remind him, though, but Anne was out of pain now and that was the one good thing to have come out of this. He wished he had been braver himself and taken it into his own hands and cut down the tree long ago, but he had been to weak, afraid of how the other villagers would have reacted to him – and yet it now seemed that so many of them had also had a secret desire that it should come to an end. Carmichael would have the gratitude of many for accepting that it had all been a prank, and would be welcome in the pub whenever he came to stay. George hoped that the experience hadn't put him off, but it was too soon to tell. And Danny Trower? Well, although his heart would be paying the price for a very long time it might very well make him a man at last and give him the chance to step out of his grandfather's shadow.

# BLOODBATH UNDER A SPECTRAL SUN

The Wars of the Roses were a series of interlinked dynastic struggles fought mainly between the rival royal houses of Lancaster and York, which devastated the fabric of English society between the years 1455 and 1485.

While not in the true sense of the phrase a civil war, the conflict was characterised by large-scale battles, savage fighting and extremely vicious treatment of those made prisoner, including the nobility. In fact, the casualty rate suffered by the English baronage during the Wars of the Roses is the highest of any conflict in the Middle Ages after the Norman Conquest of England, and it includes the death by violence of three English kings: Henry VI, Edward V and Richard III.

Owen Tudor was not a king. He was an elderly Welsh earl and a much honoured hero of Agincourt, but he lost his life under the headsman's axe in February 1461 after he watched his entire army of 5,000 men be massacred in the gory disaster that was the battle of Mortimer's Cross, near Wigmore in Herefordshire.

The fighting at Mortimer's Cross typified the Wars of the Roses in that there was deep enmity between the commanders of the two sides and, as both employed extensive use of mercenaries – ruthless bands of killers and cutthroats who could never be relied on to show mercy to the enemy – the actual engagement was followed by a series of atrocities which today would be labelled 'war crimes'.

The Yorkists were under the control of Edward, Earl of March, only eighteen years old but already a hardened veteran, and burning for vengeance after hearing about his father's death at the battle of Wakefield two months earlier. The Lancastrians were led by Owen Tudor, and his son, Jasper Tudor, Earl of Pembroke, who were bringing a large body of Welsh reinforcements into England when the Yorkists blocked their route.

The battle was extremely bitter and prolonged, knights and men-at-arms going hammer and tongs at each other for almost an entire day, using the most ghastly weapons – swords, flails, maces, pole-axes, mauls and mattocks. By mid-afternoon, eyewitnesses described corpses stacked shoulder-high, piles of severed heads and limbs, and streams of fresh blood flowing down into the nearby River Lugg, turning it purple.

After a failed attempt to flank the larger Yorkist force, the Lancastrian line finally broke and most of the troops turned and fled. Mainly on foot, they discarded their weapons and even threw off their encumbering armour to aid their escape.

But the fight was not yet over. In fact, the real horror was only just beginning.

Edward was determined to have a complete victory and sent his mounted knights in pursuit, under orders to spare no-one. The resulting slaughter was protracted over sixteen miles between Leominster and Leintwardine. Bands of panic-stricken soldiers, many wounded and exhausted, were attacked from behind as they stumbled along the muddy lanes – cut down by the failing, iron-shod hooves of battle-enraged stallions, or hacked and slashed until they were dead. The carnage was prolonged and horrific. Terrified peasants, who had lain low during the course of the main battle, finally emerged from hiding in the evening – to see mutilated bodies littering the Cotswold meadows for as far as the eye could see.

The Lancastrian army that fought at Mortimer's Cross had been annihilated. Owen Tudor was one of a very small number taken prisoner. He was promptly dispatched to Hereford, where, to his amazement, he was handed a writ for his own execution. Tudor had felt that because he'd been a favourite of the former royal family, he was likely to be saved. Only when his head was forced down on the block did he accept the truth and wryly comment: "The head which once lay in Queen Catherine's lap will now lie in a basket."

Perhaps it's no surprise that many eerie stories surround the battle of Mortimer's Cross. Before the fighting commenced, witnesses testified to seeing a bizarre vision in the sky: the sun dividing itself into three separate glowing bodies. This was possibly a parhelion – an atmospheric condition in which a 'halo' encircles the sun, creating glowing orbs to either side of it, though at the time it was deemed to be a portent of victory for the Yorkists and was later celebrated by William Shakespeare in his play 'Henry VI Part Three', with the quotation:

> Three glorious suns, each one a perfect sun;
> Not separated with the racking clouds,
> But sever'd in a pale clear-shining sky.

Needless to say, even now in the 21$^{st}$ century, mournful ghosts are said to roam the extensive battlefield. Few visual manifestations *have been reported, but late at night the most terrible screams are heard – the frightful cries of men who are quite literally being butchered alive.*

# THE SILENT DANCE
## Joel Lane

Beyond Solihull, the view opened up: the streets and tower blocks gave way to sloping fields and woodland. Thin birches lined the railway bank like crusted railings. The train plunged through a crumbling red-brick bridge, and Daniel felt his hands begin to shake. He hadn't been outside the city in years. The landscape seemed unreal in the hazy August light. The sloping graveyard, the old church, the dark cradle of foliage that held his gaze. It was all familiar, but somehow not in perspective, as if it had been painted onto a different landscape where there was no sunlight. As the train neared Hatton, he glimpsed something hanging under a bridge: a length of rope, blackened by rain, a noose tied in its end.

"Please mind the gap," the driver said as the train stopped. For nine years he'd made this journey every working day. And almost from the start, it had been *don't* mind the gap – between the rules for management and those for staff, between what people said and what they meant. Like the view, his memory was opening up. Behind the innocent façade of a children's publisher, a world of cats and hedgehogs and girls in long scarves, the vicious reality: relentless bullying of staff, worship of schedules and budgets. The train rattled on past a fringe of poplars, a mound of bracken, a cheaply-built factory with corrugated iron walls. Its chimneys had been pouring out smoke five years ago, but now it was obviously derelict: the walls dull with rust, starting to come loose around the darkness they held. Uneasily, Daniel realised he'd forgotten to get off at Warwick. The habit of years. He'd have to get off at Leamington and come back.

At the station, the light on the old buildings reminded him how beautiful the town was. Why should he let bad memories drive him out? The Neotechnic offices were nearly a mile away, and besides it was the weekend. Angry with his own fear, Daniel walked down from the platform and through the paved tunnel to the park. Ivy coated the low walls. Trees filtered the daylight into many shades of green. He paused on the bridge over the river Leam and looked down into the flat grey water. It was always a slow river, apart from one year when it had overflowed its banks and flooded the nearby houses and shops. A willow tree growing out of the bank trailed its yellowish strands over the bridge. He walked on, past the metallic shell of the bandstand to the main road, beyond which he could see the waterfall over the stone steps and the fragile suspension bridge where he and Alice had walked together in the days before Laura Ferguson.

There was no holding back the memories now. The peaceful, rather naïve atmosphere of the books department in that first year. Then Laura's arrival, and her promise to "shake things up". Within a few months she'd established a rule of fear through her private meetings, her destructive appraisals, her use of sycophants to fight her vicious little wars. Her cyan-dyed hair had earned her the nickname 'Blue Ice' among the designers. Blue ice was airline slang for the frozen human shit that fell from a plane, smashing whatever might be in its way as it reached the ground. In eight years she'd driven eleven people out of the company; three of them had brought tribunals, but Neotechnic had backed her to the hilt. It suited the directors to have a ruthless office-based manager to police the staff.

One of the young workers forced out by Laura was Alice, the kind of quiet and friendly young woman she'd liked to victimise. Daniel should have done more to protect her. He was too afraid of confrontation, always had been. Couldn't take sides. Only when Alice had left Neotechnic and the country had he realised how much he'd let her down. How badly he missed her. Laura had moved upward in the company, but had engineered the closure of the books department by directing one of her sycophants to write a report damning the department's performance. That review meeting had put the writing on the wall in Helvetica Black.

For months, Daniel had been convinced he was about to be called into her office for a private meeting and told to clear his desk. He'd imagined himself walking back to his desk and sitting down, then slowly pushing his computer forward until it crashed on the floor – and as everyone jumped up, saying: "There. My desk's clear. Want me to clear yours?"

He'd given the company the best decade of his working life, using all the skill he'd ever had to fine-tune books and get the best out of authors. But Laura had made sure the only editors who got on at Neotechnic were smug jobsworths whom the authors hated. And in the end she'd destroyed a whole department so she could remake it in her image.

But it hadn't quite worked like that. A week after Daniel had left the company, the caretaker had opened up the Neotechnic offices one morning to find Laura lying at the foot of the staircase. She'd fallen and broken her spine, was still breathing but never spoke again and died in hospital a few days later. Daniel might have tried to rejoin the company after a year or so, but some of his friends at Neotechnic had told him things were even worse. He'd lost touch with them since, shedding the good memories along with the bad.

The sky had clouded over, and suddenly the trees were shivering. It wasn't late summer any more. He'd thought he could defeat the past. Another mistake to add to the list. Turning back towards the station, Daniel saw the old hotel crusted with scaffolding and wire nets. He needed a drink. Better get to Warwick first, see what else was happening in the festival apart from the concert he had a ticket for. He waited on the platform and caught the Stratford train. As it passed the ruined factory, he looked the other way.

The Warwick platform was fringed with oaks that wore dense sleeves of ivy. Daniel walked down from the platform to the curved road that led to the town centre. When he reached the bottom of Smith Street, the festival procession was still going on. He stood outside The Roebuck to watch the floats and marching bands. The call of the bar was too strong to resist, so he slipped inside and bought a Scotch, then went back to the doorway. The crowded street was bathed in amber sunlight.

The procession halted near the end of the street, leaving a blank space in front of a line of drummers and flute-players. A troop of Morris dancers assembled from nowhere and began their routine. It wasn't as formal as any Morris dance he'd seen before: there was a wildness to it, a gypsy energy designed to match their flamboyant red and gold outfits, their long hair and silver bracelets. After a few minutes, they stopped and were replaced by dancers in black with faces painted dead white. Their clockwork routine made him think of clowns, though there was no humour in it. He sipped his drink.

The sky must have clouded over, because the third troop of dancers were unclear: shadows hung over their slow movement. They were dressed in the semi-formal outfits of office workers, and seemed to be going through the motions of using keyboards and other machines. There was a small dark woman with nervous movements who made him think of Alice. And a plump man with spiky copper hair who looked like Daniel. Then a middle-aged woman with a blue wig strode into the dance and everyone turned to stare at her admiringly – except the two he'd already recognised. She didn't really look like Laura, just like an actress playing Laura. He realised the music had stopped, and the people around were silent.

Laura wagged her finger at Alice in dignified reproval. The younger woman burst into tears and ran away. Daniel saw his own unconvincing double walk up and down in a state of hysterical rage. Then everyone disappeared but him and Laura, and the light continued to fade. Laura, moving with the grace of a ballet dancer, put on a coat and hat. Then the Daniel-figure tiptoed up behind her and pushed hard. She fell down invisible steps, landed in a contorted position. Her upturned face was white with pain as he stepped over her and into the crowd.

The procession continued. Daniel turned away. The glass fell from his hand; he heard it break on the pavement. Suddenly there was only one thing in the world he needed, and the source of that was a few yards away. He stumbled to the bar and ordered a large gin. It burned his throat going down. Almost choking, he pressed the back of his hand to his mouth. *What the fuck?*

With the caution of experience, he went though to the next bar to buy another drink. A dozen or people were sitting around a long table, where an old man was singing a folk ballad. Some of them had guitars. A singers' gathering. If he'd been calmer, he might have joined in. While he loved concerts – and the duo he'd come to see today were old heroes of his – these informal sessions were where the most interesting songs turned up. He bought a pint of Landlord's and sat at a nearby table as the ballad ended.

The next singer was a young woman without a guitar. Her thin hands locked together as she began. It sounded like a Scottish ballad, some plaintive story of murder and guilt, though her accent was pure Warwickshire. Slowly the words filtered through his half-drunk mind:

> *There was a beautiful lady*
> *Her hair blue like the sky*
> *And none of all her friends knew*
> *How soon she would die*

> *For a young man named Danny*
> *All eaten up with spite*
> *He crept up behind Laura*
> *And out went the light*

In the silence that replaced an instrumental break, nobody even seemed to be breathing. The singer continued, her voice soft and beautiful:

> *Young Danny he went to ground*
> *But there was nowhere to hide*
> *For Laura's broken body stayed*
> *Forever by his side*
>
> *Stronger than words of love*
> *Silence keeps its faithful grip*
> *And on some dark staircase*
> *He'll take a trip*

There was no applause. Before he broke the silence, or something else, Daniel rose to his feet and staggered out of the pub. Up the street, past a guitar shop, a second-hand bookshop, a drum shop, under a preserved medieval bridge, on to a more modern road and an ordinary hotel bar, where he bought a bottle of wine and took it to a solitary table where nobody could bother him, or disapprove, or mock him with silence. He couldn't go to the concert: he knew what song they would sing, or what dance the audience would perform to a tune only they could hear. Nothing was real but his glass and the light it held.

A random memory came back to him, something a Neotechnic designer had told him. One Christmas, they'd used a photo of the Board of Directors for the card they sent to important clients. The next year, instead of taking a new photo, they'd asked the designer to touch up the old one in Photoshop. That meant replacing the faces of directors who'd lost their jobs with the faces of their replacements. And as a final touch, making sure every face had a suitably festive smile.

As often happened, drinking restored his sense of normality. The recorded music in the pub, a medley of 1980s pop hits, filled his mind with surfaces in place of the aching void opened up by traditional ballads. The Morris dancers were the ghosts of nothing, he reflected. The ghosts of failure and betrayal and wasted time. Alice had gone on to a new life; it was time he did the same. When had he last picked up a man? Surely he wasn't too old for that. But Warwick wasn't the place. He needed the city. He needed dance music. He needed another drink.

After the second or third vodka, he realised he'd better eat something. It was getting late. In the toilet, he splashed water over his face. The flecked mirror showed him a pudgy red-eyed loser he wanted to punch. The walls around him glittered with broken glass. *Time to go.* As long as he kept away from live music, he'd be safe. There was another pub just across the road. But as he approached the bar, he could sense people watching him. The barman spoke into a phone. A woman laughed too deliberately. He caught the glint of a chain, turned and walked out.

The evening light cut through the buildings at an angle. Daniel tried to remember the way back to the station. Surely this was the road: under an old stone bridge, past a mock-Tudor house and down a street that plunged so steeply it should have had steps. An office crowd emerged from a nightclub in one of the side-streets, laughing and flirting. A girl sang a line from some musical. Then they were around him, suddenly quiet. He tried to walk away, but their slow dance blocked him. He could just make out Laura at the back, passively directing the others. A replica of himself waved an empty bottle and knelt to throw up. Daniel pressed a hand to his mouth, then realised it looked like he was keeping a secret. He wanted to tell them the truth. *I wasn't even in Leamington that day. I had nothing to do with it. She lied all her life, and now she's lying after her death.* But as long as they kept the silence, he had to follow suit.

As the group reached the bottom of the street, Daniel noticed how their hands and faces blurred in the sodium light. The dance couldn't quite make them real. A blind panic gripped him and he lashed out. His hand touched something that felt like old newspaper. The nearest figure fell back, losing definition. As the others closed in around him, he turned and sprinted towards the crossroads. Black shadows flickered across his view. He forced himself to keep running until he reached the narrow side road that led up to the station. Was nothing in Warwick fucking level? Choking, not daring to look back, he staggered through the entrance and down the stone steps to the brick-lined tunnel, through to the far side, climbing into the light, reaching the platform just as the train was drawing in.

Struggling not to be sick, he fell into the nearest seat and gripped his head. There was nobody else in the carriage. He didn't look at the doors. If they caught him here, that was it. But nobody came. He wiped away tears and took a deep breath as the train, with a dreamlike slowness, began to move. Ivy-clad trees slipped past like giants in a folk tale. The darkness behind them held no threat. They couldn't reach him in the city. He only wished he had another drink. It wasn't until he saw the angular black shape of the derelict factory that he realised he'd gone to the wrong side of the platform: the train was going back to Leamington.

# WHAT WALKS IN ETTINGTON PARK?

*'No live organism can continue for long to exist sanely under conditions of absolute reality; even larks and katydids are supposed, by some, to dream. Hill House, not sane, stood by itself against its hills, holding darkness within; it had stood so for eighty years and might stand for eighty more. Within, walls continued upright, bricks met neatly, floors were firm, and doors were sensibly shut; silence lay steadily against the wood and stone of Hill House, and whatever walked there, walked alone.'*

> ### The Haunting of Hill House
> ### (opening paragraph)
> ### by Shirley Jackson

The above extract is probably one of the most famous openings in the history of horror writing. Shirley Jackson's 'The Haunting of Hill House', published in 1959, is rightly regarded as one of the most frightening ghost stories ever written. Stephen King referred to it as one of the best horror novels of the late 20th century.

The very faithful film adaptation, 'The Haunting', directed by Robert Wise in 1963, had a similar impact in the movie world, delighting and petrifying its audiences in equal measure, and is still regarded today as one of the most intelligent and disturbing horror movies of all time – but disturbing in a subtle way, for there is no gore or profanity in this motion picture, just a steadily increasing sense of unease, which eventually rises to some exceptional crescendos of terror.

Both the book and the film tell the story of a paranormal investigation at a remote country house where there is a history of suicides and fatal accidents. One member of the team – Eleanor Vance in the novel, Eleanor Lance in the film – is mentally incapable of withstanding the mind-numbing fear they are subjected to, with disastrous consequences. The big question remains all the way through: is there a genuine supernatural presence at Hill House, or do the fatal phenomena have a psychological explanation?

So far, this must all seem a long way from the Cotswolds. After all, Hill House was set in Massachusetts. However, Robert Wise chose to make his movie adaption in England, at MGM Borehamwood, near London. Given that Hill House is an important character in its own right in the narrative, the interior he created at the studio was a masterwork of statues, shadows and long, dark corridors where what you couldn't see was more frightening than what you could. For the exterior he needed something equally special. Wise went searching for a magnificent Gothic edifice which as well as looking astonishing, positively exuded evil. He finally settled on Ettington Hall, in Warwickshire – in the heart of the Cotswolds.

Those who've seen the film will agree that he made the correct choice.

Of course Ettington Hall – now the exquisite Ettington Park Hotel – is not nearly so sinister in daylight, or when seen by the naked eye rather than through the lens of a skilled horror movie maestro. And yet it does have a creepy history in its own right. Built on the site of a medieval manor house, it was never associated with any famous tragedies, but the spectres said to wander its grounds and corridors include both a grey and a white lady, a pair of weeping children, and a book containing a curse which is said to regularly fly across the library on its own, and always fall open at the same page – the one where the curse is inscribed.

Despite all, these stories on their own might have been insufficient to create the sense of awe with which the magnificently ominous looking mansion is now regarded. But then the 1963 movie, 'The Haunting', was made. It was screened again as part of a special event at the Ettington Park Hotel in 2010, with one of its original stars, Richard Johnson, in attendance. Afterwards, a local journalist wrote: "I'd heard all the local ghost stories of course. But I'd never considered Ettington Park to be a spooky place until I saw that movie. Now I'll never think of it any other way."

# WAITING FOR NICKY
## Antonia James

L illian hadn't planned to murder her husband.

It just *happened*.

Afterwards, when she tried to remember the details, she couldn't. There were just small snapshots; the chill wind on her face as she rushed toward him, the cloying odour of his sweat, his startled expression as she pushed, followed by a soft thud as his body collided with rock on the way down.

Then, there was only silence and a dull echo in her brain: *"And that was the end of that."*

It was true that she had often felt like killing Nicky, but she never thought she would *actually* do it. In truth, she wasn't entirely sure what had gotten into her that day; but now, as she reflected on the events leading up to the murder, she suspected it had more than a little to do with the Devil's Chimney.

Across the Cotswolds, the land is gentle and sweeping. It lacks the drama of the Highlands, and the jagged, chalk cliffs of the coast seem very far away. Instead, verdant pasture rolls prettily from Broadway to Bath, only occasionally interrupted by sleepy villages of honey-coloured limestone.

Consequently, when Lillian first saw the Devil's Chimney, she found it ugly and forbidding.

The crooked column reared from the foliage like an obscene cenotaph, naked and conspicuous for miles around; in this part of England, where the topography was eminently well behaved, the Devil's Chimney was almost offensive.

Nobody really knew how the seventy-foot needle of rock had come to be there, although the theories were plentiful. Geologists propagated the opinion that it was all that remained after countless millennia of differential erosion. Historians seemed to favour the tale that local quarrymen had left the landmark deliberately, as some kind of ill-conceived joke. And then there were *other* stories; strange, dark stories that Lillian had barely registered when first hearing them.

Now, as she stood again before the twisted rock pile, she wondered at how flippantly she had dismissed the warnings. That said, she had suspected even then that it would all end badly.

As a brilliant crust of snow settled across the ridge of

Leckhampton Hill, Lillian cast her mind back to that night, the night when Nicky had first heard about the Devil's Chimney, the night when it had all started.

*

It was the end of a freezing December day when they arrived in Chipping Campden. She remembered how the town seemed strangely deserted, as they passed along the High Street. Pale winter moonlight silvered the rooftops, now soft with the first breath of frost, and a carpet of mist pooled across the road. She peered at the shuttered shop-fronts rolling by and wondered how it might look in the daylight. She knew of its reputation: a bustling market town, where ancient inns nestled cosily alongside boutiques and art galleries. Now swathed in darkness, the town was dead and lonely and she felt only disappointment, as she might with anything that failed to meet her expectations.

Her spirits lifted slightly as they turned off the High Street and passed through a set of elegant gates, into the grounds of the hotel. The drive swept for at least a quarter of a mile through topiary, which, even in the gloom, was quite lovely.

As always, Nicky had booked them into the most expensive hotel he could find and, as the tyres of his four-by-four crunched along the driveway and the inn came into view, she couldn't help being impressed. Seeing the gleam in her eyes, his face split into a grin.

"I knew you'd like it here."

"It's exquisite" she said, aware of the strain in her voice. If Nicky noticed, he didn't comment and instead concentrated on finding his way to the car park; where row upon row of gleaming new vehicles stood proudly in line. Killing the engine, he turned to her, raking a hand through the mop of his blonde hair. His expression was serious. "Let's try to enjoy ourselves this weekend Lillian."

She paused and then nodded. "Of course."

"I mean it ... I need this break. Let's make the most of it."

"We will," she said with forced enthusiasm, but she could tell by the look in his eyes that he was no more convinced than she was.

Inside, the hotel was equally splendid; an elegant tableau of oak panelling, deep carpets and gleaming brass. As they crossed the reception area toward the desk, she noticed other rooms breaking away; vast sitting rooms with roaring fires and sumptuous sofas, and everywhere the air was rich with the aroma of coffee and leather and sweet pastries. But try as she might, Lillian could take no pleasure in such opulent surroundings and as she followed her husband into their lavish suite, she could tell by the stiffness in his thick neck and shoulders that her detachment was starting to irritate him.

Over dinner and then afterwards in the bar, they barely spoke and, as he always did when they were on holiday, Nicky drank too much.

He was just approaching a state of total inebriation, when an old photograph caught his eye. He had been about to launch into an offensive; Lillian was well accustomed to the signs – the sour expression, the mumbling under his breath, but the sepia print on the wall distracted him and he quickly forget his anger.

"Look at that!" he said, his eyes suddenly bright with interest.

She turned to inspect the photograph, in which a towering stone needle stood erect and incongruous against a backdrop of tumbling meadows.

He eyed the image curiously, all the while sipping at his whiskey.

"It's called the Devil's Chimney sir ... impressive, isn't it?"

The voice seemed to come from nowhere and they turned to find a waiter, who had silently appeared beside them. He looked to be in his early sixties and had the wiry, weather-beaten countenance of a man who spent most of his time outdoors.

"What was that?" Nicky spluttered.

"The Devil's Chimney sir ... it's about fifteen miles from here; between Cheltenham and Leckhampton. It's just off the Cotswold Way. Fancy your chances, do you?" Lillian winced. That sounded distinctly like a challenge, and Nicky was never the one to shirk a challenge.

"I've climbed worse than that."

She smiled thinly. She could see where this was leading.

"I'm sure you have sir. Can I get you another drink?" The waiter spoke with the pleasant melody of the region and was obviously a local.

Nicky's eyes flashed. "Don't you believe me?'

The waiter bowed slightly. "Of course, sir!"

"I've bagged some right monsters in my time ... Mont Maudit ... Ben More ... in gale force winds, that one, too."

The waiter seemed genuinely interested. "Really? I used to climb a bit myself. Thought I recognised a fellow mountain man."

Nicky visibly swelled at the compliment and Lillian almost pointed out that, in fact, he hadn't climbed for years and, when he'd first met her, he hadn't known the difference between a karabiner

143

and a carbuncle. But as always, she said nothing.

Nicky, however, was hooked. "What about this one?" he asked, pointing to the picture. "Ever been up there?"

The waiter's eyes sparkled. "Actually sir, I have. I *even* left a penny at the top. Of course that was years ago ... when they still let people climb it."

"What? You mean they don't now?"

"'Fraid not sir," he sighed. "It's strictly forbidden. The limestone's all crumbling, you see. Too dangerous, they reckon ... a couple of lads chanced it last year," and at this his eyes seemed to darken. "One of them was killed. Apparently a handful of rock came away ..." Then suddenly the waiter turned his attention to Lillian, as if seeing her for the first time. "*And that was the end of that.*"

Nicky took a long pull from his glass, his eyes still fixed on the small photograph, but the waiter continued to watch Lillian, smiling his small, strange smile.

She finally spoke. "Why did you leave a penny at the top?"

"For old Nick. Nobody would dare climb the Chimney without leaving a coin at the top for *Him*." Lillian frowned and the waiter laughed lightly. "But of course ... you're not from round here. You wouldn't know the story. Local legend has it that the Devil's Chimney is the chimney of the Devil's home, deep beneath the ground. Supposedly, in the olden days, the Devil would sit on top of Leckhampton Hill and hurl stones at Sunday churchgoers. However, the stones were turned back on him, driving him under the ground and trapping him there, so he couldn't bother the good villagers anymore. Everyone who visits the Devil's Chimney has to leave a coin on top of the rock as payment. In exchange he stays underground, unable to leave and spread his mischief."

For a moment nobody spoke and then Nicky roared with laughter. 'What a load of old shite!" The waiter's mouth remained fixed in a polite smile, but his eyes were unexpectedly cold. "I can't believe that people still believe that rubbish!"

When the waiter replied, his voice was soft and serious. "Of course ...you're right sir, it is only a legend. But I know of someone who didn't pay the toll ... he lived to regret it."

This only served to fuel Nicky's amusement and he guffawed again, slapping his thigh and rolling in his chair. "Brilliant!" he howled, the tears now rolling down his cheeks.

Lillian tried to catch the waiter's eye, to show him that she was sorry and that they meant no offence, but he was still watching

Nicky, his expression difficult to read. Finally he nodded. "As you say ... just a silly story. Probably better to stay away from the place altogether, sir. Now... how about that drink?"

An hour later, Lillian's initial misgivings were confirmed when her husband shambled to Reception, demanding an Ordnance Survey Map.

That night, as he lay unconscious across their enormous bed, she watched him from a chair in the farthest corner of the room. She knew what would happen the following day. Nicky didn't like to be told what he couldn't do. She could have packed her case right then and disappeared into the night and she had often wondered since why she didn't, choosing instead to stay, sitting up all night, watching him snore. She'd been asking herself the same question for years. Why didn't she just leave? Of course, it was the money that kept her there, but she liked to tell herself that they were "working at it" and that "all couples had their ups and downs".

*

The following morning, she meekly accompanied him when he insisted they pull on their hiking gear to "just have a look at it". The days had long since passed when she had raised her voice against Nicky's schemes. He always got what he wanted in the end; initially that was what she had found so attractive about him. When they were first getting to know one another, his determination to succeed had seemed sexy as hell, but those days had been brief and fleeting. Latterly, his bull-headed obstinacy served only to push her more deeply within herself; so much so that occasionally she felt as if she were looking down at him from the darkest end of a very long corridor. That morning, as he pranced excitedly around the base of the needle, squeezed into an old fleece and a pair of climbing shorts that even the year before had been too small for him; she felt nothing less than loathing for him.

"Piece of cake," he said, gazing up toward the summit. "We'll get up there in no time."

Lillian started. "*We*? You never said anything about *me* climbing it with you!"

He turned his attention to her then, his cheeks still flushed from the previous night. "Oh come on Lillian! This is easy for an old pro like you. You could get up there with your damned eyes shut."

"But we're not supposed to climb it!" she protested, looking up at the Chimney's pock marked surface and rutted buttresses. Perhaps there had been a time when she could have climbed it with her eyes closed, but that time had gone. That said, it wasn't too high and didn't appear especially technical. The conditions were good too; it was a crisp, still day, and the skies were clear. "But I'm not wearing the right gear."

He chortled. "You're kidding, right? Stop making excuses. This is *nothing* to you. You climbed the Eiger, for Christ's sake!" His voice softened and just for a moment, when he smiled, he seemed younger. "Come on sweetheart … it'll be just like the old days."

And suddenly she was right back there; that glorious spring in the Dolomites, when they had first met. She had been a mountain guide attached to the hostel where Nicky was staying; he a cocky graduate, travelling through Europe, in search of adventure. The attraction had been instant and intoxicating. But that was then and this was now, and the two seemed a million miles apart.

"I don't really want to, Nicky. *You* do it … I'll wait here for you." He regarded her silently and seeing that familiar look in his eye, she felt her pulse quicken. "Okay then," she mumbled. "Let's just get it over with."

His simmering anger was instantly gone, and enthusiastically, he started looking for a route.

She watched him awhile, before finally stepping forward. "I'll lead, if you like."

"I can do it," he snapped and Lillian knew better than to contradict him.

Instead, she stood back and watched as her husband missed the obvious route she had picked out and instead, struggled to drag himself up and onto a narrow ledge. It was an easy opening gambit, but the way after that looked tricky as hell. Deciding not to follow him, she wandered around to the far side of the needle, and scrambled easily enough, until her feet were both steady in large footholds. Reaching up, she found a good grip and then, launching herself with her legs, pulled herself up, all the while taking very small steps against the rock face. Pushing down with her left hand, she leaned her body across, shifting the weight and, after grabbing a moment's rest, she straightened her elbow, lifting one foot onto the shelf beside her hand. Finding a higher hand-hold, she lifted the other foot until she was standing securely on the shelf. Exhaling loudly, Lillian took a moment to compose herself. That was a tricky manoeuvre and one she hadn't attempted for years, but it had come back to her so naturally that she wondered why she'd ever stopped climbing in the first place. With a renewed resolve, Lillian looked up at the rock face and feeling the thrill of the climb, she edged ever upward, quickly navigating through a myriad of hand and footholds which scarred the heavily eroded surface. In almost no time at all, she found herself at the top.

She swung her leg around the lip of the summit and then, with an ease that surprised her, swiveled her body around until she had both knees planted firmly on the top. Nicky was still some way back and she glanced down briefly to see him, resting precariously on a ledge, panting and sweating.

"You okay?" she asked, indifferently.

"Fine," he growled.

Smiling, she pushed herself to her feet and stepped away from the ledge. A cold wind whipped across her face and she breathed in deeply, enjoying the cool air in her throat. It was a marvellous spot, although isolated. Just as the waiter had described, the Cotswold Way path passed right beside the Chimney, but there was nobody using it right now. Instead there was only undulating pasture, rippling away as far as the eye could see on one side and, on the other, the bustling streets of Cheltenham were just visible. Lillian took a moment to enjoy the feeling of separation. It had been a while since she had bagged a summit and, although this wasn't an especially auspicious one, it felt good all the same. Some might not enjoy the exposure; it was a long way down and the flat peak, barely three feet across, but heights had never bothered her and closing her eyes, she took a moment to be still. It was only when she opened them again that she noticed the coins. They were everywhere, strewn across the peak in their hundreds: one-penny pieces, pound coins, farthings, shillings, foreign pennies that she didn't recognise, all glittering in the morning light in various shades of brass, copper, nickel and gold.

Bending over, she leaning in to examine a particularly old-looking coin. Years of exposure had melded it into the rock, and the figurehead was now little more than a formless blob. She tried to scratch it loose with her fingernail, but it wouldn't budge.

"Amazing," she said to nobody in particular, and was then distracted by a grunting, wheezing noise behind her. She turned in time to see Nicky struggling to drag himself onto the summit.

"*Jesus … Christ … Lillian,*" he gasped, his face puce from the exertion. "A little … *help.*"

147

Rushing across, she grabbed him, helping him heave his bulk over the ledge and then, staggering backward, watched him lying on his belly, panting and coughing like an old man. "Piece of cake," she mumbled and he glared at her as he struggled to his feet.

"Need to get back to the gym," he said, avoiding her gaze and stumbling a couple of steps away from the edge.

"Getting down will be easier" she suggested, watching her husband as he laboured to calm his breathing.

"Glorious views," he wheezed and then he too was distracted by the coins and bent down slowly to retrieve one. "Bloody hell," he said, holding it up and squinting in the pale, morning light. "Look at this." He flipped the coin over in his hand and smiled, as a single rivulet of sweat ran down his cheek. "Bloody yokels," he muttered, before dropping the coin and searching among the others. "By Christ! Some of these must be worth a fortune."

She watched him eyeing the coins greedily, picking them up and then tossing them aside, only to reach for another and then another. "We should probably leave one too," she murmured without great conviction, but her voice was carried away on a puff of wind.

"Bloody hell!" he roared again, dropping to his knees and scrabbling at the same coin that had caught Lillian's attention. "Look at this!" and now he was digging his fingers into the limestone, desperately trying to pry it free.

"For God's sake, Nick! Leave it, will you."

But he wouldn't and continued to fumble on his hands and knees until, with a small *click*, the coin came free. Sitting back, he held the dull, brass penny right up to his eye, studying the detail. "Can't really make it out."

An icy wind moaned about them then, and Lillian hugged her arms across her chest, still regarding him warily. "Please Nick ... just put it back."

He didn't appear to be listening and was busily rubbing the surface of the penny with his sleeve. "I think the date is 17 *something...*" he said, more to himself than to her. Lurching to his feet, he slipped the coin into his pocket.

"What are you doing?" she demanded.

He grinned. "Come on Lillian ... I doubt it's worth much. I'm just taking it as a souvenir."

"I don't think you should."

"Why not? You don't believe all that superstitious crap do you?"

"Of course not!" she shot back at him. "I just think it's wrong.

That coin must have been lying here for hundreds of years … why are you taking it?"

He began to laugh then; it was the laugh he always used when he found something particularly idiotic. "I'm taking it, Lillian, because I want it. *Alright*?"

"But what will you *do* with it?"

Again he laughed, folding his arms across his massive chest. "I won't *do* anything with it. I'll just *keep* it."

She didn't reply, but stood watching him as he turned his back on her, stretching his arms out to the panorama on all sides. "Just look at all this wonderful scenery. You really ought to lighten up a little." He took a step closer to the edge and it seemed to her that, just for a second, everything stopped moving; the birds seemed to fall oddly silent and the breath caught in her throat. All that remained was his voice, cutting through the stillness like a hatchet. "It's only an old coin. Hardly worth falling …"

And then there was another voice; an urging, sibilant hiss in her ear. "*Do it Lillian! Do it now!*"

And so she did.

Afterwards, Lillian stood for a moment, waiting to feel something, but her heart was as inert as the stone she stood upon. She wasn't sure how long she had waited there, on the summit of the Devil's Chimney, but it was only when the sky began to darken and her bones were aching with the cold, that she finally reached for her mobile and dialed 999.

When she spoke, her voice trembled very slightly. "I need to report an accident."

*

Three hours later, sitting in that small interview room, under the blinking fluorescents, the tears flowed easily enough. The story of how her husband had lost his grip sounded very convincing and the two detectives sitting across the table bought it completely. One even held her hand as she sobbed into her sleeve. After all, Nicky wasn't the first idiot to fall off the Devil's Chimney and he certainly wouldn't be the last. It was just a terrible accident.

When the younger detective, a dark fellow with kind eyes, asked her if they had been happily married, she told him honestly that they hadn't, but that wasn't a crime was it? And he had shaken his head and smiled.

As she was leaving the station, they handed her Nicky's belongings in a clear plastic bag, and as she carried them to the waiting squad car, the load felt surprisingly heavy. She climbed into the front seat, alongside the same young detective who had interviewed her and in front of another officer who was sitting in the darkness of the back. It was very late and the temperature had fallen to well below zero, causing an opaque mist to swallow up all detail from the surrounding landscape.

As they journeyed through the deserted villages, nobody in the car spoke and she gazed out of the window as the frozen streets whipped by in an iridescent haze, feeling strangely numb and detached.

Suddenly a thought occurred to her and she looked into the bag, where Nicky's clothes had been neatly placed. Reaching into the folds of his pocket, she found what she was searching for and pulled free the stolen coin. It looked very innocuous in the half-light; an old, rusty penny, *hardly worth falling out over*. And then for the second time that night, she cried, only this time the release was genuine; a sudden well of relief and regret.

Perhaps seeing her distress, the officer in the back seat, reached across and held her shoulder, but his touch was heavier than was comfortable, so much so in fact, that his grip soon began to smart. In fact, he seemed to be squeezing her harder and harder and the pressure soon became unbearable. Squirming under his grip, she reached up to push him away, but when her fingers arrived at the spot, she found that there was no hand there at all, and panicked. She spun around, only to find that the back seat of the car was black and empty.

"Everything okay?" the officer driving asked.

"Oh … oh yes." Lillian replied, gazing into the void and rubbing the tender place on her shoulder.

She turned back around and tried to focus on the road ahead, but as the time passed and the journey continued, she again began to suspect that someone was sitting in the back seat directly behind her, watching her from the darkness. She could hear them breathing, although on reflection that might just have been the engine, or the wind rattling against the windscreen. In any case, she chose not to turn around again.

The first night without Nicky was the longest. She slept fitfully, her dreams a maelstrom of climbing and falling and darkness. She was eventually disturbed from sleep by the sound of someone shuffling around in the corridor just outside her bedroom. When she sat up in bed and peered through the gloom to the shadows beyond the open doorway, the sound stopped. She sat there waiting, the silence pressing down all around her, but nothing happened. Again, she had the uncomfortable sensation of being watched, and although she now couldn't hear anything beyond the blood singing in her ears and there was nothing visibly wrong, she *felt* that somebody was standing there, just beyond the doorway, watching her from the veil of darkness. She resisted the urge to shout out; to ask if somebody was there. After all, what if somebody shouted back?

*

Now that Nicky was dead, Lillian's life should have been better. The insurance payout had afforded her an even grander lifestyle than she had enjoyed previously and she no longer had to explain the swollen lips or the dark glasses on a dreary day. But as time passed, the colour seemed to drain out of her world. It wasn't guilt, because she felt none. She wasn't even afraid of being found out, because for reasons she couldn't really explain, Lillian knew that nobody would ever discover what had happened that morning.

In fact, Lillian's mounting anxiety had nothing whatsoever to do with Nicky's 'accident'; it was because of the *thing* that was following her.

Ever since that first night, she'd been aware of it; a dark presence lingering just on the edge of her awareness. When she turned around, it always managed to disappear from sight, a shadow darting from view, but not quite quick enough so that she didn't see it.

Sometimes it was far away, a faceless shape in the crowd, trailing her silently. At other times it seemed to be closer and she could hear the soft footfalls tracking her own, just slightly out of sync. When she stopped walking, it stopped too, but always a millisecond late, as if she had caught it off guard.

Lillian knew it was coming and getting closer with every day that passed. It was only a matter of time before it finally caught up with her.

One evening, whilst she was applying her make-up in the mirror, she heard it again; footsteps padding softly up the carpeted staircase and then pausing at the top. She stopped what she was doing and listened. Now there was silence, but she was certain she had heard *something* and she focused her attention on the reflection of the

151

bedroom behind her. Everything seemed normal; the sumptuous bed was immaculate as always, her clothes were neatly laid out, the heavy oak wardrobe stood solid and still. She shifted her attention to the doorway and that was when she saw it, when she *really* saw it for the first time – a massive black entity, surely larger than a man, hovering just beyond the door. It was too dark in the corridor to make out any features, but it remained where it stood, defiantly staring back at her as if it had every right to be there. Slowly, she turned around, but by the time she had, the thing had disappeared. Climbing unsteadily to her feet, Lillian forced herself to go out there and face it; the thing that was waiting for her in the darkness. She stumbled forward, somehow managing to contain the abject terror that threatened to overwhelm her, but when she reached the spot, there was nothing there except the curtains drawn across the massive bay window, just as she had left them.

The wind moaned around the old house, and somewhere outside a dog was barking, but inside there wasn't a sound and Lillian felt suddenly more alone than she had ever felt in her life. She wandered blindly in the darkness until finally she found herself standing at the top of the sweeping staircase. She rested her hand on the banister; the smooth wood felt cool and reassuringly familiar against her palm, and somewhere in a far corner of the house the grandfather clock was ticking steadily. And then, very close behind her, there was a sigh and a cold breath touched her face. Startled, she stepped forward and briefly felt a jolt of pressure at her back, as if something had pushed her. Her foot slipped on the top step, but she caught the handrail in time and managed to steady herself.

The silence that followed was broken only by a small, metallic clink and she realized she had dropped something. Reaching down, she found the old penny and returned it to her pocket. She must have been holding it again. She had taken to doing that a lot lately.

*

The weeks turned into months, and Lillian saw it everywhere now; it sat behind her on the train, it tracked her as she wandered in a daze through the busy streets and at night, whilst she tossed and turned in her empty bed, it gazed down at her from the dark corners of the bedroom. She wasn't quite sure what it wanted, but her mind was settling on an idea; a way to end the torment.

One morning, as the sun was barely creeping above the horizon,

Lillian rose from another night without sleep and taking little care with her appearance, she dressed in a bewildered trance.

Stopping only to collect the brass coin from her nightstand, she wandered from the house and climbed into her four-by-four. She drove all the way to Cheltenham without once checking her rear view mirror. She didn't need to look behind her. She knew that it was there.

Parking as near as she could to the trail, she found it as empty as it had been that morning. It was an icy start and as her boots crunched along the stony track, the first flakes of snow began to fall. The conditions were bad for climbing, but it was with a growing sense of relief that she followed the path as it meandered through the frozen fields of the Cotswold's towards her destination.

The thing matched her stride for stride. She heard its enthusiastic footsteps in the thickening snow behind her and, as she glanced over her shoulder, she swore she could see the tip of its shadow as it closed the gap between them.

Eventually, as she stood again before the grotesque contours of the Chimney, Lillian felt that she fully understood what was required. She wondered how it had taken her so long to figure it out and, steeling her resolve, she began to climb.

Just as she knew it would be, the rock face was slippery with ice, and her bare hands glanced off the surface as she struggled to get a grip. Her shoes were equally untrustworthy and she had to dig in with her toes as, slowly, she inched her way up. Stopping on a ledge, she peered back over her shoulder and thought for a second that she saw it, a black shape scurrying out of sight, just beneath her. A sense of dread swept over her. From there, it could easily reach up and grab her foot, pulling her back down and the fall would almost certainly kill her. In a growing panic, Lillian scrambled upward, rushing to pull her feet higher up and out of reach, but she needn't have bothered. Nothing grabbed for her, and as she edged her way around toward the final ascent, she wondered if she had seen anything there at all.

Finally her hand closed around the lip of the top ledge and, with a massive effort, she pulled herself up, until she was resting on the top.

The surface was white with a carpet of snow that had settled and frozen, rendering the peak even more treacherous than she had anticipated. Still, it wouldn't prevent her from finishing what she had set out to do. She climbed to her feet and stepped across the summit. Her hands were raw with the cold and she rubbed them together, her breath pluming out before her.

Just as she approached the spot where Nicky had been standing, she thought for a split second that she saw him; his arms flailing in a futile struggle against thin air, but the memory was quickly gone and Lillian found herself alone again. She moved forward, until her toes were almost peeping over the edge.

She heard it then, the soft crunch of a footstep behind her; the distinct sound of someone approaching. The hair at the back of her neck bristled.

He was here.

This was what she had hoped for, but now that she was up here, she wasn't sure that she could go through with it.

In the distance, she could see the tiny shapes of cars as they moved like insects around the busy streets of Cheltenham. But she took no comfort in seeing life continue elsewhere; in fact the vivid colours, just visible through the ribbons of falling snow, only intensified her sense of isolation.

There was another footstep at her back, and perhaps the indistinct sound of laughter from somewhere below, but that might just have been her imagination playing tricks.

A cool breath stirred the hairs on the nape of her neck. She was certain that it wasn't just the wind. She closed her eyes and waited for the inevitable, her shoulders aching with tension – and then felt it, a slight pressure at the base of her back; the sensation of being pushed. It nudged her roughly forward and she staggered, but somehow held her balance. It shoved her again, harder this time, but still she didn't fall and then the force was constant, and it was building by the second. Lillian quickly found herself leaning dangerously forward, with only air between her and a plummet to certain death.

She hadn't known how she would respond when Nicky finally caught up with her. Part of her had suspected that she might just capitulate, meekly accepting this final act of his dominion, a fitting end to her years of silent subservience.

But could she *really* give in to him so easily? What was she doing up here anyway, if not to challenge him – to *dare* him to try and end this? A mutinous will was stirring inside her now, and with sudden rage, she pushed back, grinding against the terrible pressure, struggling hard against the unseen hands. The drop still yawned before her, but she didn't want it to end this way. She had been dead for over ten years; this was her last chance to start living again.

And at that precise moment, the pressure disappeared.

Almost toppling backwards, Lillian turned around and found that she was completely alone. No monster was lurking behind her; there were no creeping footfalls to disturb the perfect calm. There were only fat snowflakes, falling relentlessly against a yellow sky.

Stumbling away from the edge, she reached into her pocket and pulled free the old penny. She gazed at its confused façade; an anonymous mass in the centre, with a blur beneath where once there had been details of a birth date. She placed it carefully on the surface and then watched it a while, a dirty blot against the pristine whiteness, until eventually it disappeared from view.

*

In the weeks and months that followed, Lillian was vaguely aware of the dark wraith trailing behind her. She would occasionally turn and see it, scurrying to hide around the nearest corner, or behind a tree, but as the weeks turned into months, she stopped worrying about the simpering shadow traipsing in her wake. If Nicky wanted to follow her for the rest of her days, it was up to him; Lillian had better things to do.

# THE SATANIC SLAYINGS AT MEON HILL

The brutal death of farm worker Charles Walton at Meon Hill, Warwickshire, in 1945, was a celebrated mystery at the time, and still has the power to fascinate – primarily because it has never been solved.

The simple facts are these. Walton, described as a sullen, hard-drinking 75-year-old, had been working part-time for a farmer called Alfred Potter. Despite his age, he was employed mainly to turn soil and trim hedges, and on the 14th February that year, he was returning home with his usual tools of the trade: a billhook and a pitchfork. Somewhere along a country track quite near to Meon Hill village, he was accosted, beaten savagely with his own walking-stick, had his throat slashed with his billhook, and then, as a coup de grace, was pinned to the ground with his pitchfork.

An extensive investigation, headed up by famous police detective Robert Fabian of Scotland Yard, failed to reach a conclusion. Though Walton's employer was a suspect for some time, nobody was ever charged or convicted. Fabian would later tell how the enquiry had been complicated from the start by witchcraft rumours. Not only had Walton died in ritualistic fashion, but he had died on a date which under the old calendar was Candlemas Day, also known as the pagan festival Imbolc. In addition, the crime bore remarkable similarities to another pitchfork murder in nearby Long Compton. Some seventy years earlier in 1875, a certain Ann Tennant died at the hands of one James Heywood, who afterwards explained that he had killed her because she was part of a witch coven (Heywood's story was disregarded but he was spared the hangman because he was deemed to be insane).

But the supposed black magic elements associated with the murder of Charles Walton go much further than this. Many locals believed that Walton was himself part of a satanic sect. Apparently he bred natterjack toads and villagers told how he'd been seen driving them across farmland to render it barren. In his childhood, he'd reported a remarkable experience at Ilmington Hill, a place supposedly famous for demonic manifestations. The young Walton claimed to have met the same black dog at the same crossroads nine nights in succession – and said that on the last night he had been confronted by the apparition of a headless woman walking towards him. No-one had believed him at the time, but the youngster insisted it was true. Unnervingly, Walton's sister had died the next day.

Local gossips would later say that this was the point in Walton's life when evil spirits made contact with him. The Devil and his minions certainly figured in Walton's conversation throughout his life, especially when he was drunk. In his later years, he had taken to blaming witches and their familiars for every problem in both his life and the life of the surrounding community, and after his death a suspicion was aired that the local coven had grown tired of his garrulousness and had silenced him in the traditional way. Meanwhile, a parallel rumour suggested that it was actually God-fearing folk who had done away with Walton, as they feared he was a warlock.

It was true that Detective Fabian reported a wall of silence in the Meon Hill area when enquiring into the murder. It seemed that nobody was prepared to speak to him about what they knew. The case is now the oldest unsolved murder on the Warwickshire Constabulary's files. Some modern observers have dismissed the ritual aspects as a combination of coincidence and superstitious nonsense, but there is talk that the Meon Hill area is a centre of cult activity even today.

# THE HORROR UNDER WARRENDOWN
## Ramsey Campbell

Y
ou ask me at least to hint why I refuse ever to open a children's book. Once I made my living from such material. While the imitations of reality hawked by my colleagues in the trade grew grubbier, and the fantasies more shameful, I carried innocence from shop to shop, or so I was proud to think. Now the sight of a children's classic in a bookshop window sends me fleeing. The more apparently innocent the book, the more unspeakable the truth it may conceal, and there are books the mere thought of which revives memories I had prayed were buried for ever.

It was when I worked from Birmingham, and Warrendown was only a name on a signpost on a road to Brichester – a road I avoided, not least because it contained no bookshops. Nor did I care for the route it followed a few miles beyond the Warrendown sign through Clotton, a small settlement which appeared to be largely abandoned, its few occupied houses huddling together on each side of a river, beside which stood a concrete monument whose carvings were blurred by moss and weather. I had never been fond of the countryside, regarding it at best as a way of getting from town to town, and now the stagnant almost reptilian smell and chilly haze which surrounded Clotton seemed to attach itself to my car. This unwelcome presence helped to render the Cotswold landscape yet more forbidding to me, the farmland and green fields a disguise for the ancient stone of the hills, and I resolved to drive south of Brichester on the motorway in future and double back, even though this added half an hour to my journey. Had it not been for Graham Crawley I would never again have gone near the Warrendown road.

In those days I drank to be sociable, not to attempt to forget or to sleep. Once or twice a month I met colleagues in the trade, some of whom I fancied would have preferred to represent a children's publisher too, for a balti and as many lagers as we could stay seated for. Saturdays would find me in my local pub, the Sutton Arms in Kings Heath. Ending my week among people who didn't need to be persuaded of the excellence of my latest batch of titles was enough to set me up for the next week. But it was in the Sutton Arms that Crawley made himself, I suppose, something like a friend.

I don't recall the early stages of the process, in his case or with any of the folk I used to know. I grew used to looking for him in the small bare taproom, where the stools and tables and low ceiling were the colour of ash mixed with ale. He would raise his broad round stubbled face from his tankard, twitching his nose and upper lip in greeting, and as I joined him he would duck as though he expected me either to pat him on the head or hit him when he'd emitted his inevitable quip. "What was she up to in the woods with seven little men, eh?" he would mutter, or "There's only one kind of horn you'd blow up that I know of. No wonder he was going after sheep," or some other reference to the kind of book in which I travelled. There was a constant undercurrent of ingratiating nervousness in his voice, an apology for whatever he said as he said it, which was one reason I was never at my ease with him. While we talked about our week, mine on the road and his behind the counter of a local greengrocer's, I was bracing myself for his latest sexual bulletin. I never knew what so many women could see in him, and hardly any of them lasted for more than an encounter. My curiosity about the kind of girl who could find him attractive may have left me open to doing him the favour he asked of me.

At first he only asked which route I took to Brichester, and then which one I would follow if the motorway was closed, by which point I'd had enough of the way he skulked around a subject as if he was ready to dart into hiding at the first hint of trouble. "Are you after a lift?" I demanded.

He ducked his head so that his long hair hid even more of his ears and peered up at me. "Well, a lift, you know, I suppose, really, yes."

"Where to?"

"You won't know it, cos it's not much of a place. Only it's not far, not much out of your way, I mean, if you happened to be going that way anyway sometime."

When at last he released the name of Warrendown like a question he didn't expect to be answered, his irritating tentativeness provoked me to retort "I'll be in that square of the map next week."

"Next week, that's next week, you mean." His face twitched so hard it exposed his teeth. "I wasn't thinking quite that soon ..."

"I'll forgive you if you've given up on the idea."

"Given up – no, you're right. I'm going, cos I should go," he said, fiercely for him.

Nevertheless I arrived at his flat the next day not really expecting to collect him. When I rang his bell, however, he poked his nose under the drawn curtains and said he would be down in five minutes;

which, to my continuing surprise, he was, nibbling the last of his presumably raw breakfast and dressed in the only suit I'd ever seen him wear. He sat clutching a small case which smelled of vegetables while I concentrated on driving through the rush hour and into the tangle of motorways, and so we were irrevocably on our way before I observed that he was gripping his luggage with all the determination I'd heard in his voice in the pub. "Are you expecting some kind of trouble?" I said.

"Trouble." He added a grunt which bared his teeth and which seemed to be saying I'd understood so much that no further questions were necessary, and I nearly lost my temper. "Care to tell me what kind?" I suggested.

"What would you expect?"

"Not a woman."

"See, you knew. Be tricks. The trouble's what I got her into, as if you hadn't guessed. Cos she got me going so fast I hadn't time to wear anything. Can't beat a hairy woman."

This was a great deal more intimate than I welcomed. "When did you last see her?" I said as curtly as I could.

"Last year. She was having it then. Should have gone down after, but I, you know. You know me."

He was hugging his baggage so hard he appeared to be squeezing out the senseless vegetable smell. "Afraid of her family?" I said with very little sympathy.

He pressed his chin against his chest, but I managed to distinguish what he muttered. "Afraid of the whole bloody place."

That was clearly worth pursuing, and an excuse for me to stay on my usual route, except that ahead I saw all three lanes of traffic halted as far as the horizon, and police cars racing along the hard shoulder towards the problem. I left the motorway at the exit which immediately presented itself.

Framilode, Saul, Fretherne, Whitminster ... Old names announced themselves on signposts, and then a narrow devious road enclosed the car with hedges, blotting out the motorway at once. Beneath a sky dogged with dark clouds the gloomy foliage appeared to smoulder; the humped backs of the hills glowed a lurid green. When I opened my window to let out the vegetable smell, it admitted a breeze, unexpectedly chill for September, which felt like my passenger's nervousness rendered palpable. He was crouching over his luggage and blinking at the high spiky hedges as if they were a trap into which I'd led him. "Can I ask what your plans are?"

160

I said to break the silence which was growing as relentless as the ancient landscape.

"See her. Find out what she's got, what she wants me to."

His voice didn't so much trail off as come to a complete stop. I wasn't sure I wanted to know where his thoughts had found themselves. "What took you there to begin with?" was as much as I cared to ask.

"Beat ricks."

This time I grasped it, despite his pronouncing it as though unconvinced it was a name. "She's the young lady in question."

"Met her in the Cabbage Patch, you know, the caff. She'd just finished university but she stayed over at my place." I was afraid this might be the preamble to further intimate details, but he continued with increasing reluctance "Kept writing to me after she went home, wanting me to go down there, cos she said I'd feel at home."

"And did you?"

He raised his head as though sniffing the air and froze in that position. The sign for Warrendown, drooping a little on its post, had swung into view along the hedge. His half-admitted feelings had affected me so much that my foot on the accelerator wavered. "If you'd prefer not to do this …"

Only his mouth moved, barely opening. "No choice."

No reply could have angered me more. He'd no more will than one of his own vegetables, I thought, and sent the car screeching into the Warrendown road. As we left behind the sign which appeared to be trying to point into the earth, I had an impression of movement beyond the hedge on both sides of the road, several figures which had been standing absolutely still leaping to follow the car. I told myself I was mistaking at least their speed, and when ragged gaps in the hedges afforded me a view of oppressively green fields weighed down by the stagnant sky, nobody was to be seen, not that anyone could have kept pace with the car. I hadn't time to ponder any of this, because from the way Crawley was inching his face forward I could tell that the sight a mile ahead among the riotous fields surrounded by hunched dark hills must indeed be Warrendown.

At that distance I saw it was one of the elements of the countryside I most disliked, an insignificant huddle of buildings miles from anywhere, but I'd never experienced such immediate revulsion. The clump of thatched roofs put me in mind of dunes

161

surmounted by dry grass, evidence less of human habitation than of the mindless actions of nature. As the sloping road led me down towards them, I saw that the thatch overhung the cottages, like hair dangling over idiot brows. Where the road descended to the level of the village, it showed me that the outermost cottages were so squat they appeared to have collapsed or to be sinking into the earth of the unpaved road. Thatch obscured their squinting windows, and I gave in to an irrational hope that the village might prove to be abandoned. Then the door of the foremost cottage sank inwards, and as I braked, a head poked out of the doorway to watch our arrival.

It was a female head. So much I distinguished before it was snatched back. I glanced at Crawley in case he had recognised it, but he was wrinkling his face at some aspect of the village which had disconcerted him. As the car coasted into Warrendown, the woman reappeared, having draped a scarf over her head to cover even more of her than her dress did. I thought she was holding a baby, then decided it must be some kind of pet, because as she emerged into the road with an odd abrupt lurch the small object sprang from her arms into the dimness within the cottage. She knotted the scarf and thrust her plump yet flattish face out of it to stare swollen-eyed at my passenger. I was willing to turn the vehicle around and race for the main road, but he was lowering his window, and so I slowed the car. I saw their heads lean towards each other as though the underside of the sky was pressing them down and forcing them together. Their movements seemed obscurely reminiscent, but I'd failed to identify of what when she spoke. "You're back."

Though her low voice wasn't in itself threatening, I sensed he was disconcerted that someone he clearly couldn't put a name to had recognised him. All he said, however, was "You know Beatrix."

"Us all know one another."

She hadn't once glanced at me, but I was unable to look away from her. A few coarse hairs sprouted from her reddish face; I had the unpleasant notion that her cheeks were raw from being shaved. "Do you know where she is?" Crawley said.

"Her'll be with the young ones."

His head sank as his face turned up further. "How many?"

"All that's awake. Can't you hear them? I should reckon even he could."

As that apparently meant me I dutifully strained my ears, although I wasn't anxious to heighten another sense: our entry into Warrendown seemed to have intensified the vegetable stench. After

162

a few moments I made out a series of high regular sounds – childish voices chanting some formula – and experienced almost as much relief as my passenger audibly did. "She's at the school," he said.

"That's her. Back where her was always meant for." The woman glanced over her shoulder into the cottage, and part of a disconcertingly large ear twitched out of her headscarf. "Feeding time," she said, and began unbuttoning the front of her dress as she stepped back through the doorway, beyond which I seemed to glimpse something hopping about a bare earth floor. "See you down there later," she told Crawley, and shut the door.

I threw the car into gear and drove as fast through the village as I reasonably could. Faces peered through the thick fringes over the low windows of the stunted cottages, and I told myself it was the dimness within that made those faces seem so fat and so blurred in their outlines, and the nervousness with which Crawley had infected me that caused their eyes to appear so large. At the centre of Warrendown the cottages, some of which I took to be shops without signs, crowded towards the road as if forced forward by the mounds behind them, mounds as broad as the cottages but lower, covered with thatch or grass. Past the centre the buildings were more sunken; more than one had collapsed, while others were so overgrown that only glimpses through the half-obscured unglazed windows of movements, ill-defined and sluggish, suggested that they were inhabited. I felt as though the rotten vegetable sweetness in the air was somehow dragging them all down as it was threatening to do to me, and had to restrain my foot from tramping on the accelerator. Now the car was almost out of Warrendown, which was scarcely half a mile long, and the high voices had fallen silent before I was able to distinguish what they had been chanting – a hymn, my instincts told me, even though the language had seemed wholly unfamiliar. I was wondering whether I'd passed the school, and preparing to tell Crawley I hadn't time to retrace the route, when Crawley mumbled "This is it."

"If you say so." I now saw that the last fifty or so yards of the left-hand side of Warrendown were occupied by one long mound fattened by a pelt of thatch and grass and moss. I stopped the car but poised my foot on the accelerator. "What do you want to do?"

His blank eyes turned to me. Perhaps it was the strain on them which made them appear to be almost starting out of his head. "Why do you have to ask?"

I'd had enough. I reached across him to let him out, and the door of the school wobbled open as though I'd given it a cue. Beyond it stood a young woman of whom I could distinguish little except a long-sleeved ankle-length brown dress, my attention having been caught by the spectacle behind her – at least half a dozen small bodies in a restless heap on the bare floor of the dark corridor. As some of them raised their heads lethargically to blink big-eyed at me before subsiding again, Crawley clambered out of the vehicle, blocking my view. "Thanks for, you know," he muttered. "You'll be coming back this way, will you?"

"Does that mean you'll be ready to leave?"

"I'll know better when you come."

"I'll be back before dark and you'd better be out here on the road," I told him, and sped off.

I kept him in view in the mirror until the hedges hid Warrendown. The mirror shook with the unevenness of the road, but I saw him wave his free hand after me, stretching his torso towards the car as though he was about to drop to all fours and give chase. Behind him a figure leapt out of the doorway, and as he swung round she caught him. I could distinguish no more about her than I already had, except that the outline of her large face looked furry, no doubt framed by hair. She and Crawley embraced – all her limbs clasped him, at any rate – and as I looked away from this intimacy I noticed that the building of which the school was an extension had once possessed a tower, the overgrown stones of which were scattered beyond the edge of the village. It was none of my business whether they took care of their church, nor why anyone who'd attended university should have allowed herself to be reduced to teaching in a village school, nor what hold the place seemed to have over Crawley as well. They deserved each other, I told myself, and not only because they looked so similar. Once they were out of sight I lowered the windows and drove fast to rid the car of the stagnant mindless smell of Warrendown.

Before long the track brought me to an unmarked junction with the main road. I wound the windows tight and sped through the remains of Clotton, which felt drowned by the murky sky and the insidious chill of the dark river, and didn't slow until I saw Brichester ahead, raising its hospital and graveyard above its multiplying streets. In those streets I felt more at ease; nothing untoward had ever befallen me in a city such as Brichester, and nothing seemed likely to do so, especially in a bookshop. I parked my car in a multi-storey at the edge of Lower Brichester and walked through the crowds to the first of my appointments.

My Christmas titles went down well – in the last shop of the day, perhaps too well. Not only did the new manager, previously second in command, order more copies than any of her competitors, but in a prematurely festive mood insisted on my helping her celebrate her promotion. One drink led to several, not least because I must have been trying to douse the nervousness with which Crawley and Warrendown had left me. Too late I realised my need for plenty of coffee and something to eat, and by the time I felt fit to drive the afternoon was well over.

Twilight had gathered like soot in cobwebs as wide as the sky. From the car park I saw lights fleeing upwards all over Brichester, vanishing home. The hospital was a glimmering misshapen skull beside which lay acres of bones. Even the fluorescent glare of the car park appeared unnatural, and I sat in my car wondering how much worse the places I had to drive back through would seem. I'd told Crawley I would collect him before dark, but wasn't it already dark? Might he not have decided I wasn't coming for him, and have made his own arrangements? This was almost enough to persuade me I needn't return to Warrendown, but a stirring of guilt at my cowardice shamed me into heading for that morning's route.

The glow of the city sank out of view. A few headlights came to meet me, and then there were only my beams probing the dim road that writhed between the hills, which rose as though in the dark they no longer needed to pretend to slumber. The bends of the road swung back and forth, unable to avoid my meagre light, and once a pair of horned heads stared over a gate, rolling their eyes as they chewed and chewed, rolling them mindlessly as they would when they went to be slaughtered. I remembered how Crawley's eyes had protruded as he prepared to quit my car.

Well outside Clotton I was seized by the chill of the river. Though my windows were shut tight, as I reached the first abandoned house I heard the water, splashing more loudly than could be accounted for unless some large object was obstructing it. I drove so fast across the narrow bridge and between the eyeless buildings that by the time I was able to overcome my inexplicable panic I was miles up the road, past the unmarked lane to Warrendown.

I told myself I mustn't use this as an excuse to break my word, and when I reached the Warrendown signpost, which looked as though the weight of the growing blackness was helping the earth drag it down, I steered the car off the main road. Even with my headlight beams full on, I had to drive at a speed which made me feel the vehicle was burrowing into the thick dark, which by now could just as well have been the night it was anticipating. The contortions of the road suggested it was doing its utmost never to reach Warrendown. The thorns of the hedges tore at the air, and a gap in the tortured mass of vegetation let me see the cottages crouching furtively, heads down, in the midst of the smudged fields. Despite the darkness, not a light was to be seen.

It could have been a power failure – I assumed those might be common in so isolated and insignificant a village – but why was nobody in Warrendown using candles or flashlights? Perhaps they were, invisibly at that distance, I reassured myself. The hedges intervened without allowing me a second look. The road sloped down, giving me the unwelcome notion that Warrendown had snared it, and the hedges ended as though they had been chewed off. As my headlights found the outermost cottages, their long-haired skulls seemed to rear out of the earth. Apart from that, there was no movement all the way along the road to the half-ruined church.

The insidious vegetable stench had already begun to seep into the car. It cost me an effort to drive slowly enough through the village to look for the reason I was here. The thatched fringes were full of shadows which shifted as I passed as though each cottage was turning its idiot head towards me. Though every window was empty and dark, I felt observed, increasingly so as the car followed its wobbling beams along the deserted lane, until I found it hard to breathe. I seemed to hear a faint irregular thumping – surely my own unsteady pulse, not a drumming under the earth. I came abreast of the church and the school, and thought the thumping quickened and then ceased. Now I was out of Warrendown, but the knowledge that I would be returning to the main road whichever direction I chose persuaded me to make a last search. I turned the car, almost backing it into one of the overgrown blocks of the fallen tower, and sounded my horn twice.

The second blare followed the first into the silent dark. Nothing moved, not a single strand of thatch on the cottages within the congealed splash of light cast by my headlamps, but I was suddenly nervous of what response I might have invited. I eased the car away from the ruins of the tower and began to drive once more through Warrendown, my foot trembling on the accelerator as I made myself restrain my speed. I was past the school when a dim shape lurched into my mirror and in pursuit of the car.

Only my feeling relatively secure inside the vehicle allowed me to brake long enough to see the face. The figure flared red as though it was being skinned from head to foot, and in the moment before its hands jerked up to paw at its eyes I saw it was Crawley. Had his eyes always been so sensitive to sudden light? I released the brake pedal and fumbled the gears into neutral, and saw him let his hands fall but otherwise not move. It took some determination on my part to lower the window in order to call to him. "Come on if you're coming."

I barely heard his answer; his voice was indistinct – clogged. "I can't."

I would have reversed alongside him, except there wasn't room to pass him if he stayed put in the middle of the road. I flung myself out of the car in a rage and slammed the door furiously, a sound that seemed to provoke a renewed outbreak of muffled drumming, which I might have remarked had I not been intent on trying to wave away the suffocating vegetable smell. "Why not?" I demanded, staying by the car.

"Come and see."

I wasn't anxious to see more of Warrendown, or indeed of him. In the backwash of the car's lights his face appeared swollen with more stubble than an ordinary day could produce, and his eyes seemed dismayingly enlarged, soaking up the dimness. "See what?" I said. "Is it your young lady?"

"My what?"

I couldn't judge whether his tone was of hysterical amusement or panic or both. "Beatrix," I said, more loudly than I liked to in the abnormal silence and darkness. "Is it your child?"

"There isn't one."

"I'm sorry," I murmured, uncertain whether I should be. "You mean Beatrix ..."

I was loath to put into words what I assumed she must have done, but he shook his blurred head and took an uncertain step towards me. I had the impression, which disturbed me so much I was distracted from the word he'd inched closer to mutter, that he couldn't quite remember how to walk. "What are you saying?" I shouted before my voice flinched from the silence. "What's absurd? Never mind. Tell me when you're in the car."

He'd halted, hands dangling in front of his chest. His protruding teeth glinted, and I saw that he was chewing – seemed to glimpse a greenishness about his mouth and fattened cheeks. "Can't do that," he mumbled.

Did he mean neither of us would be able to return to the car? "Why not?" I cried.

"Come and see."

At that moment no prospect appealed to me less – but before I could refuse he turned his back and leapt into the dark. Two strides, or at least two convulsive movements, carried him to the doorless entrance to the church. The next moment he vanished into the lightless interior, and I heard a rapid padding over whatever served for a floor; then, so far as the throbbing of my ears allowed me to distinguish, there was silence.

I ran to the church doorway, which was as far as the faintest glow from my headlights reached. "Crawley," I called with an urgency meant to warn him I had no intention of lingering, but the only response from the dark was a feeble echo of my call, followed by a surge of the omnipresent vegetable stench. I called once more and then, enraged almost beyond the ability to think, I dashed to my car. If I had still been rational – if the influence of Warrendown had not already fastened on my mind – I would surely have left my acquaintance to his chosen fate and driven for my life. Instead I fetched my flashlight from under the dashboard and, having switched off the headlamps and locked the car, returned to the rotting church.

As the flashlight beam wavered through the doorway I saw that the place was worse than abandoned. The dozen or so pews on either side of the aisle, each pew broad enough to accommodate a large family, were only bloated green with moss and weeds; but the altar before them had been levered up, leaning its back against the rear wall of the church and exposing the underside of its stone. I swung the beam through the desecrated interior and glimpsed crude drawings on the mottled greenish walls as shadows of pews pranced across them. There was no trace of Crawley, and nowhere for him to hide unless he was crouching behind the altar. I stalked along the aisle to look, and almost fell headlong into a blackness that was more than dark. Just in time the flashlight beam plunged into the tunnel which had been dug where the altar ought to have stood.

The passage sloped quite gently into the earth, further than my light could reach. It was as wide as a burly man, but not as tall as I. Now I realised what my mind had been reluctant to accept as I'd heard Crawley disappear into the church – that his footfalls had seemed to recede to a greater distance than the building could contain. I let the beam stray across the pews in a last desperate search for him, and was unable to avoid glimpsing the images scrawled on the walls, an impious dance of clownish figures with ears and feet so disproportionately large they must surely be false. Then Crawley spoke from the tunnel beyond the curve which my light barely touched. "Come down. Come and see."

A wave of the stench like a huge vegetable breath rose from the tunnel and enveloped me. I staggered and almost dropped the flashlight – and then I lowered myself into the earth and stumbled in a crouch towards the summons. The somnolence audible in Crawley's voice had overtaken me too, and there seemed no reason why I should not obey, nor anything untoward about my behaviour or my surroundings. Even the vegetable stench was to my taste, because I had inhaled so much of it since venturing back to Warrendown. Indeed, I was beginning to want nothing more than to be led to its source.

I stooped as far as the bend in the tunnel, just in time to see Crawley's heels vanishing around a curve perhaps fifty yards ahead. I saw now, as I had resisted hearing, that his feet were unshod – bare, at any rate, though the glimpse I had of them seemed hairier than any man's feet should be. He was muttering to me or to himself, and phrases drifted back: " ... the revelations of the leaf ... the food twice consumed ... the paws in the dark ... the womb that eats ..." I thought only my unsteady light was making the passage gulp narrower, but before I gained the second bend I had to drop to all fours. Far ahead down the increasingly steep tunnel the drumming I'd heard earlier had recommenced, and I imagined that the models for the figures depicted on the church walls were producing the sound, drumming their malformed feet as they danced in some vast subterranean cavern. That prospect gave me cause to falter, but another vegetable exhalation from below coaxed me onwards, to the further bend around which Crawley's heels had withdrawn. I was crawling now, content as a worm in the earth, the flashlight in my outstretched hands making the tunnel swallow in anticipation of me each time my knees bumped forward. The drumming of feet on earth filled my ears, and I saw Crawley's furred soles disappear a last time at the limit of the flashlight beam, not around a curve but into an underground darkness too large for my light to begin to define. His muttering had ceased as though silenced by whatever had met him, but I heard at last the answer he had given me when I'd enquired after the child: not 'absurd' at all.

169

He'd told me that the child had been *absorbed*. Even this was no longer enough to break through the influence of whatever awaited me at the end of the tunnel, and I crawled rapidly forward to the subterranean mouth.

The flashlight beam sprawled out ahead of me, doing its best to illuminate a vast space beneath a ceiling too high even to glimpse. At first the dimness, together with shock or the torpor which had overcome my brain, allowed me to avoid seeing too much: only a horde of unclothed figures hopping and leaping and twisting in the air around an idol which towered from the moist earth, an idol not unlike a greenish Easter Island statue overgrown almost to featurelessness, its apex lost in the darkness overhead. Then I saw that one of the worshipping horde was Crawley, and began to make out faces less able to pass for human than his, their great eyes bulging in the dimness, their bestial teeth gleaming in misshapen mouths. The graffiti on the church walls had not exaggerated their shapes, I saw, nor were they in costume. The earth around the idol swarmed with their young, a scuttling mass of countless bodies which nothing human could have acknowledged as offspring. I gazed numbly down on the ancient rite, which no sunlight could have tolerated – and then the idol moved.

It unfurled part of itself towards me, a glimmering green appendage which might have been a gigantic wing emerging from a cocoon, and as it reached for me it whispered seductively with no mouth. Even this failed to appal me in my stupor; but when Crawley pranced towards me, a blasphemous priest offering me the unholy sacrament which would bind me to the buried secrets of Warrendown, some last vestige of wholesomeness and sanity within me revolted, and I backed gibbering along the tunnel, leaving the flashlight to blind anything which might follow.

All the way to the tunnel entrance I was terrified of being seized from behind. Every inhabitant of Warrendown must have been at the bestial rite, however, because I had encountered no hindrance except for the passage itself when I scrambled out beneath the altar and reeled through the lightless church to my car. The lowered heads of the cottages twitched their scalps at me as I sped recklessly out of Warrendown, the hedges beside the road clawed the air as though they were determined to close their thorns about me, but somehow in my stupor I managed to arrive at the main road, from where instincts which must have been wholly automatic enabled me to drive to the motorway, and so home, where I collapsed into bed.

I slept for a night and a day, such was my torpor. Even nightmares failed to waken me, and when eventually I struggled out of bed I half believed that the horror under Warrendown had been one of them. I avoided Crawley and the pub, however, and so it was more than a week later I learned that he had disappeared – that his landlord had entered his room and found no bed in there, only a mound of overgrown earth hollowed out to accommodate a body – at which point my mind came close to giving way beneath an onslaught of more truth than any human mind should be required to suffer.

Is that why nobody will hear me out? How can they not understand that there may be other places like Warrendown where monstrous gods older than humanity still hold sway? For a time I thought some children's books might be trying to hint at these secrets, until I came to wonder whether instead they are traps laid to lure children to such places, and I could no longer bear to do my job. Now I watch and wait, and stay close to lights that will blind the great eyes of the inhabitants of Warrendown, and avoid anywhere that sells vegetables, which I can smell at a hundred yards. Suppose there are others like Crawley, the hybrid spawn of some unspeakable congress, at large in our streets? Suppose they are feeding the unsuspecting mass of humanity some part of the horror I saw at the last under Warrendown?

What sane words can describe it? Partly virescent, partly glaucous – pullulating – internodally stunted – otiose – angiospermous – multifoliate – Nothing can convey the dreadfulness of that final revelation, when I saw how it had overcome the last traces of humanity in its worshippers, who in some lost generation must have descended from imitating the denizens of the underworld to mating with them. For as the living idol unfurled a sluggish portion of itself towards me, Crawley tore off that living member of his brainless god, sinking his teeth into it to gnaw a mouthful before he proffered it, glistening and writhing with hideous life, to me.

# WORCESTER'S MOST ODIOUS RELIC

I
n historical terms, Worcester is one of England's most atmospheric cities.

It was originally a Roman settlement, and later a thriving medieval market town. It was also the site of the last battle of the English Civil War. Its centre is famous for its well preserved Tudor buildings, and it boasts one of the most ancient cathedrals in the whole of the United Kingdom. Worcester Cathedral was constructed in the 11$^{th}$ century, but portions of it, particularly in the library, remain from early Saxon times. The library itself has an arcane history; and is home to a grotesque relic which hints at a degree of savagery that many of us living in our peaceful age would have difficulty associating with a corner of England as picturesque as the Cotswolds.

This relic, which can only now be viewed by special appointment, is a rotted parchment-like material that once clad Worcester Cathedral's doors. In the early 19$^{th}$ century, the doors were removed as part of a large-scale renovation project, put into storage and not rediscovered until the year 1850, whereupon the old parchment was finally taken note of. It awakened memories of a past conflict in which almost all the rules of civilisation were put aside.

Between the 8$^{th}$ and 11$^{th}$ centuries, Viking armies launched raid after raid upon the British Isles. Initially the purpose was pillage, but as the decades rolled by it transformed into a full-blown invasion. 'Viking' is an Old Norse word, and it essentially means 'pirate'. This was certainly the way the Saxon English of the Dark Ages viewed them – as sea-roving brigands and mercenaries who crossed the North Sea from their Scandinavian homes in search of riches and power. The Vikings were pagan, enthralled to a pantheon of warlike gods and spirits who appreciated aggression and cruelty rather than piety and charity. This particularly terrified the wealthy English Church, which had always been protected from home-grown robbers who feared that God would strike them down if they offended against His representatives on Earth. With the Vikings under no such compunction, churches and abbeys, still largely undefended, became regular targets.

The Vikings enjoyed another advantage. The whole of Britain was divided into miniature kingdoms which waged constant wars among themselves, thus weakening their collective ability to resist. As a result, in their early days the Vikings won many victories over the English. They compounded this military superiority with acts of terror which cowed the population. One punishment for Saxons who refused to submit was the creation of so-called 'half-men'. Victims had their limbs severed and the stumps seared with hot irons so they would be left as nothing more than a torso and head, and therefore a burden on their families for the rest of their days. Another fearful punishment was known as 'the Walk'. The victim had his belly slit open and his guts nailed to a post carved with sacred runes, which he was then forced to march around at spear-point until he'd unravelled all his intestines. On top of this, the Vikings thought nothing of raping and brutalising their female captives, and selling all the children they took into slavery. Worcester, like many cathedral cities in Saxon England, was not spared these gruesome depredations. The cathedral itself was sacked on numerous occasions, and countless venerable personages died under the axes and broadswords of the Norse marauders.

But the Vikings were not to have it all their own way. The tide turned when King Alfred of Wessex won two major victories against them at Ashdown and Eddington in 871 and 878 respectively. More victories followed, and suddenly the Vikings, who themselves were now plagued by internal division, saw many of their conquests recaptured. Often, they saved their own skins (remember that phrase – it's important) by converting to Christianity. But there were still recalcitrant elements who continued to worship the Norse gods and fought to the death.

There could be severe repercussions for these unrepentant Vikings. Reports detail the English throwing Viking prisoners into pits filled with adders or starving wolves. But the most common method of exacting vengeance involved flaying Viking prisoners alive. Because their most serious crimes were deemed to be against God, their shredded skins were then fixed to the doors of the monasteries or churches they had raided.

By the high Middle Ages, almost every cathedral in England boasted a door to which a dried-out Viking skin had supposedly been fastened, and, after the 19$^{th}$ century discovery, it seemed that Worcester was no exception. In fact, local antiquarians gave Worcester's skin a detailed background, explaining that it had been shorn from the living carcass of a Viking chieftain who had first tried to burn the cathedral, and then had taken sanctuary inside it when the rest of his men were driven off.

*However, by the 20th century, historians had become dubious about these tales. Many of the leathery fragments were tested scientifically and almost all were found in reality to be tanned cowhides. So much for the vengeance of the Saxons, it was said. But then Worcester's Viking skin was tested – much later than the others, in the 1980s – by a team from Birmingham University. Everyone expected that this too would prove to be cowhide.*

*But it wasn't.*

*It was human.*

# THE LURKER
## Gary Fry


"You'd better believe it, honey."

That was the way Kate had responded to many questions I'd asked, her rich American accent always melting my jaded London heart. We'd regularly come on walking holidays to the Cotswolds, and Gloucester had been one of her favourite cities – a place in which she could enrich her outsider's passion for all things historically English.

And now there was Pam. Who wasn't Kate, of course, because my wife was dead.

Pam had never really been interested in outdoor pursuits, though I suppose when you get to my age you shouldn't be picky. I'd met her in a supermarket, our trolleys colliding at the top of two aisles, and we'd got talking like only the bereaved ever did: warily and yet ever mindful of friends' well-meaning platitudes about *life going on*. Then we'd had coffee together, then a meal and, before we knew it, we were dating.

The weekend break in the Cotswolds had been my idea, an effective way of placating my doctor who'd told me to take some exercise to help get my cholesterol in order. It was true that since Kate's death I'd been neglecting my fondness for walking, so I'd put the trip to Pam one afternoon in Regent's Park. She'd agreed, saying walking and sightseeing weren't really her thing but that she'd give it a go. She was fifty-six and I was nearly sixty. It wasn't as if we had time on our side or the luxury of choice. Either we made a serious go at this … or we didn't.

We used trains and buses to get between picturesque locations, exploring idyllic villages in which time seemed to have wound backwards (and in idle moments, that was truer than I felt comfortable with, because I'd often imagined Kate in my company, speaking in that fine US accent). The countryside in this area was peerless, rolling hills and farm fields stitched together by crooked walls and hedges bustling with wildlife. Escarpments like slippages in memory had left limestone layers exposed, filled with fossils not yet excavated. At one point, I remembered my late wife saying –

"Arnold, are there many shops in Gloucester?"

That was Pam, standing at the bus stop in the street from which I'd just strayed to take in the glorious views. I turned and replied,

"Yeah, I believe so. To be honest, I've never really taken much notice of that. There's a quite magnificent cathedral, though."

"A cathedral. Ah, right," she said, and that was when the bus arrived, we got on, and were headed for the great city.

It must have been about four years since I last visited Gloucester, and I was immediately struck by how different it all looked. I wondered whether this was because standards in the district had slipped or because I'd committed to memory only its good aspects. This time I noticed rough places rubbing up alongside the splendid spots, noisy pubs full of yobs squeezed between fine old buildings with original features. Eventually, after steering Pam away from a bank of high street stores, we reached the cathedral and entered, she motivated by my promise of a restaurant meal later this evening.

For a building full of rich history, Pam seemed to take little interest in any of it. Not for her the tombs of ancient monarchs and bishops, nor the many century-spanning examples of sculpture. Her interests perked up a little when we entered the famous cloisters, with their arched elaborate carvings and intricate stained glass windows (she'd seen this place in films, apparently). On the final stretch a bride was being photographed, her dress almost as elegant as her surroundings. When she saw us approach, she turned away from the male photographer, caught Pam's tender look in particular, and said, "Hey, I'm not getting married, you know. I'm not *that* foolish."

By this stage, with my memories stirred by the stroll around the cathedral, I was struggling to work out what was real or otherwise, but then I realised that this young woman was a model, posing for an upmarket catalogue. Nevertheless, her comment had upset me, and Pam didn't appear too happy, either ... though I wasn't sure our responses to the model's catty remark had an identical source.

Back outside, we paced along the River Severn, admiring disused dock storehouses converted into kitschy malls and eateries. We ate pâté and lobster while seated outside, watching youths rather more interested in each other than in the rich heritage of their native environment. Pam just smiled at these embracing couples, looking occasionally at me as if remembering her own first adventures in love. I glanced away, tired and troubled.

I was very fond of Pam, but there was ... something in the way of our relationship. After the meal, we strayed back into the city centre, catching a street performance by a juggling clown and evading a number of tramps hoping to acquire some of my money. The architect game had certainly furnished me with plenty of that, but not a penny of it had helped combat the cancer that had taken Kate so quickly, so brutally.

Shoving aside in my mind the hurtful past, I tried to interest Pam in a local attraction I recalled from my previous visits. This place of archaeological interest was the base of a Roman tower located underground at the end of one of the city's main shopping streets. Little more than the bottom few stones had survived the inevitable ravages of history, and a glass casement had been built over it, presumably to prevent vandals from finishing off what more nobly motivated enemies had attempted in the past.

"Isn't that sad," I said to Pam, who, to her credit, had also stooped to peer into the space beneath the thick sheet of protective glass situated above the whole monument. Declining sunshine was animating the gloom down there with twitching shadows, impossible movement.

"Isn't what sad?" Pam eventually replied, as if her husband hadn't died only years ago and she was quite unfamiliar with this devastating emotion.

I tried to imagine what Kate might have said in response to my comment. *You'd better believe it, honey*, was one option. She'd always been so intimately in touch with the way I thought, and it grieved me to reflect on what I'd lost.

Nevertheless, knowing little could be achieved thinking this way, I went rapidly on. "Well, this tower was presumably erected to help protect the city from intruders, and now *it* clearly needs protecting from its own people."

At that moment, a group of hooded youths came strutting along the street, shouting and laughing scornfully. This was an element of English life my late wife hadn't cared for, and as I thought I saw something stir near the shadowy monument beneath us, I reached out an arm to reassure Pam, foolishly believing that, in the event of any trouble, I could do anything positive to protect us.

The youths soon passed on, however, and I was able to slacken my hold on my new partner and look back inside that glass-topped chamber.

It was as empty as it had been earlier: as empty as my heart often felt these days.

We walked back to our hotel, a place I'd booked online from my plush Islington office. This was an old building, three storeys high, and we'd been assigned a room right at the top. For some reason I thought this was both a good and a bad thing, as if what would keep us safe would also prevent access to something offering redemption. Once I'd unlocked the door, Pam rushed inside, marvelling quite audibly over the grand four-poster, heavy curtains of the big bay window, and – perhaps most effusively of all – a flat-screen television mounted on one wall. She activated the TV at once and watched some light entertainment show while unpacking the few items of clothing she'd brought along in her backpack.

We removed our walking gear, and after a long shower, during which I pinched the ache from my eyes with taut fingertips, I returned to find Pam dressed in her nightgown, a breeze from the dark outside blowing up the curtains with a spectral restlessness.

"Feel better now?" she asked, blinking in the way she had whenever she was apprehensive. In truth, I found this quite an endearing characteristic, which drew out my protective nature.

At the time, however, I was still a little fraught, all the events of the days – the things the Cotswolds had done to my vulnerable mind – undiminished by the hot assault of water. "Better?" I asked, and knew I was being deliberately evasive. "Better than what, exactly?"

"Well," she replied, and lowered the volume of the TV, which was now broadcasting some inane situation comedy, "better than you've been all day."

"And how's that, then?"

"*Grumpy* is how I'd describe it."

"Nonsense, Pam," I said, lying in my dressing gown beside her on the bed. "I've just been … tired lately, that's all. Pressure of work, you know. That big job for the council."

She turned and looked at me, blinking again in that cute way. But I knew I was in trouble now. "That job you finished *last* week, you mean?" she asked, though at once I realised she wasn't expecting an answer.

I was busted – wasn't that the phrase used in the loathsome modern age to describe my present situation? My late wife and I had often lampooned these moronic linguistic tendencies, deriving genuine humour and an even closer attachment from the act. Then I'd often lapsed into some faux *olde worlde* English, and that had always seduced her. For Kate, the historical heritage of this country had been a constant source of delight, and one I'd used to my advantage, never having to pretend that my pleasures were anything other than they were. But that was true of her, too – her bold

American charm had delighted me unfailingly. We'd fitted each other perfectly.

And how could anyone else ever match up to that?

I felt a little sorry for Pam as she turned away and cranked the volume of the television back up. The sit-com she was watching was, ironically, an American show, and I couldn't help feeling that she was deliberately antagonising me by now repeating some of the lines. She knew of course the nationality of my late wife. I often had the impression, whenever I was in one of my all-too-regular moods, that she was jealous of my past with Kate. Pam had never come out and said this, but there were other methods to resort to – subtler methods; more insidious ones.

"Like, oh my God," she said, and then, "Hey, really radical, dude," and then – after the line was spoken word-for-word by one of the stupid characters in the comedy whose level of sophistication did little for Kate's home nation – Pam said …

*No, no, don't say it*, I thought, with a desperately unfathomable wish to prevent this latest development.

But then my new partner *did* say it.

"You'd better believe it, honey."

I just lay there, observing her. Then she turned her head to glance back at me. She wasn't blinking on this occasion, and looked simultaneously surprised and bemused by my fierce expression. I realised that I'd rarely talked about my late wife in detail, and so could just about believe that Pam's use of this American phrase had been coincidental. But *that* was a rational conclusion. And now my emotions were highly engaged, though mainly the negative ones.

"What's … what's wrong with you?" asked Pam, her tone credulous and fragile.

I surely had to remember that she was also recently bereaved; her husband had been a solid sort who'd left her comfortably off. I had the impression that there'd been few fireworks in their marriage, but that Pam had been happy enough. Her grief was genuine, but hadn't lingered like mine had. It had been about four years since both our partners had suffered premature deaths. For Pam, the memories were fond; for me, they were unbearable. And I couldn't blame her for that.

"I'm okay," I replied at last, turning to conceal my face, hoping she wouldn't pursue the matter. If she'd just switch off the TV and snuggle down beside me, that would be good enough. With the light out and wind gusting against the open window, I could focus on the relative merits of still being alive with at least a few good things going for me, of which Pam was surely one.

But she didn't back off. She ploughed right on.

"That Roman tower we saw today," she began, a tad obliquely; she rarely talked in riddles or metaphor, though perhaps such involuntary insight dredged this sort of material from even the least sophisticated people.

"What about it?" I asked, recalling the decided lack of movement I'd perceived inside that shadowy chamber.

"It reminds me of you," Pam said, with more of that intuitive certainty.

"In … in what way?"

She blinked again as she added, "Part of you is sealed off, inscrutable. You've built a protective casing around some vital section and nobody can get close."

*You'd better believe it, honey*, I thought, and just then, that empty chamber in my mind started stirring with half-hidden shapes, or perhaps just one prowling figure, now coming into view under that glass-topped casement . . .

I dismissed this notion at once, and replied, "Leave it, Pam. It's unwise to go there."

"But … but we're supposed to be having a relationship, aren't we? You're supposed to be with *me*."

At that moment, suddenly understanding her concerns and feeling sympathetic, I reached out an arm and tried to take hold of her. But she pulled away.

"No, I'm sorry, Arnold." She used the remote-control unit to deactivate the burbling television and then flicked out the bedside lamp, plunging the room into darkness.

The curtains were again stirred by an impudent breeze from that open window, where moonlight now crept in, weak and weary. Pam's walking gear was splayed across a chair at the foot of the bed, like something sitting and watching us, patiently biding its time. She slumped down beneath the sheets, turned over with embodied emphasis, and finally said, "You may think I'm quite shallow, and maybe that's true. But I'm *here*, Arnold. I want to be with you. You just have to … well, you just have to let *her* go."

She was right, of course, but had failed to factor in one crucial detail: I wasn't keeping hold of Kate; it was she who kept hold of me. I simply had no choice in the matter. Her presence was as rooted in my mind as that Roman tower base was embedded in the

180

Gloucester ground. And if I'd built a protective casement around this experience, just as Pam had suggested, it was surely intended to keep it from being damaged by those too insensitive to know better.

I settled down beside Pam, offering no response. She seemed to be waiting apprehensively, her back to me. I imagined her eyes wide open, blinking with expectation, but still a perverse aspect of my character prevented me from reassuring her. The truth was that I enjoyed spending time with her and liked her company a good deal. Even the infrequent sexual acts we'd lately enjoyed had been an unfeigned pleasure on my part. But something was missing for me. Maybe time would heal this wound. Perhaps when my late wife had become history, I'd be able to move on, escaping the web she'd woven like some stealthy insect on the make.

Realising she wasn't about to hear what she clearly wanted to hear, Pam exhaled sharply, her body stiffening in my enfeebled embrace. And then about thirty minutes later – during which the sounds of the district filled the air around us, rich and strange – we were both asleep.

My dream when it came was predictably troubling. I was back in Gloucester city centre, though on this occasion quite alone. It was night time, pitch dark, and directly up ahead was that Roman tower covered by its protective glass-topped housing. But what, on this occasion, was being protected? Against my suddenly frightened will, I stepped up close to the place, my limbs compelled by a perverse kind of hope. Then I looked inside the chamber … and saw its solitary occupant.

Moonlight made a parody of the face pressed against the underside of that thick sheet of glass. Somehow Kate had propelled herself up off the ground beside that Roman tower's base to stare with silent fixity into the goldfish-bowl world outside, presently occupied only by me. Startled, disturbed and pitiably aroused, I snatched a quick glance behind me and saw nobody else standing in this dream-street.

Then I glanced back at the figure below.

It was indeed my late wife, now dressed in a dirty white smock, looking up at me, her mouth a slack ruin as her teeth ground against the transparent surface between us. Her muddied hands had also lifted, placed flat against the unyielding surface. I placed my own against them, each separated from what they desperately longed to touch by an impenetrable inch. In response to this obvious restriction, Kate looked furious, as if she could suddenly move worlds. Her bloodshot eyes bulged in that glass-flattened face.

And then, with the same counterintuitive compulsion with which I'd arrived, I was swept away, at first striding backwards in the direction of the hotel occupied by my sleeping self, and then turning round to flee. I heard a sound in my wake, though couldn't identify its source, and when I finally reached my now surely unwanted destination I didn't dare look back, despite every fibre in my frame telling me that this was what I should do.

When I awoke the following morning, Pam was gone.

The first thing I noticed was her walking garments strewn over that chair at the foot of the bed. In broad daylight, these no longer resembled a person looking at me, rather a vacant shell, evidence of a discarded life. I got up and examined more of the room.

"Pam?" I called, wondering whether she was in the bathroom. But after I entered, unmindful of whether she was in a state of undress, I found the room empty, just our combined toiletries populating the back of the sink unit. Would she have left all her personal stuff behind if, after waking before me, she'd decided she'd had enough and then fled? I recalled she had an open rail ticket, which could take her back to London whenever she pleased. But was Pam really the kind of woman to do that?

I returned to the main room, checking the wardrobes in which she'd placed her clothing yesterday. Her overnight bag was slumped like a dying animal on a shelf near the bottom and a few garments were folded a little higher. I hadn't paid much attention to what outfits she'd brought along for the trip, not as I might have done with Kate, who'd always looked elegant and refined and … but damn it, I was supposed to be thinking about *Pam!* I really liked Pam. She was sweet and sensitive, and although she couldn't quite engage with me in that deeper way I'd always enjoyed with my late wife, wasn't that a failing of mine and my reluctance to adapt to my altered circumstances? I suddenly remembered how I'd treated my new partner the night before and felt immediate shame. I'd been cruel and undignified. Kate would have been appalled by this lack of honour, let alone Pam.

Just then, I noticed the curtains blowing up at the window. I parted the heavy material. From this high up in the hotel, the city of Gloucester and the Cotswolds beyond it lurked implacably beyond the pane, like a face and a body pressed against restrictive glass. I turned back, examining the carpet: there was no trace of Pam's nightdress anywhere. Perhaps she'd clambered into a few new items of clothing, pushed the nightdress into one pocket, and then departed with only her essentials: money, rail tickets, keys to her house. She might have deliberately left behind her walking gear as a symbolic affront to the lifestyle I'd tried to press upon her. My reasoning was growing increasingly desperate, I knew.

I looked back at the open window letting in slithers of cool morning air. Grubby fingerprints were visible on the edge of the pane, just where the parted section stood on its metal runner. The gap was large enough for someone to have thrown herself out, I realised, and immediately jerked forwards to look down. The pavement far below was deserted except for a tramp huddled in a dark sleeping bag. I'd lapsed into melodrama, anyway. Was I *really* worth someone killing herself over? Of course not.

It wasn't until I'd rapidly packed away what few items she'd left and then hurried downstairs to settle the bill that I entertained the ludicrous suspicion that perhaps something had come *into* the room and taken Pam from her bed. The lengthy elevator ride reminded me how foolish this suspicion was. The top floor was the third storey, maybe fifty feet high. What on earth could have clambered up an external wall to enter through a window?

At reception I asked the attractive young woman working there whether my companion had taken breakfast or checked herself out. I received rather a vacant expression in response, which might denote either confusion or embarrassment. In either case, the answer was negative and so I paid in cash – £117 – received my change and left.

There was only the tramp outside, who mumbled something as I approached. "Like a pale giant insect," I thought I heard, and then, "… scrabbled up the side and entered, and then came back out with its prey …"

He was clearly deluded or drunk on cheap sherry or cider, so I handed him the three pound coins I'd received in change from the hotel and was on my way.

It was now much later than nine o'clock and the city centre shops had been open a while. This suggested one explanation that hadn't occurred to me in the hotel. Maybe Pam had gone out early for a browse around the stores and would soon return to our room. This was so unlike the behaviour of Kate – my one previous lover, the person on whom I'd based my understanding of women – that it had never crossed my mind.

I spent a good half an hour searching the shops, growing impatient in crowded aisles, and hot and sweaty under the weight of my luggage. But there was no sign of Pam. After approaching a mobile phone store, I was reminded that although I was carrying my handset, she'd yet to start using one. I hurried on through the high streets, escalating unease making me ignore the many fine old buildings preserved there.

And then I reached that Roman tower base.

I hadn't been certain that this was where it was located, either because I was insufficiently familiar with the city, having only visited a couple of times in the past, or because the crowd of people currently standing around it had concealed its appearance. I was astonished that the attraction had drawn so much interest. Kate had often bemoaned the English's lack of interest in their heritage. But here were harried housewives, be-suited city gents and even a handful of school-dodging teenagers – as well as several police officers.

It clearly wasn't history these people were now taken by; it was something that had happened in the latter-day, perhaps even overnight. When I reached the crowd, I shouldered my way through to get a good look at this spectacle.

"You can't come any closer, sir," said one of the officers – a pasty-faced youth with violent pimples. "Please, back off."

But I'd already seen what I needed to.

The thick glass sheet that covered the ancient monument had been shattered into a number of sizeable shards. I immediately wondered what could have caused such damage. The glass was inches thick, so surely only an extremely heavy object dropped powerfully upon it could have managed the trick. Meddlesome youths, perhaps – the kind Kate and I had always described as destructive of a world we'd both hankered after? Maybe we'd sometimes romanticised the past, but what in truth was the alternative? To admit that this tawdry modern cultural landscape was all we had left: shops and TV and shallow preoccupations …

Cutting away from the vandalism, I couldn't be certain I'd heard another of the police officers – a female this time – say, "It doesn't make sense. All the broken glass is on the *outside*, as if … as if something has broken *out* of there."

Fragments of my dream propelled me towards the railway station: a figure stirring in shadows, a face pressed against glass. Then, as I boarded the first train for London, I thought about Pam and how much I felt sorry for her. It really wasn't fair to have to deal with such a messed-up man like me. I pictured her now, blinking in that vulnerable way she had whenever she felt apprehensive and had to speak some awkward words. My heart went out to her, and for once my late wife didn't intervene in the form of some irrepressible memory from the past.

All this confusion and panic must have weighed heavily on my mind, because by the time the train had exited the mischievous Cotswolds with all their impish memorial prompts, I'd fallen asleep in my chair. I dreamed again, this time of two figures huddled together down a moonlit Gloucester high street. The area was deserted except for this pair, who writhed and struggled as if one was doing unforgiveable things to the other. Then my dream-lens zoomed up close to these people – and I saw they were both women.

It was Pam and Kate.

The first – my new partner – was definitely the victim. Like some terrible arachnid travesty, the second – my late wife – seemed to be absorbing Pam, or perhaps forcing Pam to absorb her. Their bodies combined with organic resistance, liquid sounds reverberating in all the hollow dream-space around them. Bones ground and muscles merged, but then at last the two were just one: a woman who looked like Pam, though a little more knowing, her eyes sharp and narrowed. Moments later, she walked away, prowling the night, hands flexing with spindly grace.

I awoke as the train was nearing Paddington Station and my change for St Pancras. I felt transformed, and I hurried from platform to platform, fresh resolutions cutting through my frame. From my professional training I was familiar with a little modern philosophy and understood something about Freudian shifts in paradigms, how a new world of meaning could open up after a single resonant experience.

And had this now happened to me?

All I knew for certain was that I had to visit Pam in her Islington home. Did it really matter that she didn't share Kate's and my fantasy of an older, finer world than this one? In fact, might that make her less dangerously deluded? What I'd surely get from Pam was stability, because it was now abundantly clear that I lacked this in myself. And the thing she'd get from me was … what? Conscious commitment, perhaps, and a real effort to – what our simplistically profound friends had termed – *move on*.

I reached her terraced house and paced up to the front door. *Kate was gone*, I reminded myself and pushed this notion deep down inside me, building an even stronger casement around her memory on this occasion. And now, looking determinedly forwards, I had to engage with Pam as who she truly was.

In response to my knock, footsteps approached from inside the property. I hadn't even been sure anyone would be home, but now realised that my initial assumption about her having left me in the hotel had been correct. I had much to make up for, and as the door opened with a stealthy creak I now had an opportunity to do so.

"Don't speak," I instructed, as the woman emerged from the house and I launched into my intuitive defence. "I'm sorry for how I've treated you. It's almost as if I've been unfaithful. But I've seen my errors now. It's *you* I want to be with. So can we possibly make another go of it? Will you forgive me? Can we try again?"

Without blinking in that customary manner she had during such fraught episodes, the woman in the house who looked almost exactly like Pam replied at once.

"You'd better believe it, honey."

# THE BEAST OF ST. JOHN'S

For several decades there have been reports from all across rural Worcestershire of a mystery predator attacking and killing both farm livestock and wild deer. From as recently as 2009, reliable eyewitnesses, including dog-walkers, forestry workers and even police officers, have described an animal similar to a panther skulking along the county's leafy lanes. Not only that, the mutilated remnants of its meals have littered the surrounding woodlands.

The general consensus seems to be that the beast – or beasts, as there must be a breeding population, though this doesn't necessarily need to be large – is a black feline, about four feet in length, but very sleek and muscular. To date there have been no reported injuries to humans, though a pair of very large paw-prints were found on a parked car near Bromyard in 2001, and later that year a farm labourer at Droitwich became the subject of an actual attack when the animal leapt at him and knocked him from his bicycle.

Of course, stories about big cats roaming the English countryside are very common, though the Worcestershire wolds, and to a slightly lesser extent, the Herefordshire borderland, have become the heartland of the myth simply because of the preponderance of reports. But no live specimens have been captured and, somewhat puzzlingly, no clear photographs or videos have been taken depicting one of these animals. Experts do not deny the possibility that these stories could be true, though they deem it unlikely the suspect could be an actual panther. More likely, they feel it is a black leopard – a very hardy brute for whom the British climate would present no problems. In fact, conditions in rural England make it highly possible that such an animal could flourish: there is plenty of water and ground-cover, and a wide variety of potential prey. As the beast's existence is denied by the British authorities, it currently occupies the top of the food chain, and could live quite comfortably so long as its numbers remain small.

There are even historical explanations for such a presence. During the 1960s and 1970s, it was quite common for wealthy folk to own leopards and jaguars as trophy pets. But in 1976, tough regulations were introduced in the form of the Dangerous Wild Animals Act, which made such ownership very expensive. Rather than having their pets destroyed, a good number of owners simply *released them into the wild. It is also true that during World War Two, US and Canadian regiments stationed in Britain kept big cats as mascots. A number of these were also released before the regiments deployed overseas. Both of these scenarios have made it quite plausible that small populations of the creatures could now have taken root in remote country areas.*

*Thus far, the apparent lack of danger to humans is a cause for encouragement. Big cats are intelligent animals, and in countries where they are common they tend to stay away from human habitation as they have learned that to do otherwise can be fatal. And if the beasts of Worcestershire actually exist, they must be of high-level intelligence to have evaded human attention for so long.*

*But don't celebrate too soon.*

*In 2009, two local men spotted one of the animals half-concealed in the undergrowth close to a highway. It snarled at them, and fled. This sighting occurred in St. John's, which is not out in the countryside, but is a busy suburb of the city of Worcester.*

*Are the intelligent beasts getting bolder? And if so, how long before there is a genuine confrontation between them and us?*

# THE COTSWOLD OLIMPICKS
## Simon Kurt Unsworth

Fillingham first saw the women by the *dwile flonkers*.

He had spent the day walking around Dover's Hill, the shallow amphitheatre where the Cotswold Olimpick Games took place and had taken, he thought, some good photographs so far. The place was heaving and he had captured some of that, he hoped; the shifting bustle as people flocked from event to event and laughed and shouted and ate and drank. The sound of cymbals, mandolins, violins and guitars filled the air, along with the smell of roasting meat and open fires. The crowd, dressed in brightly-coloured costumes, danced and moved to the beat of drums.

There were five of them and they were watching as a circle of men held hands and danced counter-clockwise around another group of men. The men in the centre of the circle had a bucket and were dipping cloths in it and hurling them at the dancers; every time one of the cloths hit its target, the crowd laughed good-naturedly. When the cloth missed, arcing into the people beyond, a cheer went up and a man dressed in a costume of rags and wearing a hat that was too big for him would shout, "Ha! Jobanowl declares a penalty!" and the cloth thrower was given a large glass of ale to drink. The women were smiling as they watched, clustered tightly together, dressed similarly in white shift dresses and with their hair long and loose.

Fillingham wondered if they were some kind of act and took their photograph, thinking that if he could catch another one of them later, in performance, it might make a nice pair, *Artists at rest and work* or something.

The women were definitely a group, seemed to be in in tune with each other somehow, their heads bobbing to the rhythms of the music slipping through the air around them, their bodies turning in the same direction as though responding to invisible currents, like birds wheeling through the sky. When one of the sodden cloths, the *dwiles*, came towards them, they danced aside as though choreographed. The crowd cheered again as Fillingham lowered his camera, a knot of people jostling between him and the women as they tried to avoid the dripping missile, and when they moved aside the women were gone.

Fillingham let the press of the crowd drift him along the field, taking more photographs, this time of men dressed in smock shirts and clogs kicking at each other's shins, and then of another team of men destroying an old piano as people around them cheered and chanted a countdown. As dusk crept across the valley, his images took on a sepia tone, bleached of colour's vibrancy, becoming timeless. This was what he was after, he thought, a set of pictures that captured some of the sense of history of this event, of people stepping back for a day to celebrate nothing but tradition and enjoyment itself. This was a folk event, owned by everyone here.

On the cusp of gloaming giving itself to darkness, someone appeared as Robert Dover, the founder of the games some time in the early seventeenth century. He was riding a huge chestnut horse, and dressed in a tunic with a heraldic crest on his breast. A yellow feather bristled jauntily from the brim of his wide hat, bobbing as he rode around. His face was a white mask hanging down from under the hat, gleaming like bone, and he was waving a wand above his head that glittered and spat sparks. It was a sign that the bonfire was to be lit and the crowd began to move back towards the huge pile of wood at the far side of the fields, following the horseman as he capered and called exhortations for people to *hurry*, to *dance on*. Fillingham took more photographs, catching a good one of Dover rearing his horse in the centre of a mass of people like some ancient leather-bound general, all buckles and gleam and leadership.

Moving with the crowd, Fillingham found himself walking behind the women in white and spent a few moments appreciating the sway of their buttocks under the thin dresses before realising they were barefoot; mud was spattered up the pale skin of their bare calves in dark, irregular tattoos. The hems of their dresses were damp and dirty as well, he saw, the material swinging in sinuous patterns as the women moved. It was surprisingly erotic, this shift of skin and muscle under skin and cotton and dirt that crept up to where Fillingham's eyes could not follow, and he suddenly felt guilty, as though he was peeping. Feeling himself blush and glad of the darkness to cover his embarrassment, he raised his eyes to deliberately look away.

The fire caught quickly, leaping orange into the sky and throwing its heat across the crowd, creating a fug of temperature and sweat. Dover cantered around the blaze, crying "To ale! To ale!" as people cheered and shouted, his motionless face reflecting the fire's colours. Fillingham took more pictures, wishing, not for the first time, that his camera could somehow catch sound and smell as well, that it could trap the intensity of the heat and the noise and the scents of mud and flame and grass, and preserve them.

From huge bags on the ground near the fire, stewards in reflective tabards began to take long white candles and hand them out. The first few they lit and then let people ignite each others', a chain of flames that stretched out in a long, snaking line as the crowds began to walk slowly back towards Chipping Campden. Fillingham declined a candle and let the line carry him, snapping all the while.

The procession ended up in the small town's market square, where more revels were starting up. Most of the shops were still open, filling with tourists buying souvenirs, and stalls along the sides of the square did a brisk trade in food and drink. Down the streets off the square, small canvas tents with open fronts nestled between the shops, offering people the change to play chess and draughts, or games of chance like three card marney or craps. The square soon became busy, clusters of people spilling out into the surrounding streets, drinking and talking and shouting, filling the tents and shops, and Fillingham photographed as many of them as he could.

Fillingham had been in the square for around an hour when he saw one of the women again; she was moving through the crowds holding a beaten pewter flask and stacks of small plastic cups. He followed her, intrigued; this wasn't what he'd expected. The women had looked like a singing group, as though they were about to launch into madrigals or choral songs at any moment, but now they were separated and were doing – what? The woman he was following, tall and dark, was doing little other than giving drinks away, pouring small amounts of liquid into the cups and handing them out. Fillingham took photographs of her, watching as she distributed the cups, dipping her head and saying something each time someone drank. Fillingham moved closer, hoping to get a clearer image and hear what she was saying, but he kept losing her in the press of bodies. Her white dress glimmered amongst the shifting masses like a faltering beacon, and he followed.

The woman moved surprisingly quickly, without apparent effort, slipping along the alleyways around the square, darting through knots of people and giving out her drinks, nodding and speaking. Fillingham wondered where the other women were; doing the same thing throughout the games, he supposed, giving out their drinks and adding to the atmosphere. The day's games were over; now the celebrations started in earnest. He took more photographs as he followed the woman, of stallholders serving, of a group of Morris

Men drinking beer from tankards, their bells jangling as their arms moved. Fillingham saw that the tankards were attached to their belts by lengths of string or leather cord; some of the Morris Men had more than one, spares hanging to their side as they supped. Children ran between the legs of adults, chasing and chased and laughing.

"Would you like a drink, sir?" The voice was friendly, the accent difficult to place, not local but redolent of somewhere hot and dry and surrounded by embracing blue seas. It was the woman, holding out one of her cups to Fillingham. He took it and sniffed at the liquid it held; it was sweet and rich and pungent. The woman was looking at him expectantly, but he held the cup back out to her.

"No, thank you," he said. "I'm not drinking at the moment." *Not drinking alcohol*, he almost added, but didn't. Instead, he indicated his press badge in its plastic sheath dangling against his chest and gave her a rueful smile, saying, "I'm working. Perhaps later."

"The celebrations go on for many hours," said the woman. Above her, in the sky, a firework exploded, showering multi-coloured flames across the stars. "You can pay fealty at any time." Another firework tore open the sky, streams of colour painting the woman's shift blue and green, throwing their shadows downwards. For a moment, the woman's shadow self moved against the shadow Fillingham, pressing to him, and then another explosion above them sent them dancing apart, wavering, their edges rimed with yellows and reds, and then the woman was moving again.

She stopped at the people next to Fillingham, offering them drinks which they took. As they drank, she dipped her head again and spoke, and this time he was close enough to hear what she said. It was doggerel, some old rhyme he presumed, intoned as though it were a prayer. *Atmosphere,* he thought, snapping a last picture of her before her head rose from its penitent's pose. On the screen in his camera's rear, she looked small and pale, the swelling of her breasts only just visible under the cotton of her dress, her hair draping down in front of her face, her neck exposed and delicate. She lifted her head, giving Fillingham a last look that he couldn't quite fathom, and then she was gone.

*

By the time Fillingham decided to go back to his hotel, the atmosphere was definitely changing; most children and their parents had emptied from the crowd, leaving only the adults who were

192

drinking seriously. The amount of dancing had increased and the town square was full of moving figures and noise. Three or four different groups of musicians were playing, with more in the pubs, and the sound of violins and guitars and differing beats and voices was creating a discordance that Fillingham didn't enjoy.

The fireworks display had lasted for a few more minutes after the woman had left him behind, and had culminated in a huge explosion of reds and greens and blues and Dover using a megaphone to cry "To Ale!" again, the wand above his head spitting like some giant sparkler as he waved it around, creating endless looping patterns in the air above him. Fillingham had taken more photographs, trying one last time to catch the feelings and the sounds and the smells of Chipping Campden, with its twisting streets and cobbles and stalls and *olde worlde* charm that managed, somehow, to seem vibrant and real and not clichéd or faked. After, he had put his camera in his bag and gone back to his room.

He was staying in a chain hotel, and not an expensive one either. He used the cheap chains unless he was on a commissioned assignment and could charge the room to someone else, and had grown used to their uniformity. Each room was the same; identical cheap veneer with its wood-grain pattern to make up for the fact that the surfaces were all plastic, identical small TVs bolted to the wall with limited number of channels available, identical beds and bedding. Everything the same, from city to city, even down to the pictures screwed to the corridor walls and the carpet with its not-too-subtle pattern of brown and skeined red. He had become almost fond of it, in the knowing what to expect and predictability of it all. At this end of the market, there were no individual flourishes in the room, no soap or shampoos in the bathroom, only two sachets of coffee, two cartons of milk, two tea bags by the small white kettle that each room came equipped with.

Like most of the hotels Fillingham stayed in, part of the reason it was cheap was that it was out of the town centre. Chipping Campden was small enough to be charming at its heart, but even this town had a business district and some minor industry, and the hotel was in this area, a ten minute walk from the cobbled lanes and town square. The view from his window was of a car park for an office block and, beyond this, the corrugated roof of a garage. The garage was also part of a chain, Fillingham noticed, his mood oddly low; after a day amongst so many people, so many colours, so much tradition and vibrancy, looking out on identikit companies from an identikit hotel was depressing. It wasn't how he usually felt, and it was unsettling in a way he couldn't quite identify. Dropping the blind down, he went and lay on his bed. The mattress was unpleasantly soft and moved under him, his book and camera, lens cap on, bouncing gently beside him. He turned on the television, turned it off again after hopping through the channels and finding nothing but blandness. Finally, he sat up, sighing.

Distantly, the sound of revels reached him and Fillingham wondered about going back and joining them and then decided against it. By the time he had left, most of the people there had been drunk and pairing off, and he'd end up feeling left behind, stood to one side and watching but unable to join in. He'd end up miserable, wishing he'd brought his camera and seeing things in terms of their composition, their visual attractiveness as flat images; the lens stood between him and these things, even when it wasn't actually there. He sighed again and put his shoes on.

Although it was late, the shop along the road was still open and happy to serve him; Fillingham bought a bottle of white wine, taking one from the refrigerator so that it was cold. He didn't drink alone often, but tonight he would, and try not to think of the women in their shift dresses covering muddy legs and taut thighs and high breasts. There was no one to betray if he did so, no wife or girlfriend; he simply knew that thinking about them would make him feel worse.

Walking back to the hotel, Fillingham smelled the scents of the day's games and the ongoing party: burning wood and paper and powder, meat, malty beer, spices and wine. The skyline ahead of him glowed orange, the dark shapes of buildings painted in shadow between him and the bonfire at Dover's Hill. Here and there, tiny yellow flickers bobbed through the gloom as people moved distantly with their candles. It would make a good picture, he thought, fireflies of light set against the solidity of the angular buildings, skittering and indistinct, a perfect metaphor for the way folk traditions survived in the modern world. He wished he'd brought his camera, and then sighed again at his own inability to detach himself from his lens.

Fillingham's room was on the third floor of the hotel, the uppermost, on the opposite side from the entrance. He was too tired to take the stairs so used the lift, emerging into a corridor decorated with featureless watercolours. He went past doors with 'Do Not Disturb' signs hanging over their handles, past the muffled dissonance of televisions and conversations, before coming around the corner to the stretch that contained his room.

One of the women was at the far end of the corridor.

It wasn't the one Fillingham had spoken to earlier in the evening; this one was taller, blonde instead of dark, fuller-figured, but she too was carrying a beaten flask and had a bag hanging at her side. As Fillingham watched, she took a small plastic cup from the bag and poured a measure of liquid into it from the flask; the drink looked thick and viscid.

"A libation," she said, holding the cup out. Her voice was deep and mellow, filled with sly amusement.

He glanced down at his bottle of wine, sheened with condensation, the neck cold in his fist, and said, "Thank you, but no. I don't like to mix my drinks." He sounded prissy, even to himself, but couldn't help it; it was late and he was tired and miserable, and whatever opportunities he had hoped the night might present felt old and lost to the past. This woman was a tendril of the event occurring down the road without him, reaching out, and her presence in the hotel was jarring, throwing his lowering mood into even sharper relief.

"You refuse?" she asked.

"Yes," said Fillingham, and went to his room door.

As he unlocked it, he was conscious of the woman simply watching him; just before he opened it, she said, "It is a small thing, a simple toast. Join me?"

"No," said Fillingham again. Even from the other end of the corridor, he could smell the drink, pungent and spicy, and the mud that was smeared across the woman's legs. The odour was cloying, unpleasant, made saliva squirt into his mouth as though he was about to vomit. He swallowed, glancing at the woman to find her still staring at him and holding the cup out. Her nipples were prominent through the material of her dress and he had a sudden strong impression that she was naked under the thin cloth. She stepped forwards, still holding the cup out towards him. Fillingham swallowed his own spit, warm and swollen, and then opened his door, stepping into the room without looking at the woman again.

Its banality was reassuring. Fillingham poured some of his wine into one of the cheap white porcelain mugs and took a large swallow, unsure what had just happened. Why was he so bothered? Ordinarily, the sight of an attractive woman, and she had been attractive, no doubt about it, would have pleased him. Even if nothing had come of it, he could have flirted, hopefully made her smile. Instead, she had disturbed him in a way that was unclear even to himself. She was out of context, yes, away from the games and celebrations, but that couldn't have been it. Her smell was strong, not pleasing, but again it couldn't have been just that. He took another mouthful of wine and realised.

Darkness. The woman had been in darkness.

The hotel, like all the others in the chain, had corridors whose lights did not remain on all the time; instead, they were triggered by movement, yet the woman had been standing in a pool of shadow. She had come into the corridor, moved along it as she spoke to Fillingham, and the lights had remained off. He drank more wine, was surprised to find he'd emptied the mug, and then started as someone knocked hard on his room door.

Hot saliva leapt into Fillingham's mouth and he swallowed again, tasting something like electricity and an afterimage of wine, and thought, *Why am I afraid? It's a woman, and a near-naked one at that! What harm can she do me?* He went to the door as the knocking sounded again, picking his camera up off the bed as he went.

The woman was standing away from his door, perhaps twenty feet along the corridor, still in darkness. Her dress glimmered in the shadows, a white smear toped by her pale face. Her lips were red, almost as dark as the shadows crowding her shoulders, and she was smiling.

"What do you want?" asked Fillingham.

"You to celebrate with us," she replied, holding out the cup again. The liquid inside slithering up and then down again, and even in the poor light Fillingham saw the residue it left in the clear plastic sides glistening and clinging like oil. "Devotions must be paid."

"What?" said Fillingham. "Look, I appreciate you've got this weird acting gig at the games and you're only doing your job, but please, it's late and I'm tired and I don't want to drink whatever that is."

"A last enquiry: you refuse?"

"Yes! I refuse! Now, just leave me alone." To emphasise what he was saying, Fillingham lifted his camera and took a photograph, the light of the flash filling the corridor with a leaching whiteness that painted the woman into a colourless mass for a moment. As the dancing ghostlights cleared from his eyes, the woman nodded and then lifted the cup to her lips and drank the liquid it contained. Keeping the cup at her lips, she thrust her tongue out into it and

196

Fillingham saw it writhe within, licking at the remaining drips of drink. It should have been erotic, he thought; he was sure it was *meant* as erotic, but somehow it wasn't, it was crude and unpleasant. Her tongue was dark and looked slimy, glittering inside the clear plastic walls of the cup. Finally, she dropped the cup to the floor, lowered her head and muttered something that sounded Latin or Greek. Before she could look up at him again, Fillingham shut his door.

Still unsettled, Fillingham sat at the counter that ran across the room under the window, shifting the mess of magazines and coins that he had dropped there and putting the camera in its place. He poured himself another mug of wine, intending to look through the pictures he had taken that day. He always found it calming, seeing his images scrolling before him, seeing the life in them reduced to tiny rectangles of colour and composition like butterflies pinned to card. He hoped that he had managed to capture the sense and energy of the Olimpick Games and the celebrations afterwards, and anticipated that he could sell some of the pictures and use others for his portfolio.

The last picture he had taken, of the woman in the corridor, was the first one he looked at, and he saw immediately that it was ... wrong. It was difficult to see it clearly on the small screen, but the air around the central figure of the woman was filled with shapes. No, with a *single* shape that had lots of pieces, he thought, something that writhed behind the woman with too many limbs too count. He wished he had brought his laptop with him in order to look at the image on its larger screen, but he hadn't wanted to carry the extra weight for an overnight trip, so he was left with the camera's display. Squinting, he tried to make out details. Was that skin? Fur? Teeth? Hands, or clawed feet? There were things curling around the woman's legs from behind her, as though the dirt on her skin had gained mass and was lifting itself towards the camera. What was going on here?

The woman herself seemed normal except for her eyes, which were entirely black and much wider than he remembered them being; it made little sense, because if she was reacting to the flash, her pupils should have contracted not expanded. Quickly, he scrolled back to the earlier pictures, to the ones of the other woman distributing drinks and then to the ones of the five females standing together by the dancing men. The same distortions were evident in all the photographs, things fluttering and shifting in the air behind them. They were clearest in the picture he had taken of the woman bending her head after giving the group of people her drinks; it was still impossible to see what it was, but it gave an impression of limbs, too many limbs, claws that curved back on themselves, eyes that gleamed like dark bone, a pelt, or skin that was rough and ridged, or possibly feathers.

Fillingham pushed his chair back and went to rise and that was when the hands fell on his shoulders.

They pushed him down into his chair, clenching around his shoulders painfully. Fillingham tried to twist and managed to shift a few inches, craning his neck around. His door was open and the five women were standing in his room; the blonde one was holding him and the brunette he had photographed earlier was by the door. The others were motionless by the bed. "What ..." he started but the women, speaking as one, interrupted him.

"You must pay obeisance to partake in Dover's Bacchanalia," they said, a single voice from coming from all their mouths. "You refuse to partake in the tribute yet drink wine. This cannot be." One of the women, shorter and red-haired, reached out without appearing to move and lifted his wine from the table. She raised it to her nose and sniffed and then upturned it, pouring the remaining liquid across his bed, dropping the bottle into the puddle when it was empty.

"Who are you?" Fillingham said, gritting his teeth against the pain of the grip; the woman's hands were extraordinarily strong and felt unlike a human hold, as though her skin were a mere covering for something else, something muscular and old and venomous.

"We are Dover's Children," they said, still in unison. Outside the room, something heavy crashed and the floor vibrated. "He is our father, the father of games themselves." There was another crash and a long, low noise like a howl torn inside out.

"I don't understand," Fillingham said, still trying to twist free of the woman's hold. There was yet another crash from somewhere out of the room but closer, and this time everything shook, the wine bottle rolling to the edge of the bed and falling to the floor with a dull thud.

"The games were a gift to Dover from that which comes, given to him in dreams so that he might, in turn, gift it on," the women said. "A gift, and all that people need do on this one night is to take the drink in honour of the gift-giver, to drink and then to worship in inebriation and heat and the movement of flesh and the knowing of each other. You refused the drink three times."

There was another crash from the corridor, still closer. Another, and the door shuddered, dust vibrating from its top and hanging in the air. The lights flickered. Another crash and the lights went out completely. In the sudden darkness, one of the woman moved and the blind was torn from the window, falling to the desk in a noisy tangle. Leaping orange reflections filled the room. *How is no one hearing this?* thought Fillingham, pulling uselessly against a grip that was getting tighter, was digging into him and tearing.

"It only comes for you," said the women, as though hearing his thoughts. "All others have given honour, or do not join the revels. All around, those who drank the tribute and heard the prayer are communing with each other through song and flesh and note, or they sleep undisturbed because they take no wine or beer." The room was suddenly filled with noises, with grunts and shouts and moans and tunes, with the images of dancing and clothed flesh and naked flesh, of people losing themselves to pleasure, and then the sounds and images began falling away, layer after layer stripped to nothing as though lenses were falling between Fillingham and them, distancing him, swaddling him away from the rest of the world.

"Give me the drink now," he managed to say.

"Offence is already taken," the women said, and the one holding him let go of his shoulders and stepped back. Fillingham snatched up his camera as he started to rise but something lashed into him, a hand tipped with claws or bone, and he pitched sideways into the wall, falling to his knees as he bounced away from it.

"He comes," intoned the women. There were more crashes from the corridor, closer and closer, faster and faster, and then the doorway was filled with a huge figure.

It was Robert Dover, only it wasn't. It was massive, having to stoop as it entered the room and the women took up a low moan, swaying. Its head brushed the ceiling as it straightened, the huge moon of its masked face glowing palely. Its eyes were completely black and in them Fillingham saw something roiling and twisting about itself, something that glittered and rasped and sweated. It stepped fully into the small space, and green and red and blue fire boiled across the ceiling above it, gathering in streamers and falling to the floor in long, sinuous fronds. Fillingham screamed and tried to rise but again one of the women struck him, sending him sprawling. He managed to raise his fist, still holding the camera, and fired off a single picture. The glare of the flash leaped across the room and for a brief moment the fire was gone, the women were reduced to pale shades, Dover to a ragged and spindly thing that capered in the light, and then the fires were back and Dover's shape was gathering, thickening, the mask dancing with the colours of the flames and it was coming towards Fillingham with its arms open wide in a lover's embrace.

> *I cannot tell what planet ruled, when I*
> *First undertook this mirth, this jollity,*
> *Nor can I give account to you at all,*
> *How this conceit into my brain did fall.*
> *Or how I durst assemble, call together*
> *Such multitudes of people as come hither ...*
> **Robert Dover, 1616**

# GOD'S DIRE WARNING

The first battle of the English Civil War was probably the least professionally managed of the entire conflict. It was fought at Edge Hill, in south Warwickshire, on October 23$^{rd}$ 1642, and it occurred when the Royalist army of King Charles 1 and Parliamentarian forces under the Earl of Essex made accidental contact with each other, and commenced a brutish slugging match with neither side operating under a firm plan of action.

Several ridiculous incidents occurred during the course of the fighting: for example, the Parliamentarian cavalry was not trained in hand-to-hand combat, and this in an era when firearms usually discharged one shot before the two sides joined, which resulted in them fleeing the field after firing off a single volley. The Royalist cavalry, on the other hand, instead of pressing home their advantage, broke the charge that would have secured them an instant victory in order to loot their opponent's baggage train.

The final death-toll was roughly about 500 fatalities incurred on either side, with perhaps four times as many wounded. It was a scene of carnage at the time, but compared to later clashes during the war this was a relatively minuscule butcher's bill. In fact, the English Civil War – fought between 1642 and 1651 – would soon escalate into a conflagration that would consume all four of the nation-states of the British Isles: England, Scotland, Wales and Ireland. The final tally of those killed in action during those nine years of constant, bitter struggle was an estimated 100,000 – an incredible figure given that this was the pre-industrial era (and that the British population at the time only numbered about six million). No attempt has even been made to reach a total for the non-combatants who died, but it's perhaps no surprise that not long after the fighting on that first day concluded, something would occur which in retrospect could be viewed as a portent of approaching catastrophe.

It's important to remember that the engagement at Edge Hill was the first major battle on English soil since 1513 (when an invading Scottish army was heavily defeated at Flodden). Royalists and Parliamentarians had skirmished a month earlier near Worcester, but Edge Hill was the first real blood-letting and certainly the point of no turning back. The news of it sent a shockwave through the entire country. Perhaps that is why folk were immediately inclined to believe the small group of shepherds who on Christmas Eve that same year claimed to have been lured back to the battlefield by what sounded like a renewal of hostilities. Baffled because they knew there were no longer opposing forces in the area, they crested a nearby ridge and found themselves gazing down on a frozen and empty battlefield. However, when one of them happened by chance to glance upward, he was stunned to behold two armies clashing fiercely in the sky over their heads.

Terrified, the shepherds fled to nearby Kineton and reported the incident to a local parson and a magistrate. The two officials hastened back to the battlefield. At first all was quiet, but then the heavenly conflict began again, and continued for several minutes. Convinced they were witnessing a sign of God's disapproval rather than a simple ghostly after effect, these august persons sent word to the Royal Court at Oxford. Charles was so intrigued that he ordered a number of his officers to the scene. All later swore testimonies that they had witnessed the astonishing event repeatedly over a period of several days. In fact some of the men – seasoned soldiers and intellectuals – were very badly affected as they had recognised friends and colleagues who had been killed in the engagement.

Needless to say, the warning apparition did not prevent the continuance of the bloody conflict, and an entire generation of Britons would soon die at each other's hands in the most terrible violence. Whether either side was made afraid by the spectral omen is unrecorded. In the way of these things, they each most likely took it as a sign that their cause was just and the other side doomed.

# A TASTE OF HONEY, A HORROR OF STONE
## John Llewellyn Probert

It wasn't really right, bringing children to a graveside memorial service.

That was what Sharon kept telling herself as the car sped south from Stratford. After all, her husband Mark's father had died a year ago and they'd all gone to the funeral. It wasn't anybody but the stonemason's fault that the stone hadn't been ready until now, and who could blame his mum for wanting a couple of people to be there while the local vicar read a few words over it? No, the children were best left with someone who could look after them while she and Mark had a rare weekend without them. Still, she had felt terribly guilty waving them goodbye yesterday, and their forlorn faces hadn't helped.

After dropping the kids off at Sharon's mum's in Birmingham, they had spent the night at a Travelodge in Stratford-on-Avon. It was always a bit of a strain for her visiting Mark's elderly mother but fortunately Mark realised it, and after all the trouble they'd been through with the burglary back in Nottingham they had figured they deserved a night to themselves before setting off for the tiny village where she lived.

Sharon looked out of the window at the countryside rushing by. Perhaps this would be a nice place to live, she thought, away from the city and the muggers and the crap schools for her kids and the astronomical rents that meant they couldn't even have a proper family holiday this year. Maybe somewhere around here would be a better place to bring her children up in. Somewhere that sounded nice, relaxed, countrified. Sharon peered at the map for inspiration and immediately grimaced.

"They've chosen bloody weird names for some of the places around here," she said.

Beside her in the driving seat of their little Nissan, Mark grinned. "Such as?" he said, keeping his eyes on the road.

"Well, how about 'Slaughter'?" She sniffed. "They couldn't even be content with having just the one – apparently there's an Upper and a Lower."

That earned a knowing nod from her other half. "I remember Dad telling me about that when I was little. Apparently Slaughter's from the old English meaning wet and muddy – nothing to do with killing at all."

"Now why does that not surprise me?" she said, flipping the page over. "Next you're going to tell me that Painswick has nothing to do with an unusual obsession with candles?"

That caused her husband's grin to widen, quite possibly from the memory of what they had been up to before leaving the hotel that morning. "I've no idea," he said, "but I very much suspect it's got nothing to do with what you're thinking right now."

Sharon threw the map onto the back seat.

"At least your mum lives somewhere that doesn't sound as if it's going to be harbouring a bunch of chainsaw-wielding loonies," she said. "So what is the derivation of 'Cornerston'? Is there something special about one of the churches there?"

"You've seen the only church they've got and it's nothing special," said Mark. "At least not in terms of its architecture."

"Maybe there was once, but it's not there anymore," said Sharon, leaning back. She spent the next two minutes fidgeting in her seat before admitting to herself the reason why. She put on her best apologetic expression before turning to her husband again. "Oh God Mark," she said. "I'm really sorry about this but I need the loo again."

Mark sighed. "Didn't you go before we left Stratford?".

She nodded. "But you know me and my small bladder. Besides, the doctor said the antidepressants could cause it as a side-effect." She looked pleadingly at him and then out of the window at a landscape that offered endless possibilities for crouching unseen. "Could you stop? I'm really, really sorry."

"Can't you wait until we get to Moreton-in-the-Marsh? It can't be more than a couple of miles down the road."

She shook her head. "I think I'll be in trouble before then."

Mark gave her a mock admonishing look. "No more tea for you if we have a long car journey planned." He pulled over to the side of the road. "Or even a short one."

She slapped his arm playfully and got out of the vehicle. The A429 was a bit too busy to risk staying by the car so Sharon eyed the small copse that Mark had stopped beside. In there would be as good as anywhere, she thought, hoping it didn't surround the cottage of some little old lady, who was about to get a bit of a shock if it did. She skipped over the ditch running parallel to the road and immediately collided with a wire fence that was almost invisible

204

against the backdrop of the trees. For the first time today she was thankful that she had worn jeans instead of a skirt on this warm summer's morning, as she levered herself over it. As soon as she was on the other side she felt a gash of pain. She looked at her left hand to see blood welling from a cut in the soft flesh below her thumb. When she examined the fence more closely, she could now see the line of sharp barbs she had been lucky to avoid. Except for one.

*Stupid*, she thought as she reached into her pocket for a tissue, only to find she had neglected to bring one. Well, it was pointless to stand here chastising herself when nature was calling. She turned and made her stumbling way across the uneven ground, regularly having to pull either one foot or the other free from long grass that was doing its best to ensnare her. The copse seemed further away than it had from the road, and by the time she was within its shadowy embrace she was out of breath from exertion. She leaned against the trunk of a tree, panting, her eyes taking time to adjust to the cool dimness. She took care of what she had come there for, and was about to leave when she saw something flicker ahead of her – a flash of yellow that, when she concentrated, came again and again.

*Shit!* she thought. *That'll be the old lady's cottage, where she's probably seen what I've done in her garden.* Under the circumstances she knew very well that Mark's advice would have been to get out of there as quickly as possible, but she had more pride than that, and if she had upset someone, living way out here in the middle of nowhere, she was perfectly prepared to apologise and ask if she could make amends. Her mother had always taught her the value of a clear conscience and she knew that if she didn't pursue the matter it would bother her for the entire weekend. She did her best to ensure that she looked presentable, and noticed that her hand was still bleeding.

*Bloody thing!* she thought as she made sure to hold it away from her clothes. Shouldn't it have stopped by now? Maybe there was something on the barbed wire. Maybe, she thought with a pang of horror, this was how tetanus started. She should probably get a shot anyway, traipsing around in the countryside like this.

She made her way towards where she thought the building was, marvelling at how abruptly the grassy terrain had changed to the dry hard-packed desiccated earth that was now beneath her feet. Despite the warmth of the day, it was so much colder within the shade of the trees that the sweat on her body had rapidly become uncomfortable. She reached round to unstick her shirt from her back, only to be rewarded with the shock of a greater chill as a gentle breeze played upon her damp skin, raising gooseflesh and making her yearn for a coat. The dampness seemed to extend to her surroundings as well, as she felt her nostrils stung by the cloying odour of mouldering vegetable matter.

*Not much further*, she told herself as more of the yellow structure up ahead began to reveal itself. *Not much further now and you'll be out of this horrible cold wood with its dusty ground and its freezing bloody winds and its trees that look like –*

She paused. The trees *did* look weird. She hadn't noticed it before, but then she hadn't really been paying attention. From the road they had looked like ordinary conifers but in here they resembled nothing she recognised. The trunks were as thick as ancient oaks and covered in tumorous eruptions, almost as if they were so old they had succumbed to warts. Or cancer, she thought with a shudder. The branches were wrong, too. Instead of reaching for the sunlight, they seemed to be pointing down towards the mottled, diseased-looking earth, their leaves so dark green they were almost black. By rights they shouldn't have been able to survive in this kind of light anyway, Sharon thought, as she looked at them more closely, realising with a shudder that with each leaf's threadlike five-point arrangement, they resembled withered claws the size of her own hand. Thankfully the path she was on kept her clear from their grasp.

She stopped, suddenly gripped by panic. There hadn't been a path when she had come in here, had there? She had just been making her way randomly through the trees. Now it almost seemed as if they had stepped aside for her to allow her to pass.

*Or were guiding her to somewhere they wanted her to go.*

She turned back only to see the trees closing in on her. Silly, she thought, trying hard to quell her rising anxiety. You've just stumbled into a clearer area, that's all. *But if that's the case why can't the sun get through?* said the voice she was trying hard to ignore. She could see more of the yellow stone just up ahead, and she decided she should run the last bit of the way, just to get out of the cold that was starting to make her shiver.

She emerged into a sunlit clearing and realised, as she was bathed in its reassuring warmth, that she was almost crying with relief to be out of that bloody awful forest. She took several deep breaths, wondering what on earth the person who lived in the cottage must be thinking. It was only when she looked up that she realised it wasn't a cottage.

It wasn't a cottage at all.

It was a circle of standing stones.

The sun glinted off them as Sharon took her bearings. There must have been more than thirty of them. Each one was easily twice her height and set at an equal distance from its neighbours. It was only when she examined one up close that she realised how uniform they were – perfect oblongs quarried from the yellow rock so prevalent in these parts it had become known as 'Cotswold Stone', which would also explain the yellow glint she had seen through the trees.

She stared at them, amber monoliths that looked so unlike those comprising the cold, forbidding stone circles she had seen elsewhere in the country. She wondered if the surface of the nearest stone was as smooth and flawless as it looked, and reached out a hand to touch it. The rock was warm and inviting to the touch – she could not think of better words to describe it, and she was surprised to discover how unwilling she felt to take her hand away. It was with a peculiar sense of disappointment that she finally withdrew it, wondering why she hadn't noticed the red blemish before until she realised she had tainted the perfect yellow stone with her own blood.

She felt a sense of shame out of all proportion to what she had done, almost as if she had defiled it somehow. She lifted her arm to wipe the blood away with her sleeve, the sun glinting in her eyes momentarily as she did so.

When she looked again the blood had gone.

Sharon breathed easily again. There couldn't have been as much blood as she'd imagined. Perhaps there hadn't been any at all and it had merely been a trick of the light that had changed a brief shadow to a scarlet stain. She raised her hand, to see that the cut had now stopped bleeding and in fact looked much less serious that it had before. She probably didn't even need that tetanus shot, she thought, as she took a step inside the circle.

If the forest had been a grim land through which she had found it necessary to journey, the circle felt like home. The closer she got to the centre the more she felt suffused by the warm glow of the sunlight and smiled upon by the vivid azure of the summer sky. She resisted the urge to lie down on the fine soft grass that grew within, permitting herself one more minute of tranquillity before she had to get back to Mark and his car and his mum and the stultifying dullness of the real world.

No, she thought, spreading her arms wide, the better to drink in the place she had found. This was the world. The real world. Out there was just a make-believe created by people with no imagination and a thirst for routine, banality and boredom. In here was life, vitality, everything that was vibrant about the world.

If only she could stay.

A loud blast from Mark's horn brought her back to the world she had managed to leave for a moment. *Stop mooning about for God's sake*, she thought, pulling herself together. As she left the circle she could feel something pulling at her, gently but insistently, not wanting her to go, and she was surprised to feel tears on her cheeks as she dragged herself back through the copse and out onto the roadside. The journey back seemed much quicker and she was careful this time to avoid the barbs on the wire fence as she hopped over and got back into the car.

"Are you alright?" her husband asked.

"Fine," she said, offering him a teary smile.

"And the way you said that means you're not. That and of course the fact that you've obviously been crying."

"I cut my hand," she said, showing him her punctured flesh, some slight bruising the only evidence now of her recent trauma. For some reason it felt terribly important to her that she not share what she had found in there, not with Mark or anyone, not for the moment. For the moment it was all hers.

"It doesn't look too bad," he said. "Have you had a tetanus jab in the last ten years?"

"Yes," she lied, unable to explain why, other than she didn't want anything of the modern world to intrude on what had just happened to her, not even on the injury she had sustained. To do so would be to somehow taint the experience. "Is there much further to go?" she asked, to change the subject.

"Not far at all," he replied, pulling back onto the road. "In fact we should be there in about fifteen minutes. A shame we had to stop really."

"I'm glad I did." Sharon looked back at the receding wood and the empty featureless land surrounding it. "I'm glad I did."

\*

"How lovely to see you again, darling." Mark's mother greeted Sharon with an exaggerated display of affection Sharon could have done without. Her sore hand throbbed as Madeleine Markham embraced her briefly. As the old woman's lips brushed her cheek, she caught a whiff of honeysuckle that almost made her cough.

"How was the trip down?" Madeleine asked, moving to take the boiling kettle from the black iron range that took up most of the far kitchen wall.

"Alright," Sharon replied, wishing Mark was here rather than taking the bags upstairs to their room. She put her handbag on the broad wooden table that dominated the kitchen and offered to help.

"Oh that's alright, my dear," said Madeleine. "You sit down and take the weight off those tiny feet of yours. Would you like a bandage for that hand?"

"Oh it should be fine," Sharon replied, wondering how on earth the old lady could have noticed it.

"You should keep it clean," said Madeleine, "or Heaven knows what might happen." She set down a steaming mug that Sharon knew the old lady would have forgotten to add sugar to. "Now you just have that and I'll see what I can find for you."

Once she was alone, a tiny sip of the tea confirmed her suspicions. She had no reason to believe that Mark's mother disliked her, but the old lady was weird and when they met it always took Sharon a little while to adjust to her mannerisms. She took a deep breath and looked around her. Perhaps she wouldn't be happy living in the country. It was far too quiet for one thing, and having no-one close by, even just a neighbour to see now and then, meant it could probably feel very lonely too. Of course, if she lived here she could always go and visit the stone circle, she thought, before giggling to herself. Perhaps that was the way people like Mrs Markham started going a bit batty in the first place. She shook her head, realising she was already missing home. Her hand had started to bleed again, and there was still no sign of Madeleine with the bandage. There were some tissues in her handbag and she looked round to see where she had put it.

Her handbag had gone.

Sharon frowned. She distinctly remembered putting it on the table. A quick search beneath and beside it yielded nothing. Perhaps Madeleine had taken it? No, she'd seen the old lady leave the room and she hadn't been carrying anything with her.

"Everything alright?"

Sharon glanced at Mark before resuming her search. "I've lost my bloody handbag," she said. "It was right here and now I can't find it."

"Never mind about that for the moment, dear," said Madeleine from behind him. "Let's get that hand cleaned up."

"I just can't work out where it could have gone," said Sharon as the old lady led her to the bathroom.

"Perhaps the piskies took it," said the old lady, giving Sharon a pointed look and tutting. "Naughty piskies."

*

"Mark, what's a piskie?"

Her husband shook his head, with a look on his face that said that now they were in bed he was keen to get off to sleep and not chat. "No idea," he said. "Are you sure you don't mean pixie?"

"It was your mum who mentioned them," Sharon plucked at a thread on the bed sheet. "She said they'd stolen my handbag."

"My mum can be a bit strange at times." Mark said, turning away from her to face the wall, mumbling about her believing all kinds of nonsense before his words were swiftly replaced by muffled snoring. It wasn't long before Sharon followed his example, crossing her fingers for a deep dreamless sleep.

But it was not to be.

Almost as soon as her eyes were closed, Sharon found herself standing in the middle of the stone circle, but instead of soft grass there was now dry earth that was dusty beneath her bare feet. From above came an unnatural heat courtesy of a sun she could not see, bathing her face in a peppery warmth that stung her lips and eyelids. The mustard glare of the sky had rendered her bleak surroundings almost the same shade of washed-out yellow as the stones themselves, which seemed to protrude from the cracked ground like the teeth of some vast and ancient creature that had been encased millennia ago in its arid solidity.

She didn't dare move.

She could not explain the fear she felt, the fear that if she were to take a step something would erupt from the ground, reaching for her with withered claws, clutching at her flesh and dragging her down into this parched land to keep it company in its dark hell.

The stone in front of her was larger than the others, and as she focused on it to take her mind off what might be lurking beneath the ground, ready to pounce at the slightest sound of a footstep, she thought she saw it move.

The second time it happened, she knew her eyes had not deceived her. It wasn't at all obvious but it was there, a gentle undulation of the surface, almost as if the stone were trying to breath.

Or, she thought with sudden horror, as if something were trying to get out.

As she watched, the undulation changed to a rippling that made her think of an insect's egg case about to burst, the hungry larvae within desperate to feed to sustain their new life. She looked around her, to see that all the stones were now moving in the same way, their waxy surfaces splitting, the winged buzzing creatures that had been contained within forcing their way through the ragged holes they had made. She tried to run but something held her fast as a thousand insectoid creatures the size of bats, each with stingers poised, bore down upon her.

*

Sharon woke with a start, gasping and clutching at the bed sheets.

For a moment she thought she was still in the dream until she realised that the blinding light was sunshine forcing its way through the curtains. She looked beside her but Mark wasn't there. A glance at the bedside clock explained why. It was well past eight. Sharon dragged herself into a sitting position on the edge of the bed and took a few deep breaths. After the third one she paused, frowning, and licked her lips. Now why should she have the quite unmistakable taste of honey in her mouth? She didn't have to think back on everything they had eaten yesterday to know she hadn't had any – not for years, in fact. She wondered if somehow Madeleine had spilled some of that awful perfume she used in here, but she knew it wasn't that either.

She remembered reading somewhere about how you could check to see if you had bad breath by licking your wrist, allowing it to dry, and then sniffing it. The odour that assailed her nostrils on performing this ritual was distinct, sweet, and definitely not perfume. Perhaps that was an effect of the antidepressants too, she thought, just like her bladder trouble, although she should have been on them long enough now for any of the funny taste her doctor said she might get to reveal itself. It remained after she had showered and brushed her teeth, although by the time she came down to breakfast she was able to convince herself that perhaps it wasn't quite as strong as it had been when she had woken.

"Up at last are you?" said Mark with an affectionate smile as she took her place at the kitchen table.

"Yes. Sorry," Sharon said in the direction of Mark's mother.

"Oh that's alright dear," said the old lady. "Mark told me you had quite a rough night."

Sharon poured coffee and saw a flicker of concern in her husband's expression as she neglected to add her usual milk and sugar and, instead, took a big swig and swilled it around her mouth before swallowing it.

"Did I?" she said, the coffee's bitter aftertaste causing her to frown.

"I should say," said Mark. "Tossing and turning all night. Are you okay?"

Sharon emptied her mug and poured another. "I think so." When she saw that made him look properly worried, she added, "I've just got a bit of a funny taste in my mouth, that's all."

"I hope the bed wasn't uncomfortable?" said Madeleine, tidying away her and Mark's empty plates as Sharon helped herself to toast.

"Not at all," Sharon replied, trying her best to smile as she spread the butter.

"Would you like some jam for that, dear?" the old lady asked, pushing a pot with homemade damson preserve dribbling down its sides towards her.

"No, thank you," Sharon said, munching on the toast and finishing off her second coffee.

"I have some honey around here somewhere."

*"NO!"* Sharon realised she had shouted and immediately apologised. "I'll be fine with what's here," she said, explaining that the bad night had given her a headache.

Mark laid a comforting hand on her shoulder. "Are you up to coming with us this morning?" he said.

Sharon nodded and pressed his hand to her cheek. "Don't worry." She picked up the empty mug. "A little bit more of this and I'll be fine."

An hour later, and a dressed and presentable Sharon joined her husband and his mother in the kitchen, ready to set off to visit Mark's father's grave. They were about to leave when Sharon noticed something on the kitchen table. She probably wouldn't have given it another thought had her dreams not been plagued by it. The

212

fact that it was in the exact position where she had left her still missing handbag seemed almost incidental.

"Is there something the matter, dear?" Mrs Markham looked concerned.

"Madeleine," said Sharon, trying hard to keep her voice calm. "Why is there a lump of yellow stone on the kitchen table?"

"Why, I have no idea," said the old lady, looking up at the ceiling. "Perhaps this old place is threatening to fall down about our ears. Or perhaps," and now she gave Sharon a look she did not like at all, "the piskies have given you a present in exchange for your handbag."

Sharon's mouth went dry at the suggestion and she licked her lips. There it was again – the taste of honey, stronger now the previously obliterating flavours of coffee and toast and toothpaste had subsided.

"Are you sure you're alright?" said Mark, putting his arm around her.

"I'm fine," Sharon lied. "Let's go and pay our respects." But after that, she thought, *I just want to get away from here.*

*

The tiny Church of St Vesper sat in the middle of Cornerston, surrounded by a cemetery peppered with teetering graves, many of them fashioned from the yellow stone Sharon was now getting sick of the sight of. They were met at the lych-gate by the Reverend Bartholomew Winston, an elderly parson with a kind face who towered over the three of them. As he led them to the grave, Sharon wondered why the cemetery took up so much space in such a small village.

"It's the oldest building in the village, you know," said the vicar as they made their way around to the rear of the church. "In fact Cornerston grew up around it, as was so often the way with many isolated communities in those days. Ah – here we are."

Dennis Markham's grave marker had also been fashioned from the butter-yellow stone. As Reverend Winston began his incantation, a ray of sunlight brushed the stone's top left hand corner before disappearing back behind a cloud.

Perhaps Sharon was the only one who was looking, or perhaps, she thought with horror, she was the only one who could see it, but as the sun's rays touched the stone she was sure that she saw an intricate carving etched into the corner of Dennis Markham's grave.

213

A cold hand gripped her heart. In that brief moment she had also recognised what it was. How could she not, having dreamed about them all night? She looked up, willing the sun to come out again, but the thick cloud cover refused her pleading eyes. She could tell from glancing at the others that they hadn't seen anything, or at least nothing out of the ordinary.

And definitely not a carving of a monstrous wasp.

A monstrous wasp, which as she watched, began to crawl across the surface of the stone.

Suddenly it was all too much – the bad night, the weird taste in her mouth, and now hallucinations. Sharon clutched at her stomach and, as her knees collapsed from under her, did her best to avoid hitting her head on Mark's father's gravestone.

*

"Ah …you're coming round. Excellent."

When Sharon next opened her eyes her first thought was that she had died and was in the waiting room for Heaven. Then she realised that the mixture of religious icons and heavy old books she could see probably meant she was in the church's vestry. A filing cabinet and a smiling Reverend Winston confirmed her theory and dispelled any concerns that she had already entered the afterlife. When she tried to speak, her voice was a honeyed croak.

"What happened?"

"You had what I think doctors call 'a bit of a funny turn'," said the vicar with a smile as he handed her a cup of tea. "I helped your husband carry you in here and said I would look after you while he took his mother home – she was most upset by the whole affair. I promised I would call an ambulance if there was the slightest chance you looked as if you were going to be properly unwell."

Sharon gave him a mirthless grin. "Properly unwell?" she said.

"You'd be surprised how many people faint in or near a church," said Winston as he used a bread knife to slit open a packet of Digestives. "I fancy myself to be quite an expert on it." He offered her a biscuit and when she declined took one for himself. "And as you can see, I was correct in my diagnosis – you seem as right as rain now."

Sharon wasn't so sure. Her head ached and there was still that bloody annoying taste in her mouth. She sipped at her tea and, suddenly realising how thirsty she was, drank the rest of the cup in almost a single gulp.

"I was right about that as well, then," the vicar beamed.

Sharon frowned. "What do you mean?"

He reached forward with his teaspoon and tapped the side of Sharon's cup. "You don't take sugar. Good thing I didn't put any in."

Her look of horror must have been obvious enough for him to ask her what was wrong.

"Oh nothing," she said. "Or at least, nothing I can explain." And then, more because she felt awkward and didn't know what else to say than because she might get an answer, she said. "I don't suppose *you* know what a piskie is?"

"Cornish things aren't they?" he said after a moment's pause that betrayed he knew more than he was letting on. "Like pixies or sprites."

"That's what I thought," said Sharon. "But Mark's mother's been going on about them since we arrived yesterday. She says they stole my handbag and left a lump of Cotswold stone in its place. And last night I had the weirdest dream about these horrible creatures, which wouldn't have been so bad except this morning, by the grave, I saw one of the things I dreamed about. It looked like a big wasp carved into the stone, but even though it was a carving it was sort of moving – you know, wriggling, as if it was trying to get out."

Sharon knew she was rambling but once she started it was difficult to stop. At the same time the vicar's increasingly darkening expression was doing little to ease her worries.

"I'm sure it's nothing," he said, "but your mother-in-law isn't having you on. There really is a legend about creatures that were called Cotswold piskies. In fact some say they are what gave rise to the modern concept of the fairy. I suspect you must have read about them at some point in the past and Mrs Markham simply caused you to remember it without realising. In fact …" he rose and took a heavy volume from the shelf behind him, "if you'll give me a moment I might be able to show you something that will jog your memory." Dust plumed from the cracking cover as he opened the book and turned water damaged pages until he found what he was looking for. He gestured for Sharon to join him. "This is probably the oldest picture there is showing one," he said. "Be careful not to actually touch the page. It's very delicate."

Sharon grimaced at the illustration. The thing in the picture didn't look like a fairy. There were two pairs of pale wings but they looked leathery rather than possessing the lacy transparency of myth, and the bulbous head appeared to possess compound eyes and a mouth from which protruded either a pair of proboscises or two horribly long fangs – it was difficult to decide which. If the picture had been drawn to scale the thing was only slightly bigger than the baby it seemed to be threatening in its crib.

"They were said to steal children," he said.

Sharon could believe it. The hooks protruding from each of its six spindly legs seemed well able to pick something as big as a baby up and the stout body from which they arose appeared sturdy enough to carry it away – for God knows what purpose.

"And people got the idea for fairies from that?" she said.

"Maybe not everywhere," was the reply, "but quite possibly around here. It's fascinating how the passage of time and the retelling of legends can make them less threatening. But I suppose it's the nature of man to want to make his environment seem friendlier than perhaps it actually is."

"Why 'quite possibly around here'?"

The Reverend Winston indicated the faded text beneath the picture. "This is an account of some kind of event that occurred here just prior to the building of the church. Quite what it was isn't clear – there's a lot of flowery language about the earth cracking and lightning and thunderbolts, that sort of thing."

"An earthquake?" said Sharon.

Winston nodded. "Or possibly a meteorite. Something that caused the ground to be disturbed. It was shortly afterwards that the foundation stones of this church were laid. I suppose it's possible that if whatever happened caused the appearance of those large insect creatures, and the people of the time might have had no other better name for them than fairies or piskies."

"But if they were real, what happened to them?"

"If they were real, then I suspect they went back where they came from," said the vicar with a smile, "and please don't ask me where. Outer space, beneath the earth, who knows? Are you feeling any better?"

Sharon said that she was as the clattering of the vestry door heralded the arrival of Mark, who looked very relieved when he saw his wife awake and talking to the vicar.

"Feeling better then?" he said, stroking her back.

"I think so," said Sharon, "but I'd like to get back now."

"Sure." Mark gave a brisk nod. "Mum's not feeling too well anyway, so I promised we'd get straight back to the cottage and just stay another night to make sure she's okay."

"I didn't mean back to the cottage, Mark," said Sharon as she was helped to her feet. "I want to go home. There's something here, something that I think is trying to get me."

"In the church you mean?" said Mark, glancing at the vicar, who shook his head.

"No, not the church." Sharon tried her best to explain, but she didn't really know what it was she was trying to tell him. "There's something here, in this town, or rather around it. I dreamt about it last night and I saw it on your father's grave this morning." She pointed at the open book on Winston's desk. "And part of it's in there as well. I know it is."

"Come on," said Mark, trying to manhandle her to the exit. "You're just a bit tired. There's nothing here that's trying to get you."

"It wouldn't have happened if I hadn't visited that stone circle," she said.

"You never mentioned anything about that," said Mark.

"When we stopped, so I could …you know," Sharon said, well aware that they were still in earshot of the vicar. "I found a stone circle just beyond the trees. I went and had a look at it. I'd never seen one made from Cotswold stone before."

"Does it have a name?" Mark asked the vicar, who was looking even more worried.

"There is no stone circle around here," he said. "Not for miles. There was one, many hundreds of years ago. That's partly what that book is about. It was the attempt of a seventeenth century writer to collect the rumours and myths concerning the event that caused the circle to be destroyed and Cornerston to be built on the site."

*

Sharon was silent for most of the ride home. Mark probably thought she was still dazed but there was so much running through her mind that she wondered if she was ever going to sleep again. She stared at the sunlit main street as Mark drove slowly, taking care to avoid Saturday afternoon shoppers, with little regard for the few vehicles that were trying to use the road. Something had happened here a long

217

time ago, something that had either brought those things in her dream, or destroyed them. Or possibly both, she thought as the car halted at a zebra crossing and a small child waved to her from a sweetshop on the corner. Sharon waved back and did her best to maintain her smile until the child's mother has whisked it away.

She could see something moving in the yellow stone lintel over the sweetshop door.

No, she thought, not something. Some *things*. As the car moved off again she tried to look anywhere except at the shop. But now she could see them everywhere. All the buildings in the main street had been built from Cotswold stone, perhaps even the stone that had come from the stone circle, and now she could see things crawling beneath the surface of every brick, every paving stone, every cornice.

"Mark, please let's get home," she said in as calm a voice as she could muster.

"I'm doing my best," he said. "We'll be there in a minute."

Sharon knew it was useless to make a scene so she shut her eyes, but there was no escape, not even behind tightly closed lids. Now she could see the circle again, the creatures that lived there, the buzzing, flying creatures with tiny intelligent faces were coming for her there, too, desperate to leave their yellow tombs and find a new home beneath the surface of her skin.

Despite Sharon's best efforts, by the time they got back to Madeleine's cottage she had started screaming.

*

"I'm telling you we've got to leave here!"

Mark looked utterly shocked, but then despite five years of marriage Sharon had never really lost it in front of him before. She drank the tea Madeleine had made for her. It was so sweet she almost spat out the mixture of sugar, honey and something else that she couldn't quite identify.

"You just had a bad night," said Mark. "You'll feel better once you've had a rest."

"I'll be dead once I've had a rest!" she screamed. "I'll go to sleep and those things in Reverend Winston's book will get me and then they'll get you and anyone else they can because they'll finally be free after a thousand years, and there'll be nothing anyone will be able to do to stop them!"

218

"And where are 'they' now?" said Mark, obviously humouring her in an effort to get her to calm down.

"They're nowhere, at least not now, but they live in the stone, or they're trapped there. I'm not sure which, but all they need is a suitable victim to let them out." Sharon was crying now, "Don't you understand!" she said through her tears. "That's me! I'm the one they want to use as a ... as a conduit to get into this world, and we've got to get away from here before they do!"

"Did you give her one of my sleeping tablets after all, dear?" said Madeline from the doorway.

Sharon looked at the two of them in horror. "Oh Christ, Mark. Oh please tell me you didn't, please!"

She was still staring at him as his face began to swim before her eyes and everything became a yellow haze.

*

It was close to three in the morning when Sharon woke. She took a deep breath, stretched, and looked around her, allowing her eyes to adjust to the dim light seeping through the window from the streetlamp outside. The taste of honey was gone, and so were the effects of the sleeping tablet that had clouded her mind. Now everything was alright, everything was as it should be, everything was clear. Mark moved in his sleep as she threw back the covers and sat up, looking at him for one last time as rows upon rows of hooked and barbed legs erupted from her arms, her body, her face, as she felt the whirring of wings in her hair and the pressure of feelers behind her eyes. As stingers the size of knitting needles began to emerge from the palms of her hands she wondered with the last vestiges of her humanity whether one in the face would be enough to kill him outright, or if she should pin him to the bed through the spine as well.

# LOVELL'S LONG WAIT

*The Cat, the Rat and Lovell the Dog*
*Ruled all England under the Hog*

Acurious bit of doggerel maybe, but it has sinister origins. Richard III, the last Plantagenet king of England, is implicated – by Shakespeare at least – in a rash of murders and unlawful trials and executions as he sought to benefit from the chaos at the end of the Wars of the Roses and have himself crowned at the expense of his nephew, Edward V (who was reputedly smothered on his uncle's orders in the Tower of London at the age of thirteen, along with his younger brother).

It is anybody's guess how true any of this is. Shakespeare was writing for the Tudor dynasty, who deposed Richard III, which may explain the Bard's memorable depiction of Richard as a ruthless and conniving hunchback. However, one thing is certain: while Richard was Duke of Gloucester and senior lieutenant to his older brother, Edward IV, he was a successful warrior, who presided over countless bloody victories against the Lancastrians, and after he became king there were many who feared his wrath.

The above rhyme lampoons Richard in reference to his 'wild boar' battle-standard (the Hog), and three knights who strongly supported him: Richard Ratcliffe (the Rat), William Catesby (the Cat) and Francis Lovell, who used a hound as one of his heraldic symbols (the Dog).

Richard was not amused. He had the lyricist responsible, William Collingborn, hanged, drawn and quartered.

But ultimately, all these powerful men came to sticky ends. Richard and Ratcliffe were killed at the battle of Bosworth in 1485; Catesby was captured shortly afterwards and beheaded. Lovell escaped the victorious Lancastrians and fled the country, only to return in 1487 in support of Yorkist pretender Lambert Simnel, whose cause was finally crushed at the battle of Stoke Field. Lovell again fled, and here lies one of our most macabre Cotswold tales.

Knowing he faced the headsman's axe if caught, Lovell dashed into Oxfordshire and took refuge in his own manor house, Minster Lovell Hall. Here there was a secret vault, its whereabouts known only to Lovell himself and a faithful if elderly servant. Lovell was locked inside with his favourite hound, just as the Lancastrian forces *arrived with a warrant for his arrest. The soldiers searched the building high and low, but still missed the perfectly concealed chamber. At length they departed, but during their stay had put enormous stress on the aged retainer – breaking furniture, making threats, promising to wipe out the entire household if the master's whereabouts was not revealed. No sooner had they left, than the retainer collapsed in a fit and died.*

*Over two centuries later, in 1708, a party of workmen was renovating the same manor house when they discovered the entrance to a hidden vault. Forcing entry, they found the skeleton of a man inside, seated at a table with a book in front of it and the skeleton of a dog lying at its feet. The stale air was subsequently disturbed and the ghoulish tableau collapsed – the table, the book and both skeletons vanishing into plumes of dust. As such no solid evidence remained, but sufficient witnesses gave voice to the evidence of their own eyes, and the case of the missing Lord Lovell was finally closed.*

# BOG MAN
## Paul Finch

At first glance it was totally repulsive. The fact that it had once been human meant nothing. It was disgusting, repellant.

Scientists, of course, had to be above such things. They knew the withered flesh was chocolate-brown in colour and slick and leathery in texture thanks to millennia of immersion in the organic acids and aldehydes deep in the sphagnum bog. Its humanoid outline had a flat, almost deflated appearance because the heavy layers of peat had slowly compressed it over the generations. In fact, any potential horror of the object was far outweighed by the professional fascination it exercised on the two archaeology students now analysing it for their thesis.

Tessa leaned down and gazed through the lamp-lit Perspex casing, getting as close as she could to the bog body's head. Considering the thing had been dead at least two thousand years, which was older than some Egyptian mummies, its face looked remarkably *un-skullish*. The features, though wizened and sharp, like carefully folded bits of charcoal paper, were clearly defined – almost reposed, as if the Iron Age man was only sleeping. His delicately closed eyelids enhanced the effect.

She tapped her front teeth with her biro.

A few wisps of wiry red hair still adhered to the stubborn thrust of bone that was the exhibit's lower jaw. Between lips shrivelled back in a black rictus, strong, even teeth were still visible, albeit brown and peg-like after so many centuries.

In the corner of the lab, Rick continued to tap away at his VDU. "Told you," he said, distractedly. "That beard's a dead give-away. If you look really closely, you'll see it's been trimmed with scissors. We know scissors existed then, but only as possessions of the select few. Therefore, our guy was once some kind of aristocrat."

Tessa threw a sidelong glance at the calendar on the shelf where the test-tubes were kept. Whichever of the professor's colleagues had been tearing the pages off, they had kept it fully up-to-date. The current one read: April 30. "Which ties in very nicely with your great theory, I suppose?" she said.

"Absolutely." He typed in more notes. "The ingredients in his belly showed he died mid-spring, which means Beltane … the big one, the guarantor for a fruitful growing season. They wouldn't have wasted someone special like him on any old festival."

"Well they couldn't have done it on Beltane every year. Otherwise, there'd have been no ruling-class left."

"Ah, but in this case we've got the Roman angle too."

"Mmm." She wasn't quite so convinced about *this* part of her boyfriend's theory, despite the carbon-dating results, which put the find in roughly the right historical period.

Bog bodies like this had been turning up all over western Europe, from the Netherlands to Ireland, Germany to Denmark, but they were especially prevalent in Britain, where they were usually uncovered during attempts to reclaim ancient, water-logged land. It wasn't uncommon for the bodies to show signs of violence – in fact, in the early days of discovery quite a few had been mistaken as the victims of modern murders. This one, recently ploughed up in the Brue Valley marshes in Somerset, bore stark evidence that he'd suffered a particularly savage demise. The strip of leather used on him as a ligature had been twisted around his neck so tightly that several of his vertebrae had actually fractured; so tightly, in fact, that it was still there, fully intact, pulled taut in a fold of shining, mottled flesh, only the knot visible at the back of his skull. Having said that, such brutality came as no surprise. It had long been established 'fact' that the bog people were, for the most part, human offerings to the Celtic gods, immortalised in death by the unique preservative conditions found under the peat. In this case however, Rick, in his wonderfully naïve undergraduate way, had gone several steps further, concluding that *this* victim had been offered up as an extra-special sop to the old British deities in order to fend off the imminent arrival of the Romans. Now he intended to put this theory on paper and forward it to the examiners.

"You see, if you were facing a major, major crisis," he said, as he worked, "like an invasion … the best thing you could do would be try and harness the powers of all the most powerful gods. Which is basically what we've got here. In Iron Age Britain, there were three key deities: Taranis, the god of the sky, Esus, the god of the underworld, and Teutates, the god of the tribe."

"You're telling me something I already know," Tessa yawned.

"Yeah, but hear me out. This is a sort of all-in-one sacrifice … the traditional way to kill for Taranis was by burning. But for Esus, it was by strangulation or hanging, which we've got clear evidence of, and for Teutates, it was by drowning in a holy pool … our guy was obviously thrown into water after he'd been garroted, because the peat bogs were originally lakes or wetland. Two out of three isn't bad. And then you go and do it on Beltane Eve, as well … what more could you ask for?"

"Well," she replied, "if that's the case, it didn't do much good."

"Nope. That's true, I suppose."

And it was. The John Morgan Museum stood at the very heart of Cirencester, now a bustling provincial town less than a hundred miles from London and in the midst of a major road network. It had been thriving, wealthy and politically active ever since its original construction as a frontier fort for the victorious legions back in the first century. Its archeological sites were among the very best, giving clear evidence of the flourishing society that Roman Britain had eventually evolved into. The tribal settlement that had previously occupied this site, like most others in the country, had long vanished.

Tessa scribbled down a few more notes, and then moved on to other aspects of the so-called 'Avalon Man'. His supple brown hands were folded together on his sunken chest. They looked soft, vaguely feminine; the fingers were long and tapering, with no signs of scars or calluses on them, the nails at their ends neatly squared off – almost as though manicured. Though she was loath to admit it, this all supported Rick's theory. Whoever this unfortunate was, he'd plainly been exempt from manual labour, which did indeed suggest that he'd held some position of respect or authority. She didn't suppose it was beyond the bounds of possibility back in those days that the bigger the problem, the bigger the attempted pay-off.

"And tonight's the night, of course," Rick added. "April 30th, Beltane Eve … lots of spirits on the loose."

She glanced across the lab towards him. He watched her from under his unruly mop of black hair, his handsome face written with youthful, impish glee.

"Are you *deliberately* trying to creep me out?" she asked.

Rick grinned all the more. They were presently ensconced in the research facility at the rear of the museum, but a labyrinth of galleries, rooms and passages surrounded them on all sides, both above and below; at this time of night all lay empty and in total darkness. Tessa didn't spook easily, but he knew she'd never have agreed to this late evening work-session if he hadn't promised to share it with her.

"Well?" she said, demanding an answer.

"Hey … how else am I going to get the prettiest girl in Paleo-Botany to put her arm around me?"

She tossed her tawny curls. "Flattery won't get you anywhere tonight, mister."

"That's why I've got to go for the scary stuff."

"Mmm."

At which point the door to the lab crashed open and a man who was more like a bear came stalking in. Balding on top, but with a dense mass of beard and wild staring eyes, the sudden sight of him might have been enough to give even the bravest heart an instant attack, despite the blue rent-a-cop outfit he wore, with its razor-sharp creases and bar of battle-braids on the breast pocket.

"Jesus … *Ralph!*" Rick complained.

"Sorry," the big security guard said. "Wasn't sure whereabouts you two were. God … that thing is *so* 'orrible." He surveyed the lean, leathery form laid out in the Perspex case.

"Take a good look," Tessa said. "It'll probably be the last time you see it. It's going permanently back into storage after the finals."

Ralph gazed at it. Much as he found the bog body repugnant – as he never ceased to inform anyone who would listen – like most other laymen, it held a grisly fascination for him. "All them bright museum lights wearing it down, I suppose," he finally said.

Tessa tittered. "I don't recall too many bright lights in the Ancient Britons' Gallery."

Up until recently Avalon Man had dwelled upstairs in a low, dark alcove designed to look like the interior of an Iron Age hut, complete with basic tools and weapons, jumbled broken pottery, flints, bones and of course a suitably meagre fire giving off the most weak and lurid light.

"Just getting a bit tatty, that's all," Rick said. "He snuffed it twenty centuries ago, remember. And he's been fifteen years out of the moss, as well. Can't do a body any good."

An involuntary shudder passed through Ralph's gigantic frame. "Best thing for it, if you want my opinion. Let it rot away to nothing, like it was supposed to."

The students exchanged smirking glances. It was well known in class, and a great source of amusement, that Ralph and other members of the museum security team, though mostly tough ex-squaddies with Gulf, Falklands and Balkan wars, not to mention multiple tours of Northern Ireland, under their belts, trod warily around the institution's more eldritch artifacts.

225

"Anyway," Ralph said, stepping back towards the door, "just letting you know I'm on my rounds. What time are you two packing up?"

"We were hoping to make last orders at The Jolly Jape, but that's a long shot now," Tessa said.

"Why are you working so late?" Ralph asked.

"Papers have to be in next week."

Ralph considered this, then threw one more nervous glance at the thing in the case. "Rather you than me ... stuck in here in the middle of the night with *him*. Anyway, you know where I'll be."

They both nodded. Whichever guard drew the night shift, he'd invariably set up base at the desk by the museum's main doors. And Ralph was no exception. That was where the security monitors were after all. And the phones, and the packs of cards, and the smokes the fellas weren't supposed to have while on duty.

"Oh listen," he said, turning before going out. "I was thinking of ordering a bit of supper later. Getting a pizza delivered, or something. Wondered if you fancied going halves?"

Tessa shook her head. "No thanks. Too late for me."

"Same here, Ralph," Rick said. "Thanks anyway."

"No problem." The security man turned to leave.

"Hey Ralph," Rick called. "Guess what our bog friend had for *his* supper?"

Ralph looked from student to student, his brow furrowed.

Rick sat back in his chair. "Tell him, Tess."

She consulted her pad. "Er ... his stomach cavity contained a rancid muck, which was all that remained of a gruel or cake mixed together from bitter herbs, oatmeal, mistletoe pollen and ground up wild flowers."

Ralph gave them a vaguely haunted look. "Cheers folks. I was looking forward to that pizza, too." And he left, his hobnailed boots clicking away down the corridor.

Rick went back to his keyboard, chuckling. Tessa resumed work on her notes, walking the length of the case. Avalon Man had been found in a slightly hunched posture, and still lay that way on his bed of earth, but his estimated height was about five feet and eight inches, which was significantly taller than most people of his era and, again, would have made him an outstanding figure in his home environment. That was the thing about these bog specimens, she supposed. They were *so* well preserved that it was impossible not to glean all sorts of detailed information from them. And to realise something else; namely, that two thousand years ago human beings had been pretty much the same as they were now. This guy was in no way ape-like or Neanderthal; by his hands and his facial expression, by the way the mouldering rags of a loincloth had covered his genitals, he was almost refined. His hair was in all the places you'd expect to find it at the dawn of the twenty first century; routine blemishes like pimples and warts could be seen on his glossy, varnished skin – there were even traces of tattoos. Muscle lineaments could be discerned; the smoothly contoured feet might very well fit into modern-day training shoes. Yet again Tessa had the eerie impression that this was just someone asleep – an actor maybe, covered in body-paint and somehow 'compressed' by refracting light in the Perspex casket.

"You know," she said, "all this ghoulish stuff about human sacrifices … it could be that you and everyone else on the course have seen too many re-runs of *The Wicker Man*."

Rick glanced curiously up. "Come on, there's plenty of evidence."

"Not really. Only one concrete piece, as I recall. That single reference Caesar made in *The Conquest of Gaul*."

"It's generally accepted that human sacrifice went on in Belgic societies all over western Europe."

"Guesswork."

"What's *your* explanation then?" he asked.

"Maybe Avalon Man just got murdered?"

"No way." Rick stood up and came over to the casket. "To start with there's no sign of a struggle. Look … his teeth and fingernails are all intact."

"You're not saying these people let themselves get sacrificed willingly?"

He shrugged. "Dunno. If the problem was dead serious maybe they felt they had no option."

"Oh, give me a break …"

"You've got to look at it *their* way. I mean, these communities lived and died at the apparent whim of the gods. You've got plague, famine, natural disasters, destruction in war, enslavement …" He went on and on excitedly.

Tessa smiled to herself. You could never play the Devil's advocate with Rick for long. *She* was just here to get some results and forge a lucrative career; but for Rick this whole thing was a life-experience. He was totally in love with the distant past, utterly absorbed by the few solid scraps that remained of it. He'd read every book and pamphlet, investigated every revolutionary new theory, and was now forwarding even more revolutionary theories of his own. He didn't want to major in his subject so much as to wallow in it. And she couldn't help loving him all the more for that, for even in a dead, dusty world of relics and fossils, his enthusiasm was infectious – not that she wanted him to know this of course.

"Anything you say, Mr. Expert," she said, moving to the window and peeking out through the blinds. "It was one big party back in the Iron Age."

Beyond the university quadrangle, through a dark hanging mass of brand new Maple leaves, the cheery lights of The Jolly Jape could be seen. Even from here lively music was faintly audible; there was laughter and shouting going on down there.

"Speaking of which," she added wistfully. "Looks like we're missing out on a bit of a bash right now."

Rick joined her. "Well … that isn't entirely the case."

She glanced round at him. "Don't tell me you've finished already?"

"No, but I didn't think it would do any harm if we took a little break. You know … have a party of our own."

She raised an eyebrow. "Oh? Just *tu* et *moi*?"

"Why not?" And he grinned, impish again. "I've got a few brews cooling nicely in the fridge."

Tessa looked puzzled, but then glanced incredulously across the lab to the large cooling cabinet where only particularly fragile specimens were contained. "You are *not* serious!"

"Go and check."

She hurried over and opened the cabinet door. Four blue and silver tins, rimed with frost, were sitting on the top shelf amid various other jars and packets. Gingerly, not even wanting to see the often grotesque oddments that Professor Holbrook kept on ice in there, Tessa reached inside.

A moment later the two students were back by the window. They cracked the tins, drank a little beer and, blowing the fluffy froth from each other's lips, kissed in the light of the half-open blind. Rick's hands roved round onto the back of his girlfriend's jeans and took possession of her pert buttocks, squeezing them gently. He sniggered.

She drew back and eyed him suspiciously. "What are you up to now?"

"Just thinking. Wouldn't it be a gas to get something going on Holbrook's table?"

"It would be an outrageous breach of trust, that's what it would be."

"But you like the sound of it … am I right?"

"Mmm …"

She kissed him again. This time it was a hot, moist one. Their tongues entwined. There was a new hunger there. Rick felt the blood start to pump, felt that familiar stirring in his loins. They broke apart and moved hand-in-hand through the door to the lecture theatre. This was a deep, circular room, designed like a small amphitheatre. Stepped aisles led down through concentric rings of hard-backed benches to the low, central table, where Professor Holbrook would habitually hold court.

It wasn't in darkness as such. Thin curtains on the tall arched windows allowed in a dim blue radiance from the floodlights outside. One could see just enough to toddle around and get up to all sorts of mischief.

"We sure there's no security camera in here?" Tessa asked, holding back.

"Sure," Rick said. "I checked it out a few months ago with one of the security lads."

She looked round at him. "Just how long have you been planning this?"

He gave her another peck. "Long enough to get my blood boiling for want of doing it to you in here … right on the spot where old Ratbag regularly gives us the fourth degree."

She let him lead her down the aisle steps to the table, which for once was clear of papers and exhibits. There they kissed again, sucking each other's tongues 'til they strained at the roots. Finally, Tessa laid back and allowed Rick to unfasten the front of her jeans. He drew them down, along with the panties underneath. The faint light sparkled on the down of golden hair between her hourglass thighs. He undid his own jeans and dropped them, then he climbed onto the table – and just as he did there came the most terrific explosion of sound from somewhere close by; an immense *crash*, as if someone had thrown a full dustbin across a room filled with furniture.

"What the hell?" Rick gasped.

They gazed wildly around the theatre, but no-one else was visible. That didn't of course mean that someone hadn't just been in and out without them noticing.

"Shit," Tessa said. "What if someone's seen us?"

Hurriedly, Rick pulled his jeans up. "It could only be Ralph, and he wouldn't say anything."

Tessa shook her head as she too adjusted her clothes. "Ralph'll be tucking into his pizza, by now."

There was another sharp detonation, followed by another, as though things were being knocked or kicked over. It clearly came from the next room.

"Someone's in the lab," Rick said in a whisper.

Tessa turned and gazed at him. "It must be Holbrook. I bet he's come back for something."

"Bloody hell … *hide!*"

They leaped from the table, darting this way and that like scared rabbits, eventually opting for the shadowy foot-space beneath one of the benches, where they had to squirm in side by side to make sure they were out of sight.

"If he's been in here and seen us, we are *for* it in a big way," Rick muttered.

"If he'd seen us, he'd be chewing our asses off by now," Tessa replied.

"On the subject of which …" For all their predicament, Rick was still in an aroused state. His fingers roved along the denim-clad cleft between Tessa's buttocks.

She shrugged him off. "Will you jack it in!" She couldn't resist a giggle all the same, and had to playfully slap at him three or four times before he'd quit making free with her body parts.

Moments of breathy silence followed – long moments. The twosome lay twisted together in darkness, listening intently. But there were no further sounds from the lab, and no tell-tale *creak* of door hinges. Not that any of this was especially comforting. Because they *knew* they'd heard something, so what exactly did the silence signify? Slowly, Rick's ardour began to cool. He now felt distinctly uneasy. He gazed at the luminous dial on his watch.

"It's not far off midnight," he whispered.

Tessa glanced around. "So?"

Awkwardly, he shrugged. "Dunno. It's just … no, nothing. Forget it."

Ralph was just finishing his final slice of Hot'n'Spicy when he thought he heard a footfall at the far side of the museum's main lobby.

He stood up and peered into the gloom. It was a big, airy, cathedral-like chamber, but even in daylight it wasn't well illuminated. The overall structure of the John Morgan was mid-Victorian, which meant neat, glazed brickwork and tall, arched doorways, but also high windows or skylights, most set with frosted glass that was now scummed over by moss and leaf-debris. If sunlight had a difficult time penetrating, moonlight failed altogether.

Ralph laid his magazine down and came round the table. With the low-key reading lamp behind him, his eyes attuned to the dimness more easily, but still nothing moved. In the immediate foreground the gigantic, articulated skeleton of a diplodocus stood on a railed-off plinth, while ranged in niches down either side of the massive room the ghostly outlines of stuffed animals once native to Britain were visible – bear, tiger, ibex, rhinoceros – all back-lit, so even with the little luminosity there was, a complex jumble of shadows was thrown in every direction.

Ralph wiped his greasy hands on a napkin. He'd expected to see the two students by this time. He couldn't imagine they'd keep slogging away at it into the wee small hours, but if it was one of them he'd just heard surely they'd have made themselves known by now? He stared through the framework of bones that was the diplodocus, trying to visualise the central staircase in the near-opaque darkness beyond it. The harder he stared, the more of the stairway he saw – the flat stone treads of the steps, the ornate balustrades to either side, *the figure coming slowly down.*

Ralph went rigid.

It was just an outline, a shapeless blot – so slight and featureless that it might not even be real, that he might be seeing things. But he knew that he wasn't because it was still moving. The figure had now reached the foot of the steps in fact, and was circling around the distant tip of the diplodocus's tail, heading straight towards him as though it didn't have a care in the world, as if it *should* be here. And of course that made it all the worse because Ralph knew that only Rick, Tessa and he should be here, and if it had been either one of the students there'd be noise: a whistling of pop songs, the idle banging of a rucksack. In this case there was nothing – except the steady, silent whisper of approaching feet.

Soft, bare feet.

*

"What the God-damn Hell!"

Rick could hardly believe what he was seeing. They'd plucked up the courage to venture back into the lab, and as soon as they'd re-entered, the very first thing they saw was the airtight Perspex case missing from the gurney. When they scrambled around to the other side, they found it lying on the floor, broken open. Its lid had literally been wrenched off. For a second they imagined that some kind of freak accident had occurred, that maybe the casket had toppled over of its own volition – they gazed around at their feet, seeing the sand, stones and twigs that made up the back-cloth for the exhibit, perhaps expecting to find the exhibit itself scattered in rotten pieces.

However, there was no trace of it.

Rick felt a creeping chill up his spine.

Tessa shook her head in bewilderment. "Are you telling me we've been in here all sodding evening, and the one moment a thief happens to come along is the moment we're next door, getting it on?"

"This was no thief," Rick replied, his breathing hard and heavy. He'd gone pale as milk in the dull lamplight.

"What else do you call it?"

He mumbled something inaudible, then dashed across the room.

"Rick … "

He reached the door to the passage and turned. There was a wild, frightened look in his eyes. "Tess … *this was no thief, okay!* Now come with me … hurry!"

Perplexed, she followed him out into the corridor, but there they came to a stumbling halt. Forty yards ahead stood the double doors connecting with the museum proper, but on the way other doorways gave in to offices and store-rooms. All were stuffed with boxes, crates and sundry items of old-world memorabilia: busy workplaces during the day, but now dark, airless recesses. Their doors hung open; black and twisted shadows fell out of them; there was a deep, tense stillness. More than anything else in the world, Rick suddenly didn't want to go down there; so many unseen niches, so many places where something could hide and jump out at you.

"I ... I must be crazy," he stammered. "Why am I not running the other way?"

"Rick ..." Tessa began, but he cut her short.

"Because there is no other way, that's why!" His face was now a mask of tortured determination. Without another word, he set off walking.

Tessa stuck with him. "Where the hell are we going?"

He didn't, or couldn't, answer, and a minute later they entered the public section of the building and found themselves at the top of the stairway leading down into the main lobby. Silence reigned below. Apart from the small pools of light around the stuffed animal displays, there was very little to see. Rick was sweating, moving uneasily from foot to foot. Again, Tessa asked what he was up to, what he thought was going on. He merely started down the stairs, insisting that she stay with him. Once they'd reached the bottom they could see the lights of the security desk on the far side of the dinosaur skeleton. But there was no sign of movement over there, no sound of a late-night radio show. Rick set off towards it warily. He took Tessa's hand in a vice-like grip, and trod with quiet precision as though unwilling to give himself away. Even in the half-light, she was able to see his chest rising and falling with astonishing rapidity – only then did it strike her how truly terrified he was.

A couple of seconds later, she learned why.

At the security station, the TV monitors had been hurled to the floor and lay in a jumble of cables and smashed glass, circuitry spilling from their broken casings. The desktop space they had once occupied now played host to Ralph, who lay flat on his back, arms and legs spread-eagled. It was immediately clear that the ligature used to strangle him was a long strip of ancient, wizened leather, evidently designed for this very purpose. It had been yanked so tightly around his neck that the security guard's head had swollen up like a balloon. The eyes were bulging duck-eggs in his bloated, florid face, his tongue a black, distended orb between gaping lips. Blood and spume was spattered all through his beard.

Tessa was barely able to stifle her screams. Rick could only shake his head, unable to shut out the vision of horror. "He ... he got in the way," was all he could say.

Tessa looked slowly round at him. "What ... what do you mean?"

Rick shook his head feverishly. "*No-one* must get in the way! Oh Jesus, this is for real!"

He released Tessa's hand, and staggered to the main doors, which he tried to open but found firmly bolted. He seemed baffled. "No-one … no-one's been out this way. I don't … I don't get it."

Tessa had retreated from the desk and was leaning against a pillar. The shock of what she'd seen was gradually receding, to be replaced by a numbing terror of the unknown. She scanned the surrounding darkness. "Rick, whoever did this might still be here. We've got to get help."

But Rick wasn't listening. He'd now fixed on a narrow door just to the left of the security station, half-hidden behind a row of rubber plants. When he spotted it and realised that it stood open, he swore volubly.

"What?" Tessa asked.

"This way," he said, again taking her by the hand and hauling her around the desk.

When they reached the door, they saw that it stood open because it had been *broken* open; the jamb was splintered, the innards of the lock hanging out in silvery twists. Rick barged his way through and descended a spiral stone stair into the very bowels of the museum, still dragging his reluctant girlfriend behind him.

"Don't you think we should at least call the police?" she said.

"Too late for that," he murmured.

When they reached the bottom they found themselves in deep, hot shadow. Despite the depth it wasn't pitch-black – for another door stood ajar there, a wavering red glow filtering around it. It created just enough light for Tessa to see the sudden defeat on Rick's face.

"I knew it …" His voice was a low, heartfelt groan. "Teutates, Esus and Taranis … *Taranis*." He glanced round at her, anguished. "I got it wrong, Tess. Not about the Britons being in serious trouble. They were in trouble alright, and it *was* because of the Romans. But they didn't go for the double sacrifice; they went the whole hog … for the triple. The only thing was they didn't get it finished."

He pushed the door open. On the far side of the vaulted stone basement beyond, the sooty hatch on the huge stainless-steel furnace was slowly being closed. Being closed from the inside.

"But they have now," he added.

Eyes downcast, he put his arms around her and bowed his head.

And outside in the town, and in all the towns of modern Britain, the lightning began to fall.

# SOURCES

All of these stories are original to *Terror Tales of the Cotswolds*, with the exception of 'The Horror Under Warrendown', by Ramsey Campbell, which first appeared in *Dark Terrors* #3, 1997, and 'Bog Man', by Paul Finch, which first appeared in *Cemetery Dance* #59, 2009.

# FUTURE TITLES

If you enjoyed *Terror Tales of the Cotswolds*, why not seek out the first volume in this series, *Terror Tales of the Lake District* – available from most good online retailers, including Amazon, and from http://www.grayfriarpress.com/catalogue/lake.html.

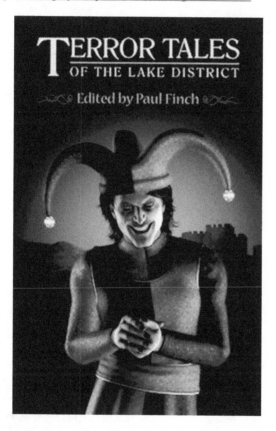

In addition, watch out for forthcoming titles, *Terror Tales of East Anglia* and *Terror Tales of London*. Check regularly for updates with Gray Friar Press, and on the editor's own webpage, http://paulfinch-writer.blogspot.com/.

CPSIA information can be obtained
at www.ICGtesting.com
Printed in the USA
BVHW040105240522
637899BV00001B/20

9 781906 331269